JIM MORGAN
and
THE DOOR
AT THE
EDGE OF THE
WORLD

BY

JAMES MATLACK RANEY

ISBN: 978-0-9858359-7-2

Typesetting by wordzworth.com

Books in the Jim Morgan Series

For my mother, my sister,
and my brother, I love you.

For my father, until the day
we see each other again.

CONTENTS

TAKE COURAGE, FELLOW ADVENTURERS.

ONLY THE FINAL DOOR REMAINS...

JIM MORGAN

and

THE DOOR AT THE EDGE OF THE WORLD

BOOK I

The Mending of the Hunter's Shell

ONE

A Chase Through the Streets of the Kasbah

The last sunset of the summer hung low over the ocean. As evening settled, a cold breeze twisted through the narrow streets of a city upon the shore called the Kasbah of the Udayas. The Kasbah stood on the desert coast of Morocco, a dry and dusty place, where an army of sea ships sat docked near cobblestone streets and clay buildings stacked upon the rocks like steps.

Through those dangerous streets, now falling into darkness, a lone figure ran. He slipped through alleyways and curled around corners, light as a feather on the ocean wind. His name was Jim Morgan. He had once been the son of an English Lord but was now a pirate and a thief, fourteen years old, survivor of countless encounters that would have been the death of men twice his age. A cocky smile stretched across his ruddy face as he flew through the city, barely reining in his laughter, on the run for his life – as usual.

No less than ten of the Kasbah's City Guard rumbled down the streets in pursuit, bearded, turbaned, and armed with curved scimitars. The troop was led by a furious shop owner named Ali, who was chattering in enraged Arabic, vowing revenge and retribution.

Just as the thought of Ali's puffed up, red-cheeked face was about to loose the laugh from Jim's lips, a second figure leapt over an alley wall and landed beside him. George Ratt, Jim's best friend in the whole world, arrived exactly on time.

"Good evening, George," said Jim, never breaking stride.

"Evenin, Jim," said George, tipping his hat like the gentlemen he most certainly was not. "Lovely night for a run, innit?"

"I suppose so, Georgie, but I really wasn't planning on running quite this fast. Ali the shop owner is quite a bit more upset than I thought he'd be."

"Oh, he's upset alright, mate. He's only about half a block back, and he's got himself about fifteen or so of them city guards."

"Fifteen? Really? I hardly see what all the fuss is about. I mean, we did offer to pay, didn't we?"

"Of course we offered to pay, just like the upstandin citizens we are!" George flashed Jim his best hurt look before a dangerous grin cracked the corners of his mouth. From seemingly nowhere, George produced a small vial of glowing red liquid, twirling it over his deft fingers. The crimson light emanating from the concoction danced over the two thieves' faces until George vanished the vial back into one of his pockets. "And the old goof said he weren't gonna sell it to us cause we looked untrustworthy. Us? Untrustworthy? Can you imagine?"

Jim's laugh finally broke free. George Ratt was the best friend a boy could hope to have, loyal to a fault. He was also one of the greatest pickpockets in the entire world, a skill which he and Jim had most recently employed on Ali the shopkeeper, relieving him of the glowing vile of magical juice. The young adventurers had a dire purpose for the concoction. But first was the small matter of their escape.

"Race you to the gate," Jim said, picking up speed.

"Jim, you ain't never been faster than me a day in your life!"

They ran as fast as they could, pace for pace, laughing as they went, as though they had not a care in the world.

Ahead, an iron-barred gate blocked the way through a thick stone wall. Behind him, Jim heard the guards growling that the foolish thieves had just run themselves into a death trap. But they were sadly mistaken. Jim and George never slowed, tearing for the gate as though it were made of air. Just before they crashed into the bars, the gate's lock clicked sharply, and the rusty bars creaked open.

As Jim and George sped through the now open archway, a shadow on the wall behind them kicked the gate closed again, then stepped into the red evening light.

"Hiya, Jim and George," said the smiling shadow, whose name was Peter Ratt. Peter was George's younger brother and lock picker extraordinaire. Ever since Jim had met the Ratts, back in London, there had never been a lock found to stump Peter. "You know," said Peter, with a cluck of his tongue. "You might be gettin a bit sloppy in your old age, Georgie. Isn't the idea of bein a thief about gettin away without anyone knowin you was even there? And if you are gonna let people know, maybe it shouldn't be a bunch of blokes with swords."

"Speak for yourself, *Peter*," said George, his smile slipping from his face as he glared at his brother. "Me and Jim almost ran smack into that gate. Took your time openin it, didn't you?"

Peter just shook his head at his brother, folded up his little pouch of tools, and tucked them into his pocket with a satisfied pat. "Gotta give meself some sort of challenge now, don't I?"

George was about to unload some boast of his own when the guards finally arrived. They slammed into the gate, tugging and pulling on it with their burly fists, cursing and spitting at the boys through the bars.

"These gates are to be locked at night!" shouted one of the scimitar-wielding watchmen. "How is it you have gotten through?"

"Well they seem locked to me, don't they?" said Peter, thumbing over at the guard. Their argument forgotten, George and Peter doubled over, hands on their sides, laughing in the guards' faces like hyenas. Jim was about to join in, when through the tangle of guards stepped a giant of a man. His shoulders filled the archway in the wall and his arms were like tree trunks. Jim's mouth fell open and the Ratts choked on their laughter as the enormous man took hold of the gate, swallowing the iron bars in his monstrous grip. When he pulled, the hinges groaned, and the bolts began to pop from the wall.

"Well," said Peter, staring with unblinking eyes. "I suppose that's another way to do it, innit?"

"Run!" Jim cried, and like a shot the three friends were off again. The boys were hardly a block down the street when the gate crashed to the cobblestone behind them, releasing their pursuers with cries of the hunt renewed. But as surprised as Jim was by this turn, he was yet to be worried. For as it happened, there were three Ratt Brothers, and the third and smallest of the trio was just up ahead. Paul Ratt stood hat in hand next to a set of stairs ascending the side of a building. He conversed with the building's owner through an open window as his two brothers and Jim came barreling down the street. He motioned to his cohorts with an expectant smile, as though they had arrived right on time.

"Ah," he said, "here they come now. See? Nothin to fear at all. Trust me, sir, when me mates and I are all finished up, your roof is gonna be the most rain proof in all the city."

"But it hardly ever rains in this place," said the man, staring skeptically at Paul and his friends. "We live in the desert. And is it not nearly night? It is too late to begin work. And what is it your friends are running from anyway?"

"The fact that it hardly ever rains is all the more reason to be prepared, old chum," said Paul, his smile never faltering. The youngest Ratt was every bit a born conman as George was a pickpocket and Peter a lock picker. "And have you ever worked on a roof in the daytime? Intolerable heat. As for me mates, they were just runnin here from our last job, weren't they? Have you ever seen such dedication? And I'll tell you sir, your neighbors are gonna be laughin at you when it rains that time later this year – cause they'll be drip free while you'll be swimmin in puddles. Trust me, friend, I'm from London, and we know our rain." With that, the building owner finally shrugged and relented, allowing the four thieves onto his roof just as Ali and his guards came pouring down the street.

"Just like London, eh lads?" whispered George, once they were all safely on the roof and looking down on the guards below. The guards' turbaned heads bobbed like onions in the shadows and their scimitars glimmered in the last bit of sunlight sneaking into the city.

"I don't recall Butterstreet and his lot wavin swords about, Georgie," said Peter, a hint of I-told-you-so in his voice.

"Well, if they don't see us, then they won't slice us, now will they, Pete?" retorted George. "Besides, I think a good run like thissun is good for us. It keeps—"

"—the skills sharp," Peter and Paul interjected in chorus. "We know."

As George balled up his fists, Jim suppressed a laugh. He foresaw yet another tussle from the three brothers, which usually ended with bloody noses and lips, and the three of them proclaiming one of themselves or the other the greatest brawler in the known world. But there was little time for more shenanigans. Darkness gathered swiftly. MacGuffy and the other pirates would be waiting for Jim and the Ratts to return to the mighty *Spectre*, where Lacey waited as well. At that thought, a quieter, sweeter smile crept onto Jim's face.

"Come on then, mates," he said. "Time to do like ghosts and vanish. That shopkeeper and those guards will simply have to remember with fondness the day they were lucky enough to cross Jim Morgan and the Brothers Ratt."

With that, Jim took a running leap over the thin alleyway to the adjacent rooftop, already imagining a hot dinner in his belly and a good sleep in his hammock. Unfortunately, Jim would soon be reminded that even the best laid plans sometimes hit a bump in the road – or roof.

Jim landed like a cat on the other side. But a string of popping cracks followed his usually quiet arrival. Jim dropped his eyes to his feet. The roof was not made of clay. It was made of thatch, only a scant crisscrossing of thin sticks. Jim whirled back with upraised hands to warn his friends – who were already in mid-air. They had leapt together, with wide obnoxious smirks plastered on their cheeks.

"Oh, bother," said Jim.

The Ratts hit the roof all at once to the sound of a brittle crunch, and with Jim, they crashed into the building in a cloud of dust, landing in four heaps in the room below. Fortunately, the thatch at least afforded some cushion – along with the stacked carpets lining the floor. The four of them had somehow managed to tumble into a rug shop. Jim picked himself up with a groan, cracking his back, coughing and hacking in the dusty air.

"Didn't you see me hold up my hands?" he asked his friends, all rubbing at bruises, wiggling their fingers and toes, and checking for anything that might be broken or unnaturally bent. "That's the universal sign for stop, you know."

"Oh sure, Jim," said George. "Not sure you if caught this, but the three of us actually stopped right there in midair and held a li'l conversation amongst ourselves about turnin back. But, wouldn't you know it, Paul just insisted we crack on!"

Jim was about to fire off a retort of his own, when he realized that silence had grown as thick about them as the swirling dust. The four thieves looked at each other, and then to the windows. The turbaned guards of the Kasbah leered from the streets outside, fingering the edges of their scimitars. The doorway to the shop creaked open, revealing the shop owner, Ali. His thin arms were folded across his chest and a vindictive smile was twisted upon his face.

"Oh, hello again," said Jim, coughing politely and wiping his filthy hands on his filthy jacket. "Did we forget to pay?" He and the Ratts laughed nervously to one another. A few of the guards laughed along – until Ali snapped his fingers, snuffing the guards' laughter like candle flames.

"Bring me their hands," he commanded.

The guards bulled through the windows, but Jim and the Ratts had other plans. Each grabbed a rolled rug, caked with dirt from the rooftop's collapse, and with four flicks, snapped them open. Clouds of thick dust filled the room. The guards coughed in agony as the grit scoured their eyes, blinding them just long enough for Jim and the Ratts to make a break for it.

They charged the shop owner, covering the man with one of the carpets, wrapping him into a neat little bundle and rolling him into the streets. Off the boys ran, with Jim pausing just long enough to withdraw a silver coin from his jacket pocket, roll it over his knuckles, and flick it to land atop the shop owner's carpet-bound body.

"Thanks for the potion," he said with a parting wink.

The guards tore after, shouting and waving their scimitars as they went.

Jim and the Ratts barreled around corners and leapt over drums, crates, and casks, fleeing the sound of thundering boots just behind them. Jim had no doubt that he and his friends could outrun the big men chasing them, as long as they didn't run themselves into—

—a dead end.

Jim skidded to a halt just before crashing into the wall. The Ratts slammed into his back and the four of them smashed into the bricks together. They searched for a way out, but quickly found the alley bereft of doors or windows. Jim looked to the top of the wall, hoping he and the others could boost themselves up. But rusty spikes lined the edge, taunting him with barbed points.

"We're stuck!" said Peter, a touch of fear flitting into his voice. The sound of tromping boots drew closer and closer.

"Got no way out!" added Paul, looking down at his hands and fingers as though already kissing them goodbye.

"No choice but to stand and fight, mates," said George, deadly serious.

"Stand and fight?" Jim asked, eyebrows raised. "George, they have swords if you didn't notice. We wouldn't stand a chance."

But George seemed not to hear Jim's warning. He was staring down the alley, toward the entrance where the guards would soon appear. His hand crept toward his inside jacket pocket, as though he kept some object there that might serve as a weapon, even against insurmountable odds such as these. What could George possibly have in there that would give him a chance against twenty armed men? But there was no time to ask. Jim balled up his fists beside his friend. What other choice was there? All the fourteen year-old arrogance finally drained from Jim's heart. He was just imagining what it might feel like to have his hand chopped from his wrist when the soft hiss of an urgent *pssst* caught his attention from the nearby wall.

"*Over here,*" the whisper called. Jim caught a sliver of light sneaking into the alley. The light traced the hairline cracks of a secret door built into the stone. "*Quick, young ones!*" cried the whisper. "*In here for your fathers' sakes!*" From the small opening in the wall, a finger stretched, curling once, twice, three times... beckoning the boys inside.

Jim looked to his friends. They looked back. The victorious catcalls of the approaching guards made up their minds. Hoping with all his heart this wasn't a trap, Jim ushered the Ratts through the hidden door. When they'd all gotten inside, and the door in the wall slid shut behind them, Jim's eyes went wide. A low whistle escaped his lips. There was a familiar smell wafting on the air of the hidden room—

— the familiar smell of freshly brewed magic.

TWO

ABDULLAH'S SHOP OF WONDERS

Jim's first thought as he surveyed the shop around him was of Egidio Quattrochi's turtle shell store in Shelltown, on Spire Island. That had been the place where Jim and his friends had learned of the Veiled Isle and the Hunter's Shell, over a year gone by. It had been from there that they had all set out on their last great adventure. The shopkeeper in this store stood no taller than Egidio. But unlike the bespectacled purveyor of magical goods from the pirate isle, this fellow was as thin as he was short, all dark skin and sharp bones. The top of his bright white turban reached only as high as the bottom of Jim's chin.

The small man crouched with his back to the boys, leaning urgently into the wall. He pressed one ear flush against the hidden door, his black mustache twitching beneath his nose as he listened to the befuddled guards outside. Jim had only taken a breath to whisper some thanks for their rescue before the silent shopkeeper waved a hand over his shoulder – the unspoken sign for *keep quiet you fools!*

So Jim surveyed the shop instead. Some time ago, this strange room might have been the most curious place Jim had ever seen. But after more than two years of adventuring through monster-infested waters and trekking over enchanted islands, the magic sales floor seemed only a bit less dull than the plain cabin Jim shared with the Ratts aboard the *Spectre*.

Two baskets, wound of thick rope and noticeably empty, stood beside a bookshelf next to the hidden door. The shelves were packed with thick volumes, spines titled with indecipherable letters. This same pattern was repeated along each wall – a single set of shelves flanked by rope-wound baskets.

One shelf was stacked with yellowed scrolls upon diamond-shaped lattices. On the next stood clay pots, symbols of clouds, rain, lightning, and the like baked onto each one. A set of twelve alarmingly active potted plants lined the final shelf, each leafy green stalk writhing and crawling in their pottery, like worms on wet ground. Twelve brass lamps burned from the tops of the shelves, and a thirteenth atop a counter in the center of the store. There, a small cauldron hung from a tripod over a flame, a glowing concoction bubbling within. The potion's smell shifted from sweet to putrid and back again. Clouds of steam puffed into the air from the tincture, taking the shapes of various animals before fading away.

"They have gone at last," said the shop owner all of a sudden. Jim nearly jumped out of his skin at the sound of the man's voice, for he had become quite entranced by the potion upon the counter. "Fear not," the little man continued, "for you are most fortunate, young pirates, that chance brought you to the alleyway behind Abdullah's Shop of Wonders. Had I not discovered you, you may have soon found your thieving fingers somewhat less useful when hung as decorations on the walls of the Khalif's dungeons." The shop owner padded around the boys, who had squeezed close together. His calloused fingers crossed before his chapped lips and his keen eyes measured the four young men before him.

"Those blokes wasn't gonna catch us, mister," George said, following the shopkeeper about the room with a suspicious gaze. "Our fingers was pretty safe then, and'll stay pretty useful for a long time to come." George wiggled his digits before his face with a snide grin on his lips.

"Good thing too, Georgie," said Paul. "I mean, how on earth would you pick your nose with just stumps for wrists? That would be a real challenge I'd wager. Might just rob some of the joy from your life." Paul shoved the palm of his hand into his nose to demonstrate, succeeding only in giving himself a piggy look on his face, with which he snorted in his older brother's direction.

"How would you know, Paul?" added Peter. "It's awful hard for you to pick you nose when you've got both hands occupied diggin into your b—"

"George, Peter, and Paul... Ratt," said Abdullah, the shopkeeper, interrupting Peter's rather awful insult. The sound of their names on this stranger's lips silenced the three brothers at once. A cold chill spilled down Jim's throat, oozing into an icy puddle in his stomach. "The Brothers Ratt? Thieves extraordinaire, yes?" Abdullah arched one eyebrow high on his swarthy forehead. A clever smile twitched onto his lips as his sights finally settled on Jim's face. "And would that not make you, oh fair one, James Morgan, son of Lindsay, Son of Earth, Son of Sea?"

"How do you know our names?" Jim demanded. The hackles raised on the back of his neck. He, like the Ratts beside him, began to search the shop for the quickest escape. Unfortunately, there was none but a single door and a single window in addition to the secret door behind them. "And where have you heard that title before?"

15

"How do I know the names of the famous Jim Morgan and his friends, the infamous Brothers Ratt?" Abdullah dropped his hands from his mouth, laughing heartily. "Your names are spoken in every pirate port from here to Tripoli, my young friends. You are world renowned pirates!"

"Did you hear that, George?" Paul whispered to Peter. "We're even more famous than Jim now. We're *in*famous!"

"I'm not sure that's a compliment, Paulie," said Peter. But Jim heard the two younger Ratts giggle as the shopkeeper approached, seizing Jim by the hand and shaking it firmly.

"You may call me Abdullah, Keeper of Lost Secrets and Knower of Magical Wonders. My humble shop is your shop, oh great adventurers!" Abdullah spread his arms wide in welcome and bowed his head low to the boys. "Now, I am no great wizard like the great Egidio Quattrochi, oh dear friends, but let us say that he and I run in the same circles, learning the same secrets, dabbling in the same arts."

Abdullah, who suddenly seemed quite flustered to be in the presence of such notoriety, began to scuttle about his shop. He popped over to the counter, reaching out for the lamp's flame. He took the fire onto his fingers and, whispering some words, transformed the flame into a fiery butterfly. It fluttered from the palm of his hand and twirled about the shop until it burst into a puff of smoke. Then Abdullah ran to the shelf lined with clay pots. He pulled off one of the lids with a flourish, ducking his head as a stray lightning bolt zipped from the jar. The bolt nearly singed off one of Abdullah's eyebrows on its way to the ceiling, where it crackled, burst, and showered the room with sparks. Lastly, the turbaned man dashed back to the counter, from under which he retrieved a quill and scrap of parchment. Upon scribbling a few words on the page, the paper folded itself into the shape of a bird and flew through the window, off into the darkening sky. Abdullah finished his magical display with arms outstretched like a showman, breathless from his enchanted exertion.

Jim and the others looked to one another, and after a brief shrug between themselves, offered Abdullah a polite round of applause. Peter and Paul's clapping came across as a bit less than enthusiastic.

"I'd give that a solid five out of ten, Paulie," said Peter. "Maybe a six. That lightnin bolt was fair sport, now weren't it?"

"Four. Four tops, Pete," replied Paul with a sigh. "I mean, once you seen green magic swallow a bloke whole, magic maps appear in blue flames, and ridden on the back of a water dragon, it takes a bit to impress, now don't it?"

"Ah, not so amazed with parlor tricks, are we, oh marvelous sailors of the sea?" said Abdullah, once more folding his hands before his face. Jim cringed inside, fighting the sudden urge to turn around and knock Peter and Paul's heads together for insulting the man who'd just pulled them out of deep trouble. But the shopkeeper merely grinned from behind his crisscrossed fingers, his eyes aglow with a glimmer of secrets. "But this is to be expected, is it not? For the great ship *Spectre* and her famous crew have not sailed all the way to the great Kasbah of the Udayas to seek out the cheap tricks of a street corner conjurer, have they? No, no, no. This is not what news has reached Abdullah's ears. The pirates of the *Spectre* have long been seeking out those who know the arcane mysteries. They have sought out those capable of greater magic. They have searched for magic deep enough to match such power as the Hunter's Shell."

Jim tried to keep the flash of surprise from his face, but the flicker of excited glee in Abdullah's eyes told him that he had been too slow. How did the shopkeeper know so much? Had word of their adventures truly spread so far, so fast? With a heavy sigh, Jim realized there was no point in trying to hide anything from the magical merchant.

"Yes," he finally admitted, "we have been looking for great magicians. We've been searching for magic as strong as the Hunter's Shell."

"Then fortune smiles upon us all again," said Abdullah, nearly squealing with delight. From behind the counter he produced a short stool, setting himself upon it and folding his legs beneath him like a djinn swirling from a lamp. "Though I am not nearly as famous as my four new friends, Abdullah has spent the humble years of his humble life in search of many secrets, and he has uncovered many spells. Perhaps the fates have brought us together for a purpose. Tell Abdullah of your mission, and Abdullah shall tell you if he can help." Abdullah set his eyes intently upon Jim. From his sleeve, with hands deft enough to impress even the Ratts, he revealed a Pungi, which was a short flute with a large bulb at the center.

At the sight of the flute, Jim's hands curled into fists. Peter and Paul pressed closer to Jim's back. And George, perhaps most noticeably of all, braced at Jim's side, ready for trouble.

"What's that for?" Jim demanded, pointing hard at the flute.

"Oh, fear not, young ones!" Abdullah said. The little man blushed sheepishly and bowed his head low three times. "Forgive an old fool. I have forgotten the details of your recent trials, and of your sorrows as well. Abdullah knows of Splitbeard the Pirate, who was in truth the magician, Philus Philonius – he of the enchanted flute. I also heard of the pain and trouble that wicked sorcerer inflicted upon you, oh Jim Morgan. But I promise you my Pungi is but an old habit that calms Abdullah's nerves. Its song is also good for storytelling. Its tune holds no sway over the minds of men." With that, Abdullah played a thin, whining trill on the Pungi. When nothing happened, Jim breathed a small, but wary, sigh of relief.

Jim looked once to George, who, after a bit of glaring at Abdullah, finally returned a nod. Jim licked his lips. Sweat slicked his palms, but he wiped them on his breeches, pressing a bit further into his story. Abdullah listened closely, every once in a while playing a tune on his flute.

"For the last year or more my friends and I have been sailing around the world, looking for powerful magic, as you said. And yes, as you've heard, we came into possession of the Hunter's Shell, taken from the Veiled Isle. But we only had it for a moment, until the Crimson Storm rained lightning on the *Spectre*, thicker than arrows. The storm's magic lightning struck the shell and split it in two."

"But that was not all it struck, was it, young one?" Abdullah asked softly.

"No," Jim said. The next words stuck in his throat, which was suddenly dry as sand. "The lightning also struck Dread Steele, Lord of the Pirates. It killed him as it cleaved the shell in half." Jim went quiet. His dry throat grew thick and chalky at the memory of Dread Steele.

"So much sorrow, young one," said Abdullah. "So much loss." Jim came out of his troubled thoughts to glance at the shopkeeper, who had stopped playing his flute and was now staring off into some nowhere above Jim's head. For an instant, a sorrow deep as Jim's own flickered on Abdullah's face. But the shopkeeper put his flute to his lips and played another trill, and the moment passed. "And now, oh valiant Jim Morgan, you seek to mend the Shell. You seek to make Dread Steele's sacrifice worthwhile. You seek to once again take up your quest for the Treasure of the Ocean."

"No!" Jim shouted. Abdullah seemed so surprised by this sudden outburst that he nearly tipped over backwards and toppled from his perch upon the stool. "Count Cromier and his son, Bartholomew, have the other half of the Shell. Even if I were to somehow stomach the idea of coming close enough to those murderers to steal back their half, I would only be giving them another chance to find the Treasure of the Ocean. Those fiends can never be allowed to have such power as the Treasure. I don't want to mend the Hunter's Shell, Abdullah. I want to destroy it. That's what we've been after all this time: a way to destroy the Shell. But no matter what we try, the shell seems resistant to any form of destruction. I think only something as powerful as the Crimson Storm will be strong enough to affect it."

"We still haven't tried havin George smash it with his head, though, have we?" Paul interjected. "I know for a fact that nothin in the world's harder than George's noggin. Nothin. It just might work."

"Shut it, Paul!" said George and Peter together. But Abdullah ignored them all. His eyes had gone wide and white, unblinking and fixed upon Jim's face.

"You, oh young adventurer, wish to destroy the Hunter's Shell? That which is one of the greatest talismans in all the world?" Abdullah recoiled in horror. "I pray you please reconsider, oh son of Lindsay Morgan!"

"I'm sorry," Jim said. "But I can't. One way or another, we're going to destroy the Shell, and with it, any chance of ever finding the Treasure of the Ocean. Then maybe my friends and I can get some peace for once. Then maybe we can find a home of our own."

"It would break Abdullah's heart to see such a glorious artifact destroyed, young one. But Abdullah also knows the love of family must come above all." Another brief wave of sadness swept over the shopkeeper's face, until he once again harrumphed it away. "Tell Abdullah what methods you have already tried to accomplish this mad deed."

"Liquid Dragonfire. Frost Giant Tears. Even a sword forged in the coals of Phoenix ashes," Jim said. "None of it so much as scratched the Shell."

"And your escape from the city guards this very evening?" Abdullah asked, an eyebrow arched high on his head. "This was surely not for sport, eh, my young friends?"

George produced the vial from his jacket pocket, shaking the shimmering red liquid to catch Abdullah's attention. "Fireberry Juice," he proclaimed. "Can set just about anythin on fire with this stuff, or so we're told. And it'll burn 'til nothin's left but ashes." At this boast Abdullah snorted back a mouthful of laughter.

"Fireberry Juice? Oh pray, young thieves, do not tell Abdullah that you have been thieving from that charlatan, Ali? Fireberry Juice will hardly burn a blister on your clever little fingers."

"We told you, George!" Peter and Paul declared together. Their older brother just sighed, rolling his eyes and slamming the vial back into his pocket.

"Can you help us, sir?" Jim asked, allowing himself a glimmer of hope after so many frustrations, near misses, and disappointments. Abdullah sat stone still on his stool, eyes fixed on the floor. It seemed to Jim the magical shopkeeper was thinking back on some long forgotten knowledge, tucked into a dusty corner of his mind.

"Yes," Abdullah finally uttered, in no more than a whisper. "Abdullah knows what to do." The shopkeeper's eyes slowly lifted from the floor, meeting Jim's own and holding the gaze as if for dear life. "Tell me boy... Have you brought the Shell with you?"

Now, Jim Morgan had lived on the run for over three years of his life, from the streets of London to the high seas of pirate waters. During that time his senses had grown sharp indeed, especially those mysterious powers that warn of danger. There was a hint of *something* in Abdullah's eyes, or in his voice, or perhaps in the question itself, that set those senses ringing like church bells at noontime.

"No," Jim said. "We wouldn't just go running around with something like that in our pockets, now would we?" Already Jim was motioning to the Ratts behind his back toward the door on the far side of the counter.

"You must bring the Shell here, young Morgan, for Abdullah knows what to do." The shopkeeper's gaze tightened on Jim's face. His grip squeezed on his flute, turning his knuckles white. "Abdullah is the only one who knows what to do."

"Could you just give us the potion?" Jim said. He and his friends inched their way toward the exit. "I promise you we'll pay — and if it works, we'll double whatever you ask when the deed is done."

"No!" Abdullah rasped. "Abdullah wants not gold or treasure. I only wish to help the great Jim Morgan finish his quest. But you must bring the Shell here. You must bring it to me. Where is it, boy? Tell Abdullah, for your father's sake!"

"I'm terribly sorry, but I'm afraid that won't be possible." Jim's heart began to slam at his ribs. There was a hunger lurking at the edges of Abdullah's eyes now – a hunger like a starving wolf's. Foolishly or not, Jim was beginning to wish that the city guards had caught him and his friends after all.

"Thanks for getting us out of that tight spot earlier. We really do appreciate it. But for now, I'm afraid we must be leaving."

"And I am afraid," said Abdullah, his voice growing hard, "that I cannot allow you to go."

Abdullah set his flute once more to his lips. Jim and the Ratts bolted for the door, but the fleet-footed thieves would be a step too late. The sharp notes of a tune began to play. Jim realized all too late that the flute indeed held no sway over him and the Ratts, neither over their minds nor their bodies.

But it was a magic flute nevertheless.

Its power commanded the ropes wound into the baskets by the shelves.

The baskets unspooled into long coils. The living ropes sprang like striking snakes, seizing the Ratts by the ankles, wrists, and waists before they could reach the door. George, Peter, and Paul slipped and struggled against their binds – all to no avail. Jim tried to yank one of the twists from George's ankles, until he felt a serpentine cord wind about his chest. A second rope slipped about his throat, strangling his startled cry.

Jim's eyes watered. Blackness crept onto the edges of his vision. The wicked cord began to squeeze.

THREE

IN THE SHOPKEEPER'S CLUTCHES

The cord that held Jim by the throat dragged him to the center of the room, slowly turning him to face Abdullah. The treacherous shopkeeper controlled the young thieves like a merciless puppeteer. Jim and George struggled with all their strength, while Peter and Paul dangled helplessly above the shop floor.

"I must beg your forgiveness, young Morgan," Abdullah said, taking the flute from his lips. "But there are some treasures worth more than silver and gold – a lesson Abdullah is most certain you have learned before." Jim tried to unleash a flurry of curses against the villainous little man, but the coils drew too tight about his throat, choking the words into gurgling rasps.

"There are some treasures worth even more than right or wrong, oh young adventurer," Abdullah continued. "But fear not, for I shall only hold you here in ransom for a short while. The pirates of the mighty *Spectre* will surrender your half of the Hunter's Shell to me. Then Abdullah shall in turn surrender you and your friends. At least those of you who survive."

It was then Jim realized what purpose the enchanted ropes served and why the baskets stood empty along the walls. The cords pulled the thieves back toward the baskets, where the ropes would cocoon them like flies in a spider's web. Peter and Paul were very nearly imprisoned already, kicking and thrashing to no avail. But Jim noticed something else at the same moment. When Abdullah paused his song to speak, the ropes were drained of some of their vigor.

From the corner of his eye, Jim saw that George had not missed the moment either. The eldest Ratt reached for his coat pocket once again, as he had when Jim and the others found themselves cornered by the city guards. What did George have? What besides magic could possibly help them now? Whatever it was though, Jim thought, now would be a good time to use it.

But Abdullah the shopkeeper was no fool. His dark eyes were sharp as well.

"I think not, oh clever thief! Abdullah must not lose his prize!" The flute leapt back to Abdullah's lips, unleashing its furious tune once more. The ropes about George crawled from his ankle and waist to his wrists, pinning his arms. George twisted and turned, gritting his teeth, pulling with all his might for his pocket. His fingertips crept just inside the lapel of his waistcoat – within inches of whatever he carried, but the ropes were strengthened by Abdullah's song. They won out in the end and George's arms were wrenched into the air.

But George's gambit did not wholly fail. As the furling binds yanked away his arms, one small object did fall from his pocket – a slender vial filled with glowing, red juice.

"Curse you, you blackguard!" George railed. The ropes dragged him toward his own basket. Jim felt his shoes losing their grip on the wooden floor, losing their battle against the living tangles. He managed to glance down to his feet. The vial from George's pocket had rolled on the floor just beside him. He would have only one chance.

Jim reached into his pocket, for the ropes still had him about his throat and his chest. He prayed that he still had one coin left, that he had not given his last away to that fraud Ali. Jim's fingers clutched a single farthing in the folds of his dirty pocket – one small stroke of luck.

Jim loaded the coin onto his thumb. Abdullah's attention was still on George, who was unleashing all manner of foul language at the little shopkeeper. Jim's eyes were nearly watered blind, but a year of picking pockets on the streets of London had given him deft fingers indeed. He shot the coin off his thumb, and was rewarded by a sharp plunk as it struck Abdullah on the forehead.

Abdullah's song faltered for but two or three notes. The binds loosened for a brief instant. Jim twisted in his coils, reaching for the floor, the rope burning the skin around his neck as he stretched. Abdullah recovered from his surprise, striking up his tune again. The ropes redoubled their grip on Jim, squeezing a choked gasp from his lungs. Jim had one finger on the vial, but the ropes were pulling him away.

Purple-faced and light-headed, Jim pushed on the floor with all his might – just enough to take the vial in his grasp. With his thumb, he uncorked the glass bottle, praying that Abdullah had been wrong, and that the Fireberry Juice held a bit more kick than would blister a finger. Jim splashed the cord that wound up around his neck.

Nothing happened.

Jim's heart sank...

...until a bloom of heat rushed up against his cheeks. A flame snapped to life on the stretch of rope, burning through the cord in an instant. The coils about Jim's neck went slack and fell to the floor. The length of twine still running from the basket flapped like a beheaded serpent in the throes of death. A streamer of smoke trailed behind its flaming end. The rope about Jim's chest went next, and the moment it burned away Jim stole a deep gulp of air. His vision cleared and his mind grew sharp.

There wasn't enough time or Fireberry Juice to free all the Ratts. And already, Abdullah's eyes were set on him, blazing with fury. The shopkeeper's fingers danced along the flute, driving the song faster. Two cords released the younger Ratt Brothers and wriggled along the floor toward Jim's ankles.

But if Jim had learned anything in his numerous dealings with magic, it was that the magician never had as much control over the black forces as he thought. That was why magic things were always kept locked up tight, in boxes, in vaults, or in clay jars. Jim dashed to the shelf lined with lidded pots, seizing the side and grabbing on tight.

"You should have known the moment you brought us in here, Abdullah," Jim said. "You called us famous thieves. Well, thieves only get famous if they're good at not getting caught!" Jim threw all his strength against the shelf, just as the ropes reached his ankles. Abdullah's eyes went wide with terror. The flute dropped from the sorcerer's lips as the shelves went crashing to the floor.

"No, you fool!" Abdullah cried. But it was too late.

The clay jars shattered against the floor, bursting into a hundred shards. All the magical forces held within erupted into the shop. A great wind blew Jim back against the wall, whipping at his coat and pulling his hair. A black cloud gathered on the ceiling, spinning and swirling. Rain, hail, and snow flew, thunder shook, and lightning flashed. Abdullah was nearly swept away when a wave of water spilled from another one of the broken pots, all but drowning him. He raised his hands, shouting spells into the air to harness the out-of-control forces unleashed within his store.

But when the shopkeeper lifted his hands, he was forced to drop his flute. The ropes fell from George, Peter, and Paul. Even in the midst of all the madness about them, irrepressible smiles lit their mousy faces.

"Well done, mate!" George said, rushing to Jim's side, his brothers just behind him.

"Not bad, Jim," added Peter.

"Not bad at all," finish Paul.

"Let's make a break for it!" Jim cried over the peals of thunder. He and the Ratts splashed through the ankle deep water, fighting the hurricane winds to the front door.

"Think you have escaped already, oh crafty Morgan?" Abdullah raged. The shopkeeper had given up on restraining the wild forces and stalked toward the counter in the center of his ruined shop. "Do you think you have undone all of Abdullah's magic by pulling down one shelf, foolish boy?"

Abdullah reached for the cauldron that had been burning on the counter. He lifted a ladle from the cauldron's edge and tossed two dollops of boiling concoction onto the counter. The goopy puddles bubbled and frothed, congealing into solid forms.

Jim watched in horror as two great dogs grew to full size on the counter top – snouts lined end to end with glistening fangs.

"Well," said Paul with a sigh, "maybe the old boy rates a bit higher than a four after all."

"Run!" Jim screamed, yanking hard on the door. The Ratts had no need to be told twice. The four friends tore into the streets. The warm air of the city washed over them, and the cold wind and enchanted water rushed at their heels. Jim and the Ratts had gone but a few steps when they heard the snarling dogs leap through the window and land on the cobblestone street behind them.

If these had been ordinary boys, those raised in stuffy school clothes, with harpsichord lessons in the morning and Latin classes in the afternoon, then the magically produced hounds would have caught them by the ankles within the first block. But these were no schoolboys. Through windows, down alleys, over tables, barrels, and walls the four thieves fled like deer.

Several times the dogs snapped at Jim's ankles, nipped at

George's fingertips, and threatened to run down Peter and Paul in the streets. But the nimble youths were just quick enough to leap out of the pursuing pack's reach. At last, when even the fleet friends' breaths grew labored, Jim saw a chance to put some distance between the clan and the dogs.

"George!" Jim shouted, pointing to an aproned kiosk at the edge of the market, closed and covered for the night. Jim's best friend nodded and slid up behind him. In one leap the two of them reached up and tore the apron from the kiosk frame, casting it behind them as they fell back to the street.

The apron floated down like a blanket. The dogs ran into the folds. The tangles of cloth tripped the hounds, ensnaring them within the thick fabric. The trap lasted only for a moment – but a moment long enough for the Clan of the Ratt to sprint ahead.

"Good throw, gents!" Peter said, coming to run between Jim and George. Paul whooped from just behind them, laughing at the top of his lungs.

"Was there ever any doubt?" he said as the four of them rounded a corner into the closed market and toward the docks. "I mean, honestly, who's going to catch us? We're the most famous thieves in the world. We are George, Peter, and Paul! The Brothers—"

"Rats!" Jim screamed, interrupting Paul's solo cheer. He skidded to a halt, grabbing Peter's elbow and feeling Paul slam face first into his back.

"You interrupted the cheer, Jim," Paul yelped, rubbing his nose. But all Jim's attention was focused on the wall of men blocking the way ahead.

"Famous thieves indeed, young ones," said a voice. "And the hands of famous thieves will make famous trophies on the dungeon walls of the Kasbah." Ali, the shopkeeper from whom the boys had stolen the Fireberry Juice, stepped between the heavily muscled frames of two guards. "Thought we had given up, my young friends? Oh, foolish ones, Ali never gives up. Ali always gets what he deserves."

A dose of dread dripped over Jim's heart. "Ah yes, well hello there, old chum," he said, backing away from the guards with George and his brothers. "We were actually on our way back to thank you. Your Fireberry Juice was in no way as fraudulent as Abdullah made it out to be. It worked wonders against some nasty magic ropes just a few minutes ago." Jim held up the empty vial, smiling as best he could. "And I would even give you a whole extra coin just to say thank you, but I unfortunately had to flick it against Abdullah's head."

"I do sell the Fireberry Juice by the coin, oh little thief," growled Abdullah, a dark cloud passing over his face. "One coin for one drop."

"Oh, right," Jim said. A sick feeling welled up in his gut. He turned to run back the way they had come, but this time it was he who slammed into Paul's back.

Slather dangled from the hounds' lips as they stepped into the market. Growls burned behind their long teeth. The dogs stalked toward Jim and his friends. The guards closed in from behind. Jim wondered if the dogs would leave enough scraps of him and his friends for Ali and his guards to imprison. Jim turned to George, and once more found his friend reaching for his jacket pocket.

"George," Jim whispered. "What have you got there?"

"Just a li'l somethin to even the odds, mate," George said. Jim wondered if perhaps George still had a fog seed or two from Egidio Quattrochi's shop. Yet something in George's face told him this was something stronger – something darker.

But a caw from the air froze both Jim and George where they stood. "Preoleum!" cried a shrill voice. It was the voice of a raven – a talking raven circling just above Jim's head. The bird's name was Cornelius Darkfeather, and not only could he talk, but he could fight. The raven dove from the air into the line of guards, clapping his wings and clawing at their faces. The guards clumsily swung their scimitars at the flitting bird, hitting nothing but air.

The dogs, excited by the sudden flurry of action, sprung forward, jaws snapping. Jim and his friends squeezed together when another voice sounded over the marketplace.

"You boys may want to jump in just a moment!"

Jim snapped his head to the side and found a slender, hooded figure atop a stack of barrels, which were lashed to a wall with thick rope. With a flick of a knife, the figure cut the ropes and the barrels tumbled forward. Jim, George, Peter, and Paul leapt out of the way, letting the barrels crash and rupture against the far wall, spilling water and fresh olives into the square.

The attacking dogs hit the olives and water and slid on the slippery ground, stumbling in two rolling balls of snapping jaws and flying fur. Jim and the Ratts rolled aside as the dogs bowled into the guards behind them, knocking them down like pins.

"Scramble!" Jim cried. He hit the ground running with the Ratts close behind, leaping over the pile of dogs and guards. As the clan fled the market, Ali the shopkeeper howled after them, swearing that he would one day have their hands as trophies.

The hooded figure that had come to their rescue caught up with the clan as they made for the docks, running light as a feather.

"What kept you, Lacey?" Jim said, unable to keep a smile from his face. The shadow running beside him pulled the hood from her head, loosing a long tangle of curly auburn hair, and letting her blue eyes shining in the evening light.

"I believe your exact words, Jim Morgan, were 'feel free to sit this one out, Lacey. The *boys* will handle it.' Or am I mistaken?" Jim snuck a glance to the side and found Lacey giving him the smallest of smirks.

"Well, those *were* the words, I said, Lacey, but I think you may have missed the meaning. 'Feel free' was just a nice way of saying, we'd love to have you along. Wouldn't you agree, fellows?"

"That's the way I took it, Jim," said Peter, nodding convincingly even as he ran.

"I was asking where you was the entire time, Lacey," added Paul. "The *entire* time!"

"Well I didn't need or ask for your help, Lacey," said George. "We're always runnin, it seems. One of these days we're gonna have to stand and fight. And I was ready." George's usual smile never appeared as he spoke. Jim noted the firm set of his friend's jaw and the dark squint of his eyes. Jim was just about to ask again about whatever it was George had hidden in his pocket, when a whirl of black feathers zipped between the two of them.

"I think not, Master Ratt," squawked Cornelius, gliding just above their heads. "Battle is indeed an unfortunate solution to some challenges, but only as a final choice, and hopefully with at least some form of a plan in mind, young sir."

Jim thought he heard George grumbling something about not needing a plan when he had... something. But he could not make out the last word.

"So, how many times have Cornelius and I saved you in the last few months, Jim?" Lacey asked. "You know, for being pirates and thieves and all, the four of you certainly end up on the run quite a bit, don't you?"

There was a time, Jim knew, when he would find Lacey's eyes aglow with flashing anger during just such a moment. But as of late, Lacey had replaced those furious glares with a curious sort of smile, the very one she was wearing then. It was the most perplexing and infuriating smile Jim could imagine. But for some reason he couldn't help but return it, and it held more sway over him than a thousand flashing stares.

"I don't know, Lacey," Jim said with a shrug. "Twice?"

"It would be ten times, Master Morgan," cawed Cornelius. The raven came to fly just over Jim's head and swatted him with an outstretched wing. "TEN! And this makes twice in this very city. In fact, I think you may have now worn out our welcome in the Kasbah. MacGuffy and the Khalif were once good friends, you know, when Dread Steele was alive. But even those ties hold only so strong. And don't expect me to stick up for you with the old salt this time either." Cornelius gave an irritated squawk. "He was quite put out when the four of you failed to return at sunset... again." Jim nearly laughed out loud at the thought of MacGuffy's scarred face going purple and the string of creative curses spilling from his ruined lips.

"Oh come on, Cornelius," said Jim. "I'm sure MacGuffy will hardly have noticed our absence at all. And besides, what's life without a little excitement?" At those words, Jim and his friends crested a small hill. The great docks of the Kasbah spread out before them, the last lip of the setting sun still glowing off the ocean waves. There, moored to the longest pier, mast stretched tall to the sky, the mighty ship *Spectre* stood proud in the bay.

"Home, sweet home," Jim said to himself. His smile faltered only a little at the thought.

FOUR

SHADOWS FROM THE DARK

Abdullah swept the ruined floor of his once tidy shop. He'd managed to gather a small pile of wet ash, drowned plants, and broken pottery at his feet, but when he looked at the calamity that still covered the rest of the floor, he sighed with despair and threw the broom to the ground.

How many years had he spent collecting the magic of the four winds, the spring rain, the winter snow, and the summer storm? To how many shores had he sailed to collect the rarest of plants, those with which be brewed his elixirs? Abdullah had lost count of all those deeds. But he was sure of this – he had neither the strength nor the time to accomplish them again.

A forlorn whine mewled from the door. Abdullah turned to find his conjured dogs limping back from the hunt, heads down, ears low and tails dragging behind them.

"Ah, so you have returned, my beauties," Abdullah said. He forced a quivering smile over his face, as though trying to cheer them up. "But you return empty handed, or empty jawed, as it were." Abdullah coughed a laugh at his own pun, but the laugh nearly became a sob. The dogs whimpered about his ankles, and Abdullah leant down to scratch behind their drooping ears. When he brought up his hands, he found his fingers coated with slimy potion. The dogs had tracked the sludge in prints back to the door and out into the street. The magic was failing.

"Away with you for the night, oh courageous ones." Abdullah took the ladle from the cauldron and scooped through each of the animals. The ladle's touch turned them back into a perfect dollop of potion each. With two plops he deposited them back into the simmering brew.

Alone once more, Abdullah pulled the turban from his head, releasing his bedraggled, gray hair. He covered his eyes with a shaking hand, ashamed of his own tears. But before Abdullah had the chance to weep, a cold wind swept through the door, flickering the remaining lamp flames and dimming their glow. The wind snatched the breath from Abdullah's lungs and stung his tear-filled eyes. It was a wind too cold to have been born of the Moroccan desert.

It was a wind from a far off place.

Abdullah uncovered his face, but he was afraid to lift his eyes. Wisps of grit blew in from the door, carried on the back of the icy gale. They were not grains of sand from the Moroccan soil. This was fine black powder – magic black powder – used by only a few in all the world. Abdullah's aching heart sank even lower.

"Where are they, Abdullah?" said a voice from the doorway, the graveled, cracked bark of an old man. "Where are the thieves?"

Abdullah summoned his courage and lifted his face to meet his visitors. Two men melted from the deepening night. The man who spoke came first, a black coat over his shoulders, waistcoat and breeches dark as a starless sky. His face was scarred and puckered. He wore a gentleman's wig of bright, blood red curls. Behind him appeared the other – more ghoul than man, and far too young to have earned the red captain's coat he wore. He had hair as black as a raven's wings, skin like fallen snow, and ice blue eyes that stabbed wherever they looked. Count Cromier and his son, Bartholomew, had come.

"You said you had them here," continued the count. "You said you had Morgan here." The count held out a gloved fist. He unfurled his fingers one at a time, revealing the crushed shape of a paper bird, the magical note that had flown with uncanny speed to Shade Manor, in England, that very night. Cromier dropped the smashed wad to the floor. "Where are they, Abdullah?" Abdullah's throat went dry as the desert. His hands shook. He began to wring the turban in his grip like a wet towel.

"Abdullah did have them here, oh masterful one," Abdullah said, the words sticking to his tongue. "Can you not see the evidence of their skullduggery in the mayhem that was once my shop?"

"Did I not warn you of the consequences of failure?" Not a breath of pity carried on the count's voice. The purple scar quivered upon the his rucked face.

"Please, sir," Abdullah begged. "For pity's sake." But he knew he would find no kindness from the count. Over the last year, ever since that cursed night when the count and his pale son had come to the Shop of Wonders, Abdullah had learned the hard way that the Red Count did not know the meaning of mercy.

It was rumored that Cromier's unending schemes to unearth The Treasure of the Ocean had begun to take a toll on his vast wealth. It was even whispered that his failures to find it had begun to take a toll on his mind and on what little remained of his soul.

"There are but three men in all the world who possess the magical knowledge to mend the Hunter's Shell, Abdullah," the count said.

"As you may have heard, Wong of the Far East failed me but a few months gone by. So now we are down to two. Of those two, Abdullah, I thought surely you would be the one to succeed in the end."

"Please, sir," Abdullah managed. "Do not harm them. Please do not hurt my family. They are innocent." Abdullah fell to his knees before the count, shaming himself for his family's sake, and begged. "I plead with you, oh merciful Count. Please!"

"Their lives were in your hands, Abdullah, not mine." Only then did a smile touch the count's withered lips. Cromier reached into his pocket and withdrew two wooden shapes – stick figures of a woman and a small child. Tears brimmed in Abdullah's eyes. He wrung the turban until it nearly ripped in two. The count curled his fingers over the shapes, ready to squeeze.

"Can you truly do it?" Bartholomew's voice suddenly rang out. The surprise of it stole Abdullah's breath away, but it also paused the count's crushing grip. Bartholomew brushed past his father, coming to stand over the miserable heap that was Abdullah the shopkeeper. "Can you truly mend the Hunter's Shell, you cur? Or have you been lying all along?" Bartholomew tore his sword from its scabbard, holding the glimmering blade to Abdullah's throat.

"Yes, oh pale son of the great Count! Yes, Abdullah can do this thing. I swear it!"

"And Morgan is still in the city, or has the coward already fled to sea?"

"The city guards chased him and the Brothers Ratt this very night, after they thieved from a magical charlatan named Ali. But I know that the old sailor who pilots their great ship is a friend of the Khalif. If the pirates leave, they will wait until morning, sir. Please... Please let Abdullah have this one last chance." Abdullah cared no longer about his pride. He let his tears fall down his face, wiping them from his cheeks with his ragged turban.

Bartholomew turned then to his father, keeping his blade pressed against Abdullah's neck. "Father," he said, "if Morgan and his pirate scum are still in the city, we may have time. Let us allow our new friend a chance to do what he says he can. If we find the shell, then perhaps, this very night, you might yet gain your prize."

The count's burning eyes lingered on Abdullah's face. The scar on his face writhed. After a moment – one that seemed to Abdullah like a hundred years – the count relaxed his fingers from around the wooden dolls and placed them back into his pocket.

"Thank you!" Abdullah sobbed, brushing the blade from his neck and falling at Bartholomew's feet, kissing the toes of his boots. "Thank you, oh merciful one!"

"Get off me, swine!" Bartholomew kicked Abdullah away from him. "I seek only the means to undo the house of Morgan once and for all, and to finally claim the birthright of power meant for me."

"And Abdullah shall assist you, oh merciful one!" Abdullah scrambled to his feet, throwing his wrinkled turban back on his head, careful to keep his eyes to the floor. "I shall go to the docks this very hour. I still have many tricks, oh great son of the count, many potions with which I can force that renegade, Jim Morgan to give up the Shell. I shall–"

"You shall do nothing!" The count thundered. Abdullah choked his offerings in his throat. "You shall do nothing but prepare the magic that will make the two halves whole again. We no longer have need to force Morgan to say anything, I think. In fact, I believe we need but ask him for what we seek. Isn't that right, Janus Blacktail?"

From behind the count, all but camouflaged in the night, a svelte shape slunk through the door. Green eyes, aglow like flaming emeralds, shone from a smiling face – the smiling face of a gleeful, black cat.

"Of courrrse, my dearrr Count," purred the cat, running a pink tongue over his sharp teeth. "Of courrrse." The cat's laugh ran like claws over Abdullah's soul.

FIVE

BACK ABOARD THE *SPECTRE*

Jim, Lacey, and the Ratts arrived at the *Spectre* just as the moon rose over the ocean. Cornelius sat perched upon Lacey's shoulder, ruffling his feathers as she scratched him beneath his beak. The mighty ship was moored to the pier, her sails tied down, but her noble bowsprit pointed toward the horizon, as though the ship itself longed to take to the waves for another adventure.

Up the gangplank the five youths ran, greeted with silent nods by Murdoch and Wang Chi, the best lookouts in the entire crew. A lively tune kicked across the deck, cranked out by a red-bearded pirate who called himself the Organ Grinder. The other sailors, both young and old, tapped their feet, clapped their hands, or bellowed out the words to the song. They laughed and joked, clanked cups of ale in toasts of good health, and afterward drained them dry.

But as merry as the crew seemed, Jim heard their voices lower as he and his friends passed by. He saw their eyes drop to their feet. He heard their furtive whispers behind his back. It had been this way ever since the death of Dread Steele, just over a year ago. Cursed, the crew would whisper among themselves. The name of Morgan was cursed, as was the one who still carried it.

"Hullo there, me friends. Good to have you all back safe and sound, it is, it is!" Mister Gilly appeared from behind the mainmast, his round belly poking out from beneath his striped shirt, his bulbous nose as red as a plump tomato. He held two tins of ale, one in each hand. "Old Gilly would offer ye some grog if ye was old enough, I would. But since you can't have any, I'll settle for havin some more meself." With that the joyful seaman toasted the young clan with both cups and took a sip from each, leaving a foam lining about his sleepy smile.

"Thank you, Mister Gilly," said Jim. If there was one pirate who was forever happy to see Jim's face, it was Gilly. That was often enough to make Jim feel at least a little more at peace aboard his floating home. As much as all the other pirates laughed at Gilly's odd sayings and his overfondness of ale, they also knew there was no better pilot on the ocean, so Gilly's opinion carried some weight.

"Greetings, little sea Ratts," another voice boomed over the deck. This one belonged to a bald giant of a man named Mufwalme. The great man's skin was dark as midnight, but his smile shined bright as the moon. "Returned from inciting yet another riot in yet another city, have we, young ones?"

"Oh, hello there, Mufwalme," said Paul, crossing his skinny arms over his skinny chest in a fairly good imitation of the way Mufwalme crossed his enormous arms over his enormous chest. "No, no, nothin so excitin as all that. Pete here and I were just tryin to find you some magical hair growin lotion this time out. Unfortunately, both Ali and Abdullah were clean out. Promise we'll get you next time though. You've got our word." Peter slapped his hand over his mouth in an attempt to stifle a giggle. But Mufwalme had only to growl in the direction of the two boys to still their laughter. Peter and Paul actually liked Mufwalme a great deal, and Jim knew that jokes were their way of showing it. Jim was only slightly nervous that they would take it too far one day and end up overboard.

"We heard the bells calling out the city guard from here, little sea Ratts," rumbled Mufwalme. "For who else would they ring but the four of you?"

"It really wasn't as bald–I mean, bad as all that, Mufwalme," Peter said, almost spitting with laughter.

"Nothin too *hairy*. Just the usual," said Paul with a bored sigh. Peter giggled again and Lacey just rolled her eyes. "Scimitar wieldin guards, magic ropes tryin to choke us to death, storms breakin out o pots, and magical dogs huntin us. Did I miss anythin?"

"Only the part where Cornelius and I had to save your lives, Paul," said Lacey, pulling her curls behind her ear to give the two younger Ratts a warning look.

"Indeed, Master Ratt," squawked Cornelius. "Every time you four cause a scene in a port city, you attract unwanted attention. Beyond that, it was fortunate for you that dear Lacey and I arrived when we did, or I would be giving the four of you new nicknames to commemorate your sudden lack of hands."

"We didn't need your help!" George barked. The harshness of his voice caught Jim and the others off guard. His hands were balled up into fists at his side, and some hot color had risen into his cheeks. "Me and Jim had it under control, dinnit we, Jim?"

"It was a rather tight scrape, Georgie," Jim said softly. "I mean, you really saved us earlier by getting that Fireberry Juice out of your pocket, that's for sure. And you and I can still put on some good moves when on the run."

"But when are we gonna stop runnin, Jim?" George said loudly enough for some of the pirates nearby to hear. "Are we gonna live our whole lives on the run? We're no better off now than we was when we were in London. But at least there we had a plan to get away, to find a place where we could live a bit easier."

"But that plan was a lie, George," said Lacey. "A lie told by the King of Thieves."

"But at least it was a plan!" The color in George's cheeks went even darker. "One of these days we're gonna have to stand up and fight, or we're never gonna have no home for ourselves."

Neither Jim nor Lacey said anything. Jim hated seeing his friend so angry, but more than anyone else, he understood what George was feeling. A tingle in the palm of Jim's hand, where a scar in the shape of a blooming white rose marked his flesh, was a constant reminder of that. It was a reminder of when he had nearly given in to anger – given in to revenge. He pricked his finger with a magical rose thorn, a decision that had nearly cost him and his friends their lives.

"Well then, Master Ratt," said Mufwalme in his booming voice. "Perhaps you would like to explain this plan of yours to MacGuffy. If I were the four of you, I would find my way below decks and make myself as useful as possible before—"

"Blast ye, ye scurvy sea Ratts!" a railing old voice cried over the deck. The pirates went back to their singing, Gilly went back to his drinking, and the three brothers Ratt groaned together, dropping their heads in unison.

"Too late," said Mufwalme. A wide, beaming smile split his face.

MacGuffy limped toward the little clan from the quarterdeck, his faded greatcoat billowing out from his shoulders and his one good eye glaring out from his ruined face. Younger pirates fell over themselves to clear a path, and Jim braced himself for an epic lecture – again.

"How many times have I told ye to go without bein seen?" MacGuffy raged. "How many times have I told ye to return to the Spectre before the settin o the sun? How many times have I told ye to raise no flags nor alarums to our presence whilst in port? How many? And yet here we be standin yet again. Here we be forced to set sail from yet another port, thanks to yer foolhardiness!" MacGuffy stood over the four boys, his wrinkled old face nearly purple as the scar that ran from his eye patch down to his cheek. "When a cap'n gives an order, he be givin it only one time. One! And if a sailor be disobeyin the order, he be given the lash or the plank. But you three, you three be some kind o demons o disobedience! Some kind of devils of foolish rebellion! Sent from on high by the almighty to punish old MacGuffy for the sins o his youth!"

"Remember those nicknames," Peter whispered to Paul from the corner of his mouth. "They're not half bad really." Jim sighed to himself. Now it was going to be worse.

"And now we start with the jokin!" MacGuffy shook his head and raised his hands to the heavens. "Would that Poseidon send a sea beastie to pluck me from this very deck to put me out of me cursed misery. Would that Neptune hisself summon a great wave to wash me to the depths of the ocean, n' drag me old bones down to live with the fishes of the deep. Would that..." With each 'would that', MacGuffy's pirate accent grew thicker and thicker, to the point that Jim could hardly understand a word the old man said, which probably included a fair sampling of the vast array of curse words the old salt had in his repertoire. At last, with spittle flying from his now crimson face, MacGuffy took a deep breath and finished with: "Have I made meself clear, ye rascally sea pups?"

George kept his eyes glued to his feet, his hands shoved into his pockets. But Peter and Paul stared at MacGuffy, who was sucking in long, labored breaths, their faces scrunched up like quizzical bulldogs.

"I missed everythin after that bit about Neptune," said Paul, exchanging confirming nods with Peter.

Jim thought this would be the last straw, the one that finally sent old MacGuffy over the edge. But a slow smile, one twitching at both corners pulled at the thin lines of MacGuffy's lips. He leaned over, bringing his scarred face within an inch of Paul's, turning to glare with his one good eye.

"I said, Paul Ratt, that if ye and yer two scurvy brothers don't get yer skinny arses below decks by the time old MacGuffy counts to three, I'm goin to poke a hole in that empty coconut ye use fer a head, and drink out yer soul from it. Be that a bit clearer for ye?"

Paul's eyes went a bit wider than tea saucers, and for a half moment, Jim thought the smallest Ratt actually believed every word MacGuffy had just said. Without another peep, Peter and Paul scampered off for the steps that led below decks. George followed after, head low and hands in his pockets, scuffing at the deck with his feet. Whether he admitted it or not, George had taken a stronger shine to old MacGuffy than he let on. The old man had been the closest thing George and his brothers had to a father since they became orphans in London, and MacGuffy's lighthouse the closest thing to a real home.

Jim and Lacey turned to go as well, when MacGuffy's voice caught Jim from behind. "Not you, young Morgan," MacGuffy said. Without looking Jim in the eye, the old pirate hobbled past on his way to the *Spectre's* fore, calling over his shoulder as he went. "I'll be havin yet a few more words with ye at the prow, if ye please." Jim loosed a long sigh, bracing himself for the continuation of the evening's lecture. But before he could turn to follow MacGuffy, Lacey caught him by the wrist.

"Go on then, Jim," she said. "I'll talk to George. You know how he can be sometimes. I'm sure he'll be all right." But it was another moment before Lacey released Jim's hand, and for a long breath, Jim wasn't sure whether he wanted her to let go at all. The warmth of her fingers scattered his thoughts and had his heart skipping every other beat. But she finally did let go and turned to leave, her auburn curls swaying over her cloak.

"Lacey," Jim said so suddenly he had to scramble to remember what he was going to say. She stopped and threw him a glance over her shoulder. "Thanks for saving my neck again. Wouldn't have gotten away if it weren't for you."

"I know that, Jim Morgan. I think it's written in the stars that I'll have to save you from death for the rest of my life." Lacey gave Jim that infuriating smile of hers before turning once more to follow the Ratts below decks.

Jim might have stood there staring after her the rest of the night if Cornelius had not flapped over to his shoulder and reminded him it was time to speak with MacGuffy alone.

SIX

OLD MACGUFFY

Jim found old MacGuffy leaning against the railing at the bow, his scraggly hair waving in the salty wind and his hardened gaze fixed past the bowsprit, like some sort of scarecrow warding off evil spirits in the night. Out over the sea, the stars poked holes in the night and the moon lit a path over the water to the dark horizon.

"Sorry about the alarms and the guards," Jim said after watching MacGuffy quietly for a while. "I'm sorry we have to leave again. It wasn't really George, Peter, or Paul's fault. I—"

"Ye just did what boys do, Jimmy," said MacGuffy. "Ye did what boys are supposed to be doin, anyways." All the fire and brimstone had left MacGuffy's voice. His words were quiet now. MacGuffy turned from the sea and sat down with a groan on a barrel. His one good eye fell to the deck. He rested his old arms on his knees, bowing his tired back. "I carry on too much sometimes with the sea Ratts, I do. Like 'em I do, Jimmy, 'specially Georgie. Minds me of meself, he does. Minds me of when I was a rascally sea pup, if ye can imagine this rurnt face young again. Shouldn't be blamin a boy for doin what boys do."

"You're just trying to keep us safe, MacGuffy," Jim said. Pirates were not really the apologizing sorts, Jim had learned early on. But he could tell that was what MacGuffy was after. "One day you won't have to. One day, everything will go back to normal."

"One day. Aye, one day." MacGuffy reached into his coat and withdrew a small flask. He took a long sip, wiping the drippings from his scruffy chin with the back of his sleeve. Then he took another. "Know what the crew be sayin about ye, Jimmy? Know what they be whisperin behind yer back?"

"They're not very good whisperers," Jim said. "They say I'm cursed. They say that if I stay aboard for much longer, eventually my curse will take us all. They say it was my curse that killed Dread Steele."

"And if they ever say that when old MacGuffy stands near, they should cover up their hollow heads afore I box their ears in to fill up the empty space between." Some of the thunder returned to MacGuffy's voice, and some lightning to his eye. But only for a moment. "And what do you think, Jimmy? Do you think you be cursed?" MacGuffy at last looked Jim in the eye.

Jim opened his mouth. But then he closed it again, settling for a shrug of his shoulders. His throat hurt as he thought about Dread Steele, and about his father.

"In a way, ye are cursed, Jim. But here me outright afore ye mistake me meanin. Remember when I told ye, back at the lighthouse, that there be storms in the world, and that ye know not what kind of man ye be until ye've sailed through 'em? Remember?"

"I remember, MacGuffy."

"A man cannot always choose the storms he'll face. Sometimes the storms choose him. The storm that has chosen you is a dark, merciless fiend if I ever seen one, boy. That be your curse indeed. But that don't make it yer fault."

Jim swallowed hard. "Dread Steele told me once that sometimes to sail through a storm, you have to turn into it. You have to turn into the waves, or they'll tip you over and drown you."

"Aye, lad, aye." MacGuffy took another sip from his flask. "Spoke true, he did."

"So George is right? We should stop running? We should stand and fight the Cromiers?"

MacGuffy shook his head, holding up his withered, bony hand. "Hear me, hear me, Jim, afore ye start thinkin rash thoughts about war, and fightin, and battles. The scar ye carry on yer hand should be reminder enough to think twice on such things. Now, there's not much MacGuffy remembers from his lessons back at school, long ago. But there was a proverb from the old book that read: 'The battle be not against flesh nor blood, but against the powers, and against the darkness of this world.' That's how I remember it, anyhow. No, you can't run from your storm forever. But the Cromiers ain't the storm, boy. Oh, they're bad, they are, and they've allied themselves with the dark, they have. But the real storm is cruelty and greed, one man thinkin he got a right to rule over another, and one man thinkin he knows what's best for all the rest. That be the battle, boy, 'specially when ye feel those things creepin up inside yerself. Remember that, and you'll know when to stand and when to run. Aye, you will. Understand me, boy?"

Jim managed to nod. "You'll be here to help me remember though, won't you, MacGuffy? You'll help me know when to stand and when to run?"

A small smile wiggled onto MacGuffy's lips. His lone eye searched Jim's face and somewhere beyond, into that place of memory.

"I still remember sayin somethin the like to me old pappy, I do. One day yer askin old men when to turn right and when to turn left. Then ye fall asleep one night, and ye wake up and some young pup is askin ye the same questions. Makes ye wonder where the years went in between.

"I'm an old man, Jim Morgan, an old man that mayhaps has faced more storms than he shoulda survived. I fear for ye, Jim Morgan. I fear for ye. I fear fer little Lacey and the sea Ratts as well. When old MacGuffy is gone, me thinks it will be you that'll have to lead 'em on. It'll have to be you, Jimmy."

"How will I know what to do, MacGuffy?" Jim asked. The words came out thick and quiet, for his throat was tight and burning. "How will I know if no one is here to tell me?" At this, MacGuffy smiled again, but this time for true, his old, yellow teeth gleaming in the moonlight. He got up from his barrel and came to stand beside Jim, resting a hand on his shoulder.

"A good heart is a sure compass, and wisdom a sail that catches the wind. You were born with a good heart, Jim Morgan. But wisdom can be bought by only two manner of coin – time and pain, and it costs a great deal of both. But MacGuffy will stand by yer side a while longer. And who knows? Mayhaps we'll find a way to destroy our half of the Hunter's Shell after all. Mayhaps we'll find a way to escape this storm afore it strikes again."

Jim managed a grin. But the sliver of hope he held in his heart was as thin as the slight smile upon his face.

SEVEN

An Intruder in the Dream

That night, as the moon rose high over the Kasbah, Jim Morgan tossed and turned in his hammock, grappling against a familiar nightmare.

Jim rode Destroyer, his old pony, through the haunted forest beyond his old home, fighting through wind and rain, fleeing the Crimson Storm. Some nights the dream ended at the river, possessed by the black rose thorn's poison, which had nearly killed Jim on the Veiled Isle. The pitch-black water reached out for Jim like a living hand. It caught him by the arm and dragged him below the surface. But the Fairy Queen never came to rescue Jim as she had on the Veiled Isle. He sank to the bottom alone. There, he found the ghosts of his father, Lindsay Morgan, and Dread Steele waiting for him.

"Welcome home," they would say. Jim would wake then – sometimes screaming, sometimes gasping for air, every time slicked with sweat.

Other nights, however, Jim escaped the poisoned river and broke through the tree line of the haunted forest. He thought he had been running away, but always found himself back at Morgan Manor, her ivy-covered walls again appearing before him. The Crimson Storm would lance out with a finger of lighting, burning the building to ash in a whirlwind of red fire. Towers of smoke climbed into the night sky. Count Cromier's face appeared in the flames and Bartholomew's in the black billows. Their laughing faces poured derision on Jim as his home crumbled to the ground. This too would often be the ending of the dream.

But sometimes the dream went further still. Jim watched from Destroyer's back as his home fell. When the fires died, in their wake, an ancient ruin remained where the manor once stood. But it was not the ruin of Morgan Manor. Broken arches and crumbling columns rose up before Jim, becoming the skeleton of a derelict building. It was like some kind of temple, carved from stone as old as the world's birth.

Through the ruined arches, at the temple's heart, Jim saw an altar. Speared into the altar was the Treasure of the Ocean, the golden trident.

Jim rode down to the temple upon Destroyer and dismounted. The moment his feet touched the ground, stone steps tore from the earth before him, leading up to the jagged archway. Jim could feel the Treasure pulling him, dragging him by the heart to the altar. So he climbed the steps.

Statues lined the stairs – statues of Jim's friends – Peter and Paul, old MacGuffy, Mister Gilly, Cornelius, even Phineus the tutor. At the very top, at the entrance to the temple itself, statues of Lacey and George waited for Jim. Their faces were so sad, especially Lacey's. Her mouth was open, as though trying to speak, and her hands raised, as though reaching for Jim, trying to hold him back. But the pull of the Treasure was too strong.

Jim came to the foot of the altar. He reached for the trident and took the golden rod in his hand. His touch ignited its power.

A rip in the fabric of night tore open before Jim's eyes, a hole blacker than midnight – starless and moonless. A great wind rose up from nowhere, whipping at Jim's coat and dragging him toward the tear. This was the final ending of Jim's dream… until tonight.

Tonight the dream did not end.

A shadow flickered at the edge of Jim's vision. He whipped his head about, but the shadow was no longer there. An icy cold, like a touch of death, stung the back of Jim's neck. He whirled in the other direction – only fast enough to catch the shadow disappear behind a crumbled column.

"Who's there?" Jim shouted over the roar of the wind. Something was wrong about this shadow. It was not a part of his dream. It was not a part of Jim. It was an intruder.

"Jim Morgan," a voice whispered. Even in the gale winds, Jim heard the whisper as if the speaker's lips were pressed against his ear. "Jim Morgan, why are you afraid?"

"You don't belong here," Jim shouted. He flicked his eyes to the right and to the left, each time capturing only the tail end of the shadow, like the hem of a dark cape. "Get out."

"Oh, but I'm not here to harm you, my old friend, Jim," said the voice. "As always, I am here to help you, to guide you." Jim heard a hint of something familiar in that voice – a hint from the past.

"Guide me where?" Jim asked. "This is the end of the dream. It doesn't go any further than this." The shadow laughed, a quiet, smooth laugh.

"Yes, yes this is the end of the dream, my boy. But only the beginning of the adventure – the final adventure. Now, I shall ask you again. Why are you afraid?"

"The tear in the sky," Jim said, swallowing hard. "I can't see what lies beyond it."

"Rarely can we see what lies beyond doors through which we have not yet passed."

"A door?" Jim asked. "The tear is a door?" The shadow laughed again, clucking its hidden tongue in disappointment.

"Did you learn nothing from our time together, Jim Morgan? Nothing at all? Cast your eyes at the altar before you. Observe the Treasure of the Ocean. What do you see?" Jim did as the shadow asked. The trident was driven down into the heart of the altar, the three points fitted into three slots in the stone.

"It's like a key," Jim said. He had not noticed this before, even after a hundred dreams just like this one. "The trident is a key and the altar is the lock."

"And beyond both lies a door. Did you learn nothing from me at all?" The whisper began to grow in volume, rolling into a full voice. "Did I not tell you, young thief, all those years ago, that every treasure is just a key? Just a key to something greater and deeper, lying just beyond man's reach? Did I not offer to share such treasures with you, my boy? Like a father to a son?"

Jim's fingers and toes went numb. He knew that voice. He knew those words. But it could not be. Cold fingers crawled over Jim's shoulders and around his neck. Jim forced himself to turn around. He wanted to shut his eyes, but he forced them to stay open, even against the fear welling up within his heart.

Black rivulets, misty as a dark fog, flowed from behind the columns of the temple. They crawled along the ground like black snakes and dark spiders. The shadows pooled together before the archway in a murky puddle. The puddle of pitch took shape and grew. It stood taller and taller, waxing into the form of a man – a shadow man with long, spider fingers, thin, spindly legs, a shimmering split coattail, and a satin hat upon his head.

"No!" Jim cried. "You can't be here! You're dead!"

A line of white split the shadow's face. A smile Jim knew all too well – the honey-dripped smile of the King of Thieves.

"I have returned."

Jim screamed again and finally flew awake.

EIGHT

JANUS BLACKTAIL'S SECRET

Jim jerked from his sleep, thrashing in the dark and kicking off his blanket. His nightclothes clung to his body.

Peter and Paul lay in their hammocks beside him. Peter was turned sideways, his head dangling off one edge and his feet hanging off the other. Paul lay face first in his hammock, folded backwards like a human banana.

Jim turned to his other side, where he expected to see George, fast asleep as well, but there was only a blanket and pillow, lying in a little pile where George should have been.

Something moved in the moonlit shadows against the cabin wall.

Jim froze. For the span of a heartbeat, the shadow in the soft blue light took the shape of the spider-limbed King of Thieves. Jim gripped the rope lining of his hammock, ready to spring out and

57

defend himself and his sleeping friends. But as his hammock swayed, the shadow before him shifted and the ghostly shape disappeared.

Jim loosed a long sigh. He closed his eyes and wiped the cold sweat from his brow. *The pressure is getting to me*, Jim thought. That was why his dream was worse tonight. Time was running out. He had to find something to destroy the Hunter's Shell, and fast. Only then would it all be over, only then could he sleep in peace. Jim flipped his pillow to the cool side, hoping to find a bit of rest before dawn. But as he reached to the floor for his fallen blanket, another voice from the past snatched any hope of slumber from Jim's grasp.

"Nothing worse than a bad dream, eh, Morgan? They're purrrfectly miserable, aren't they?"

Jim looked back to the shadow that had only a moment ago been a shade of the King of Thieves. Two green orbs bloomed to emerald life from the darkness, bobbing into the moonlight on a bristling black body. Jim knew that voice and recognized those eyes in an instant. His stomach coiled within him. Janus Blacktail had come back.

"You?" Jim rasped. "I was hoping you were just another one of Philus Philonius's disguises, and that I'd seen the last of you. What are you doing here?" Jim kept his eyes fixed on the long black cat as it stalked toward his hammock, leaping without a sound onto the big knot at Jim's feet. Over a year ago, on the *Spectre's* prow, Janus Blacktail had been the one to tell Jim that his own father had once been a pirate, a Pirate of the Black Skull, along with Dread Steele and Count Cromier. Janus had told Jim it was his father who had first stolen the Treasure of the Ocean and started all this trouble.

"Alas, you cut me to the quick, Jim Morgan." The cat shot Jim a hurt look – one quickly cut with a sneaky smile. "Is it so bad to see old Janus after all this time? Why all this hostility? Did I lie to you? Did I mislead you? You seem to have come out of your last adventure none the worse for wear." Janus's eyes flicked to Jim's open hand, where the white rose scar bloomed upon his palm. "Well, almost none."

Jim snatched his hand shut and shoved his fist behind his back. "You didn't tell me everything, cat. And you left me that scratch on the back of my hand, which bloody well hurt, by the way. Then you took off and left before all the real trouble started. You're nothing but a lying, eavesdropping stowaway. This time I'm going to make sure MacGuffy and Cornelius catch you and pitch you overboard in a bag, you mangy liar."

"Why, Jim, what scurrrrilous things to say to an old acquaintance. And just when I thought we were going to become pals." Janus laughed again, running his pink tongue across his teeth. "But since we can't be friends, then I suppose I should just get down to business."

"We don't have business, cat. So just slink off before I call the watch."

"Oh, but dirty, pirate boys have such short memories, don't they? We do have business, Jim Morgan. I gave you a secret, remember? I gave you the secret to the Pirates of the Black Skull, on the deck of this very ship, when you were whining and moping at the prow, all by your lonesome. I told you their identities, including that of your own father, Lindsay Morgan. Now, you owe me a secret in return. The time has come to settle our debt."

"I don't owe you anything."

"Oh, but you do. But you do." The round green orbs on Janus's face narrowed into thin crescents. The smile on his face twisted into a snarl.

Jim felt a prickling sting crawl across the back of his hand, needling the place where the cat had scratched him a year ago. The heat crawled up his arm and into his chest. Jim's face flushed. Sweat beaded on his forehead and upper lip.

"Where is your half of the Hunter's Shell, Jim? Where have you hidden it?"

Jim fought as best he could. He struggled to contain the burning pain in his hand, growing hotter and hotter by the second. He clamped his mouth shut. He tried with all his might to keep it closed. He shook his head at the cat.

"Where is it, boy?" Janus's smooth voice now whipped like a lash. Each word fanned the flames burning in Jim's blood. "Where is your half of the Hunter's Shell? Tell me now!" The dam broke within Jim. The searing heat ignited into a wildfire in his bones, burning out of control from his hand up to his head.

"In the crow's nest!" Jim heard himself scream through gritted teeth. "We hid it in a box in the crow's nest!"

"See, Jim Morgan?" Janus said. "Was that so hard? If nothing else, you may at last rest easy, knowing you and I are finally square. I thank you for the secret and I bid you adieu!" Janus leapt from the hammock. The force of his kick twisted the ropes and sent Jim tumbling to the floor. Jim tried to scream for help, but the fire in his blood was slow to cool. His head swam as if in a fever. His body shook from head to toe.

Finally, after what Jim feared had been too long, he found the strength to reach up and shake Paul's hammock. He shook it once, twice, but still the smallest Ratt snored away. Jim gave the hammock one last heave, dumping his friend onto the floor beside him.

"Oy, Jim!" Paul grumbled, rubbing the back of his head. "You coulda just poked me shoulder a few more–" Paul stopped griping the moment his waking eyes caught sight of Jim's pale, sweaty face. He hopped up to his feet at Jim's side, helping him up. "Jim, what's wrong?"

"The Shell, Paul," Jim managed. "They've come for the Shell." But even as Paul roused his brother, and even as the two of them shouted the alarm to the ship's watch at the top of their lungs, Jim somehow knew it was already too late.

NINE

THE MENDING OF THE SHELL

The *Spectre's* warning bell rang in the night, calling the ship's crew to action. Peter and Paul helped Jim onto the main deck and Lacey appeared beside them, throwing her hooded cloak over her shoulders. Her eyes filled with concern when she saw Jim's ashen face.

"Jim, what's happened to you? What's happening now?"

"It was Janus Blacktail," Jim said, "that blasted cat from before, the one who told me about the Pirates of the Black Skull. He's after the Shell. I tried not to tell him, but he made me."

Just then George landed beside the clan, having leapt down the steps from the quarterdeck. Pirates poured onto the deck from all sides, pulling on their clothes, rubbing sleep from their eyes, loading their pistols and drawing their blades.

Jim was about to ask George where he'd been, but his friend cut him off with a pointing finger to the crow's nest. "No need to ask what this is all about, is there?"

A dark shape moved along the lip of the bucket at the tip of the mainmast. Janus had somehow managed to take the Hunter's Shell from its locked box, but the treacherous cat struggled to drag the shell's weight behind him.

On the main deck, the *Spectre's* pirate crew, led by MacGuffy and Mufwalme, drew a tight circle around the center mast. Their pistols, knives, and cutlasses all pointed up. Whether most of the sailors still believed in Jim's mission or not, the sanctity of their ship had been violated, and a talisman under their keep had been compromised. Such crimes could not go unpunished. Murdock and Wang-Chi were halfway up the riggings, closing in on the black cat upon his precarious perch.

"Looks like you didn't quite think things through, cat," Jim shouted up to Janus. "You're surrounded. There's no way out. Now that you've gotten your secret, you no longer have any power over me. So come down quietly and I'll try and talk these fellows into going easy on you." The crew growled and cursed at the cat, brandishing their weapons and wicked grins. "Well," Jim added, folding his arms over his chest. "I'll try anyway."

But in spite of the army of pirates gathered at the base of the mast, and in spite of Jim's taunts, only a raspy laugh fell down from Janus, the shell resting between his paws.

"Oh no, young Morgan," the cat said. "It is you who has not thought things through. Do you not remember what it is that I do? I am a dealer in secrets. I am a trader in treasures of the tongue. For there to be a trade, there must also be an interested party. Did you think I wanted the Hunter's Shell for myself? No, I am but on an errand for some new friends. And I will tell you, boy, this party was most keen on this secret. They have protected their investment well."

A rustling and popping, like a flag in the wind, sounded from somewhere above Jim's head. Jim craned his neck and, in the light of the moon, caught a dark shape soar over the ship, streaking to a hovering stop beside Janus Blacktail.

"I don't believe it," said Peter, his eyes going wide.

"It's a flyin carpet!" finished Paul.

Indeed, the dark shape floating in the air above the *Spectre* was a tasseled rug, very much like those that had covered the floor of Abdullah's shop. The enchanted fabric rustled on the ocean wind. Janus shoved the Shell onto the carpet and then leapt on himself, just in time to evade Wang-Chi's grasp. From over the edge of the carpet, the black cat stuck out his head, throwing Jim one last toothy smile.

"Too-da-loo, Jim Morgan," purred the cat. With a crack, the flying carpet shot off into the night, sailing on the air into the heart of the Kasbah.

An ice-cold tendril curled about Jim's heart. He stared after the shrinking shape in the sky, trembling. It was gone. The one chance for Jim to keep the Treasure of the Ocean hidden forever, the one chance he had to end this madness and find some peace, had just been stolen. The vision of Janus's taunting smile stung and the rose blossom scar on his palm tingled. Jim would not allow the villain to escape so easily.

Jim said nothing, not to the pirate crew, not to his friends, not even to Lacey. He only ran. He rushed for the gangplank and leapt over the railings. Keeping his eyes fixed on the quickly escaping Janus Blacktail, Jim tore down the pier and into the Kasbah streets.

"Wait, Jimmy!" MacGuffy called. But there was no time to pause, or even to call back over his shoulder. The *Spectre's* sailors were a bold bunch to be sure, and fierce fighters to the man, but they were nowhere near as quick as a young thief from London. Jim could still hear MacGuffy and Mufwalme bellowing orders to the men when he was off the docks and two blocks into the city.

What Jim never heard, however, were the voices of his friends calling to stop him. That was because they never did. The Ratt Clan was already behind him. To Jim's right, Lacey's auburn curls flowed over her cloak as it trailed behind her. As tall and strong as the boys had grown, Lacey was every bit as fast and determined as they. And to Jim's left, the Brothers Ratt, led by George, sprinted beside him.

A shrieking caw split the night above the Kasbah. Down from the sky swooped a familiar, winged form. Cornelius had returned, just in time, from his nightly patrols over the city.

"What madness is this, boy? What madness now?" Cornelius said. "I heard the bells toll from the far side of the city – the warning bells of the *Spectre*! Are we under attack?"

"It was Janus Blacktail, Cornelius," Jim said, throwing his chin toward the carpet in the sky. "He's got the Hunter's Shell and he's getting away."

"That blackguard," Cornelius squawked. "That garrulous fiend. That overly verbose, vile, black hearted, deceitful merchant of gossip and lies! That—"

"Yes, Cornelius, we know!" Jim interjected with an exasperated shout. "Climb higher, will you, and keep us on his trail."

Without another word, Cornelius beat his wings hard and lifted himself above the roofs of the city. Even in the dark, Jim could see the raven flitting across the starry sky, guiding them deeper into the heart of the Kasbah. The clan ran quietly as they could, desperate to avoid rousing the Kasbah's guards. But when Cornelius led the clan past a domed mosque and into an empty square, Jim realized that it might not be him and his friends who would attract unwanted attention.

Across the square stood a tall, palatial inn for the Kasbah's wealthiest visitors. Arched windows, their sills covered thick with plants, lined the inn's walls, which stood four stories high. When Jim's eyes reached the roof his mouth dropped open and his heart sunk low. Glowing blues, purples, and reds flickered and burst against a rising column of smoke, which climbed into the night. Some dark magic was at work atop the inn. The Cromiers were there, and they had wasted no time. They were going to mend the shattered halves of the Hunter's Shell the moment it was in their grasp.

"Our enemies have congregated atop the roof," Cornelius cawed, dropping down to land on Jim's shoulder. "They gather about a cauldron boiling over with some enchanted brew."

"We have to stop them," Jim said.

"We should wait for MacGuffy, lad," Cornelius cautioned. "I can handle the cat, and it would give me some pleasure to have a peck or two at those diabolical green eyes of his, I might add. And perhaps the Ratts could tackle the old count."

"We'd like to peck at his eyes," George said, pounding a fist into an open palm, to his brothers' glee.

"But Bartholomew is up there, young Morgan, sword at his side," Cornelius warned. Jim's veins filled with ice. How many times could he throw himself in the way of Cromier's pale son, eyes so full of murder and hate, and expect to survive? The Brothers Ratt stopped their giggling. Lacey put a hand on Jim's shoulder.

"Maybe we should wait, Jim," she said.

Jim swallowed hard. There was no denying the fear gnawing at his courage. But he had a small idea of what power the Treasure of the Ocean could unleash, and he could not, fear of death or no, allow such magic to fall into the hands of Count Villius Cromier.

"There's no time," Jim said. "George, do you think those plants growing off those windows are strong enough to hold us? It's been a while since we scaled ivy back in London."

"Only one way to find out," George said, an all too eager gleam in his eye. "Just remember, mate: Don't look down."

Jim and his friends charged the inn. With running leaps they reached the first windows, grabbing hold of the hanging stalks from the sills above. The plants were thick and hearty, and while leaves ripped and roots sometimes gave, they made for true holds. Floor to floor the young thieves climbed to the ledge. Jim hoped that whatever spells the Cromiers were attempting to complete were long and tedious. But when he and the others pulled themselves onto the roof, a wave of dread washed those hopes away.

Abdullah the shopkeeper stood before a black cauldron, large and deep, floating free of hooks and chains above a magic flame. The boiling blend within the great pot frothed and rippled, spitting smoke into the air and flashing from color to color. To either side of the small magician stood a Cromier, and at Abdullah's feet sat Janus Blacktail. The count, shadows carving deep into his withered face, stepped up to the cauldron. In each hand he balanced a half of the Hunter's Shell. He placed the fragments together, forming the single conch over the potion.

"Cromier!" Jim cried. "Don't do it!"

At the sound of Jim's voice, Bartholomew's hand leapt to his sword and old Abdullah hung his head. But the red-wigged count only turned and smiled at Jim through the potion's smoke, as though he'd been expecting Jim the entire time.

Without a word, he dropped the shell into the cauldron.

"No!" Jim cried. He leapt from the ledge, thinking he might be able to ram the cauldron, knocking it over to prevent the shell's restoration. But when shell dropped into the concoction, the cauldron exploded with a thunderclap. A blinding wave of magic, purple and blue, like a spreading bruise, blew across the roof. The force knocked Jim and his friends off their feet.

A deathly silence settled over the roof. Jim opened his eyes, blinking away the spots and dazzles. He found the magical explosion had bowled over Abdullah, Bartholomew, and the count as well. But as the smoke cleared, what Jim feared most came into view. The cauldron lay in two halves upon the roof, edges burning orange like hot coals. But between those two halves lay the Hunter's Shell, forged anew, restored of all its power.

Jim watched, horrified, as the count climbed to his feet. The old man leant over the shell, took it in his hands, and raised it above his head. A violet aura swam in the air. It seemed to Jim that the shell was gathering the power back into itself, like a long-sleeping giant drawing in a great, waking breath. Then came the exhale. With a great thrum the shell erupted with mystical force, hurling a column of violet into the heavens.

When the shell finally stilled itself again, the only sound on the rooftop was laughter, scraping from the throat of Count Cromier. The count pulled the shell into his chest, hugging it close like a newborn child.

"You see, boy!" The count declared, leveling his crazed eyes on Jim. "Destiny cannot be thwarted. Your father failed to stop me. Dread Steele failed to stop me. Now you have failed as well. The Treasure of the Ocean is mine. It was I who first discovered its existence, and it is I alone who remain of those who sought it. With the shell restored, the greatest power on earth will soon be in my grasp. You will watch, Jim Morgan, as I assume the throne of the world."

From the corners of the roof, somehow hidden from Jim and his friends in the shadows, a troop of Corsair pirates stepped into the moonlight. Scimitars and daggers hung from their belts. Tattoos crawled across their sun-darkened chests. Terrible smiles split their faces as they closed in. Jim scrambled to his feet. He felt Lacey squeeze in beside him, her hands gripping his arm. George and his brothers gathered about as well.

"Take them!" Cromier commanded. The Corsairs raised their eager hands to seize their young prisoners.

"I think not, curs! These young ones are under the protection of men with more honor apiece than you poltroons hold amongst the lot of you." Cornelius swooped to a landing on Jim's shoulder, ruffling his feathers and cawing at the Corsairs.

"Ah, Darkfeather," said Janus Blacktail, slinking around the count's ankles. "I was wondering when you might turn up. What are you going to do? Bore these poor blokes to death with another story? Fill their heads with idle, empty talk of honor and chivalry?"

"I shall teach you the meaning of honor, Blacktail – in but a moment. As for these fiends, I shall leave them to my friends."

A shout roared over the roof. On the ledge, from one end of the roof to the other, rose the crew of the *Spectre*, weapons in hand, and a thirst for battle on their lips. From their center strode MacGuffy, a dark smile spread across his scarred face.

"Argh, Cromier, ye slime, I've come for yer miserable, fiendin life!"

The *Spectre's* men stormed the roof, clashing with the Corsairs. Cries, curses, and blood spilled into the night, sweeping Jim and his friends under a tide of battle once again.

TEN

JIM AND BARTHOLOMEW

Jim, Lacey, and ye sea Ratts, back to the *Spectre* at once with ye! Run, for yer lives, ye young fools!" MacGuffy fired his pistol with one hand and crossed his blade against a Corsair pirate's with the other. He shouted commands as he waded through the fight, slowly forcing his way to Count Cromier. The count, cradling the Hunter's Shell, screamed a graveled cry at MacGuffy and ran to meet the old salt in battle.

"Across the roofs then?" said Lacey, flicking her eyes to the next building. She had already pulled Peter and Paul close to her, shielding them with her arms.

"As good a path to the docks as any right now," said Jim. He turned to lead the way, but George stood fast, fists clenched.

"Jim, we can end this now. The count has your shell – the

whole, mended shell – the one that can find that Treasure of your dad's, right? It's there, right in front of us, ripe for the pickin. If we run now, we might miss our one chance for it. Let's take it while the takin's good. Me and you, Jim, just like old times."

"George, no!" Lacey shouted. She was already pulling the two younger Ratts toward the ledge. Jim took George by the arm, intent on dragging his friend along, kicking and screaming if need be. But at the last moment, he hesitated. He caught the look in George's eye, the hungry eyes of a young wolf. The look set a spark to Jim's blood. He turned from the roofs to survey the battle, looking for an opening.

More and more Corsairs poured into the fight, but Mufwalme, Murdock, Wang-Chi, and the rest were more than a match for them. Cornelius, his avian cry of "Preoleum" cawing over the din, descended upon Janus Blacktail. The two of them rolled in a black ball of flying feathers and fur. Abdullah the shopkeeper sat curled up by his cleaved cauldron, head hung low in shame. Count Cromier fought old MacGuffy, the two men circling each other in tight turns, swinging for life and death.

No one was watching the Clan.

For a brief moment, Jim *knew* he and George could creep through the battle like shadows, right up behind old Cromier and pluck the shell from his arms. They would be off before the Red Count ever knew they were there. Jim nearly said as much to George, when a pair of ice-blue eyes cut through the fight, chilling Jim's courage.

Someone was watching Jim and his friends after all – Bartholomew Cromier. The pale captain stalked through the battle toward Jim and George. Jim knew the look in the young Cromier's face. He had good reason to fear it.

"We need to go," Jim whispered. "We need to go, now!" George resisted Jim's pull only once – only until he saw the murder in Bartholomew's face.

The five friends took off in a mad dash, leaping over a narrow gap to the next roof. They were halfway across when Jim looked back and saw Bartholomew land in perfect stride behind them, chasing the Clan down. Jim had never seen Bartholomew run before, not like this. He had never seen Bartholomew so close behind him – hunting him. Bartholomew was younger than he sometimes seemed, and fast.

A realization pierced Jim's thoughts as he looked from Bartholomew to the younger Ratts, Peter and Paul. Bartholomew was going to catch them. They were too slow all together. And when Bartholomew did catch them… Jim didn't even want to think about that.

"Break off," Jim shouted at his friends as they flew across to the next roof. "Break off and get back to the ship. I'll meet you there."

"No, Jim!" Lacey stole a fiery glance in Jim's direction. "We stay together, no matter what."

"I'll go with you, Jim," George offered. But Jim cut them both off.

"There's no time for this! We're slower as a group. I'm fastest alone. That, and Bartholomew wants me. Trust me, Lacey. I can outrun him. You four just get back. I promise I'm just behind you." Jim gave his friends no chance to argue. He broke right and charged across the roof in the other direction, throwing himself onto another building.

A soft skid whispered behind him. Then he heard Bartholomew's boots hammer after him again.

Of all the sensations Jim could feel in a moment such as this, with a man intent on his death but steps behind him, it was relief that came first. George and the Ratts would reach the *Spectre*, with Lacey – and Lacey would be safe there. That would be enough.

Jim breathed deeply of the ocean breeze. The salty smell seemed to give him strength. He churned his legs, jumping from roof to roof. He could hear Bartholomew behind him, breathing hard, but the sound of those breaths was getting farther away.

I'm faster, Jim thought. For the first time since he laid eyes on the wraith that was Bartholomew Cromier, a thrill of confidence surged through Jim's veins. *Bartholomew is bigger and stronger... but I'm faster*. The realization gave Jim even more speed. He loosed a whoop over the city streets with his next jump. But the joy of that discovery lasted only as a long as the echoes of his shout.

As Jim landed, he glanced to the docks, toward the *Spectre,* and safety. His eyes drifted past the ship's mainmast and sails, out over the ocean—

—and into the lightning eyes of the Crimson Storm.

Some awful burst of hot and cold flared in Jim's chest. Just as on that terrible night, over a year ago when Philus Philonius had inadvertently called the Storm, so Count Cromier had called it again. The storm boiled over the sea. The black clouds, rimmed in blood red, rolled like an inky stain toward the shore. Jim was wondering how he and his friends could possibly escape the storm again, when the roof ran out beneath his feet.

Jim pushed off the very edge of the bricks at the last instant. But fear had robbed his legs of their power. He tumbled through the air. His arms spun in wheels. Somehow, only by luck or fate, Jim caught the ledge of the next building, by no more than his fingertips. His chest slammed against the wall. He might have been knocked down to his death, but fear of plummeting to the streets below gave Jim's fingers iron strength. He held on for dear life, scrambling to climb back onto the ledge.

A black shape sailed over Jim's head.

Boots landed on the roof above. They crunched on sticks and gravel, stepping to the edge. The heavy breaths of a man who had been running at full speed panted above the footfalls. A face, pale as the moon and eyes blue as ice, appeared over the lip of the roof.

Bartholomew Cromier stared down on Jim. Jim chanced a look to the street below, daring himself to let go of the ledge and fall to escape. But it was four stories down. Only death or shattered limbs awaited on the cobblestone below. Jim swallowed a panicked gulp. There was no escape.

"So here we are at last, Morgan," Bartholomew said. "Just you and me." Bartholomew pressed Jim's fingers into the brick with his heel. "Wouldn't want you falling, now would we? I need you to hang on, Jim. Hang on for just a moment longer."

Jim strangled a cry. Pain sang in his fingers. His eyes watered. But he refused to cry. Not this time. Jim summoned up all his courage and pride. He willed his eyes open to meet Bartholomew's murderous glare.

"Good," Bartholomew said. "You've learned some courage after all."

"You didn't see it before?" Jim challenged. "Maybe it was hard to catch looking at my back, while I was facing the horrors from which your daddy protected you." Jim may as well have reached up and slapped Bartholomew's face. The pale captain's blue eyes widened. The barest hint of color flushed his alabaster cheeks. Bartholomew drew his sword slowly and lowered it over the roof's edge, pressing the point into the soft place below Jim's eye. The sting of cold metal set Jim's teeth on edge, but he refused to look away.

"Look at you," Bartholomew rasped. "You cling to life by your fingertips while I hold you beneath my boot. You sacrifice yourself, your birthright, for that street trash you call your friends. Now you'll die a failure, not even a shadow of what you could have been. You are your father's son, Jim Morgan."

"And you are yours, Bartholomew Cromier," Jim spat back. "So go on then, *Captain*. I can see his strings tugging at your arms."

Bartholomew's lips peeled back from his teeth. Jim felt the sword point bite into the flesh above his cheek. A teardrop of blood ran down to his chin. But then *something* passed over Bartholomew's face, like a thin cloud over the moon. Jim could not say what he saw there, but perhaps, he thought, a boy's face behind the wolf's. Bartholomew looked up from Jim, toward the ocean and the

Crimson Storm. The thunder rumbled in the near distance. Bartholomew's black ponytail whipped in the rising wind. The boy and the wolf wrestled on the young Cromier's face, and for the briefest instant, the boy won.

The sword point pulled away from Jim's cheek, the small cut left behind stinging. The boot heel lifted from Jim's fingers and a gloved hand took his wrist in a strong grip. With a heave, and some help from Jim's churning legs, Bartholomew lifted Jim to the safety of the roof.

Jim knelt there on the ledge, his arms and legs trembling. His breath came in great gulps. He stared at Bartholomew Cromier's face, where the boy still lingered for another moment.

"My father told me what happened on the Spectre," Bartholomew said. "What you did. How you pulled me up. He would not let me forget it." Bartholomew's fingers went to his cheek and felt there, as if for some invisible scar. He ran his finger down his face – so like his father. "He will never let me forget. But I am my own man. Do you hear me, Morgan? I am no one's puppet. Now we are even. Understand? My debt is paid. The storm does not come for the shell anymore, Morgan. It comes for us. We are the only two that might undo its power. We are the only two that might control the power hidden with the Treasure of the Ocean. But there can be only one. We are destined to end this way, Morgan, one on his knees, and one with a sword in his hand. We are even now. When you find yourself on your knees before me again, there shall be no mercy. Now run. Run!"

Jim opened his mouth to say something. But Bartholomew gave him no chance. He shouted once more at Jim, then thrust his sword in the air toward the approaching storm before dashing off in the other direction.

Jim climbed slowly to his feet on shaking legs. It took him a long moment before he could run again. And run he did, back to the *Spectre*, just as the first drops of rain from the Crimson Storm began to spatter on the streets of the Kasbah.

ELEVEN

THE RETURN OF THE CRIMSON STORM

By the time Jim climbed the gangplank to the *Spectre's* deck, an angry rain lashed the docks. The Crimson Storm's long tendrils clawed at the sky above the city, pulling its black heart close behind. Fleeting glimpses of the hateful face that lurked within the clouds burned in flashes of purple lightning.

Exhausted, drenched, and still stunned from his encounter with Bartholomew Cromier, Jim dragged himself aboard, where he was beset by Peter and Paul.

"Jim, you made it!" Peter said, shaking Jim by the arm.

"Thought for a second that maybe old Bart finally got the best of you," added Peter.

"Never in a million years," said George, coming up from behind his two younger brothers. "Jim's got the moves now, thanks to me. Taught 'im everythin he knows." George offered Jim a hint of his old rogue's grin. But when another volley of thunder shook the ship's timbers, all smiles fell and the four boys looked with fear to the sky.

When Jim managed to tear his eyes away from the storm, he found Lacey beside him. Not a trace of that infuriating smile graced her lips. Her eyes were wide, glaring hard at Jim, falling almost at once to the fresh cut on his cheek. Jim stepped closer to her, half expecting her to throw her arms around his neck, or perhaps to wipe the thin stream of blood from his face. But she did neither. She stood still as a statue, pursing her lips into a tight, thin line.

"So, you've made it back then. All on your own. And with nothing but a scratch, I see, which I'm sure you got from a piece of gravel or something you kicked up along the way. Glad you didn't need us after all." Lacey's set chin twitched only once as she spoke. She pulled her cloak around her tight, turning away from Jim and hiding her face.

"Lacey—" Jim began, but he was cut off by a great clamor. Scores of boots pounded up the gangplank. The *Spectre's* crew had returned.

Jim and his friends leapt aside as the sailors rushed aboard. Not a man among them had escaped some form of injury. Cuts, bruises, and gashes covered their arms and faces. A handful of the men had to be helped aboard by their mates. But it was not their wounds that worried Jim most. Rather, it was their eyes, cast up to the Crimson Storm. Their eyes were filled with fear, haunted by doom and defeat.

Last of all came MacGuffy, a fresh cut upon the crown of his head, dripping a stream of rain-slicked blood down his face, which ran along the edge of his scar. Cornelius sat upon his shoulder, feathers mangy and matted from both rain and combat.

"Avast, Mr. Gilly!" MacGuffy screamed over the rain. His old voice rattled like a rusty chain. "Cut us loose from this god forsaken pier, for the love of Poseidon. Every man to his post. Cast down the sails and get us out into the water."

"You want to take us out into this?" a terrified sailor cried with dismay. "You want to take us up against the devil storm?"

"Face the devil storm on the sea or face the Corsair horde in the streets, ya sea whelp," MacGuffy roared. "If it be the devil at my back or the devil in my way, I'll always choose to fight the latter. Now stand fast or stand aside."

"Mister MacGuffy! Mister Cornelius!" Lacey cried, rushing past Jim and the Ratts to the old salt's side. She grabbed MacGuffy's arm and touched her fingers to the raven's ruined feathers. "You're both hurt so badly. Are you all right?"

"We will both assuredly live, sweet Lacey," Cornelius croaked. "As will, less fortunately I think, those villains, the Cromiers. As for Janus Blacktail, however… that blackguard shall tell no more tales." Jim shivered in the rain, thinking of the evil in the black cat's smile. "But we have lost the Shell, I'm afraid, and that wound stings worse than any of the others."

"Aye, we shall live, little Lacey," said MacGuffy. "But not for much longer if we cannot escape the demon squall above our heads. So stand aside and let an old sailor do his duty." MacGuffy left Lacey with Jim and the Ratts, climbing the sodden stairs to the quarterdeck. He came to stand by faithful Mister Gilly at the great wheel. As the *Spectre* tilted and leaned against the waves, lumbering her way out to sea, Jim and the clan ran to help the pirates hold the sail to the wind.

The *Spectre* pitched on the spiking waves, fighting with creaks and groans to make the open waters. But the ship was crawling far too slowly. The Crimson Storm held her in its black grasp, pinning the ship to the harbor with whirling winds. The clouds above began to spin. The cruel face burned to life with white-hot lightning and erupted from the storm's dark heart.

Jim's courage melted. His knees quaked and his arms trembled. There would be no escape. The storm's eyes blazed brighter than two moons, gathering whips of lightning with which to tear the *Spectre* to kindling.

"MacGuffy," Jim screamed. "The eyes! The eyes are about to strike!"

"Still yourself, young Morgan," MacGuffy bellowed. "Old MacGuffy has but one trick left up his sleeve, learnt him by Dread Steele himself." Jim looked to the quarterdeck to find MacGuffy standing forth by the railing. The old man reached into his pocket, pulling out some white stuff in his fist. He rubbed the substance between his palms, whispering words hopelessly lost to the wind. From his hands he blew a fine powder into the sails.

Aeolus Feathers.

"Hang on!" Jim shouted to his friends. He gathered them up in his arms, throwing them tight against the mainmast.

Only the briefest pause came before the magic feathers did their work. The *Spectre's* sails suddenly went taught on an enchanted wind, yanking the great ship forward with a jolt. Even holding against the mainmast, Jim had to bend his knees and squeeze tight to Lacey and the Ratts to keep from tumbling backwards. He snuck a glance back to see two lightning blasts lance down from the Crimson Storm's eyes, striking the empty place in the harbor where the *Spectre* had been only seconds before.

Powered by the magic of the feathers, the *Spectre* knifed through the choppy waves at impossible speed. Wind and rain whipped at Jim's face, stinging hard as they flew sideways in the ship's rush. The clan held on for dear life for the next several minutes, until the *Spectre* made her escape.

When the magic finally faded, Jim looked back to the Moroccan Coast, far behind. The roiling black mass of the Crimson Storm was now nothing but a stain against the starlit sky. Even from so many miles away, Jim saw purple lightning sparking in the distance. He heard the storm thundering, pounding the sea in fury over its escaped prey. The storm would try again, Jim knew. It would keep trying until it caught him and buried him beneath the sea.

TWELVE

DESPERATE DECISIONS
IN THE CAPTAIN'S QUARTERS

I've failed ye, Jimmy," said MacGuffy. The old man leaned against the wall in the captain's quarters. Candles burned in a rack on what had once been Dread Steele's desk and cast stark shadows about the scars and crags on the old salt's face. MacGuffy looked so old, Jim thought, older than he had ever seemed before.

"You haven't failed us, MacGuffy," Jim said. He and the Ratts stood on the other side of the desk, while Lacey sat in Dread Steele's red leather chair, cradling Cornelius in her lap. "You did your best."

"You haven't failed anyone ever," said Lacey. "You've taken

better care of us than anyone in our entire lives, MacGuffy. That's the truth. Please don't say otherwise. It's awful."

Lacey reached out and patted the back of MacGuffy's hand. Jim tried to catch her gaze in that quiet moment, but Lacey met his eyes only long enough to make the point that she would *not* be looking back. Instead, she returned her attention to Cornelius, who had come away from his fight with Janus covered in cuts and scratches.

Lacey had said next to nothing to Jim since their escape from the Kasbah. As much as Jim wanted to figure out why, there were other, more pressing matters that required their attention – matters of life and death.

"If anything, it's my fault," Jim finally managed. "Janus Blacktail scratched me on the back of the hand when I first met him on the *Spectre* last year. When he asked me where our half of the shell was hidden, I tried to say nothing, or even to lie, but the scratch burned worse than anything I've ever felt before. It burned until I couldn't help but tell him the truth."

"Janus Blacktail was a lying, conniving trickster, my boy. He had been for his entire life – all nine of them, actually," said Cornelius, weakly ruffling his feathers. "An absolute maelstrom of manipulative deceits and entrapments. Do not hold yourself to fault where that villain was concerned."

"Well it don't really matter whose fault it was, now does it?" said George, the candle flames burning hot in his eyes. "'Cause one way or the other, them Cromiers got the shell now. So what are we gonna do about it?" No one said anything for a long moment. The *Spectre's* hull groaned against the waves. The candle flames whispered to one another. In the midst of all that silence, Jim felt the answer well up within him.

"No more running," he said, quietly at first. He swallowed hard, gathered a deep breath, and then said it again, louder. "No more running. Now that the Cromiers have the shell, they'll find the Treasure of the Ocean before long. If they unlock the Treasure's power, we won't be the only ones in danger. Everyone in the world will be. We have to stop them."

MacGuffy opened his mouth to speak, and by the look in the pirate's eye, Jim thought it was a protest against such recklessness. But in the end, MacGuffy only shook his head.

"So be it," he said. "So be it, Jimmy."

"But how will we even know where them Cromiers are?" asked Peter. "That Treasure of the Ocean could be hidden anywhere in the world, right? And they got the shell, which, if I remember right, is the only thing that can find that Treasure in the first place. So what can we do?"

"Maybe they still won't be able to find the Treasure at all," Paul suggested. "All the other times Jim's had to find magic stuff, it's been pretty near impossible to knick, hasn't it? If this is the grand daddy of all magic stuff in the world, then shouldn't it be the hardest of all to get?"

"Undoubtedly, Master Ratt," said Cornelius. "The Treasure of the Ocean is a talisman of ultimate power. It will surely be guarded by forces equal to the task. Even with the Hunter's Shell, taking hold of the Treasure will be a most dangerous quest indeed."

"They'll get it," Jim said. He remembered the look in Bartholomew's eyes atop the roof, where he had held Jim at the mercy of his sword. "One way or the other, they'll get it."

"Then we're right back to where we started," said George, kicking at the floor with his toe. "The Cromiers got the shell, which'll take 'em to the Treasure, and we got no way of knowin where either of 'em are."

"There's a place," Jim said, his mouth suddenly very dry. In his mind's eye he saw the ruins from his dreams. He felt the touch of the golden trident in his hand. "There's a place where the Cromiers will have to take the Treasure of the Ocean. The Treasure isn't the source of the power – it's just the key. They have to open the lock to unleash the magic."

A deeper silence shrouded the cabin. Jim felt the eyes of all his friends upon him, even Lacey's. But when he met her gaze, she dropped it back to her lap. Her curls fell across her face, hiding it from him.

"How do ye know, Jimmy?" asked MacGuffy.

"I just do. I've seen it in my dreams."

"Dread Steele spoke of a place once," said Cornelius, his oft bright squawk not much more than a whisper. "A ruined temple, barely more than a pile of stones on a desolate rock, somewhere out on the deep ocean. He told me this tale but one time, of how he and his comrades went there – went there to deal with the Treasure of the Ocean. Is this like the place you saw, Jim?"

"Yes, Cornelius, it is. Janus Blacktail also told me about it in his story of the Pirates of the Black Skull. He said it was the place they all went, the place where the fourth pirate, Lord Winter, was killed. But did Dread Steele tell you where the temple was? That part I never see in my dreams."

"Nay, lad. In truth, it sounded to me as if Dread Steele hoped never to return there again. Whatever it was that happened there was more horrible than he liked to remember. He also told me the island was cursed, that it cannot be found by any magical seeker. One must know the way, and only that way can it be reached."

"I know who can tell us the way," said Jim. The knot in his stomach twisted another turn. "In the story Janus told me, there was someone else who knew the location of the temple. He chased the Pirates of the Black Skull there to retrieve the Treasure after they had stolen it from him."

"Curses of Neptune," MacGuffy muttered, standing up from the wall. He ran his hand through his mess of white hair, staring into the candle flames. "Nemus."

Jim nodded. Nemus, King of the Sea Folk.

"One does not simply knock on the door of Nemus's palace, Jim," said Cornelius. "Especially not one whose father earned a death sentence from the very same king. We would only gain audience by invitation."

"Jim's necklace," Lacey said. She glanced at Jim excitedly for a moment, but then caught herself, as though remembering she was still angry with him. She finished her thought to MacGuffy and the raven instead. "Queen Melodia, when she was saying goodbye after Dread Steele's funeral, told Jim that if he ever needed her help, he only had to dip his necklace into the sea's foam on an island called the Tower's Top. She will take Jim to Nemus."

MacGuffy stood silent for a long time, staring into the flickering candlelight. "Cornelius," he finally said, "fly up to Mister Gilly at the wheel. Tell him to make for Spire Island. We go there to take on a few extra souls, roughnecks good for a fight... and also to take on a new captain."

"A new captain?" Jim exclaimed.

"Aye, Jimmy, a new captain. One younger and more able than I. One that will not fail ye when it matters most. Now, get ye all below and to sleep, for it has been a tryin day, and there be many more of those yet to come." With that, MacGuffy strode from the captain's quarters, with Cornelius just over his shoulder. Jim rushed out behind them, yanking hard on the pirate's sleeve to turn him back around.

"MacGuffy, you can't leave. You can't abandon us!" Panic fluttered at the edges of Jim's voice. He felt a thick knot swell in his throat.

"Ah, Jim, I'm not gonna abandon ye," said MacGuffy. It seemed to Jim that the old man's heart was breaking as he spoke. "I could never leave ye and little Lacey or the sea mice, not ever, especially not a time as dark as thissun. But look at me, Jim. I'm an old man. Me body has nearly given up on me. Me greatest deeds were done long ago. If Dread Steele had been here this night, it would be we who possessed the healed Hunter's Shell, not them blasted Cromiers."

MacGuffy knelt down, setting his old hands upon Jim's shoulders. "What we go to face now is no game, boy," he said. "This is a race for somethin real, Jimmy. At the end of this road is a power that old MacGuffy can scarce comprehend. Power – real power like this – drives men mad. It can turn good men wrong, and bad men – it can turn them to monsters, Jimmy – monsters who care not who they hurt. Truth is, I'm afraid for ye. I'm afraid for Lacey and Georgie, Peter, and Paul. I'm afraid of what's gonna happen to ye."

Jim's heart beat hard. His lips and throat were dry. When he swallowed, it was like choking down a stone. "But I know you'll look after us, MacGuffy. You always have."

"One day, I won't be there to look out for ye, remember? One day you must be the one to look out for yerself, and for the others."

"But you'll stay as long as you can, won't you? Like you said?"

MacGuffy finally let a smile wrinkle onto his ruined face. He pulled Jim close, squeezing him tight, and held him for a long moment.

"Aye, lad," he said. "As long as I can. Now, off to bed with ye. Smile to Lacey and the sea Ratts for me. Tell them not to fear. Old MacGuffy still has some adventurin left in him yet."

With a pat on his back, MacGuffy sent Jim off for the stairs to the belowdecks, to the cabin he shared with the Ratts. When he reached the steps, Jim threw one last glance over his shoulder. He found MacGuffy still watching over him from where he stood on the deck, like a gnarled gargoyle, standing guard against the darkness in the pale light of the moon.

THIRTEEN

MAGIC ON THE *SEA SPIDER*

Across the sea from where the *Spectre* sailed to Spire Island, the Corsair ship called the *Sea Spider* crested the waves. Her hull was the color of a dead tree and her mainmast was as jagged as a leafless branch in winter. The turbaned pirates who helmed the ship attended carefully to their riggings and sails. They sang no pirate songs nor laughed at sailors' tales. Fear had robbed them of all the sea's joy – fear of their dark master, his pale son, and the cursed magic brought aboard in the port of the Kasbah.

Below decks, behind closed doors and protected by powerful wards and spells, Bartholomew Cromier watched his father, the Red Count, withdraw the Hunter's Shell from a black box. Whether he admitted it aloud or not, Bartholomew felt his heart beat faster and his blood curdle in his veins. He and his father now drew close to the end of their journey, close to the ultimate prize. But the two of them had been closer even than this to the Treasure of the Ocean once before. Bartholomew had held the golden trident in his bare hands. The heat with which the magic had burned his skin still haunted him in his secret dreams.

"So close, my son, so close," said the count. His voice was a whisper. His gaze was fixed on the purple shell's polished surface. A shimmer of magic ran across the conch, the violet glow sparkling in Cromier's mad eyes. "All of Lindsay Morgan's schemes and plots and traps have failed him at last. Dread Steele is dead. Now even the young Morgan has failed to keep us from our purpose. Our quest is nearly at an end, Bartholomew. The hour of your destiny – of our glory – is at hand."

A shiver crawled up Bartholomew's back.

Count Cromier removed his leather gloves. He touched the shell with his bare skin. A violet aura pulsed around the conch, throwing hard shadows on the walls. The count squeezed the shell in his fingers. His lips peeled back from his old, yellowed teeth. He spat a command at the enchanted talisman, as though it were his slave.

"I seek the Treasure of the Ocean. I seek that which was taken from Nemus. I seek the golden trident. Show me its hiding place, that I might make it mine."

From the Shell, a finger of magic unfurled in a violent arc. It lanced through the black room, nearly blinding Bartholomew, forcing him back from his father with an arm over his face. When Bartholomew dared look again, he found the purple beam had carved a hole through the ceiling, all the way through the deck of the ship above, trailing into the black night.

"Look Bartholomew," the count shrieked. His old eyes were wide. His mouth hung open, teeth bared. "Can you see? Can you see?"

Bartholomew could see. In the pulsating glow of the shell an image took shape. It was England – the north of England that became

Scotland. The image soared over the land, past rivers and lakes, all the way to the highlands, all the way to one particular mountain. In the mountainside, the mouth of a cave opened in the purple glow. The glamor allowed Bartholomew and his father to see into the blackness, to see what stood watch over the Treasure of the Ocean.

Bartholomew felt his guts curl into a slippery knot.

The count slowly lowered the shell into its box. The moment he released the talisman, the purple beam pointing the way to a cave in the mountain went dark, and the room was plunged into blackness. When Bartholomew's eyes adjusted once more to the dim light, he saw steam rising from his father's hands. The twisting tendrils danced before the old count's eyes, those mad, dark-circled eyes.

"Perhaps, Bartholomew," said the count, "your most recent failure to kill Jim Morgan and his friends will prove of some benefit after all."

Bartholomew gritted his teeth. He wanted to say something. To tell his father how he had held Jim Morgan at his mercy. To tell him how he had let Jim Morgan go, like a plaything to be toyed with. But he held his tongue. His hand instinctively reached to his cheek, where a dull ache marked a swelling beneath his eye. When Bartholomew had returned without the blood of Morgan on his sword, his father had not been pleased.

"Why, father?" He finally dared to ask. "Why must it always be him? Why must it always be him that you send into the darkness? Have you no faith in me? Have you not seen the man I've become?"

"You are still but a boy," said the count. The sharp tone of his voice stung that place on Bartholomew's cheek. "A boy and a fool. Did you not see what waits for us in the shadows of that cave? Did you not see what stands watch over our prize?"

Indeed Bartholomew had. The image had run his blood cold. But something else flowed through Bartholomew's veins besides the ice – something hot.

"I can do it," Bartholomew whispered. "We don't need—"

"Silence!" Cromier snapped. Bartholomew's head dropped. He stepped back from his father, toward the wall. "You will do as I command. Nothing more and nothing less. If left to you, this entire quest would have failed years ago. It is I who have brought us this far. Now, bring me the old tome I have there on shelf – quickly now."

Bartholomew kept his eyes on his feet as he stalked over to his father's shelf. There he withdrew a thick, heavy volume, its yellowed pages bound in cracked black leather. He had hardly offered the book to his father before the count snatched it from his grasp. Cromier threw it open and snapped through the pages, all but ripping the leaves from the binding. At last, the count found what he was looking for. He closed the book with a soft tap, a dry cackle running over his lips.

"Fortune smiles, my son. Your failure may be our salvation. The challenge guarding the Treasure is the greatest we have faced yet – but all challenges have a weakness. The chink in this armor may still be within our grasp. We will have need of the street trash once again."

"Morgan." Bartholomew spat the name like a curse. Always it was Morgan.

"No, my son. As it turns out, your earlier words may be correct. It is not that whelp, Morgan, of whom I have need this time. It is another."

Bartholomew said nothing. He finally found the courage to look to his father. He found the count staring back at him, his unblinking eyes quivering in their sockets.

"We will need this one whole and unspoiled – it is of utmost importance. Go to the wheel. Command the first officer to turn us about. The *Spectre* will undoubtedly head for one of two places. Spire Island or the waters of the Merfolk. We will track them. We will catch them. We will take what we need."

Bartholomew licked his lips. He wanted desperately to argue once more for his chance, just a chance to be the one to walk first through the door of discovery, of danger, or even of death. But "Yes, Father," was all that came out. On his way to the wheel, Bartholomew tried to convince himself that it would not besmirch his honor to stand by as his father offered up a mere child to the great beast that guarded the Treasure of the Ocean.

BOOK II

TO THE KINGDOM
BENEATH THE WAVES

FOURTEEN

THE EMPTY TURTLE SHELL

After two days with the wind in her sails, the *Spectre* made berth at Spire Island. Albatrosses and gulls circled on a gentle breeze about the stone tower that gave the island its name. But even under the warmth of the morning sun, a cold shadow hung over Jim, Lacey, and the Ratts as they made their way down the pier and into the bustling streets of Shelltown.

The voyage to Spire Island had been long and tiresome. After the Crimson Storm's attack, much of the crew became all the more eager to pitch Jim and his friends overboard, desperate to save themselves from the Morgan Curse. Everywhere Jim went on the *Spectre*, whispers and distrustful stares followed close behind. It was all MacGuffy could do to keep the peace. All that saved the ship from mutiny was MacGuffy's allowance for any sailor who so desired to abandon the quest and find a new ship in Shelltown.

The moment the ship had docked, no less than a third of the crew walked off, duffle or locker in hand. As they went, some of the sailors threw Jim hateful stares. Others refused to look him in the eye at all. Only one old salt paused to lay a hand on Jim's shoulder. He opened his mouth to speak, but in the end, offered only a look of pity, shaking his head with tears in his rheumy eyes as he walked away.

"Pay ye no mind to these craven slugs, Jimmy," MacGuffy had growled, spitting on the deck. "I would not be sharin our triumph no ways with such poltroons as these. When we finally win the day over that murderin tyrant, Cromier, I'll not be mentionin none of these curs among the names of the brave!"

"They're just scared, MacGuffy," Jim said, watching after the old pirate as he hobbled down the pier. "Hard to fault them for that with all we've seen."

"We'll be seein worse afore the end, Jimmy, I can tell you that for certain." But even as he said those words, MacGuffy must have seen the crestfallen look on Jim's face. So to take Jim's mind off his worries, MacGuffy sent him and the clan to go visit Egidio Quattrochi and collect a few more Aeolus Feathers for the journey.

"Meet me and Cornelius at noontime in a small inn called the Splintered Forecastle," MacGuffy had said after placing a few coins in Jim's hand. "There we shall see what manner of man we might find to aid us on our way."

So Jim and his friends had set out, but even on the streets of Shelltown, Jim felt curious stares at his back and heard whispers in his wake. All pirates, it seemed, knew the name of Morgan and the unending tragedy that followed wherever it went.

"You think Egidio has got anymore of them fog seeds lyin about?" asked Paul. "I'd like to get a hold of some of them. A pocketful of them little marvels goes a long way, now don't it?"

"Fog seeds won't help you hide from me, Paul," said Peter,

sneaking up behind his brother and flicking him on the ear. "I can smell you in the dark."

"Ouch, Peter! We had a truce while we was in town." Paul tried to slug Peter's arm, but Peter flitted just out of reach. "And I don't smell." The two younger Ratts had been playing ear flicks for the last two days, if for no other reason than to keep their spirits up. Usually, Jim thought, George would have played as well, changing the rules every so often to ensure he won. But the eldest Ratt seemed less playful of late, wandering off to be by himself more often than not.

"We're not here for fog seeds, Paul," said Lacey. "And I think, in a way, Peter might be right. I'm not sure fog seeds could hide us from the Crimson Storm – or from the Cromiers. The count has his own magic – dangerous magic. We're going to buy Aeolus Feathers. They're the only things that make us fast enough to run away."

"But we're not running, Lacey," said Jim, hoping for at least a small response from her. She had barely spoken to him for the last two days. "Even MacGuffy says so. The Cromiers will get the Treasure of the Ocean. The count won't let anything get in his way. When they take the golden trident to the temple, we'll be the only ones that can stop them."

"If MacGuffy says we can't run no more, then why are we buyin them feathers?" said George, head down and hands in his pocket. "Why did he let all them crew just walk off like that? We're not gettin ready for a fight. Just like Lacey says, all them feathers is good for is runnin. We should use that money and buy somethin stronger. Somethin more like a weapon."

"Magic is dangerous," said Lacey. She was looking at George, but Jim knew she was talking to him as well. "You saw what happened to the King of Thieves. You saw what happened to Philus Philonius. And you just saw what happened to that poor shop owner, Abdullah. Every time we've seen magic, the one who used it got destroyed by it in the end." Finally Lacey looked back at Jim, straight into his eyes. "Every time," she said.

"Well they got magic, Lacey," said George. "Them Cromiers do. Maybe the only way to fight magic is with more magic of our own. So I'm askin Egidio, whether you like it or not."

But neither Lacey's concern or George's defiance were going to make any difference, Jim soon realized. They were going to return to the *Spectre* empty-handed, without having even asked Egidio for anything at all.

As Jim rounded a bend in the cobblestone road, walking into the shadow of the island's spire, a warning bell rang at the back of his mind. At the edge of the rocky beach, splashed by high tide, a ruined pier came into view. Beneath the pier was a single structure, built not of brick or stone, but from the shell of a massive sea turtle. The holes once meant for enormous, scaly limbs served as doors and windows. It was the wonderful, bizarre shop of Egidio Quattrochi.

But something was amiss. No smoke climbed from the chimney. The windows were dark in the shadow of the spire. The red hue of the shell's plates had somehow dulled to nearly gray, as though life had faded from the very building itself. Jim ran the rest of the way to the front door, the Ratts and Lacey behind him.

The shingle that once read *Egidio Quattrochi's Shop of Magical Books, Potions, and Artifacts* lay broken in pieces on the ground. The bright green door, the very one through which the clan had snuck to eavesdrop on Dread Steele and Egidio over a year before, was snapped in half, as though caved in by a giant's boot.

"Oh no," Jim whispered, "Egidio."

Jim kicked the shattered remains of the door aside, rushing into the darkened shop. "Be careful!" he heard Lacey say, but she was nearly as close behind as George.

Broken shelves, shredded baskets, and shards of smashed pots littered the floor. Dust motes floated like fireflies in the shafts of light sneaking through the filthy windows. None of the wondrous concoctions, mysterious plants, or bubbling cauldrons remained. They had all been taken or destroyed as far as Jim could tell.

"Egidio!" Jim shouted into the shop. The shadows returned no answer.

"Maybe he just moved shops," Peter suggested quietly, as though afraid to disturb whatever wickedness had wrought this destruction. "You know, found a better shell or somethin." But Jim knew better. The little shop did not feel abandoned. It felt violated.

"Jim, over here, look." George was standing a few feet away, in the middle of the wrecked shop. He was staring down at the floor. A sick feeling rose in the back of Jim's throat when he saw what George had pointed out. It was a nearly perfect circle, burned into the floor. Inside the ring and all around it were leftover grains of black powder. Jim had seen such a circle before – left behind on the deck of the *Spectre* the night Dread Steele died.

"Cromier," Jim said through gritted teeth. "He was here." Jim picked up a broken board from the floor, raised it above his head, and smashed it against the ground with all his might. "Maybe there is a Morgan Curse," he finally said. His throat felt thick and hot. "Everyone I know ends up getting hurt… or worse."

"This wasn't your fault, Jim," said Lacey. She came to stand beside him, close for the first time in a while. "It was the count. He did this to poor Egidio, and it was him alone."

Jim nodded, glad to hear Lacey's voice again, but he was hardly sure he believed what she said. "Let's at least look around a little," he suggested. "Maybe we can find something of use left in here. Or maybe just something to remember old Egidio by." Jim was sure he would never see the old shopkeeper again.

The five friends spread out with hardly a word between them. The Ratts searched about the counter. Lacey began to comb through the remains of the broken pots on the floor. But Jim, who felt like being alone, wandered down the hallway at the back of the shop to a small room where he and his friends had once spied on a secret conversation between Egidio and Dread Steele.

Jim found the sitting room in much the same shape as the rest of the shop, looted and empty. A single beam of light came through the room's lone window. Jim ambled through the door, scuffing up puffs of dust. He was wondering what had become of kind, old Egidio when the round spot of sunshine disappeared. For a moment, Jim thought that a cloud had come between the shop and the sun.

But the darkness sank deeper.

A cold wind kissed Jim's skin. The icy chill crawled up his arms and legs, wrapping about him like a cloak. Jim shivered to his bones. Black tendrils sprang from the floor. They climbed the walls, slithered along the ground, and wound across the ceiling.

Jim tried to run. He tried to shout to his friends. But the cold froze his legs and the darkness swallowed his voice. The black cloud invading the room trapped him all alone. At last, when the whole of the room had fallen under the shroud, the lightless tendrils gathered at the floor before Jim's feet. The blackness grew, taking shape and rising up to the roof to loom over Jim.

Spindly legs and spidery arms came to life. A long face protruded from beneath a black hat, with a hooked nose, and a smile that stretched from pallid cheek to pallid cheek.

"Well, hello there, James Francis Morgan," the shadow said, tongue dripping honey. "So good to see you again after all these years."

It was the King of Thieves.

FIFTEEN

THE KING OF THIEVES

Y ou can't be here!" Jim said. "I saw you... I saw you swallowed whole by the green fire from the broken Amulet of Portunes." The shadows crawling along the floor had slipped around Jim's ankles, and those climbing the walls were about his wrists. They pinned him to where he stood, piercing his muscles like icy needles.

"It doesn't seem possible, does it, my boy? But yet it *is*." The King stretched his wiry arms wide, reaching through the magic-soaked air, grabbing at the world with his fingers. But there was still a dreamlike quality to the King, even standing there in the room with Jim. He seemed almost translucent, as if the light could not quite stick to his skin.

"I remember that night, you know," continued the King. "I remember it as though it were yesterday. The green fire burned. It burned like real flames, only worse. That burning scorched deeper than my flesh. I could feel it burning *me* – my thoughts, my feelings… my soul, if you will."

"Didn't you think you had that one coming?" Jim growled. But the King only laughed. He threw his head back and howled. The spidery man began to gleefully circle around the room. His footfalls made no sound upon the stone floor.

"Oh, the more things change, the more they stay the same," said the King. "You still have that haughty tongue, don't you? But you're not wrong. Perhaps I did have that one coming, and in more ways than one. All my life, if you recall, I searched for treasures of magic and power." The King's eyes widened into a deep staring gaze, traveling through Jim, to somewhere beyond the confines of the room. "Because of you I found more of it than I ever dreamed possible."

"But you haven't fully come back to our world from wherever you went, have you?"

"No indeed, my boy. I have not." The King rounded on Jim, so fast that it seemed more like stretching than walking, flowing through the air in a dark puddle. "Do you know that place between dreaming and waking? That place, lying in your bed, when your eyes are open but you cannot quite trust what you see? That is the place where I find myself. I am so close to being *here…*" The King unfurled one of his long, bony fingers, reaching it towards Jim's face. But where the finger should have pressed against Jim's cheek, there was only a dull cold. It was like the imagining of touch rather than the touch itself. "But not quite."

"How have you come back, then?"

"I cannot fully explain it. One moment I was mostly there. The next I was mostly here. But what is important is that I know *why*. I have returned with a purpose, with a mission, if you will. I have come back to aid you in your quest."

Jim nearly choked with laughter. "You? Aid me? The way you were going to aid the clans? The way you aided me into the Vault of Treasures? You sure have an odd way of showing you want to help." Jim twisted his wrists in their misty bonds. The King turned one half of his mouth into a knowing grin and waved his hand. The dark vines retreated from Jim, loosing his arms and legs.

"Forgive me, lad," said the King, bowing his head. "But we both know that due to our past… misunderstandings, you would have fled the moment you saw me. I tried to speak to you in your dreams, but you woke too quickly."

"Invading someone's mind doesn't exactly come across as charitable, King." Jim challenged. But his thoughts flicked back to that image from his sleep, back to the altar in the temple and the yawning mouth of blackness floating in the air.

"But did I not explain your dream to you? Did I not open your eyes to what you were seeing?" The King dropped down to one knee, hands held out. "I have seen so much since I've been gone. In all that time I spent beyond the veil of this world, I began to understand things in a different way. I have seen this poor, wretched earth from the outside, young Morgan. I have seen its sorrows, its injustices, its wickedness—"

"You were plenty part of that wickedness when you were here, King." Jim thrust a finger toward the King's face. "You never saw the looks on their faces, on the faces of my friends when they learned that you'd lied to them and used them. You never saw their tears, did you?"

"Yes, I did." The King whispered his confession, head down, eyes to the floor. "I told you that I saw this world from the outside. I saw the pain of each and every child I ever wronged – children like poor, George Ratt. Poor George, lied to by his parents, lied to by his friends, lied to by me, made to feel so alone and defenseless in the world." Jim felt a small pang in his chest. Once, he had been one of the friends who lied to George, when he had failed to tell him about the Treasure of the Ocean, back in London. "Together, though, we could make all those wrongs right."

Jim licked his lips. Even in the cold, sweat began to slick his clammy palms and bead on the back of his neck. "How do you mean, make wrongs right?"

"What the world needs is a light to show the way," the King said, daring once more to lift his eyes. "But not a lone candle of goodness that will be snuffed out by the first strong wind. No, this world needs a wild fire! It needs a leader with enough power to *force* his goodness upon even the vilest evildoers. I told you in your dream that the Treasure of the Ocean is but a key and the altar a lock. Together they open a door – a door that leads to the world of magic. But the magic cannot simply pour out into the world. No, no, that would destroy and overwhelm everything. The magic is like water. It requires a cloud through which it will bring its rain. It requires a vessel. You are that vessel, young Morgan. It is what you were born to be. It is what your father meant you to be."

The King's words rang in Jim's mind. He had heard them before, when Janus Blacktail told the story of the Pirates of the Black Skull. The Thief and the Sailor, otherwise known as Lindsay Morgan and Dread Steele, had wanted to use the Treasure of the Ocean to make the world a better place. So this was Jim's purpose? His destiny? Was this really what his father had wanted from him?

"Why would you want to help me do that?" Jim asked. He was digging through the King's words, looking for lies, but everything the spidery man said seemed to align with all Jim had learned thus far. "What's in it for you?"

"Redemption," The King proclaimed. He stood back up, swirling about the room like bleeding ink. "Do you remember that night outside the Pirate Vault of Treasures, when I asked you to come with me? I offered to be a father to you, and make you a son to me. I was a fool then, and a thief, just as you say. But now I could at last make good on that offer. Your father meant to be here for you through all of these trials. He meant to guide you as you took hold of the power. He meant to be a voice of wisdom in your ear, to help you know when to turn right and when to turn left. Don't we all need that? To know the right thing to do at the right time?"

"But you're not my father."

"What does a father do, Jim? Does he not give his son a name? Who was it that called you Jim for the first time? Wasn't it me? Does not a father set his son on the road to manhood? Did I not do that when I put you on the path you now travel? Have I not done all these things?" The King went back down on one knee before Jim, reaching out with his long fingers for Jim's face. The King's eyes were wide and soft, full of sorrow. His voice was sweeter than honey.

"I could be a greater advisor to you than your real father ever could. He never saw the worlds I have seen. I could show you all of it." The King's fingers reached Jim's head. Jim could feel the cold points on the side of his face. "I could see through your eyes, and you could see through mine. We could be as one…"

Jim suddenly saw a picture in his mind's eye. The King was knocking at the door of his thoughts – no, he was pounding. He was slamming his fist against that door to be let in. But if Jim let him in, there would be no sharing. There would be no advising. There would be only control. Jim would become nothing more than a mask. Behind that mask would be the King of Thieves.

"Liar!" he cried. The white rose scar burned on Jim's palm. Strength hummed to life in his arms and legs. The shadows retreated and a few rays of light once more trickled into the room. "You don't want me for a son. You want me for a slave. You don't have a real body in this place, so you want to take mine. You're just like Philus Philonius. But I wasn't his puppet and I won't be yours either. Not ever!" With every shout, Jim and the light grew stronger, and the shadows grew weaker. The King shrank back from him. With each step the false kindness melted from his pale face, revealing the hideous snarl beneath.

"You are a fool, Jim Morgan," The King shrieked. "Twice now I have offered you the keys to a life free of fear. Twice you have chosen the path of pain and sorrow. Remember this when there are tears pouring down your face and the faces of your friends. For you have forgotten one of the first lessons of thieving – a thief only rarely enters through the front door. There are windows, cracks, and hidden passages into your life, Jim Morgan. You cannot keep them all locked. You cannot forever keep out the King of Thieves."

"Get away from me!" Jim cried out at last. The darkness finally lost its hold on the room. The shadowy tendrils gathered up unto the King of Thieves, clinging to him like a cloak of serpents. He flowed away, flying through the window and leaving no proof of his being behind.

When the King was gone, Jim staggered to regain his balance. He felt exhausted, as though he had been running for hours on end. The sun glared harsh in his eyes. His head ached. He turned a full circle, looking about the barren room and finding not a trace of anything that had just happened.

"Jim! Jim, are you alright?" Lacey appeared from behind Jim, grabbing his shoulders to turn him around. She was looking him up and down, searching for some wound or injury. George was just behind her, flanked by his brothers. The three of them looked about the room for any sign of danger. "What happened? You walked down the hallway and suddenly you were shouting about getting something away from you."

"Just came down the hall?" Jim asked. "I haven't been down here for some time? You didn't hear me talking or shouting?"

"Talkin or shoutin?" George asked. He raised one eyebrow on his forehead, analyzing Jim closely. "You been back here for just a second, mate. You feelin alright? Maybe there's still some magical dust or somethin floatin in the air from when Egidio was still here, and it's got to your head."

"You have only been back here for a moment, Jim," said Lacey. "But something happened? What was it?"

"I... I thought I saw something," Jim said. "I thought I saw the King of Thieves."

"The King of Thieves?" Lacey and the others suddenly drew closer together. She and the Ratts looked nervously around the room for any trace of their old enemy, as though searching for spiders dangling above their heads. "But Jim, he's been dead for ages."

"Got what he deserved... Right?" said George. But he and his brothers seemed suddenly wary all the same.

"I don't know," said Jim, shaking his head. "It felt real when it happened. But you said I've only been down here for a moment or two. And it wasn't like he was really here. It was more like talking to a ghost." Jim met Lacey's worried eyes. She had already been so concerned, worrying about magic consuming people, he thought. This was only making it worse. "Maybe it was just a shadow or something. Or maybe just a leftover part of some bad dream. Nothing to worry about, Lacey. I'm fine."

"You shouted aloud and you think maybe it was just a shadow?" Lacey dropped her hands from Jim's shoulders. "Well, one doesn't need any help with that, does he?" With that, Lacey spun about on her heel and marched through the door and into the hallway. "Come on, you lot," she called over her shoulder. "We're leaving. As Jim just pointed out, there's nothing here but shadows!"

"Lacey," Jim called after, but she was already in the hall and headed toward what was left of the shop's front door.

"You really did see somethin though, dinnit ya?" George whispered, squeezing the back of Jim's arm, holding him fast as Peter and Paul followed after Lacey.

"Yes, I did," Jim whispered. "But I don't want to scare the others. I almost didn't say anything at all – know what I mean?" Jim pointed toward George's chest, to his inside jacket pocket, where he kept that something hidden. A bit of guilt stole into George's grim expression.

"Yeah, I know," he said. George was about to release Jim's arm and walk away, but now it was Jim's turn to take his friend by the elbow.

"George, remember back on the Veiled Isle, when I'd nearly walked us to death in the dark forest because of the black rose's poison? Remember when you had to carry me all the way to the faeries' country to save my life?"

George nodded. A bit of color seemed to creep back into his cheeks. "Course I remember that, Jim. And you remember that time when you coulda used that Amulet of What's-it to unlock your box, but instead you set me and me brothers free? Remember that?"

"I do," said Jim. He and George smiled again, smiled the way they used to, back in London when the world never seemed so dark.

"I trust you, George. You're my best friend."

"I trust you, Jim. As long as we're together, ain't nothin that can stop us. I know it."

"Then when you're ready, I hope you know you can tell me," said Jim.

"Alright, I will. But later," George said with a nod. "Just the two of us."

"Just the two of us."

Jim and George shook on it, still smiling. Together they strode from the shop and joined the others. But it would be only a day before Jim would wish more than anything that George had not waited to tell him his secret.

SIXTEEN

THROWING KNIVES
IN THE SPLINTERED FORECASTLE

I f the Inn of the Wet Rock, where Jim and his friends first met Dread Steele, had a harsher, uglier, and meaner older brother, it would have been the Splintered Forecastle. From twenty paces away, a foul twist of odors – spilt ale, dried blood, unwashed bodies, and a hint of seaweed – assaulted Jim's nose. The building itself was indeed comprised of a forecastle – the back portion of a sailing ship – shorn from some unlucky vessel and dumped on the cobblestone corner. A steering wheel sat atop the roof, where a haggard, wind-worn pirate propped himself, his head stuck through the wheel's spokes and two empty tins of ale dangling from each hand.

"Well, this looks promising," said Paul, saluting to the unconscious seaman on the roof. "Only the sharpest minds on the island in here, I can tell already."

"Right, Paul," said Peter, nodding to his brother. "Only the highest quality captains for us. Qual-i-ty."

"We're better off with just us and MacGuffy," added George, grumpily. "We won't find nobody worth a lick in this dump." The clan turned off the street and made their way up the walk to the front door. It was so dented and bent that it seemed it was only ever opened by kick. The raucous chorus of a pirate shanty, accompanied by a melody of rough laughter, greeted the clan's arrival. As they neared the entrance, Jim pulled Lacey back by the arm.

"Stay close," he whispered. "It may get ugly in here."

"Oh, don't worry, Jim," replied Lacey, brushing off Jim's hand and offering him a look as warm as snow. "If I run into anything dangerous, I'll just take care of it by myself." With that, Lacey stormed ahead and kicked open the door as though she'd been a founding patron. Jim sighed and the younger Ratts laughed as they followed her through.

The ribald cacophony within the inn exploded in Jim's ears. Pirates, sailors, and scoundrels from every ship on the ocean packed themselves onto benches, atop tables, and even stretched themselves out on the floor. They poured ale down their gullets and shoved food into their mouths. Fortunately, Jim had spent the last couple of years living amongst such salt of the sea, for the crude language alone would have been enough to pink the cheeks of even the worldliest London gentleman.

Jim and the Ratts made themselves as small as possible and wove through the jostling pirates. Half the sailors in the pub hung on each other's necks like old friends, while the other half brandished weapons and vowed revenge. Every few moments or so, the two halves switched, and the hugging pirates turned to fighting, and the fighting pirates turned to hugging.

The pirates offered Jim and the Ratts nothing but hateful glares or growls, but just ahead, Lacey moved through the crowd like Moses through the Red Sea. The scalawags parted the way for her, voices dropped to whispers and faces gone red, as though caught by their mothers at playing dice or fighting. Jim did his best to follow in her wake until the clan broke through into a clearing, only to find an even saltier inner circle gathered about a long table.

A glimmering pile of opulence lay gathered on the table in the midst of the shouting and cheering mob – stacks of gold doubloons, glimmering jewels, and strings of pearls from the deep ocean. The pirates were gambling, Jim realized. The contest was knife throwing. One pirate at a time had a turn, taking position beside the end of the table and hurling three blades into a target on the far wall, without any heed for passersby. A hush fell over the game each time a set of blades was thrown. After a hit or miss, the hollering erupted again, louder with each passing round. Just outside the circle of players Jim spied MacGuffy, Cornelius Darkfeather perched upon his shoulder. The old sailor was propped against a post, studying the knife throwers with his lone, dark eye

"Did ye buy us the Aeolus Feathers, Jimmy?" asked MacGuffy, barely turning his head, as though he had smelled a less foul scent upon the air and knew the young clan drew near. "And did ye ask after Egidio for me? How is the old rascal?"

"He's gone, MacGuffy," said Jim as he and the others gathered close. The pang of yet another loss stung deeply.

"When will he be back, I wonders? We cannot be wastin much time here. Once we find our new captain and crew, we'll be needin to cast off at once."

"No, you don't understand. He's gone. It must have been Count Cromier. The black dust he uses to vanish from place to place was in a burned ring on the floor."

MacGuffy jerked his head about to face Jim, some flash of fury or fear, or both, ablaze in his eye. The old man and the raven shared a silent conversation in a glance. Jim thought he saw MacGuffy's frail shoulders slump a little further.

"Darker and darker by the day," MacGuffy muttered, his white-whiskered chin quivering. But remembering himself in front of Jim and his friends, the sea worn sailor straightened up again and nodded to the rowdy contest before them. "Well, all shall be set right afore the end, fates be willin. So let us set our sights on the task at hand. If we're goin to venture once more upon the deep ocean, and if we're goin to face the Cromiers head on, then we need a Cap'n up to the task. Every month, only the best cap'ns from the best ships gather here, to try their hand at some contest or another. Knife throwin it be today, and today, I hope to find one of the sort we be needin."

"We have a handful of decent candidates in mind already," said Cornelius. The raven flapped down to sit on Lacey's shoulder, motioning Jim and the Ratts closer for a better look. "I'm feeling quite encouraged in spite of things, really. MacGuffy and I were hoping that a few, certain chaps would be in port today, and we've had a stroke of luck. Most of the captains on our list are here."

A slender pirate, robed in gold and crimson silk, a pearl medallion hanging about his neck, glided up to position at the end of the table. His head was shaved bald, save for a long, black braid that trailed from the crown of his head down to his waist.

"First up, we have Lo Fang," said Cornelius, "a pirate captain from Wang Chi's part of the globe. Dragons are still fairly prevalent in that corner of the world, or so they say. Wang Chi told us that this Lo Fang once sailed alone to a far eastern island, one forever shrouded in mist, where a blind dragon, wearing a crown of pearls, lived upon a mountaintop. For three days and three nights, Lo Fang disguised himself among the gusts of ocean air, always staying down wind, always keeping quiet as the fog. He crept nearer and nearer, until he was close enough to whisper in the Dragon's ear. The Dragon, impressed by Lo Fang's cunning, gave him a pearl from his crown, which Lo Fang wears, even to this day."

Graceful as a swan upon the waters, this Lo Fang took all three daggers in one hand. He spun in a single whirl, throwing one knife behind his back, one over his head, and the last as he came back about. All three found the target with satisfying thunks.

"Not bad," said George, he and his brothers nodding as though that throw was nearly as good as what they could have done.

"Although, Georgie," said Peter, stroking his chin, "I might have been a bit more impressed if he had actually taken the entire crown off that dragon's head, you know? Not a really strong finish to just sneak up and whisper. I mean, not to take anythin away from him or anythin, disguisin oneself as a gust a wind ain't a bad trick, but anybody could have whispered." Jim did his best to suppress a chuckle, but Lacey snorted as loud as she could and rolled her blue eyes.

"Now, next up is a fearsome captain indeed." Cornelius pointed a feathery wing to a short pirate, hat pulled so low over his face so that only a single curve of an unshaved jaw could be seen. "This pirate comes with a reputation hard to match, my young friends. Found more buried treasures than old John Silver, they say. Raided more ports than Blackbeard himself. Has horded more gold than the kings and queens of some nations. They call her Golden Ginny."

"Her?" Jim, George, Peter, and Paul said together. On cue, the pirate before them tore away her hat, casting it aside with a shake of her head. A shimmering wave of golden hair came spilling down over her black-vested back. She sauntered to the throwing mark with all the grace of Lo Fang and twice the swagger.

"I told you there were girl pirates," said Lacey, unleashing the most uncontainable smirk Jim had ever seen.

"Yeah, well, that don't mean she's any good, now does it?" George said. But he tugged at his shirt collar as though it had gotten suddenly quite warm inside. His question was answered by three rapid strikes on the target. Golden Ginny had landed all three blades on the board, as had Lo Fang, but two of her daggers now quivered in the bull's-eye.

"You were saying?" said Lacey. Golden Ginny turned about, her yellow hair trailing behind her like a shining ribbon. When she caught sight of Lacey, she paused, flashing her a white smile and wink of an almond eye. The Ratts immediately whipped their hats from their heads, holding them in their hands and babbling like baboons.

"We was rootin for you the whole time, Captain Golden," Peter stammered.

"Brilliant throw, ma'am," said George, craning his neck and trying to make himself look as tall as possible. "Just brilliant."

Paul, meanwhile, just stood with his widest smile frozen in place upon his cheeks, winking back at Golden Ginny. Once Ginny pulled her hat back upon her head, and her hypnotic spell over the Ratts was broken, Peter and Paul slapped their hats back on their heads and seemed ready to leave.

"Well, I think it's a clear choice, don't you Cornelius?" said Peter.

"I mean, I'm sure the rest are all right and everythin, but I think we've seen what we needed to see," agreed Paul, half of his ridiculous smile still glued to his face.

"Well, there is one more." Cornelius's black-within-black eyes were still fixed on the contest. "It has been many years since we have seen him. He once ran in the same circles as Dread Steele. Of all the pirates we have seen thus far, Steele said it was this fellow that knew magic best, and he was also most well known by the merfolk. If he is still game, he may be our best hope. His name is F.W. Pennington Sharpe."

As though at the sound of Cornelius's voice, the crowd parted like a curtain, revealing the dandiest pirate Jim had ever seen. His feet were crossed and propped upon the table beside the mound of glimmering bets. His shoes were polished until they shone. His stockings were white as lace. His breeches were a spotless tan and his coat a perfect, powdered blue. A cascade of brown curls tumbled from his robin's egg hat. In one hand, Sharpe delicately held an all but empty bottle of wine, and in the other, balanced on his fingertips, a fully drained goblet.

"Ogh," said the captain, flashing his pearly smile and pinking under all the sudden attention now fixed upon him. "Gis it my turn, algready?" The captain stood quite suddenly, knocking his chair down behind him and setting his bottle in a row of three others. In some blend of a shuffle and stagger, Captain Sharpe somehow managed to make his way to the throwing mark, but along the way, he saw MacGuffy, leaning against his post.

"Well, hoist my sails!" said Sharpe, laughing a little too loudly. "If it igsn't my good friend, ogld MacGuffy!" When Sharpe said MacGuffy's name, he did such a perfect imitation of the old salt's voice, that Peter and Paul nearly exploded with laughter. "Good to see you still kigging, and glad to know that you are, apparently, still eating soglid foods at your age. There's hgope for ugs all!"

"Aye," growled MacGuffy. "We was, in fact, hoping to have a word with ye, F.W."

"A word?" Sharpe whispered loudly enough for everyone in the inn to hear. "Is igt a segret? I do love segrets. Gimme jus a moment, ogld man. I need to done these fools how it's shown." With that, Captain Sharpe whirled unsteadily, his hat and wig falling over his eyes, and stumbled up to the throwing line.

"Well," said Jim. "This should be interesting."

"Maybe it's some kind of trick?" said Paul. "You know, like a con?" Jim was just about to accept that possibility when Sharpe seized the three daggers from the table and took a long steadying breath. He readjusted his hat and drew back his arm to throw. The circle of pirates went quiet. With three quick flicks Sharpe launched his knives.

A glass shattered in a barmaid's hand, a cat squalled, and the last dagger stuck a rather portly pirate directly in the hindquarters, which he announced with an ear-splitting howl.

"Oh, boy," said Jim aloud, just as the entire table of throwers burst into uproarious laughter. Peter and Paul were practically rolling on the floor beside Jim, hands on their sides, and faces turning various shades of purple. Only George kept calm, barely hiding the look of contempt crawling over his face.

"Oh, he's tip top, Cornelius," said George. "Tip. Top."

"Oh, drop my anchors, sorry about that Billy," Sharpe called to the unfortunately knifed pirate, who was hopping around the inn, gingerly pulling at the dagger protruding from his rear. "I don't suppose One-Buttock Billy will make much of a pirate name, now will it?" As opposed to seeming ashamed of his awful display, Sharpe was smiling even more ridiculously than before, laughing right along with the pirates who were mocking him.

"I'd say we've seen enough," Jim said to Cornelius and Mac-Guffy. "Whoever this fool was when he ran with Dread Steele, I think he's drunk most of it away." Cornelius looked up to Mac-Guffy, and the old salt nodded sadly. The aged first mate was about to make his way to Golden Ginny, who was just raking in her winnings, when Sharpe roared loudly and slammed his fist down on the table.

"Waigt," he said. "Nouble or duthin'! Nouble or duthin!"

"You've bet everythin you haven't drunk, Sharpe," said the pirate running the game. But the Captain held up a perfectly manicured hand.

"Not everything, my friend. Not everything." He reached into his pocket and withdrew, with some reverence, a pearl the likes of which Jim had never seen. It was as perfect as the one that hung around Jim's neck, but three times the size and surely worth more than all the treasure currently gathered upon the table. The entire inn fell under a hush at the sight of the flawless jewel.

"I think ye've had enough fun fer one day, F.W.," said Mac-Guffy, trying to collect the dandy sailor from the table. "Don't be givin away such treasures in a place like thissun." But Sharpe shrugged off MacGuffy's hand, looking Golden Ginny in the eye, twirling the pearl on the tips of his fingers.

"Nouble or duthin," the captain said again, once more whispering loud enough for every ear in the pub to hear.

"Double or nothing," said Golden Ginny, and again the pirates around the table burst into laughter. Sharpe set the pearl down on the table. Once more he staggered to his place at the thrower's mark.

"I don't wanna watch," said George.

"I don't either," said Lacey. "It's shameful."

But Jim set his sights on the pearl, sensing almost at once from its perfect shape and stunning glow that it had come from the deepest ocean, plucked by the hands of the folk that lived beneath the sea. When Jim at last tore his gaze away from the precious stone, he found F.W. Pennington Sharpe's eyes focused back upon him. A small flicker of a smile twitched at the corner of the captain's mouth. A shadow of wink blinked over one eye.

Sharpe turned and threw. Three thunks later, each knife quivered at the very center of the bull's-eye, not an inch of space between them.

SEVENTEEN

F.W. PENNINGTON SHARPE

The key to life, lads," pronounced F.W. Pennington Sharpe, "as with any other game, is to never show your cards to the other chaps. Then they'll only believe what they see on your face. There are more bad hands than good in this world, and that's a fact. But you can always control your face. The right man can make even the worst cards winners if he has the constitution to keep up a broad enough smile."

"That sounds like somethin our father would have said," cried Peter.

"Don't you think so, Georgie?" asked Paul. After the knife-throwing contest, the two younger Ratts had become so instantly enamored with Captain Sharpe that they had abandoned the idea of sailing under anyone else on Spire Island. Even Paul had given only the slightest hesitation when the party had left the Splintered Forecastle, and that was to wave goodbye to Golden Ginny, who was kind enough to blow him a kiss.

"I suppose so," said George, walking with his hands in his pockets and still squinting in the bright sun. "But I knew he was foolin the whole time." Jim could tell that his friend was playing it cool on purpose and that even George had been impressed by the con the dandy captain had played. It took a lot to impress George, Jim knew. It took even more to pull the wool over the clever Ratts' eyes.

As Jim and the others followed Captain Sharpe through the cobblestone streets of Shelltown, Jim noted that Captain Sharpe walked in a straight line, spoke with a silver tongue, and met Jim's suspicious gaze with clear eyes.

"You don't agree, young Morgan?" F.W. asked over his shoulder, sparing Jim a casual glance.

"My life isn't a game," said Jim. "Maybe it used to be. But not any more. If the Cromiers find the Treasure of the Ocean – if Bartholomew places the golden trident into the altar at the ruined temple – you'll see just how serious all of this is."

"Well of course life is a game, my dear boy," replied Sharpe with a laugh. "But that doesn't mean that the stakes don't get raised every now and again, does it?"

"Game or not," Jim said. "How can we trust you to help us if you've just come out and said that you put on a false face all the time?" At this, Captain Sharpe stopped dead in his tracks in the middle of the street. Peter and Paul, who had been walking on Sharpe's heels in newfound idol worship, crashed into his back.

"All men wear masks, Morgan." Sharpe leaned over to look Jim in the eye, that gleaming smile stretched across his face. "In fact, men wear only masks. The hour you see a man's true face is the hour of his doom. All you can really trust is what men want... and what they'll do to get it. Which brings us to the point of the matter." Sharpe straightened again to address MacGuffy and

Cornelius. "It's been some time since I've seen either of you out this way. Even longer still since either of you have sought out the likes of me. Which means two things. First, you're planning on sailing into something outrageously foolish, and second, this unbelievably foolish quest is serious enough for you to ask for my help."

"Aye, Sharpe, aye," growled MacGuffy. "Foolish it be, but necessary. Cromier does indeed have the Hunter's Shell. Find the Treasure he will. Use it he will. And if that happens, the boy is right, twon't be no more games. We sail for the deep ocean – for the Tower Top. We sail to seek the aide of Nemus and his folk."

Sharpe stared at MacGuffy for a long, silent moment. The smile on his face never wavered.

"Steele told me once that ye was an honorable man," continued MacGuffy. "Told me, he did, that ye was handy with the blade, and handier still with spells and enchantments and such. He also said that ye were familiar with the Sea Folk."

"Foolish indeed," said Sharpe at last. "And such foolishness is quite expensive. One thousand gold pieces for the trip to the Tower Top."

"A thousand gold pieces?" Jim exclaimed. Cornelius squawked with him from MacGuffy's shoulder. "We could hire an entire new crew for that much."

"True," said Sharpe with a shrug of his shoulders. "And that's only for the trip out. The trip back will be another thousand on top."

"Two thousand?" crowed Cornelius. "It matters not one whit what cards you hide now, Sharpe. I can assure you they aren't worth half that much. We could hire both Golden Ginny and Lo Fang together for a quarter that am—"

"And yet, here you stand, in the middle of the street, talking to me," Sharpe interjected. "And I cost two thousand gold pieces."

"Why so much?" Jim demanded. "That pearl in your pocket must be worth thousands of gold pieces all by itself." Jim pointed his finger to the dandy captain's pocket. "You could sell it anywhere and live off the—"

Fast as a pistol hammer, Sharpe snatched Jim's pointing hand by the wrist, turning it painfully in the wrong direction until Jim winced. For half a moment, even in his pain, Jim saw that everlasting smile on the captain's face fail.

"The pearl, is not for sale – ever," the captain said, eyes afire. But the flame on Sharpe's face died faster than it flared. He released Jim's arm with a pat on the shoulder. "My services, on the other hand, are. But, it would seem, not to a high enough bidder today." Sharpe straightened his coat, fixed his hat atop his wig of curls, and bowed neatly to MacGuffy. "MacGuffy, Cornelius, always a pleasure. My young friends, you are also well met. Hopefully, you all outlive this bout of idiocy with which you currently find yourself afflicted, and stop by the Splintered Forecastle in another few years or so, with enough gold to bet on me in another game of knives. Until then, I bid you good day."

Sharpe spun on his heel and took one step down the street before MacGuffy's rough voice caught him like a hand on the shoulder.

"Two thousand pieces of eight it be, Sharpe. Two thousand in gold, for the trip out and the trip back."

"Have you gone mad, old friend?" Cornelius cawed.

"MacGuffy, no," Jim pleaded as well. But MacGuffy silenced them both with a nasty glare from his good eye, twisting his scar on his cheek.

Sharpe rotated slowly back around, one eyebrow arched high on his head. As clever a conman as the pirate captain was, Jim felt certain that Sharpe had made his ridiculous demand in full confidence that MacGuffy would never pay it. But now, with the offer on the table, the dandy captain paced over to the aged salt, searching MacGuffy's lone eye for any trace of deception.

"Are you serious, old man?"

"Do ye know me to be a jester, Sharpe? Look me in my one

good eye and dare call me a liar if ye think otherwise."

Sharpe stood facing MacGuffy and Cornelius for a long moment. Jim caught the captain sneak his hand into his coat pocket – the coat pocket where the great pearl rested – and there the hand stayed until Sharpe finally spoke again.

"Done," he said. "I shall see you aboard the *Spectre* in one hour's time. Before the sun sets on this day we shall sail for the deep ocean and the Tower Top."

"MacGuffy, why *not* take Golden Ginny and Lo Fang for a quarter of the price?" Jim complained for at least the second time since he and the others had parted ways with Sharpe. But MacGuffy answered Jim's protest with nothing but a vague growl as they made their way back to the *Spectre* and up the gangplank. "And where did we suddenly come up with two thousand gold pieces, anyway?"

"Do we have enough gold pieces to get both Captain Sharpe *and* Golden Ginny?" asked Paul, sneaking up beside Jim's elbow. "That would be really worth it if you ask me."

"Well, he's not asking you, now is he?" retorted George, shoving his younger brother aside. "We're better off with just you, Mac-Guffy. You and us, just like—"

"All of ye just clamp yer traps and leave an old man's ears in peace for St. Elmo's sake!" MacGuffy finally shouted, turning to face them. His cheeks had gone so purple that his scar blended into the rest of his face. "The deal is struck, and it cannot be unstruck. That is the pirate way of things. And that includes you as well, ye feathered devil!" MacGuffy pointed a stubby finger at Cornelius, shrugging the bird from his shoulder. The Raven flapped down with a squawk to light upon Lacey's instead. When the pirate spoke again, his voice was quieter and calmer, like the sea after a storm.

"It don't matter a fig whether we like this man or no, Jimmy Morgan. We need him. He knows and is known by the Merfolk, accordin to Dread Steele. That matters much. And as for the gold,

MacGuffy was never as much a fool with money as perhaps ye took me for. After all the buried treasure we found, and after every ship we raided when I was a lad, I stored most of it away in a secret spot, and I'll be makin good with F.W. Pennington Sharpe."

"MacGuffy," this time it was Lacey who protested. "You can't give away all of your life savings. How will you live after all this is done?"

"Oh, sweet little Lacey, if only you knew how good ye've done this old sailor's heart these last few years." MacGuffy pulled Lacey close with one arm over her shoulder and rested a hand on Jim's shoulder, looking each of his young charges in the eye.

"All of ye have done me well. Even ye, George Ratt – even ye." A hint of color found George's pale cheeks, and he offered Mac-Guffy a shy smile. "I knows how much I been yellin and shoutin at the five of ye these last years. God in heaven knows how many times ye used me good long johns fer pirate flags. But sometimes an old man remembers only shoutin and yellin, and he forgets about whisperin and laughin. But ye have reminded this foolish old salt of both. So worry not for MacGuffy. Let MacGuffy worry for ye. When I close my good eye at night, I see ye Ratts goin to school – aye, don't laugh, Paul! Ye've minds good enough to use for better deeds than thievin. Lacey, if they chose queens by their virtues, I'd have ye as mine. And quaint as it may be, what can an old man wish but that he could be there to give ye away when ye take a prince to be yer own? Jim, I see yer father in ye... but more than that, yer mother, too. Ye have it in ye not just to be a great cap'n of the sea, but to be a great man. What is two thousand gold pieces compared to all that?"

By the time he was finished speaking, MacGuffy's eye was red and swimming. A lone tear trickled onto his ruined face and fell to the deck. Jim's throat burned and his nose stung. Neither he nor any of his friends could think of anything to say.

"Argh, that be the whole of it!" MacGuffy barked, as though

commanding his pesky feelings to harden – and they obeyed. He quenched the tears in his eye and restored his nearly permanent grimace. "Now, let us get this ship prepared to sail. Every sailor to his station! Stow the gear and ready the lines!" MacGuffy turned his back on the clan and stormed off to the quarterdeck, from where he shouted orders to the crew for nearly the next hour. But as the old man went about his business, his head was held a little higher, and his shoulders pulled back a little straighter.

An hour later, when every neck upon the *Spectre* glistened with sweat, the sound of whistling carried up the gangplank. The cheerful tune was followed by the appearance of the merry-faced F.W. Pennington Sharpe, just as pristine as he had been in the Splintered Forecastle. The dandy captain carried a single duffle, slung over his shoulder, a sword at his side, a fresh bottle of wine in one hand, and a fancy goblet in the other. He was seemingly more prepared for a party than an adventure.

"Ah, good afternoon, all," Sharpe announced, lifting his goblet in salute to the crew. "Permission to come aboard?"

"Permission granted, Sharpe," growled MacGuffy, who Jim could tell was less than enthralled by F.W.'s overly cheery disposition. MacGuffy hobbled down the steps of the quarterdeck to meet Sharpe, who stepped aboard, immediately dropping his duffle at his feet.

"That would be Captain Sharpe, now, don't you think, Mac-Guffy?" He threw the old salt a wink, which reddened MacGuffy's face. "Per the terms of our agreement."

"Per the terms of our agreement, if ye disrespect yer position, our mission, or any member of the crew, includin meself, I reserve the right to punt yer dandy ars overboard, at any time of my choosin... Cap'n."

Jim and George, who had come over with much of the crew to meet the new captain, could barely conceal their snickers at Mac-Guffy's retort. But if the old man's words had at all perturbed Sharpe, such consternation remained buried beneath the man's flawless smile.

"Well spoken, MacGuffy. We are off to a marvelous beginning. Now, let's set sail, if you please. We need to be on our way." Sharpe waved his wine bottle about and stepped over to a barrel. He hoisted himself upon it to have a seat and crossed his legs, as though reclining on a Sunday afternoon. He was just refilling his goblet when he seemed to realize that the crew was still staring at him, expectantly. "Well," he said to the half circle of confused faces. "Shall we not get a move on?"

"And upon what course would you set us, Captain?" cawed Cornelius, who flew down from the topmast to rest on MacGuffy's shoulder. "You have not even given us a point on a compass."

"Ah yes, apologies," said Sharpe, shaking his head at himself with a laugh. "Just out into the water a bit will be fine, and point us westward, if at all possible." The captain waved his goblet vaguely out toward the ocean.

"Westward... if at all possible?" Jim questioned aloud. He and George shared a disbelieving smirk. "Do you even know where you're going?" Sharpe loosed an overly long sigh, followed by a slurping sip of his wine. After the drink, he smacked his lips and threw MacGuffy a sidelong glance.

"MacGuffy, we have yet to debark. If you wish to change your mind about our agreement, then so be it. Now is the time. But if you are going to bring me aboard as captain, then I trust that the crew – all of them," Sharpe leveled his eyes at Jim, "will obey orders when given."

Jim looked to MacGuffy, with hope in his eyes that the old pirate would toss the dandy captain overboard that very moment. But MacGuffy only returned Jim's glance with another one-eyed glare.

"Ye all heard the Cap'n," MacGuffy bellowed. "Get yer scurvy hides to yer duties and let us be underway." Jim's shoulders slumped. He was about to return to work when he heard Sharpe call his name.

"Ah, Mister Morgan, perhaps you and your friends might join me at my barrel."

Jim and George groaned together. Jim knew MacGuffy had made his decision, so like it or not, he was stuck with F.W. Pennington Sharpe for the duration of this journey. The clan gathered around their new captain, who was happily bouncing his crossed legs and sipping on his wine.

"Hello, my young friends," said Sharpe gaily, with a nod of his head to Jim. "You know, Morgan, it is considered bad form on most ships to question your captain." Jim folded his arms over his chest. He knew that MacGuffy had struck a deal, but he was really beginning to dislike this Captain Sharpe.

"You're not really our captain," Jim said. "You're more like a hired hand if you think about it. Nothing more than a sellsword."

"A very expensive hired hand," Sharpe replied, his smile somehow widening. "And all men are sellswords. Some of us just know what we're worth, that's all."

"You don't seem to have a very high opinion of anyone, do you, Sharpe?"

"Oh young Morgan, just give it time. It isn't what other men do that will make you lose faith in mankind. Rather, it's what you find yourself capable of doing that will do the trick. But you already know that, don't you?" Sharpe flicked his eyes down to Jim's scarred palm.

"Well, Dread Steele wasn't a sellsword," said Jim. He could feel his ears getting hot and that very scar on his hand beginning to tingle. "Nor was my father. They sailed for greater causes than gold. If you ask me, you're nothing like them."

"And glad for it!" Sharpe proclaimed, finally hopping off his barrel. He set his goblet and his bottle on what had just been his seat and then proceeded to stretch his arms upward and outward, as though warming up for a bit of exercise. "Dread Steele and your father are dead. I am alive. If anything, I would imagine they wish they were more like me at the moment."

That was it for Jim. The scar on his hand was no longer tingling.

It was on fire. He gritted his teeth and all but pounced on Sharpe. Only George at one arm and Lacey at the other held him back.

"That was an awful thing to say, Captain Sharpe," Lacey snapped, glaring at the dandy captain. Even Peter and Paul, who had so admired Sharpe's display at the Splintered Forecastle, cast dubious glares at him from behind Jim, George, and Lacey.

"You're not worth two hundred gold pieces, much less two thousand," Jim challenged through gritted teeth. But not a mite of Jim's anger, or Lacey's rebuke, or the Ratts' disappointment seemed to bother Captain Sharpe in the slightest.

"Let's just see about that, shall we?" Sharpe reached into his pocket, but instead of withdrawing the priceless pearl, he produced a coil of delicate string, which glimmered like a strand of silver in the afternoon sun. A touch of curiosity stilled Jim's anger for a moment. He begrudgingly fell in step behind the captain as he strode all the way to the fore of the ship, the rest of the Clan following along.

When Captain Sharpe reached the prow, he came to a sudden stop. He stood with both feet together, hands at his sides and eyes closed, as though listening hard for a single drop of water on the ocean's surface. The captain took three deep breaths, raised the coil of string to his lips, and whispered a nearly silent incantation. When Sharpe opened his eyes, he took one end of the string, which was tipped with a small hook, and hurled it into the sea. The hook seemed to do nothing but sink beneath the waves at first, until, quite violently, it must have caught hold of something, as though Captain Sharpe had been fishing and managed to catch himself a whale.

The hooked end of the string shot out from the ship like a cannon ball. But as fast as it began to unspool, snapping coil after coil from Sharpe's hand, it never reached its end, nor did the loop of string ever seem to shrink in size. Finally, after some moments of winding out to sea, the slender cord went taught, snapping with a musical twang like the highest note on a violin.

"Stand back," commanded Captain Sharpe to Jim and his friends, not a hint of jovial laughter on his lips. Then he raised his voice to the rest of the crew, who had drawn closer to watch the man with the silver string. "All of you stand fast. Take hold of your lifelines or the railing for your fathers' sakes."

Sharpe took the string in both hands and again whispered some indecipherable spell. In his grasp, the string began to grow. It popped and sprang and twisted into a thick cable, gleaming like steel in the sun. On this cable the captain began to pull. He groaned at first, as though pulling against the weight of the world. As much as Jim was already beginning to hate this man, he started forward to help. But Sharpe ordered him off.

"Do not touch the string," he managed, through grunts and gasps. "I alone must touch it now."

Jim backed away, staring in astonishment as Captain Sharpe began to gather momentum, pulling faster and faster at the rope. Jim felt the ship shift beneath his feet. The ocean wind began to whip at his face, pulling at his clothes and his hair.

"Jim, look!" George cried, jumping to Jim's side and pointing toward the horizon. "We're really movin now." The line at the edge of the world was drawing closer. The waves blurred around the *Spectre's* sides. The clouds in the sky streaked over their heads.

"Hang on to something," Lacey shouted. Jim and George ran to where she and the other Ratts clung to a row of barrels, lashed fast to the deck. "Look behind us," Lacey said. Jim looked back to where Spire Island should have been. He saw only a shrinking speck in the distance.

Soon, the roar of the wind and the groan of the ship against the sea drowned out all other voices. Jim saw that even the hardened men of the Spectre, Mufwalme, Murdoch, Wang Chi, and the rest, had gone pale, their mouths opened wide in screams that Jim could not hear.

As suddenly as it had begun, it ended. With a great crash and a spray of seawater that spouted as high as the topmast, the *Spectre* rocked to a halt. The Clan pitched forward and tumbled onto the deck, spilling into a tangle on the rough wood. When Jim scrambled back to his feet, he found himself staring at a small circle of white sand, surrounding a great rock rising into the air, one that indeed resembled the top of a tall castle turret. In but a few seconds, Captain Sharpe had brought them all the way to the Tower Top.

When Jim once more looked to Captain Sharpe, he found the man calmly respooling the string on his hand. The rope was once again a thin loop of string, tipped by a slender hook. The captain's shoulders rose and fell with deep gulps of air, his face flushed from exertion. But the wide smile still curved the corners of his mouth.

"Like I said, young Morgan, never let them see your cards." Sharpe threw Jim a wink, slapped him hard on the shoulder, and sauntered back to his barrel. The crew of the *Spectre* gave him a wide berth, nodding their heads as he passed.

EIGHTEEN

THE SECRET OF THE TOWER TOP

The red, swollen sun fell to the sea, leaving the sky on the far side of the world darkened and bruised. The closer the sun neared the horizon the more the pearl that hung from Jim's neck seemed to tingle. It was almost time for Jim to call upon King Nemus to guide him and his friends to the ancient temple, where the Treasure of the Ocean could unleash its power.

Jim stood at the Spectre's prow, watching the sunset and thinking of the long, strange road that had brought him to this place. Reaching into his pocket, he felt for the sharp corner of his father's old box, as he often did when he grew nervous. He slowly traced the etched drawing on the lid with his finger – the ancient symbol of the Treasure of the Ocean.

Only a few years ago, Jim had hoped to take this very box before another king, the King of England, to ask for help restoring his family fortune. Instead, it had fallen into the hands of the King of Thieves. Later, the box had kept safe the Black Rose Thorn, the poison of which had nearly killed Jim on the Veiled Isle. His father's box had traveled with him the entire length of his journey.

Now it was empty. The last item it had ever held, the necklace, was looped around Jim's neck. His father's letter was gone. The Black Rose Thorn was gone. But Jim couldn't leave the box behind. It reminded him of his father. It reminded him he had a job to do. If only the box could tell him how to do that job, though. Should he hide the Treasure? Should he use it himself? But the box was silent to those questions. So Jim only tightened his grip on it to still the butterflies in his stomach.

"Are you ready, Jim? It's almost time to go ashore."

Jim snatched his hand from his pocket, rubbing his sweaty hand against his britches, suddenly feeling as though his thoughts were visible to everyone on the ship.

"I think so, Lacey. I have everything I need, I suppose."

"Have you thought about what you're going to say? To the king, I mean. Have you thought about what you're going to ask King Nemus?"

"Oh, yeah, of course," Jim said, his voice cracking as he tapped the side of his head. "Got it all right here."

"You haven't a clue what you're going to say, do you?"

"Not even a little," Jim admitted. He laughed at himself and Lacey laughed with him. Even with the end of the world quite possibly at hand, just hearing Lacey's laugh gave Jim hope, even if only a little.

"Jim Morgan," said Lacey, turning her eyes out to the red sun above the sea, "always running off, opening doors you shouldn't open, climbing down into dark places you shouldn't risk, picking battles you shouldn't fight. And all this magic..." She shook her head, her auburn curls aglow in the dying light. "It's gobbled up everyone, you know. Sometimes I'm afraid it will gobble you up as well."

The box in Jim's pocket felt suddenly heavy. Its weight gave Jim a long pause before he said anything in return. "Before I met you, just before I got to London, there was this gypsy, the gypsy who locked up my father's box. She told me this would happen. She told me I was a Son of Earth and Son of Sea, and that so much hung on me finding this Treasure. Even my father's last words to me were about keeping it safe. Maybe the Treasure was why I was even born. Like... like a destiny. Do you know what I mean? It's like I don't even have a choice."

"Jim, I was born in London, I lived on the streets in London, and if it weren't for you, I don't think I ever would have seen another place in the world besides London for my whole life. I don't know much of a thing about destinies or all that. I just know that in some way, the whole idea of a destiny scares me a little, like the thought of being in prison, or something like it."

"What do you think happens after you've fulfilled your destiny, Lacey?" Jim asked. He stuck his hand back in his pocket, grabbing at his father's old box. "What if you never end up fulfilling it at all? Would you even know?"

"I just told you I don't know, Jim," Lacey said. But she drew closer to him then, so close they were almost touching. "But either way, don't you think it's better to find out together, than alone?" She reached out and took Jim's hand from his pocket, and held it in her own. It was ever so much softer and warmer and more alive than the sharp, roughened edges of that old box in his pocket.

On the other end of the ship from where Jim and Lacey stood together, at the aft, which looked away from the sunset to the darkened horizon, George Ratt climbed down onto a little nook at the back of the forecastle. He had discovered this place some months ago. It was the one corner of the ship where he could go to be alone. Not that George liked being alone – he hated it in fact. He never felt quite whole when his brothers weren't around, and that included his best pal, Jim Morgan. Friends and family were all the riches George had ever possessed. Like any wealth, George would do anything to protect it.

That was why it was so important that he go to be alone from time to time. To practice. To be ready for anything.

George nestled himself onto his nook, which was really nothing more than a decorative curl of wood on the back of the ship. There he waited for the right moment. Nearly every day, just before sunset, the Organ Grinder would start up his song, providing George with his chance. As if on cue, the whistling, cranking, hooting, tune caught the air, all to the rhythm of pirates finishing another day's work. George would have to be quicker today, for Jim, Lacey, and the others would soon be going ashore to call on the merfolk. Who knew when George would next have a moment alone?

He reached into his jacket pocket. Out George pulled a thin tube of wood, split halfway down, like a fork. At first, George wasn't even sure why he'd snatched this little object off the *Spectre's* deck in the first place. Perhaps out of habit, he thought. Though it hadn't really been stealing, had it? The owner of this particular object had already been dead.

No, it hadn't been stealing when George took the flute of Philus Philonius for his own. No, not at all. And under cover of the Organ Grinder's tune, George placed the twin piped flute to his lips and began to play.

George had been awful at playing his new instrument at first. He never quite covered the holes all the way, nor quite held a note long enough. On more than one occasion he nearly pitched the flute into the sea, sure that either he would never learn to play it properly or that even if he did, the magic it had once held would have long abandoned it.

But George was blessed with clever fingers and a dogged will. These things at least he knew about himself. So he kept on with it, every chance he could find, until the day he managed to string a few chords into something of a melody – and a window had cracked open in his mind. In that brief instant, George had gotten a taste of magic.

As the days stretched into weeks and months, George forced open that window in his head a bit further each time he played. He was hardly any sort of wizard, that was certain. He'd also grown up a little too much to invent a cheer and declare himself the greatest magician of all time. But although George lacked the skill to transform himself into a great owl, a talking lizard, or a wicked pirate captain, he did find that he could reach out and touch the thoughts of other creatures in the world about him.

He began with a small mouse he found lurking about the ship one afternoon. It was less that George could control the mouse's thoughts and more that he could convince it to try some braver antics than it normally would have dared. George almost showed Jim and Lacey then. How amazed and proud they would have been, he was sure, once they'd gotten over telling him what a bad idea playing with magic was. He would show them how he could make the mouse balance a bit of cheese on its nose, or do backflips, or hang from a beam by its tail.

One evening, when George had been playing with the mouse, there on his nook, the mouse did one backflip too many. George thought about diving in after the poor creature when it fell beneath the waves. But the *Spectre* was moving too fast, and George himself would have been left behind. He wept that night, all by himself, turned into his pillow, pretending to be asleep. Once more he thought about throwing the flute overboard.

The problem was, he needed it. The day was coming when he and Jim would finally stop running from those murderers, the Cromiers. The day was coming when he and his brothers and his best friends would be forced to fight. George was going to be ready. He was tired of letting grown ups hurt the ones he loved and tired of letting them hurt him. The next time, he would be strong enough to hurt back.

So George quietly practiced his song. He managed to cajole a few fish from a passing school to swim in circles beneath his dangling feet. He even got them to jump one at a time from the waves, turning a somersault in the air before splashing back into the sea. George took the reed from his lips and started to put the flute away when he heard the sound of his name on the wind.

"George Ratt."

George took a start, nearly fumbling the flute into the ocean. He thought for sure he'd finally been caught and would look up to find MacGuffy's lone, disappointed eye, glaring at him from the deck. But when George peeked over his shoulder, he was still alone.

"Why, George Ratt, just look at what you've made of yourself."

George looked all around, wondering if his brothers were playing a trick on him. But he could always tell when Peter or Paul were using a voice. They were never very good at keeping themselves from laughing. But there was something familiar to the whisper, like the aftertaste of a particular drink that won't go away.

"Who's out there?" George whispered back, just loud enough to be heard over the waves on the Tower Top's shore.

"I'm hurt by that, George," said the voice. "Have you so quickly forgotten your first friend on the street? Your first mentor? Your first king?"

As a ring of shadows surrounded George, he finally recognized the voice. A dark misty column took shape before him, hovering over the waves, revealing a face long lost to George's memories. The air grew cold about George's body, frosting his breath.

"No," George said, trying to convince himself his eyes and ears were lying. "I don't believe it. I saw that magic fire swallow you up." So Jim hadn't been seeing things in old Egidio's shop after all, he realized.

"Indeed you did, George, you magnificent boy. But I have returned. I have returned to make amends for all my evil ways. I have returned to tell you that I'm sorry."

"I don't believe you," George shouted as loud as he dared. He suddenly wished he had not hidden himself away so carefully. He wished he would find Jim, or Lacey, or MacGuffy over his shoulder. But George had begun to understand magic as he had learned the flute. He knew that he and the King of Thieves were alone. "You're nothin but a cheat and a liar. Me and Jim've seen far worse than you. You ain't nothin compared to what we seen since we left London. So take your sorry and choke on it."

"I deserve that, George Ratt. I know I do." The shade of the King of Thieves bowed low. He floated closer to where George sat on his nook, his dark eyes gleaming with sorrow. "I once laughed at you. I once lied to you. I once thought you were nothing but a dirty thief. But look at what you've become. I must admit, never would I have thought that you, one of the Ratt Clan, might decipher the secrets of magic. But here you sit. I can see the power dancing at your fingertips. It is sad, that only now, after I was consumed by the magic I sought, that I have come to more fully understand it. I was banished, George, banished to that place beyond the window you've opened in your mind. But somehow I have been granted this one last chance to come back. I've been granted one last chance to make things right."

"You're a liar." George said again. But he did not move from his nook.

"Once I was," said the King. "But if ever you believed me, believe me now. I have come back to aide you and Jim Morgan against your enemies. He will need you, George, before the end. More than he knows, Jim Morgan will need your help. It is a great weight your friend carries. Now you're strong enough to help him lift it – if you allow me to teach you what I have learned."

"Go away," George said. "Just go away." But even as he spoke,

George could feel that he was asking instead of telling. There was a small part of him, a very small part, that still needed to learn more about the magic flute – more than he could learn on his own. But the shadowy King of Thieves bowed his head again as his body started to lose its shape. The shadows about George began to lose their hold.

"As you wish, my young friend. But know that they are coming. The Cromiers are coming. They're coming for Jim. You can help him. There is more power in the flute than you yet know – power you could use to save Jim and everyone you love."

The dark and the cold finally broke, allowing the last touch of sun to warm George as he shivered on the nook. One more whisper from the shadow reached George's ears as he climbed up from his hiding place and onto the *Spectre's* deck.

"I can show you the way, George Ratt. I can teach you the power."

George tried to shake the whisper from his ears and the vision of the ghostly King of Thieves from his thoughts. How had the King come back from beyond the grave? Did he really know if the Cromiers were coming? George told himself he wasn't going to listen, not to that liar. The King of Thieves had abandoned him before. He had left him and his brothers out in the cold in London, just like George's father.

But George's father had never come back, had he? Nor had he ever apologized. Nor had he ever offered to give George the power to protect his friends. All these thoughts weighed heavy on George's mind as he ran to catch up with Jim and Lacey, descending the gangplank to the shores of the Tower Top. He would wait to tell Jim what he had seen. He would tell him when he was also going to tell him about the flute. Little did George know that by then it would be far, far too late.

NINETEEN

THE CRYSTAL TOWER

Jim and the clan, along with MacGuffy, Cornelius, Sharpe and some of the *Spectre's* crew, stood on the beach of the Tower's Top. Jim held the pearl in his hand, glowing red in the waning sunlight. MacGuffy gave Jim a nod. It was time. With a deep breath to calm his nerves, Jim stepped to the surf's edge. He knelt down in the sand and, as Melodia had instructed him, dipped the pearl into the white foam.

Once, twice, three times, Jim touched the pearl to the waves. He listened for the boom of thunder and searched the waves for sparks of magic. But there was nothing.

A few moments crept by, and Jim's heart began to sink. They had come so far to ask for help, and MacGuffy had spent everything he had to get them here. They could not afford to fail.

"Maybe you gotta dip the pearl in after the sun is already down, Jim?" offered Peter.

"Or maybe don't dip it, but just leave it in the water," suggested Paul.

Jim, having no better ideas, knelt down to give it another go. But he had only dangled the chain above the surf a second time when a spout of water erupted with a clap, twenty paces out on the water. The explosion threw Jim into the sand. He scampered backwards like a crab to the feet of his friends.

A slender needle pierced the ocean surface. It grew into a tower as it rose into the air – the true Tower's Top. Glowing embers danced up and down the tower's length, reflections from the setting sun, for the tower was cut from pure crystal.

When the crystal tower had reached higher than the great rock in the center of the island, the outline of a door appeared in its side. A line of white foam cut the waters straight to the shore. A bridge emerged from the tide, making a path from the beach to the door in the crystal tower.

All along the bridge, scores of coral spears came forth, gripped in the powerful fists of merfolk warriors. Gold and blue tattoos traced their bearded faces and broad shoulders. Sparkling jewels hung about their necks.

"You there!" cried the foremost merman. "Son of Morgan!" The leader of the warriors swam closer to the beach, pointing to Jim with his spear. Jim recognized the merman as one who had been with Melodia on the day she had visited with Dread Steele, the day the merfolk had driven off the Kraken and saved the Spectre. Fulkern, was his name. "What business have you with the Sons of the Sea?"

"Queen Melodia told me that if I ever needed her help," Jim began, scrambling back to his feet, "that I should come here, to this island, and dip this in the surf's foam." Jim held forth his silver shell charm. As it swayed beneath his hand like a glimmering pendulum, each of the mermen, even Fulkern, bowed his head and lowered his eyes.

"Her majesty will hear your words, son of Lindsay Morgan." Fulkern's voice was hard, but he nodded toward the door in the crystal tower. "You may enter."

Jim glanced over his shoulder at his friends. Though their faces had all gone white, they were still behind him, ready to cross the bridge. MacGuffy and Cornelius came along as well, but as the pirates made for the crossway, Fulkern jabbed his spear toward Captain Sharpe.

"Your face is known to me as well, boat man," growled Fulkern. "But why have you come here? Should you not be enjoying your great wealth upon the shores of the earth? You were well rewarded to leave these waters and never return."

"Just chaperoning my young friends here, Fulkern, old chum," said Sharpe, the familiar smile still fixed to his face. "I wouldn't dream of breaking a promise, you know. Pirate's honor and all that. These two chaps and I," he nodded toward Murdock and Wang-Chi, "will just be heading back to the ship now. Toodles, Jim." Sharpe waggled his fingers in Jim's direction. "Do be home for supper now, won't you?"

With that, the pirate captain turned on his heel and strode off to the *Spectre*, Murdock and Wang-Chi just behind him. Jim then knew for certain where Captain Sharpe had procured the magnificent pearl he carried in his pocket. He had taken it from the people of the sea. But for what had he been paid?

"Quit yer ponderin, young Morgan," said MacGuffy, apparently catching the furrow on Jim's brow. "It's a long trip down to the City of the Sea Folk. We best be gettin on with it."

So, with a deep breath, Jim led the way onto the bridge and over the waters as night fell. He paused at the door for only a moment before entering the crystal tower.

Just inside the door, a stairwell descended down the crystal structure. No handrail lined the steps, and over the naked edge, the length of the tower fell farther than Jim could see, to the center of the earth, it seemed.

The small party worked their way down the stairs. Some of the crystal was rough and lightless as brick, but other stretches were smooth as marble and clear as glass. Through these windows the evening light seeped through the waters, outlining the shadow of the Spectre above. Fulkern and his warriors glided down beside the tower, twisting their way into the depths. To Jim it looked like flying, or dancing on nothing but blue space.

As they descended, the ocean beyond the wall grew darker than night. A blue-green light hissed to life from the walls, bathing the stairwell in a soft glow. Small orbs clung to the crystal, casting a pale light into the tower and out into the black waters beyond.

"How you think them lamps have light without fire?" asked Peter.

Unable to resist curiosity, as Paul passed by an orb, he reached out a finger to gently poke it. The orb gave an agitated snort, then opened two, even brighter eyes and scampered up the wall to escape further prodding. Paul gave an equally surprised grunt, reeling back and nearly tumbling off the steps. Only MacGuffy's strong hand on the scruff of his neck kept him from falling.

"Keep your wanderin fingers in yer pockets, if ye will, Paulie," growled the old pirate. "The next beastie ye touch may take one of 'em with him when he goes."

"Too right, MacGuffy," Paul agreed. "What kind of creepy crawlie glows in the dark anyways? It ain't natural."

"We are entering the deep waters, Master Ratt," crowed Cornelius from MacGuffy's shoulder. "There are many such creatures beneath the waves – animal life that few eyes of the earth have ever seen. We are entering not only another kingdom, my friends. We are entering another world. You have yet to see anything at all."

As if summoned by Cornelius's words, fish and other beasts approached the tower from the black, like shapes melting from a fog. Some of them lit the dark with glowing bodies. The bones and organs of others were visible through transparent skin. Lone eyes dangled off the ends of antennae, mouths yawned wider than bodies stretched long, and teeth the length of spears glimmered in open maws.

As Jim rounded another turn in the stairwell, a wall of light shone through the crystal windows from down below, brighter than the orb creatures within the tower or the bizarre fish outside. Jim and George rushed ahead a few more turns in the staircase to get a better look. What they saw stole the words from their lips.

"My friends," said Cornelius, "here is Aquila, underwater metropolis of the Sea Folk, and Nemus, King Under the Sea."

"Would you look at that," said Peter, having rushed down to stand by George.

"It's a little like lookin at London from the top of Primrose Hill, ain't it?" added Paul. "'Cept with more swimmin things."

Towers rose into the waters as far as the eye could see, stretching out until the depths swallowed their light. The vibrant blues, greens, and yellows seemed to grow up the sides of the buildings. Everything that shone was alive, whether fishes that swam or plants that grew. Everywhere Jim looked, merfolk bustled about, not as though there were streets to walk, but swimming above and around the towers in flowing rows.

"It's beautiful," said Lacey, squeezing up against Jim's side by the window.

"I think we're almost to the bottom," said George. The sight of the city and the thought of reaching the end of the long stairs restored some of Jim's hopes. He and the others began to rush, taking the steps two or three at a time.

The dark stone bottom floor glistened in the city light from outside the tower. In the center of the stairwell they had descended, stood a stone pylon, etched with pictures from some ancient time. The images told a story – a story Jim had seen once before, in the painted cave on the Veiled Isle.

Above the carving of a city falling into the sea, the Treasure of the Ocean's symbol appeared. *Everyone who has played with magic has been consumed by it*, Lacey had said to Jim. *Everyone*. But there was no turning back now.

As Jim reached the bottom of the stairs, a great hall opened up before him. In its center, a wide pool stretched across the floor, a raised dais before it, with seven steps leading up to the stone platform.

"Go on, lad," said MacGuffy. He was leaning against the tower wall, breathing heavily from the long climb down, nodding his chin toward the dais. "Time to pose the question ye come all this way to ask. Ask it well, boy."

Jim took a deep breath. His hand found its way back into his pocket and he squeezed his father's box tight, just for a little courage. He mounted the stairs to the dais. From the top he looked down into the pool below, wondering if there was something he needed to do to gain his audience. He was about to open his mouth to call into the pool, when a shadow darkened the glowing waters.

Queen Melodia rose up from the water, pearl crown upon her head, bejeweled necklaces in rings about her neck, green raiment wrapped around her body. An unexpected smile crossed Jim's face at the memory of Dread Steele flicking the back of his head. This time he remembered to bow.

"Your majesty," he said. "I'm sorry it took so long, but I've come back. I dipped my mother's pearl into the waters of the Tower Top. I've returned to ask for your help." But as Jim raised his head, he found the Queen's face, more beautiful than those carved in statues of old, etched with worry.

"You are well met, Jim Morgan," she said. "But it is not me you must ask."

A watery column burst from the pool. As the seawater rained back down, a figure appeared in its mist. His shoulders stretched twice as broad as giant Mufwalme's. His arms looked strong enough to crush stone. In his hand he gripped a spear twice as long as Jim stood tall. Black hair, veined with shimmering silver, fell down from beneath his coral crown, and a black beard, two silver stripes running down the center, flowed over his chest. Like Queen Melodia's, his eyes glowed gold. Their hard gaze fell heavily upon Jim.

"Jim Morgan," announced the Queen, "may I present to you the leader of our people, and my husband, Ruler of the Sea, King Nemus."

TWENTY

THE KING UNDER THE SEA

And so, Son of Morgan, you have returned at last." Nemus's voice filled the chamber. His golden eyes seemed to pin Jim in place. "And after all this time, what has brought you to the City of the Depths, to the country of my people?"

Jim shivered on the platform. His knees quaked. He redoubled his grip on his box, still held in his pocket, and somehow managed a trembling answer. "I've traveled far, your majesty. I've sailed all over the world. I hoped this day would never come... I tried... but I failed." Jim shook his head. The words were coming out all wrong. "I've come to ask you for your help, sir. We need your help to—"

"You need my help?" The king cut Jim off. His golden eyes burned hotter and brighter. He surged closer to the platform, until he loomed over Jim. "How dare you, boy? How *dare* you?" Nemus reached for Jim with his empty hand, as though to take him by the throat.

"Nemus!" Melodia gasped. "Remember yourself!"

"Silence, Melodia," roared the king. But he withdrew his threatening hand. "I will not have my pain mocked at the steps of my own throne."

"He's only a boy."

"The look of a man blossoms on his face even now." Nemus leaned close to Jim, glaring at him, smelling his fear. "He has the look of his father."

"He does not know, Nemus." Melodia swam closer to the king in the pool, but only so close.

"Doesn't know?" Nemus's golden gaze narrowed on Jim. "Tell me boy, is this true? Do you plead ignorance to the crimes your father committed against us? Against my queen? Against me?"

Jim swallowed hard. Sweat formed like dew on his lip and his forehead.

"I think… I think I know a little, sir," he whispered. "I think he stole three treasures from you."

"You make it sound as if he picked a pocket, boy." The king sneered. "That is your human expression, is it not? To pluck trinkets from another man's purse? Tell me, Son of Morgan, what did your father steal?"

"The Treasure of the Ocean…"

"And?"

"I was told another was called the Flower of Nemus. But I don't know what that is. Nor do I know anything about the last."

The king's eyes flickered. He drifted away from Jim, as though Jim had reached out and struck him. Nemus's shoulders slumped and his spear dipped into the water. The silver in his black beard seemed to spread like frost before Jim's eyes, transforming him into an older and frailer man in only the span of a few breaths.

"Then you truly do not know, do you? It seems I must be the one to instruct you. The first treasure your father stole from me was indeed the Treasure of the Ocean, that mystical golden trident that has been at the center of all this trouble. The stone pylon behind you tells its story – a story of madness and ruin. The second treasure you wear around your neck, even now." Nemus nodded toward the silver shell charm, dangling from its chain at Jim's chest.

"The pearl?"

"Not just a pearl," the king said. "Unlike any other jewel in the world, only a pearl is grown. Only pearls are created by a living being. The creatures within the shells hold their pearls to their breasts and protect them with all their strength, like a man keeps his own soul. There are some pearls, grown in the deepest crevices of the ocean, which can do just that. They are called Soul Stones. You carry one about your neck. Have you not felt the stone thrum at your touch? Have you not ever seen its glow?"

"Yes, your majesty. I have." Jim took the silver shell in his fingers, twisting it back and forth, as his father had always done.

"That was the second treasure your father stole. But both of those, even the Treasure of the Ocean, pale in comparison to the last."

"The Flower of Nemus?"

The old king nodded. His eyes fell to the pool, as though searching the waters for something long lost. "Yes," he said. "Her name was Venia."

"Her name?" Jim's blood went still. His breath grew shallow. "The Flower of Nemus… was a person?"

"Yes, a person. She was my daughter." The king swam close again to Jim, towering over him. "And are you so dull that you have not guessed it yet, boy? Guessed why I have not drowned you the moment you came into my throne room? Guessed why my wife looks after you so tenderly? She was your mother."

The platform seemed to fall out from beneath Jim's feet. He felt like he was falling, plummeting through the air but never hitting the ground.

"No," Jim cried. "How can that be? I'm a human... I'm not... not one of you!" Jim looked over his shoulder, terrified to see his friends' faces. What was he if he was not a man? What sort of creature? But to Jim's surprise, Lacey, the Ratts, and MacGuffy all stood still as statues, with blank faces, as though trying to understand what was going on.

"They cannot hear us, boy," said the king. "You alone stand on the platform. You alone hear my words. But your eyes betray you. You fear your friends will reject you for what you are – especially her." Nemus looked past Jim to Lacey. A pang stung Jim's chest. "And you should be afraid, young Morgan. Men are petty creatures."

"Maybe you're lying," Jim said. "How do I know this is true?"

Queen Melodia took a start, as though such an accusation might send the king into a rage that would end in blood. But the king only smiled, though cruelly.

"You know in your heart that I do not lie, *Son of Earth and Son of Sea*." The old gypsy's cackle, from the back of that wagon so long ago, rattled in Jim's memory. "But you may be surer still." Nemus reached out his enormous hand and pointed to Jim's shell necklace. Jim thought he saw tears swimming in the old king's eyes.

"If you wish to know for certain, you may ask your mother for yourself."

TWENTY-ONE

THE SOUL STONE

Nemus pointed to the far side of the pool with his spear and spoke some words in the merfolk tongue. At his magic command, his spear glowed. The platform beneath Jim's feet stretched out before him, crawling like stone vines to the other edge of the pool. With a crunch of stone on stone, a bridge formed for Jim to cross.

Jim glanced back only once, to where his friends stood, deaf to Nemus's words. There was no time to explain. He took a deep breath for courage and stepped onto the stone bridge. No sooner had Jim descended the steps on the other side than Nemus pointed again with his spear. An archway rumbled open in the crystal wall before Jim, leading to a hidden room.

"Your proof lies through yonder door, young Morgan," said the king.

"But I don't know how to make the magic work, sir," Jim said, forgetting to say 'Your Majesty.' But Nemus said nothing about it, nor did he lend Jim any instruction. Without another word, he dipped into the pool and swam away.

"Wait for me beyond the archway," Queen Melodia offered after watching the king's shadow disappear. "I will show you how." She nodded toward the doorway before silently slipping into the pool herself.

Jim's mouth grew dry and his palms wet. He gripped the box in his pocket so tightly he thought it might break to pieces. In his other hand he cradled the silver shell charm, the magic pearl kept within. Jim found he was far more fearful to meet whatever waited for him beyond this archway than he had been facing all the magical dangers he had confronted before.

When Jim finally passed through the arch, Queen Melodia was floating in a small pool, waiting for him. In the center of the room, beside the pool, stood a lone vessel, formed of white coral. It grew up through the stone floor like strands of grass piercing a cobblestone street. The coral tub brimmed with water, but this water was clearer than glass and smoother than polished stone.

"This is the Well of Spirits, Jim Morgan," said the Queen. "It is filled with sacred waters. These waters must be kept separate from the waters of the sea. If ever they mixed, the magic would fail, and our ability to speak with the souls kept in the stones would be lost. All you must do is touch the pearl to the waters, Jim, but be careful not to dip your hand below the surface."

Jim crept to the lip of the coral bowl. He leaned over the edge and found the still waters cast no reflection, not of his face, nor of the crystal ceiling above his head. Jim took the silver chain and opened the shell charm. When the pearl tasted the chamber's salty air, it began to thrum. A glow sparked to life from within the sphere. Jim's fingers trembled as he held the stone above the magical waters.

"I'm afraid," Jim said to the Queen. Was he really about to meet his mother? What would she say to him? What would she think of him – of what he had become?

The Queen only nodded again toward the well. Carefully, Jim stretched his shaking arm toward the waters. When the pearl touched the surface, a single ripple, cast out in a flawless arc, sprang from the stone. A shimmer, like a drop of liquid gold in the water, spread through the well. Jim retreated, his heart plummeting to somewhere deep inside his chest.

A misty tendril rose from the well, twisting and curling in the air until it took the lithe form of a mermaid. Like a painting come to life, the shifting mist took clearer shape and color. Golden hair fluttered like autumn leaves in the wind. A long tail, blue as the cloudless sky, snapped against invisible waves. The tail's scales suddenly took flight like a hundred butterflies, rushing out and returning to lie upon the woman like a thin gown, revealing feet where there had once been fins. Upon these feet the woman from the mist stepped from the well, treading down through the air onto the stone.

Jim was locked in place, motionless, save for shaking arms and legs. He was startled to find that he already stood taller than she, that his mother had to look up into his face, with eyes green as spring grass. Whenever he had dreamt of her, it was she who had looked down on him.

"Jim," she said. "For so long I have hoped for this moment. But oh how you look like your father."

"Mother," Jim said. He fought to still his chin, to hold back the hot drops brimming behind his eyes. He had never seen her before, not even in a painting. But the moment he saw her, he knew it was true. She was the Lady Morgan. Jim thought of something to say, but all that came out was, "Mother, what happened to your tail?"

His mother laughed – a perfect laugh. Jim could not help himself but to laugh along, in spite of his aching throat and burning nose.

"That is a question your friend George might have asked, I think," she said, her smile glowing.

"But how do you know George? You've never met him… You've never met me. How do you even know to call me Jim?"

"But of course I've met you, Jim," his mother said, shaking her head and laughing again. "I held you when you still fit in the crook of my arm. You did not cry. Did you know that? The first sound you ever made was a laugh, at least that is what I believed it to be. Your father was so proud. Jim, I've been with you all this time, with you and your friends, on all your adventures, ever since your father…" the Lady Morgan caught her breath, closing her eyes and pursing her lips. But at length she spoke again. "Ever since your father left you the Soul Stone."

"Ever since?" Jim said. He shrank back from his mother, curling his left hand behind his back, hiding the rose scar that bloomed forever on his palm. "You've seen then? Everything I've done? Everything I've thought and everything I've said?"

"Yes, Jim. But I am not ashamed." The Lady Morgan rushed forward and took Jim by the hand. Jim gasped when he felt her touch. He thought perhaps she was nothing more than a ghost, nothing more than a memory person as his father had been in the Vault of Treasures. But Lady Morgan gently touched the scar on his skin. She was warm, as though she were truly alive. "Yes, I've seen the things you've done, Jim. No mother ever gave birth to a perfect man. But some are blessed enough to have given birth to those who try."

"Am I even a man? What am I, mother?"

"Of course you are a man. You are my son, and you are your father's." Lady Morgan took her hands from Jim's and cupped his face. "You are whatever you have it in yourself to be. That is all, and that is so much. You mustn't believe the things Count Cromier said about him – about your father. Or even the things Dread Steele said about him, Jim. Lindsay was a good man, good enough for me to leave all that I knew to follow him to the world above the waters. But the magic we used to cross such lines came at a greater cost than either of us could have known."

"But King Nemus, and Janus the cat, they told me father stole you, that he betrayed everyone. They told me he was a thief."

"As I said, no mother ever gave birth to a perfect man. Your father and I were young, Jim. He believed that if he had the power of the Treasure of the Ocean, he could make the world a better place. He believed that if a good man had the power of the sea itself at his command, then the world could at last have justice and peace. He would put an end to wars, he said, an end to injustice. It was a beautiful, foolish dream."

"What changed his mind? Why did he hide the Treasure after all that?"

"We changed his mind, Jim."

"We?"

"You and I. My death and your birth. Our love was a pure thing, but as I said, the magic we used to cross the bridge between our worlds was more than my body could stand for long."

"It killed you?" A pang struck Jim's heart. Did magic destroy everything it touched?

"He didn't know it would, Jim. Neither of us did. That taught him that magic and power always come at a cost – even when used for good. But more than that, when your father held you in his arms and imagined your future, he found a better way than force to change the world."

"Me? Change the world?" Jim asked. "Then he did want me to use the Treasure of the Ocean. That's why I was born."

"No, Jim, no." His mother pulled Jim closer. "Do you remember what your father said to you on the beach that day he came home from his long journey? Do you remember?"

Jim did remember. He would never forget. "He asked me if I still played in the sands on the beach. He asked me if I still daydreamed like a child."

"He was asking if you still believed in all the good things that children believe. When children wage battles in their minds, they don't really battle other men. They fight the forces of evil. They battle for the light. Don't you see, Jim? For every child that grows into a good man or a good woman, another light shines in the world, like another star in the night sky."

"But I haven't been good, mother." Jim felt a tear burn its way down his cheek to his chin. How many times had he imagined, even though he knew it was impossible, to stand before all the people he had ever known, as a hero, as the true Lord Morgan? He had imagined standing before his mother and father most, seeing their proud smiles as they looked on all he had done. But now he met his mother with nothing but the clothes on his back and his father's empty box in his pocket. How could she be anything but disappointed in him? "I've been a thief... and a pirate. I've been a fool. I've hurt my friends. I've—"

"You've never failed to make amends, Jim. You have fought to be good. You have struggled for so long." His mother touched his hair. Jim felt a sudden weight fall on his shoulders, crushing his chest and bending his back.

"I'm tired, mother. I'm tired of fighting."

"I know, Jim. I know. But you must fight on a little longer. Count Cromier will use the Treasure of the Ocean. He will claim to use it for good. Perhaps, even in his twisted mind, he truly believes that. Even the wicked want good things, Jim, they've just forgotten that it is what we do to get those things that makes us heroes or villains."

"I don't know what I can do. If Nemus won't help us, how can I stop Count Cromier? He has too many pirates. He knows too much magic."

"He doesn't know as much as he thinks." Lady Morgan's eyes sobered. The bright spring green turned dark, like the sea. "To Cromier, his son Bartholomew is only a means to an end, no less a tool than the golden trident itself. Cromier believes he will be able to control his son once Bartholomew uses the Treasure at the temple. But he is wrong. Tell me Jim, what is the Treasure of the Ocean and what is the altar? The one you have seen in your dreams?"

"The Treasure is a key," said Jim, "and the altar is the lock."

"Keys and locks are used to open and seal doors. But the one who wishes to allow the magic to pass through must hold the door open, or it will shut behind him. The magic must pass through a vessel to truly enter our world. Do you understand, Jim?"

"A vessel for the magic," Jim said to himself, turning it over in his mind. Had not the King of Thieves said the same thing, that the magic needed a vessel? He was not sure he understood. He was about to ask Lady Morgan to tell him more, when he found she was no longer looking at him. Her eyes had gone wide. Her lips were pressed tight together. Suddenly, she released Jim's face and turned to Queen Melodia.

"Mother!" She cried. "At the surface – something is wrong." Queen Melodia said nothing, but quickly dove into the pool with a splash.

"What is it, mother?" Jim asked, grabbing at his mother's hands. Already he missed her touch on his face.

"Trouble has followed you faster than I thought it would, Jim," Lady Morgan replied. Queen Melodia returned to the pool, her golden eyes ablaze.

"He is here," she said. "Count Cromier has come with an armada of Corsair ships at his back. He has come for Jim."

TWENTY-TWO

WHILE JIM WAS IN THE CHAMBER

While Jim met his mother for the first time, Lacey, Peter, Paul, and MacGuffy waited for him in the chamber at the bottom of the spiraling stairs, growing more restless and worried by the minute. George, however, had wandered off on his own.

Like the others, George had wondered at first why none of them could hear anything between King Nemus and Jim. Peter and Paul had screwed up their faces, as though wiggling their ears might help. And Lacey had begun wringing her hands. George had never seen her do that before. Certainly not when he or his brothers had ever been in a pinch. She'd only ever tossed them that lightning glare of hers.

Then the bridge had stretched out under Jim's feet. He'd gone right over, barely looking back. And Lacey kept right on wringing her hands. But George hadn't been worried. Part of this was because he knew Jim could take care of himself. He had, after all, taught Jim everything he knew about keeping oneself alive, and on the streets of London for that matter, which was no easy trick.

But it was also because there was some other feeling stirring around in George's chest. He would not call it jealousy – no, no, he told himself – not that at all. Jim was George's best mate, like his third brother, just like Lacey was like his only sister. But sometimes, in moments like this one, George wondered if there would ever be someone who would wring her hands for him. That would be quite something, to have someone feel the need to wring her hands raw for a bloke, he thought. He also wondered what it might be like to be the one crossing bridges and wearing magic necklaces, and not the one left behind.

George had been left on the steps of a church by his own mother and father. That was his first memory. All he had ever been good at was thieving. How important were thieves, after all? So George wandered off by himself, to wait for Jim, and to wait for these pesky feelings poking the inside of his chest to go away.

He came to the stone pillar in the center of the winding stairwell and began to shuffle around it. George had seen similar monuments when he and Jim had been on the run from some magical shop owner or another in Egypt. The ones in Egypt had been more square than this one, though, with a little pyramid on top. What had Jim called them? Obelicks? Obelisks? Something like that. Not even Jim had been able to read the symbols on those stones, George recalled. But the pictures on this one, even a thief could understand them.

There was the great city of giants, a city bigger than London, towers like castles from end to end. Then there were two giants standing next to one building, built on top of a mountain in the middle of the city. They had that symbol above their heads – the symbol from the lid on Jim's box. Then came the cloud, the wind, the lightning, and the waves. In the next carving the great city fell into the sea. Then there was only one giant left, standing on top of the altar in that funny looking building…

…that symbol of the Treasure still hanging over his head.

"It will destroy him, George. It will destroy everything."

The whispering voice caught George by surprise. He spun around, his hand leaping all by itself to his inside coat pocket, where he kept the magic flute. A tricky shadow crept between a crevice in the crystal. A long, spidery limb stepped from the dark spot, followed by two spindly arms, a long hooked nose, and a dark-eyed face.

"You again?" George said to the King of Thieves. "I thought I told you before to—"

"Hush!" The King hissed to George, pressing one bony finger to his pale lips. "Did you see any coils of shade surround you, my boy? Did you feel any touch of cold upon your skin? I have not shielded us in darkness as I did before. That was a mistake… but old habits die hard, you know. We are out in the open, if you will, a dangerous place for a pair of retired thieves like us, wouldn't you say?"

George took a step to his left. He felt no slower than a moment before. The light about him seemed no dimmer.

"Then what's to keep me from shoutin out and showin you to me friends, eh?" George challenged – but he did it more quietly than he first intended.

"That might be a bit of an awkward conversation, don't you think? To find you here with me, to have it known that we talked before? To have it known that you said nothing? As Jim said nothing to you about our conversation in Egidio's shop. Oh yes, we spoke, my boy. We spoke at length."

So the King of Thieves had gone to Jim first, George thought. Of course he had gone to Jim first. George felt another poke at the inside of his chest.

"You musn't blame Jim," said the King, shaking his head. "It is a tremendous burden he carries. Such weights as those, the weights we most need to share, are the most difficult to let go. But no matter how brave and how selfless Jim may be, the Treasure of the Ocean will destroy him if he attempts to use it, for he does not know how to wield its power."

"But you do, I suppose?"

"I told you before, George, I was banished to a world beyond this one – a world of magic. Only fate has allowed this ghostly version of myself to return. Fate has allowed me a chance to make all my wrongs right."

"Then why tell me? Why did Jim turn you away if you wanted to help him so much?"

"Because, like you, he did not trust me, George. Who could blame him? But there is a reason more than that. I am but a shade in this world – a shadow." The King flitted through the crystal walls, out into the ocean and back again. Then he poured himself into the heart of the stone, only to have his face reappear, right through the symbol of the Treasure of the Ocean, above the ruins of the once magnificent city. "You, on the other hand, are real. And you, like me, are a master thief. On top of that, now you are also becoming a master of magic. What better friend could Jim have than you? It isn't an easy job, being a hero, George. Even heroes need friends… friends that might become heroes themselves."

George's fingers twitched beside his pocket. They itched for the feel of the flute. But after a moment, George let his hand drop just a little. "What exactly would I need to do, if I were to even trust you at all?"

"There are only two who might use the Treasure, George. Is that not so?" The King melted out of the stone, swirling about George, the traces of his shadow wrapping about George's feet like a long, black cloak.

"Jim," said George, thinking hard about everything his friend had told him over the years. "Jim and Bartholomew."

"That's right. So why have Jim risk so much only to fail and die? Why risk all that when the Cromiers are so eager to do it for us? Let the young Cromier try and fail. Let him be destroyed, George. Convince Jim of the wisdom of this. Then, with time, I will train Jim how to use the Treasure properly. There will be plenty of time to prepare him for the great deeds he will one day accomplish. And, for saving him, you will be his most trusted friend, his advisor, the right hand man to the most powerful being on earth."

George tried not to let his mind wander to the pictures of this future. But thoughts are harder to hold than fresh caught fish. George saw himself beside Jim. He wouldn't be the most important person – but that would be all right. It was okay for Jim to be that one... but George would be close. He would still be important. Jim would still need him. But George's heart still tingled with a warning. The King had lied to him before. Lied to him cold.

"How do I know this ain't a trick? How do I know I can trust you?"

"For one, I have nothing to gain, my boy. I'm a ghost, remember? What need have I for gold, or treasure, or food, or water, or power? The only hope I have is to make right my wrongs."

"And for two?" asked George.

"For two, I will prove myself to you by a good deed. I will give you a chance to rescue your friends from great danger, even now. Look."

The King held out his arms in a circle, his long fingers stretching to touch at the tips. His elbows lost their points. The crooks of his wrists twisted into smooth curves. His arms intertwined like two black serpents and in the midst of the circle appeared a rippling image.

It was the *Spectre*, bobbing beneath a bright moon on the ocean. A fleet of Corsair ships surrounded her. On the prow of the foremost enemy vessel, sword in hand, stood Count Cromier.

"Cromier!" George hissed.

"Yes. He has come for Jim, lad. Even now, your friends are noticing the massing of the merfolk's warriors outside the tower. But it will take too long for them to mount an attack. Your friends will rush up to the Tower Top to see what's the matter, and there the count will catch them all. He'll catch them all and cut their throats until he gets his hands on Jim."

"No!" George cried, his stomach twisting.

"Go then. Warn them now. Warn them not to take the stairs. Then, do what the mermen will be unable to do. Save the crew of your ship."

"Me? What can I do against a whole fleet of pirate ships?"

"Use the flute, George. You are in the deep ocean now. Do you remember what the Kraken did to the *Spectre* on your last adventure? Oh yes, from my place of torture beyond the magic veil, I saw this too. There are such monsters that lurk in the depths. They could fall under your command. They could be your soldiers, your weapons with which to strike."

At last, George pulled the flute from his coat pocket. He stared at it, trembling like a leaf on the tips of his fingers. "I've never tried anything that big." His voice shook worse than the flute. His thoughts flicked back to his little friend, the mouse. "I don't know if I can."

"But you must, George," said the King, his dark eyes pleading. "This is what heroes do. They do those things they are not sure they can, because they must. I leave the choice up to you." Then the King faded away, drifting into nothing through the crystal wall.

George stood still as stone, his eyes fixed upon the flute. He might have stayed that way for hours, frozen by the impossible choice before him, when his brothers' panicked cries woke him from his indecision.

"Georgie, Georgie! Come quick!"

George slipped the flute back into his pocket, swallowed hard, and ran back to join the others.

"Look at all them mermen, George," Peter said, pointing through a window in the crystal tower, his face white as a sheet.

"They're lookin like those chaps back in Morocco, ain't they?" said Paul. "Lookin like them guards gettin ready to chop off some hands."

"There must be some trouble on the surface," said MacGuffy. "The *Spectre* may be in danger. We must be gettin back."

"No!" George shouted, so loud it surprised even him. "We can't."

"George is right," Lacey agreed. "We can't leave now, Jim is still in that other room. We must wait for him."

"The Queen'll look after him, little Lacey," said MacGuffy. "If ye like, ye young'uns might wait here. But me and Cornelius must make for the *Spectre*."

"No, don't," George shouted again. "MacGuffy, you can't. Count Cromier is up there. He's waitin for you, like a trap and everythin. If you go up there, you'll just get killed."

"That would be some trick to know such a thing from down here, wouldn't you say, Master Ratt?" squawked Cornelius, flapping his wings on the old pirate's shoulders.

"He's right, George," said Lacey. "How could you possibly know that?"

"I... I just do."

MacGuffy regarded George for a long moment, his scar twitching on his ruined cheek. His gnarled fingers tapped the battered bell of his old cutlass.

"You know I thank ye for yer care, ya sea rat," MacGuffy finally said. "But I'm afraid me old eye needs to see fer itself. Ye all wait here. If the raven and I do not return, keep safe here in the protection of Nemus and his folk." With that, MacGuffy turned to climb the stairs. But the thought of the old salt, who had been the closest thing George had ever had to a father, falling at the hands of Count Cromier, was more than George could bear.

"No, MacGuffy, wait. I can stop them. I can do it!"

George pulled the flute from his pocket. Lacey put her hands up to her face. Cornelius crowed. Even Peter and Paul fell back from their brother.

"Oh, George, what is that?" Lacey asked. But George could tell from her eyes that she already knew.

"Stay your hand, young Ratt," cried Cornelius. "That is an instrument of dark magic you hold."

Their warnings came too late. George would not let Cromier hurt his friends. He would not let Jim be destroyed by the power of the Treasure of the Ocean. The Cromiers were evil. They had taken Jim's home from him. They had taken his father from him. They were the ones who deserved to be destroyed. George put the flute to his lips and began to play.

TWENTY-THREE

BEASTS FROM THE DEEP

A t first, George feared the crystal tower's walls or the sea beyond them would dull the flute's strength. But if anything, the water gave his magic song even greater reach. That little window in George's mind opened wider, and through it he touched the minds of more creatures than he ever had before. These were old beasts, creatures undisturbed by men since the dawn of time. Some were small and quick, others great and powerful. All answered his call.

One by one, they began to swim to the crystal tower.

Old MacGuffy, Lacey, or even George's brothers, might have stopped him if they had tried, but they all became hypnotized by the gathering army of sea monsters above the underwater city. Even

Fulkern and his warriors drifted in awe on the other side of the crystal windows, pointing wildly with their spears.

George was flush with the joy of newly discovered power. He sent his brigade of great fishes to the surface to deal with the Cromiers and their scum. But his moment of triumph would not last long. He had tasted success, but he was not a master of magic yet.

He never noticed the sweat pouring down his face until it was too late. He never felt the pain burning in his lungs until after disaster had struck.

It began with some of the smaller schools of fish flitting away, more afraid of the predators George had summoned than loyal to the magic song that had called them. George let them go. It was the giant beasts that would do the most damage. The greatest of them all was a true terror, longer than a whale, skin aglow in purple and blue, with countless rows of teeth as tall as men.

This creature was a king of the sea, like the lion in the jungle. He was not prone to following commands. He lived his life as he pleased. Feeling the magical fetters on his mind, the great fish bucked against them. George fought to hang on. He played faster and louder. He tried different tunes to different rhythms. But when his newfound strength abandoned him, it abandoned him quickly.

The sea monster tore loose of George's control, breaking the spell over all the other fish as well. Most of them swam away, terrified to be caught in such shallow waters, frightened to be so far from their dark homes. But not the great one. He was not afraid. He was angry. All he knew was the source of his fury had come from the crystal tower.

As the beast charged the tower. Lacey screamed. Cornelius cried for the party to fly for the stairs. But an icy claw had seized George's heart and frozen his legs. What had he done? Oh, what had he done?

A thunderous bang shook the crystal tower, rattling it like windows in a storm, nearly shaking Jim to his knees.

166

"What was that?" he cried. Another tremor threatened to toss him to the floor. Then another. And another.

At last, the explosions ceased. All Jim could hear was the hammer of his heart. He was about to ask his mother and the Queen what was happening when another sound cut him off – a splintering, like ice crunching beneath large boots. Jim watched as cracks crawled across the crystal wall. They branched out in long, bony fingers. Water began to spit and spring into the chamber through the cracks.

"Mother, no!" Jim screamed. He ran to the well, trying to shield its waters from the ocean spilling into the chamber. "The waters cannot mix. We have to save the waters."

"Jim, oh Jim, stop!" Lady Morgan took Jim by the shoulders, turning him to face her. Jim tried to shrug her off and reach for the waters with his bare hands, perhaps to carry just enough of it to the surface, enough to see his mother again. But his mother would not let him. "Jim, you must stop and listen to me. Please, if you love me, listen."

"I'll never see you again," Jim said. He began to tremble from head to toe. Finding his mother had been like remembering the words to a beautiful song, long forgotten. Now he would have to forget it again.

"One day you will, Jim. One day, on the far side of the invisible ocean, once your journey is complete. I will wait for you there, on those shores. Your father and I will wait for you. But not today. Please, not today. Hear me now. My father is a hard man. After this, he will surely refuse to help you. He may even try to harm you. But you must find a way, Jim. You must reach the temple and stop the Cromiers. But it is not the count you must stop, Jim. Do you understand me? It isn't the count you must win over."

A shower of seawater stuck Jim, raining down from the cracks in the wall. It stung his skin and stole his breath, for it was cold as ice. The water also sprayed into the pool. As the pure waters began to spoil, Jim's mother began to return to mist.

"But I still don't know the way, mother." Jim grabbed his mother's wrists, but her figure began to slip through his fingers. "I don't even know how to reach the temple."

"There is another who knows," Lady Morgan said, her voice growing almost too soft to hear. "There is another who can show you the way. As I do not want to lose you, so she will not want to lose her son. I believe she will help you. Her name is Legeia. She lives on the deep ocean, on a stretch of sea called the Wastewaters, on the Island of the Silver Pool. You must find her, Jim. She will show you the way."

"Mother, don't leave!" Jim cried.

"There is more than one way to change the world, Jim. Remember me, please. You are your father's son, and mine. Goodbye." Jim's mother drifted like steam off the street in the rain. A hole finally broke through the tower wall. A chunk of crystal, propelled by the flowing water, smashed the coral well to pieces and spilled the sacred waters to the floor.

Jim fell to his knees, where the freezing water had already begun to pool and climb above his legs. He struck the bubbling foam with his fists, crying out above the cracking crystal and roaring water.

"There is no time to mourn, Jim," said Queen Melodia. "You must fly. Fly to your friends. It is not too late. Even now, even in the face of this loss, I will help you if I can. I will try and convince Nemus to help you, for your mother's sake, and for the sake of all that is still good in the world. Now run!"

Jim took only the time to loop the necklace and the pearl, now dead and bereft of power, about his neck. He also took one of the shards from the coral well, put it in his father's box, and then ran for the archway that led to the great chamber and the stairwell beyond.

When Jim reached the bridge over the great pool, he found that Lacey, Peter, Paul, and MacGuffy were already running up the winding stairs. George was nowhere to be seen. A great, white spiderweb of cracks covered the wall, crying tears of seawater, threatening to shatter under the weight of the ocean. Whatever it was that had caused the destruction, however, was gone.

"Jim!" Lacey screamed. "Come on!"

"Hurry, boy," urged Cornelius. "Make haste, make haste!"

Jim splashed through the freezing waters, rising over his waist. His lips and fingers and toes were beginning to shiver. When he reached the stairs and climbed from the water, Lacey rushed up and pulled him into her arms. Her auburn hair was slicked to her face, but her eyes were red and wet with more than seawater.

"Where's George?" Jim asked.

"He's gone, Jim," Lacey said, her voice cracking. "He disappeared in a swirl of black smoke. I don't know how."

"Disappeared?" Jim asked. But Cornelius's crow reminded him this was not the time for mysteries.

"We must fly," He cawed. "We must fly to the Tower Top, and fast!"

The clan began to scale the stairs at once. For a half moment, as they cleared the top of the stone pillar, marked with the ancient carvings, Jim held on to hope that they might just make it.

But the crystal tower had taken too great of a beating. It finally surrendered to the strength of the sea. An awful cry screeched through the tower. The water roared in after with the thunder of ten-thousand stampeding horses.

Lacey pulled Peter and Paul close to her. Jim reached out to take her by the arm or by the hand, to hold her close when the end came. But the water reached him too quickly. The sea's cold hands took Jim by the legs and yanked him down into the frigid black.

TWENTY-FOUR

THE BANISHMENT OF JIM MORGAN

Jim coughed and spat. He thrashed about and sucked in a greedy gulp of poor air. When he opened his eyes, he found the ocean surrounded him, but he was not drowning. Jim stretched out his hand. Just when he thought he would reach the water he found a slippery surface instead. The invisible wall bent around Jim's fingertips, but it was strong enough to keep him safe from the crushing power of the ocean.

Jim was in a bubble.

He slid around on his back until he sat up, searching the ocean around him to find five more bubbles floating beside him, illuminated in the shimmering glow of Aquila. Lacey, Peter, Paul, MacGuffy, and even Cornelius Darkfeather, in the smallest bubble of them all, hovered nearby. Jim shouted for Lacey through the clear wall. His voice sounded stale and weak. Lacey could not hear him. She was not even looking in his direction. She was staring past Jim's bubble with her hands over her mouth.

Jim turned around. What he saw stunned him.

The crystal tower lay in a glimmering heap, like a bristling pile of shattered bottles. Some shards still drifted down, landing and breaking on the ocean floor. Within the rubble, buried at the bottom of what had once been the bridge between the worlds above and below the waters, were the crushed remains of the Well of Spirits. The sacred waters were spoiled and ruined. Jim would never again see his mother's face or hear her voice.

A blurred shape rose up in Jim's teary vision. Jim drew the back of his hand across his eyes, wiping them clear to see Queen Melodia swimming up to the bubbles, arms outstretched and fingers spread wide. It was she who had formed the protective spheres. She had used her magic to save Jim and his friends.

"I'm sorry," Jim cried through the bubble. "I'm so sorry." Unlike Lacey, Melodia could hear Jim through the waters.

"This was not your doing, Jim," he heard her say. Her voice was thick and full of sadness. "This was not your fault."

"But the Crystal Tower and the Well of Spirits, they're gone—"

"Yes, gone!" a voice boomed, so loud Jim feared his bubble might burst and leave him to drown after all. "Destroyed forever!" King Nemus swam up beside his wife. His black and silver hair spread about his head in the water like a lion's mane. His golden eyes, so sad and tired but a few moments ago, now burned like molten coins. He leveled his great spear at Jim's face, nearly piercing the bubble with its jagged point. "Had you never come here, Jim Morgan, this tragedy would not have befallen my city. How much longer must the house of Morgan torment me? You stole my treasures. You destroyed our tower. Even the great gift of your mother's essence, kept safe in the Soul Stone, is wasted.

Because of you and your father, even your own world will be thrown into darkness when the Cromiers use the Treasure of the Ocean."

"I never meant any of this to happen," Jim cried, pounding his fists against the bubble. "I don't want the Treasure of the Ocean anymore. I don't want its power. I'll bring it back to you, I swear it. But if you don't help us, nothing will stop the Cromiers. Things will only get worse."

"Even now you have the gall to ask for my help. Even as you look upon the ruins of our tower, and even after you, a human, were the last to look upon the face of my own daughter, the princess of our people. You think only of yourself and the people of the world above the sea."

"It's all one world, isn't it?" Jim said. "If the Cromiers unlock the power of the Treasure, then won't they wreak just as much havoc here as on the surface? We need to work together."

"How dare you lecture me?" Bolts of power lanced from the king's spear, dancing in the water. Even Queen Melodia, powerful as she was, shrank back from her husband. "You are exactly like your father – an arrogant fool. You think you know what is best for others. Do you not see my power? Too long have I allowed sorrow to dull my anger. The race of men has caused my people too much suffering. I will go to the ancient temple, Jim Morgan. But I go to wipe out any who approach. But first, I shall start by punishing the house of Morgan for its crimes."

Nemus drew back his coral spear, aflame with burning magic. He fixed his sights on Jim. Jim pressed himself against the back of his bubble, as though there was any hope of escape. At the last moment, Queen Melodia threw herself between Jim and the king.

"Stop this, Nemus," she shouted. "This is your grandson. He is all that remains of Venia. Can the boy be blamed for all the crimes of men? Do their crimes outweigh our own? How long did we keep the Treasure of the Ocean here, when we could have hidden it or tried to destroy it? We too were tempted, Nemus, tempted by the promise of power."

The king held his spear high, poised to strike. Jim thought Nemus might throw the queen aside and destroy him in spite of her pleas. Yet Nemus relented in the end and lowered his spear. But fury still burned in his eyes.

"So be it," he said. "For the sake of our daughter I will spare the boy's life. But I will not help him. He will go back to the surface to face his own kind. And if any man, Morgan or Cromier, tries for the temple, I will make him suffer. And not him alone – all men! They will learn to fear the ocean once more. I will trap them on their islands of dirt for all time."

"Nemus, please—" Melodia began. But the king already had his fill of mercy.

"Silence! I have spoken. Be gone from my sight, Jim Morgan. Let fate do with you what it will. I disown you as my grandson. I toss you to the waves." Nemus swung his spear. At his command, the bubbles holding Jim and his friends began to rise.

"Your majesty, please!" Jim cried as he was lifted away. "Please don't do this!" But Nemus no longer listened. As Jim drifted up from the city of Aquila, he saw Nemus gather his warriors. The number was growing as merfolk swam from the city by the hundreds, by the thousands. Nemus's angry voice carried through the water, his cry taken up by those rallying to their king.

"War! War! War!"

The bubbles burst at the surface, spitting Jim and the others onto the waves – surrounded by Corsair ships. There was nowhere to swim and nowhere to hide. The Corsairs threw down ropes and dragged the clan onto the deck of the *Sea Spider*. The pirates tossed Jim in a heap beside his friends, dripping wet and staring at a pair of polished shoes on the feet of Count Cromier.

"My, my, my," said the count, tracing his purple scar with a gloved finger. Bartholomew stood behind him, hand on his sword, icy eyes fixed on Jim. "What a fine catch this is. So, even the merfolk have turned you away, eh, Morgan? You truly have no safe harbor left on the earth."

Jim raised himself up on his knees, looking around for any last hope. He found none. Some twelve Corsair ships surrounded the Spectre. Her crew, lessened by the number who had abandoned her at Spire Island, stood helplessly on the deck, weapons at their feet.

"Looking for Dread Steele to come save you?" said the count. "Looking for Queen Melodia to appear? Perhaps even the ghost of your father? Let's see, who's left? How about you, F.W. Pennington Sharpe? Any tricks left in your pocket for young Jim Morgan?" Sharpe stood on the deck of the Sea Spider, his hands behind his back, two Corsair pistols pointed at his head. When Jim's eyes met Sharpe's, the roguish sea captain threw him a wan smile.

"Sorry, old boy," he said. "Sometimes a man can bluff his way to victory, but other times, he must know when to fold. Cromier has allowed the crew of the *Spectre* to live in exchange for you and your friends. I wish I could say I had more honor than that, but I came here for the gold – might as well leave with my life."

"Coward!" raged MacGuffy. The old man climbed to his feet, swaying on his old legs. He shook a gnarled finger at Sharpe and the crew of the *Spectre*. "Cowards, all! Do ye not remember? We swore an oath. An oath to Cap'n Dread Steele, Lord of the Pirates, to look after this boy and see his quest to an end. Do ye give up now? Even in the face of this villain? Have ye forgotten yer honor?" The *Spectre's* crew hung their heads. Jim could not blame them. They would surely die to the last man if they fought.

"I'm afraid I don't even remember what it was like to have honor, old friend," said Sharpe. For the briefest instant, Jim thought he saw the captain's stiff smile twist into a frown.

"Then to the Devil with ye all!" cried MacGuffy. "I shall at least leave with me honor in tact."

He drew his cutlass. Jim shook his head no. With a desperate look he pleaded with MacGuffy to sit back down and sheath his sword, to join the other members of the crew and just sail away. But the old man, thin wisps of silver hair flying about his head, shouted his last battle cry and charged the count.

"For Morgan! For Morgan! For Mor—"

The last cry caught in MacGuffy's throat. He stood still as a statue on the deck, his sword held high in the air. But he never brought down the blade. When the count stepped away from MacGuffy, the old salt tipped on his feet and fell to the deck. In Count Cromier's hand was a short blade, covered in red.

"No!" Jim cried. He could hear Lacey screaming behind him. He crawled to MacGuffy's side, cradling the old man's head in his hands. MacGuffy, wheezing with some effort, managed to look up with his one good eye, struggling to keep it open.

"Forgive me," said MacGuffy. "Forgive an old fool… I was not strong enough to see ye through to the end."

"You don't have anything to be sorry for, MacGuffy," said Jim. Tears rolled down his cheeks. "You were like the best grandfather I could ever have."

"Remember…" MacGuffy's voice began to fail. "A boy knows not what kind of man he'll be until he's sailed through the storms… Sail on, Jim Morgan, as I do." Then MacGuffy closed his eye and breathed his last breath.

"Well, so much for that," said the count, laughing. The Corsair pirates laughed with him. "Let Captain Sharpe go." The count waved his hand without looking. "Let the Spectre go. They cannot stop us now. We set sail at once. The Treasure of the Ocean is within our grasp. We have but one last test to pass before the world falls at our feet."

"Cromier, you murderer!" Jim screamed. "If you think I'm going to help you… If you think I'm going to do your dirty work after this, you—"

"You?" Cromier interjected. "Do you still think it's all about you, Jim Morgan? You are more like your father than I thought. Bartholomew and I do require some assistance through our final obstacle. But the help we need isn't yours."

A smile stretched across the count's withered face. His eyes drifted past Jim, to where his friends sat, weeping for MacGuffy – to where Lacey sat.

"It is written in a very old tome of mine, the story of the beast that stands in my way. He has a weakness, Morgan. Hair like autumn, eyes like summer, spirit like spring – she will be my key."

"No!" Jim screamed. He tried to stand and charge the count. But Cromier was still as quick as he was evil. He struck Jim on the top of the head with the butt of his knife. As Jim staggered, the count seized him by the collar, dragging him across the deck. Jim could hear Lacey and the Ratts crying out for him. He blearily saw Lacey reach for him. But before she could come close, Bartholomew grabbed her by the arm. Jim stretched for her. Their fingers never touched.

"I would love to finally kill you, Morgan, but since you are the only other person in the world who can unlock the power I seek, and since I will most likely need the leverage of your life to coerce your lovely young lady to do my bidding, you must live. There is another place I shall keep you for now. A place from which there is no escape. A place reserved for those for whom even a dungeon is too kind a punishment."

The count threw Jim down on the deck and reached into his pocket, withdrawing a fistful of black powder. Cromier poured the powder in a ring around Jim's body.

"You will only see me again if I need you, Jim Morgan. If not, you will live out the rest of your life in the Dark Hole, where you will never see the sun again. In that place, the line of Morgan will end forever."

"Jim!" Lacey screamed.

"Lacey!" Jim shouted back. He reached for her again, but before he could do anything more than say her name, the last of the black powder fell from the count's hand.

"Goodbye, Jim Morgan," said the count.

A black whirlwind swallowed up the world. Jim felt his body ripped from the deck of the *Sea Spider*, thrown into a place between places. He was carried away on a dark wind, far from those he loved, who were left trapped in the Cromier's clutches.

TWENTY-FIVE

PRISONERS

In the belly of the *Sea Spider*, trapped in the brig behind iron bars, Lacey felt the weight of the entire world on her shoulders. She feared she might be crushed beneath it. The two remaining Ratts, Peter and Paul, sat opposite her, knees hugged to their chests and hands clamped in rusty manacles. The Corsairs had even cinched shut Cornelius's beak, ceasing his unending string of curses and vows of vengeance with a twist of copper wire. And all three of them, the talking raven included, were looking to her.

"Where are they takin us, Lacey?"

"I don't know, Paul. To wherever Jim's Treasure is hidden, I suppose."

"What are they goin to do to us, Lacey?"

"I don't know, Peter. Use us to find the Treasure, I suppose."

"Is Jim dead, Lacey?"

"Do you think... Do you think George is dead?"

"I don't..."

Lacey caught herself. She thought back to George, standing there by the steps, the flute in his hand. A ribbon of black had flown in from nowhere, wrapped around George's body, and unraveled to reveal him gone. Then she thought of Jim, of the sound of his voice, calling her name. She thought of the black whirlwind that had taken him away to someplace awful. Hot tears curled under her eyes. That weight on her shoulders pressed down harder still.

But Lacey would not allow herself to be crushed. She clenched her fists and told those tears in her eyes to go back from where they came. She took all her sadness and put it away in a closet in her heart... for later. This was her clan, she thought. She was the leader of the Ratt Clan now.

"No, Jim and George are not dead," she said. "Do you hear me? They are not dead!" Lacey spoke as much to the fates as to her friends. "They are alive. And they're going to need us. They're going to need us to do our jobs. Count Cromier wouldn't have kept us alive for no reason. Remember how he made Jim go into that cave, the one with the serpent's mouth? He made Jim go in and get that shell for him. He did it because he's afraid to do it himself. The count and Bartholomew need us – and that gives us a chance. So look sharp!"

Peter and Paul took a start and bolted upright against the bars. Peter wiped his eyes with the back of his filthy sleeve. Paul sucked back any remaining tears with a huge sniffle. Even Cornelius ruffled his feathers, squawking a muffled crow through his clamped beak.

"Peter, you're the greatest lock pick in the world. We're going to need that. And Paul, you're still the premier trickster on all the seven seas, aren't you? That'll come in handy, believe me. We also have Cornelius, who knows more about magic and the world than even the count. We're not weak and helpless. We're the Clan of the

Ratt. We're not done yet. We're going to get Jim and George back if it's the last thing we do. We're not going to let the Cromiers unleash darkness on the world. We're going to fight."

On the deck of the Sea Spider, in morning's first gray, the Corsair pirates shrank from their black-clad captain, Count Villius Cromier. Bartholomew watched their faces, taking note of their fear, their lips moving in silent prayers. It was the magic that terrified them so.

The count held the Hunter's Shell over his head. Violet magic rippled over the polished surface, pulsing with bright flames. A strong wind whipped across the deck, as though summoned by the shell. But Bartholomew did not shrink away from either his father or this display of power. It was not fear he felt.

Once again his father had allowed Jim Morgan to live. Oh, he claimed it was merely to force the girl to do his bidding, that little brat who had cried and screamed as the count had hurled Morgan off with the black powder. And that was his father's way, wasn't it? The two little dolls in Bartholomew's pocket, the figures in the shapes of Abdullah the magic shopkeeper's wife and child were proof of that. But it was not for the little girl alone that his father kept Jim Morgan alive. No, his father kept Morgan alive for Bartholomew, to remind him that there was still another who could wield the Treasure's power – to remind him that failure would still come with consequences.

Jim Morgan was imprisoned in the Dark Hole, but he could still be brought back. Bartholomew shivered in the morning wind. Even for Jim Morgan he shivered. The Dark Hole would break him. It broke all men. Then Morgan would be just another puppet, a puppet for Bartholomew's father.

"The Treasure of the Ocean," Cromier shrieked into the ashy dawn, shattering Bartholomew's thoughts. "Show me that which I seek, oh Hunter's Shell! Show me the way to that which I desire!"

Even the bravest Corsairs hid their faces and covered their eyes.

The violet beam shot from the Shell, arcing through the gray sky like a rainbow to where the Treasure was hidden. Bartholomew still refused to back away. His eyes drifted from the beam, to his father – to the puppet master.

Bartholomew squeezed the hilt of his sword.

Far away from where Lacey, Peter, and Paul began to plot and scheme in the brig of the *Sea Spider*, and from where Bartholomew watched his father seek the Treasure of the Ocean with the magic shell, on the edge of the horizon, there was a dark spot of night that refused to brighten in the morning.

A black cloud boiled over the sea, throwing the waves below into shadow. Crimson streaks burned at its edges. The cloud sensed the magic of the Hunter's Shell. It felt the Treasure of the Ocean was at risk of being found.

Hate roiled within the cloud. Vengeance crackled with purple lightning. The cloud surged forward in the sky. The Crimson Storm went on the move.

BOOK III

IN THE DEPTHS OF THE TWO CAVES

TWENTY-SIX

THE DARK HOLE

Jim awoke face down on cold rock. His head throbbed. His arms and legs felt beaten black and blue. The count's whirlwind had tossed him about, rolling him like a stone down a hill, and spat him onto a rocky floor. He struck his head, and all had gone dark again.

Jim groaned and tried to lift himself up. The ground was sharp and unforgiving, biting into his hands and knees. A wet slime coated the floor, dampening Jim's clothes and slicking the side of his face. Water drops echoed in shallow pools somewhere in the dark beside him. Jim blinked his eyes, searching for a glimmer on the puddles, but wherever he lay was utterly lightless.

"Well, well, well, wouldja look at this?" a voice croaked in the black. Jim froze. He was not alone. "Anover one. You'oulda thought we was some sort of hotel, eh, lads? What with the steady stream of new res'dents that red fella been sendin us of late.

Wouldn't ya say, Bog?"

"Oy, I would, Slag," growled a second voice, like a body being dragged down a wet road. "Feels like we don't do nothin but work, work, work anymore. Don't even remember the last time I just sat me bones down on a wet rock and let meself enjoy the dark, eh? But that's life innit? So just whaddarya smilin about, Grime? You plannin on lettin me and Slag do all the heavy liffin again?"

"Ohhhh, you know me, Bog. I also long for the simple pleasures in life, ahhhh." The third voice wheezed and sighed, where the first two slogged and croaked. "Buuut, if a bloke can't enjoy his work, how can he enjoy life, eh? There *are* pleasures in work, my friends. Great pleasures." The third voice drew in a deep breath so greedy Jim thought its owner was all but drinking the dank air. "Do you smell it, boys?"

Hungry sniffing scratched eagerly at the black. After the sniffing came the laughs, hacking, coughing, and retching.

"I do smell it, I do, Grime," said the one called Bog.

"Leave it up to you, old chap, to remind us ungrateful buggers of the good things in life. And this one smells sooo good."

Jim trembled where he knelt. Unless his ears deceived him, these three brutes were intent on eating him whole. Jim thought frantically for some means to defend himself. He had no pistol, no sword, and no knife. All he had was his father's box, his mother's necklace, and a brittle coral shard from the Well of Spirits. With nothing left to his defense, Jim scampered backward until he struck a rough wall behind him.

"Goin somewhere, are you, lad?" said the one called Slag.

"Leavin so soooon?" hissed Grime.

"This place may indeed be the death of me," Jim said, trying to sound brave. "But I don't intend on dying as your dinner."

The choking laughter erupted again.

"Dinner? Did you hear that, Bog? Dinner?"

"Oy, I did, Slag, I did. Don't worry about that boy. We's are good employees, we is. Eatin of the res'dents is strictly forbidden by man'gement."

"Besides, whaaat do you take us for, boy?" wheezed Grime. "Monsters?" There was a flick, a snap, and hiss. A flash of torchlight seared Jim's vision. When the stars finally cleared, Jim wished he had remained blind.

Three wart-rotted faces, like withered frogs, loomed in the fire-light, eyes that were filmy orbs, smiles of wrinkled folds, yellow, stubby teeth like poisonous mushrooms. They all wore waterlogged straps about their scaly hides, from which rusty knives hung at their sinewy hips.

Jim screamed. The creatures laughed again.

They wrapped their sticky hands about Jim's arms and grabbed him so hard by the back of his neck that he nearly fainted. The three ogres, for that was all Jim could think to call them, dragged him down a narrow corridor, lined with rows of rocky teeth, that led deeper and deeper into the heart of the cave.

The stony hallway opened into a large chamber. Torches hung high in the damp cavern. Shallow cavities lined the walls, and in these hollows, cowering like mice in holes, huddled men, clothed in rags, with filthy beards hanging down to their dirty feet. The men hid their faces from the ogres. They pressed into their little cells as though they might push through the stone and somehow escape.

"What is this place?" Jim cried.

"What is this place? It's a bloody cave, innit? *Where* is a much better question, ain't it, Bog?"

"Where indeed, Slag? One can't never tell. Don't even know meself annnymore." Bog and Slag burst into laughter again, their croaking voices breaking into cackling howls. But Grime, who was the thinnest, most gnarled, and most horned of the three, leaned his face close to Jim's, running a sickly yellow tongue over his rotted teeth.

"Those few from the outside world familiar with this haaapy little pit, call it only the Dark Hooole, boy. But for my mates and me, it is heeearth and hooome."

Grime and his two mates lugged Jim toward the far wall. On the way, they passed through an even icier draft in the damp air. Jim looked between the ogres' green arms and found a gash in the wall, a tear ripped in the stone. It was a chasm into the deepest black Jim had ever seen.

The ogres gave each other a look and on the spot dropped Jim to the floor. They were on him again in an instant, ripping away his shoes and his coat. Like greedy pickpockets they rifled through his clothes. They took his mother's necklace. They plucked his father's box from his pocket.

Grime knelt down before Jim, shoving Jim's last holdings into his face, one at a time. He dangled Jim's mother's necklace before his face, the silver duller now, bereft of all its magic. Then Grime threw the necklace into the chasm.

"No!" Jim screamed, but his cries were drowned out by the ogres' uproarious laughter. Next came the coral shard. Not content with throwing it after the necklace, Grime crumbled it to dust in his hand, sprinkling the remains into the chasm. Jim struggled and fought. He cursed and snarled, but the ogres held him down. Last, Grime held the empty box under Jim's nose – his father's box, once more his final possession.

Jim stopped struggling. He stopped fighting and shouting. Two tears rolled down his cheeks and he grew still.

"Theeere it is," said Grime. The ogre did not throw the box into the chasm. He set it gently on Jim's lap. "Heeere you go, my boy. Why don't you just keep that?" Bog and Slag finally released Jim. All he could think to do was pull his box to his chest and cry for all his sorrows.

The ogres then descended upon Jim like vultures. They did not bite him, scratch him, or devour him. They hardly touched him at all.

But they *breathed* him. They snorted and sniffed. They ran their noses within an inch of his flesh. Jim reeled back from the creatures, but they surrounded him, refusing to let him escape. The ogres gulped down his scent. Their rucked flesh began to plump, their pale skin greened like leaves in spring. Their filmy eyes grew clear and their bodies swelled like mosquitos full of blood. At the last, Grime ran his lumpy tongue down the side of Jim's face, shuddering in ecstasy.

They were drinking Jim's despair. These awful things were gorging themselves on his sorrows. Of course they weren't going to eat him, Jim realized. As long as he was alive in this prison, he could be a feast for them that would never end.

Finally, when the foul keepers of the evil cave had sucked down their fill of Jim's heartbreak, they dragged him to his feet. Grime appeared with a length of rope, tying it tightly about Jim's waist.

"We wouldn't want you floooating away, now would we, young sir?" said Grime, looking so much younger than he had only moments before, rejuvenated by Jim's pain.

"Floating away?" Jim asked.

"Oooh, this isn't to keep you from escaping, my delicious young friend. No, no, feel free to attempt an escape whenever you like." Grime stretched a slimy finger over Jim's shoulder, to the gaping chasm in the wall. "The way out is right through there. In fact, I heeear there's even a boat tied to a wharf on the other end, just waiting for the soul brave enough to reach it." Bog and Slag chortled – low and naughty, like wicked little boys who knew a secret.

"What's really down there?"

"Soooemething worse than us. Trust me when I say that screeeams of horror are a tasty dessert for us whenever we gets the chance to have it." Bog and Slag howled louder and louder. "You'll see about floooating away for yourself, once at dawn and again at dusk. Every day, at morning and at night. But for now, why don't you make yourself at hooome?"

The ogres yanked Jim to an empty cavity, with nothing but the wet stone for a bed. They tied the other end of his rope to a metal ring, which was pressed into the rock. There they left him and walked away, rubbing their swollen bellies. But not before Bog pinched Jim's cheek, like a farmer testing the plumpness of a prize pig.

"See ya again soon, my tasty little friend."

Then Jim was alone. He slumped against his prison cell wall. He gripped his father's empty, useless box in his hands. Silently, he wept.

TWENTY-SEVEN

THE KING'S OFFER

Upon the shores of a desolate island, a black smear appeared.

The swirling pitch ribbons released George Ratt, dropping him to his knees in the sand. Tears ran down his face, so many more than when the poor mouse had fallen from the Spectre. George was sure the great fish, which he had summoned from the deep with the flute, had badly injured itself by ramming the Crystal Tower. And the tower itself had begun crumbling to pieces, just before the King of Thieves had whisked George away.

Worse still had been the way Lacey, Peter, and Paul had looked at him. George had never been much for words or their meanings – he left those sorts of things to Peter and Jim. But he knew the word for what Lacey and his brothers had done. They had recoiled from him, like from a spider, a lizard, or a snake.

What have I done? George thought. *What have I done?*

George took the magic flute in hand and pulled it over his shoulder. He was ready to smash it against the ground. He wished he had never laid eyes on the cursed thing. He wished he had never heard of magic. But as George readied to rid himself of the enchanted instrument, the King of Thieves swooped before him, splaying his long, thin fingers, pleading with George to stop.

"Wait, young George, wait! Do not be so hasty. To destroy such a useful tool as that marvelous flute would be a great loss indeed."

"Destroy?" George shouted, flinging a hateful glare at the King. "I just destroyed a whole tower! I just brought this big fish up outta the sea and watched it ram its head over and over against a wall. I just…" George's tirade caught in his throat. A horrifying thought occurred to him. He had escaped drowning in the ruins only by help of the King's power. How had his brothers gotten away? How had Jim and Lacey? What if… "Oh no!" George shouted. He felt all within him go empty and dark.

"Fear not, young George," The King said. "They are safe." The King once more formed his arms in a ring, fingertips touching. His arms lost their crooked points, curving into a smooth circle, wherein images from far away appeared.

Jim, Lacey, and both his brothers floated in the water, but they were not drowned. Magical bubbles protected them from death in the cold ocean. They were alive. Slowly, George's heart began to beat again. His lungs drew breath.

"What's going to happen to them?"

"Hard to say for certain," said the King, breaking the circle and scattering the vision. "Nemus will most surely be furious after your disaster. He will probably send them up to the surface, where they will be taken prisoner by Count Cromier."

"My disaster?" George wanted to both hang his head and fall fighting upon the King in equal measure. "Why did I listen to you? Why did I listen to your lies? That's all you are, is a liar. You tricked me." George dug in the sand beside him until he unearthed a rock and hurled into the King's face. George hoped the rock would break the King's nose and send the spidery man sprawling in the sand.

But the stone splashed through the King's head like a pebble in a pond. A misty hole appeared in his pallid face. In a blink, all the King's features rippled back into place, only his expression affected, forming a deep frown with sad eyes.

"You see, George," said the King. "I wasn't lying. Look at me. Look at the result of my crimes. This is my punishment. I'm not a man anymore. I'm just a shadow, only an echo of what was once the King of Thieves. What good would lying do me? What could a ghost possibly gain in the world of men?"

"Then why did you tell me to summon up the fish? Why did you make me call up that... that disaster?"

"I told you, my boy," said the King. He blurred through the air to sit in the sand at George's side. "I was trying to help you, and to help Jim as well – to help all mankind. I thought that with the power of the flute, perhaps you could be the one to turn the tide. So perhaps you're right. Perhaps this is my fault. I pushed you too far, too fast. You just weren't ready, and that's not your fault."

The King let his pointy chin fall to his chest. He shook his head, eyes cast to the ground. George, meanwhile, stared off toward the ocean. His tears blurred the sea and the sky. He did not know what to say, and even less so what to do.

"Don't worry, George," said the King. "If I know your friend, Jim Morgan, and you know him better than I, he will find some way to escape. He won't let the Cromiers do what they will with him, or with the Treasure of the Ocean."

"But you said if Jim used the Treasure, it would destroy him." George snuck a wary glance at the King. He knew he could not trust the dark man, but hadn't he seen the carvings in the rock with his own eyes? And what about the paintings in the cave on the Veiled Isle? They both showed the Treasure of the Ocean bringing nothing but destruction. Hadn't the calamity with the flute just proved the point?

"We could warn him," George said. "You could transport us to where Jim is. We can tell him. We can help him escape! He didn't believe you before, but he'll believe me. I know he will."

"Will he?" the King asked, meeting George's gaze. "How long has Jim been after the Treasure of the Ocean? Even longer than he's known you, isn't that so? Sometimes, George, when a man gets an idea in his head, when he sets his hopes on something for too long, there's no talking him out of it. Believe me, I know. One thing you must learn is that when you care about someone, and when you know what's good for him even better than he does, you must be ready to force him to do what's best."

"Force him?" George inched away from the King. "Jim is my friend. He wants to help people. He wants to do what's good."

"I know he does! But he can't help it that he's mistaken, now can he? That's why you must *force* him to do what you know is best. You don't have to hurt him, or that sweet girl, or your brothers. No, no, no. You must only be prepared to keep them from hurting themselves. I cannot do it, George. As I said, I'm just a shadow. But you…" The King flicked his eyes to the flute.

"What about the Cromiers?"

"Ho, ho, ho," said the King, laughing into the air, "the Cromiers! They are proper villains, aren't they? Usually, I would say that you must force the wicked to do what's right just as much as the good. Or punish them, like Jim punished me with the Amulet." A tremble flew over the King's face at the mention of that incident, but he was quick to hurry past it again. "In this case, why not let the Cromiers fall prey to their own wickedness? Let them use the Treasure of the Ocean. Let them be destroyed by it. That would only be fair, wouldn't it? That would be justice, right?" The King smiled at the thought, with sudden, terrible glee.

George was thinking hard, about Jim, Lacey, and his brothers. Hadn't Jim been reckless with the Black Rose, when he had stabbed himself with its poisonous thorn to get back at the Cromiers? Jim had been trying to do what was good then, hadn't he? And he'd nearly gotten himself killed. George had saved him then. He'd been a hero, hadn't he? He could do it again. He could prove that the Crystal Tower was just a mistake, that he hadn't meant to harm anything, that he was better than that.

"What if I mess up again?" asked George. The flute felt very heavy in his hand.

"Ah, now we come to where I can finally be of some use, George Ratt." The King folded his shape again, coiling through the air to rematerialize before George, down on his knees in the sand. "I can't, wish though I could, do anything with this shadowy body of mine in this world. Magic alone can touch me, and I alone can touch magic. But, I can also teach magic. I know magic better than any man on earth. I could show you how to wield it. If only you would give me this chance. If only you would give me this one opportunity to redeem myself."

George lifted the flute again. It was so heavy. His thoughts were heavy too, of Jim, of Lacey, of his brothers. He could save them. He could show them.

"All right, King," said George at last. "I'll let you show me. But if you try to trick me, if you try to use me like you did before..." George pointed the flute at the King's pale face.

"George, my boy," said the King, that honey smile stretched over his cheeks, "by the time you've learned what I can teach you, you'll be far too powerful for me to trick ever again."

So George put his flute to his lips and played. To help him along, to push him further through that window in his mind, the King placed his spidery fingers at George's temples, just to guide him on his way.

TWENTY-EIGHT

A Friend in the Dark

Jim Morgan?"

The whisper caught Jim by surprise, jerking him from a dreamless sleep. He scrambled deeper into his cell, until his back hit the wall. Wiping his tear-crusted eyes, Jim looked around, but he saw no one else in the dull torchlight. The other prisoners of the Dark Hole lay asleep in shivering lumps in the damp cave. The black chasm in the wall was all that stared back at Jim.

"Jim Morgan, is that you?" the invisible voice said again. Jim refused to answer. He wondered if, in addition to losing his hope, he was also losing his mind. But when the voice asked a third time, Jim at last risked a response.

"Yes," he said. "It's me. Who are you? Just another creature come to torment me?"

"No, my poor boy, no," said the voice. "I'm just an old friend, good for nothing though I might be." Around the corner of Jim's cell peeked a plump face. White hair sprouted in wings from his head, and he wore glasses so round they turned his eyes into those of an owl's. It was Egidio Quattrochi, the shopkeeper who lived in the shell on Spire Island and once taught Jim's father the workings of the Hunter's Shell.

"Egidio?" Jim asked, not believing his eyes.

"Yes, Jim, it's me." The old man inched his way into Jim's cell, pulling his own dirty rope behind him. "I was banished here by the Red Count for refusing to mend the Hunter's Shell, for refusing to aid him in his mad quest for power."

"It didn't matter, Egidio." Jim struggled to still his chin. "He mended the halves anyway. He killed MacGuffy. He has Lacey, Peter, Paul, and Cornelius. He sent me here, and now there's nothing to stop him from finding the Treasure of the Ocean. I've failed, Egidio. I've failed my father. I've failed everyone."

"Do not say such things!" Egidio seized Jim tight by the arm. "Our troglodyte guards can smell even the slightest hint of sorrow. They can smell despair and hopelessness like sharks smell blood in the water. It is worse when they hear you speak it aloud. They'll fly to your cell and fall on you like dogs to meat."

Jim shuddered, remembering the starved sniffing at his flesh and Grime's rough tongue on his face.

"How long do they keep people here?" Jim asked. "How long can they feed on a man?"

"For as long as he has even a mote of hope left in his heart, Jim." Egidio sat down beside Jim, speaking in hushed tones and keeping a lookout for Bog, Slag, and Grime. "I've watched them, those three slugs that keep guard over us. They thrive on suffering. But just as our sadness and sorrows feed them, so I think our hope, our courage, even the faintest wisp of our joy is like a deadly poison to them. But they can't stamp that all out completely. They work to keep the flame alive just enough so that you are reminded of the world outside, of your loved ones, of your dreams. They do this so that every time you doubt you will see any of them ever again, your sorrow will be that much deeper and that much more satisfying when they drink it down. That's why they let you keep your box, Jim. That's why they let me wear my apron." Egidio pointed to the filthy shopkeeper's apron, now not much more than a rag tied about his waist. "It reminds me of my work," he said. "It reminds me of what I love to do, and might never do again."

Jim squeezed his father's empty box. Like Egidio's apron, the box was accomplishing just what the ogres intended. It reminded Jim of his quest, of his friends – and how he had failed them all.

"Is that why the guards say you can escape through the chasm? Just to keep you thinking you could get out?" Jim flicked his eyes to the gash in the wall. The deeper blackness that cut the rock filled him with dread. The longer he stared at it the more he feared that the cave floor itself might betray him, tip him over, and feed him to the chasm.

"It is possible that it is only another cruel lie. But who knows? It may be true. I know this for certain though – something lives down there. When a man's hope is all used up, and his despair loses its decadence for Grime, Slag, and Bog, they throw him into the chasm. They wait for an hour or two, sometimes more, until screams eventually follow. Then those foul beasts feast on the echoes. Nevertheless, more than once I've been tempted to risk the chasm of my own free will – if only I weren't such a coward."

"Why?" asked Jim, grabbing Egidio's shoulder, desperate to keep the old shopkeeper from leaving him alone. "You said it yourself that there only *might* be a way out, but that there is for certain a creature down there, just waiting to devour men. Why would you even think about going down there?"

"Don't worry, lad." Egidio patted Jim on the hand. "I may have been dear friends with both your father and Dread Steele, but unlike them, I am a coward. I can't make myself cut free of this rope. But if

I were a bit braver, I do think I would at least have a chance that few others do."

"What chance is that, Egidio?"

"When you came here, did they take anything from you? Anything other than this box to which you now cling so tightly?"

"My mother's necklace," Jim said. He tried not to think of her face. If he thought of her here, in this place, of losing her forever, the ogres would feast for days. "The guards threw it into the chasm."

"Indeed. So it was when they found me." Egidio leaned even closer, speaking into Jim's ear. His great glasses glimmered like full moons in the torchlight. "But if only I had been a bit quicker in realizing these fiends' game, I could have escaped already. All I had with me when Cromier banished me here was my apron and my satchel, which I had been wearing when the Red Count came to call. When the creatures tore the bag from my arm, they found it empty. So they threw it into the chasm. But the satchel is not empty Jim. That little bag is more like a door – a hatch that leads to a great chest I kept hidden away. The chest contains my most prized possessions, not the least of which was one your father—"

A loud groan broke from the chasm in the wall, a rumbling like far off thunder. It cut Egidio off before he could finish. The old man took the rope that bound him to his cell and gripped it tight.

"What's that sound?" Jim asked.

"It is the clock striking the coming of night. The only clock we have in this awful place. It is our sunrise and sunset."

The cavern trembled. The vibrations hummed beneath Jim's seat, harder and harder until his arms and legs shook. The sound of *something* coming, like an avalanche or a thousand running feet, rushed toward the black mouth of the chasm.

"Egidio…"

"Hang on, Jim!"

The water burst from the chasm. It filled the cavern at once, slamming Jim and Egidio into the cave wall, throwing them under an instant flood. The water was so cold it shocked the breath from Jim's lungs. The icy sting hurt his skin. The beating he took against the rock walls bruised his bones. Jim took in a mouthful of water, salty as the sea, but tinged with some rotten taste it gathered from the tunnels. Jim began to choke. He tried to swim for the surface, but he was lost in the swirling tide.

In his panic, the box slipped from his grasp.

A terror, greater than even that of drowning, seized Jim by the throat. He thrashed about and opened his eyes, though they burned in the foul water. All was blackness beneath the wave. He began to swing his arms wildly, searching with his hands, desperately grabbing in the water.

When the air in his lungs was all but spent, he reached out once more, and his fingers found something hard and square – his father's box. Jim clutched it to his chest.

The tide began to recede, escaping back into the chasm. The draining pull yanked Jim hard against the end of his rope. Then it was over. Jim lay on the cave's cold floor as the water cleared away, choking for air, gulping it in, poor and stinking though it was. This would happen twice a day, every day, for as long as Jim lived in the Dark Hole. His heart sank. That was when the ogres appeared. They ran through the cavern, pausing by the fallen prisoners to lap up every last taste of misery.

"My, but fresh anguish do taste so fine in the evenin, don't it, Slag?" said Bog, leaning in over Jim, running his nose over Jim's shoulder. Slag leapt in beside him, doing the same above Jim's face.

"So scrumptious, Bog, so hearty and fillin and satisfyin, runnin all the way down to me core, just like what me own mum used to brew in our cave."

Jim gripped his box tight, hoping for it all to be over soon. But even then, still coughing out seawater, his hopelessness sopped up by two, soul-stealing ogres, Jim's eyes flicked to the black chasm. The darkness was staring back at him – calling to him.

TWENTY-NINE

LACEY AND BARTHOLOMEW

For the better part of a day, Lacey cradled Cornelius in her lap while Peter toiled over the copper ring holding shut the raven's beak. They were all prisoners on the brig of the *Sea Spider,* which made all speed for England, where the Treasure of the Ocean was hidden in a dark cave.

Peter cut himself more than once and wore his fingertips raw fiddling with the wire's sharp ends. But in spite of the injuries, the task was at least something to occupy his restless mind. Paul, on the other hand, had nothing to do but pester Peter the entire time, giving unwarranted advice about how Peter should twist left instead of right, or push instead of pull, or asking every few minutes if he was quite done already.

"Would you just shut it, Paul?" Peter must have said a dozen times. "I'll be finished when I'm finished."

Lacey, when she once would have lectured the boys on brotherly love, just let the tufts go. She knew the two of them were tired. She knew how they missed their brother.

Lacey missed George too... and Jim.

She swallowed the thick lump in her throat and went back to patting Cornelius's feathers. The poor bird could hardly breath with the copper ring about his beak. He certainly could not eat or drink. After a day and night, locked in the steel cage, Lacey had begun to fear for Cornelius's life, prompting Peter to do whatever he could.

Before that, the two Ratts had been focused on retrieving their coats, or more specifically, Peter's coat, from the floor outside the cage. Neither of them was cold, nor looking to use the coat as a pillow. What they really wanted was the leather pouch hidden in Peter's left pocket – the leather pouch containing a particular set of pins.

Paul had successfully conned a Corsair guard to let him and his brother out of the cage to inspect the hull for termites. Unfortunately, the guard's overseer was not nearly as dull. He arrived just as the Ratts were making a play for the coat and boxed them both on sides of the head – Peter on the left and Paul on the right – leaving them with a swollen black eye each.

"If I only had me pins," Peter grumbled again after cutting another one of his fingers. "We'd be out of this bloody cage already."

"And go where, Peter?" Lacey said. "We're in the middle of the ocean, remember? I don't think any of us could swim all the way to Spire Island."

"I'd like to make that count go swimmin," said Paul, slamming his fist into his palm. "Him and his creepy son, both." Lacey half wanted to remind Paul not to say such awful things. But then she thought of MacGuffy, and of Jim, banished to who-knew-where, and realized she was only pretending to not want the same thing. A sharp plink snapped those dark thoughts as Peter finally undid the copper ring.

"Got it," he cried, sitting back against the cage and wiping his brow with the back of his hand.

"Oh, well done, Peter," said Lacey, squeezing his arm. "Well done."

"Good job, Pete," Paul added. For the first time in a day the two brothers shared a smile.

Cornelius stretched open his beak and drew in a long, thirsty breath. He tried to speak, but only a dry croak scraped over his little tongue. Lacey had been saving a single sip of water from the lone tin the Corsairs provided her and the Ratts. She poured the few drops into her palm and let Cornelius drink.

"Oh, that is so much better," Cornelius finally managed. "Thank you sweet Lacey for the drink. And my dear boy," Cornelius flapped with some effort to Peter and patted his leg with a feathered wing. "Thank you for the gift of your deft fingers and clever mind. I don't think I would have lasted much longer if you had not freed me."

"You know, old Darkfeather," said Paul, "you may not believe this, but I was actually beginnin to miss the sound of your voice, and maybe even one of your stories to pass the time."

"Lad, should we manage to escape these villains," said the Raven, "you and your brother will play a part in the greatest tale I will ever tell."

"I think even George would appreciate that, Cornelius," said Lacey. "He *will* appreciate it, I mean," she corrected. "Once we're all together again."

"Well, for better or for worse, my friends," Cornelius said, hopping back up onto Lacey's lap, "I know for a fact your bother is alive, Master Ratts. But what worries me is the company in which he now finds himself."

"What do you mean?" Lacey asked. "George had the enchanted flute, Cornelius, the one that used to belong to Philus Philonius. Surely he used that to disappear, didn't he?"

"Ah, but Lacey dear, I do not think George escaped by the power of the flute. In truth, I don't believe he left the Crystal Tower of his own accord at all."

"If George had disappeared with the flute, he woulda taken us with him. I know it!" said Paul.

"Precisely," said the Raven. "But what is more, in that instant your brother was whisked away, I was sure I saw a form in the black magic. It was a face I had seen only once before, of that sallow thief that caused you so much trouble in London."

"The King of Thieves?" Peter leaned forward, eyes wide. "Jim said he thought he saw the King's ghost back on Spire Island. But how could he be here? How can he be alive?"

"The King certainly seemed to know a great deal about magic, even back in London," said Lacey. "But even so, I don't understand how he could be back. He was swallowed whole by green fire when Jim broke the Amulet, wasn't he?"

"Indeed, sweet Lacey. But swallowed to where? I will tell you this – I thought I had seen much in the presence of Dread Steele, all those years we sailed the seven seas. But since I met Jim Morgan I have seen more magic, monsters, and miracles than I ever dreamed possible. With a talisman as powerful as the Treasure of the Ocean at stake, who knows what forces might be in play? Forces of good – and of evil. A great battle is brewing, my friends, one that may decide the fate of all people for a thousand years."

The thought of such a battle turned Lacey's stomach and set her teeth on edge. It reminded her why she could not lose hope. It reminded her that she and the clan still had to do all they could to thwart the Cromiers. But it also made her think of Jim, and all those carvings of destruction and ruin she had seen on the stone pylon in the crystal tower.

"The bird is right you know," said a voice from beyond the cage. Lacey and the Ratts cringed. From a shadow by the wall stepped Bartholomew Cromier, sword at his side, skin pale against his blood red coat. "There is a battle coming. Do as you're told and you may even live long enough to see it."

"Please don't put the ring back on," Lacey cried, slipping her fingers over Cornelius's beak to keep the raven from saying something they might all regret. "He can hardly breath in that ring, and he can't get any water either. It will kill him if you do."

"Leave it off for all I care." Bartholomew said. "The bird can squawk his head off day and night. It makes no mind to me. Of course, if he says the wrong thing around my father, it will be off with some head or another." Bartholomew stalked to the cage and peered through the bars at Peter and Paul, smiling cruelly. The two brothers backed away from him, Paul's hands trembling at his sides.

Lacey had seen enough. She stood up, handing Cornelius to Peter, and placed herself between Bartholomew and the boys. She locked her fiery blue eyes with Bartholomew's. It was just like standing up to Big Red, she reminded herself. It was like standing up to any bully – even one that was a sword-wielding son of a mad count.

"So, is that all you came down here for, then? To frighten people in chains? To pick fights with unarmed prisoners?"

"You know, I remember your face, little girl. You were there, outside the Pirate Vault of Treasures, in London, when Dread Steele saved your life. You were also there on the deck of the *Spectre*, when the Lord of the Pirates was struck down dead."

"No thanks to you," said Lacey. "I seem to remember helping Jim pull your body back onto the deck about that time. Of course you wouldn't remember that would you? You were knocked out cold."

A dark flush crested Bartholomew's pale cheeks.

"You didn't see me run from him though, did you? The greatest pirate to ever sail the seven seas, they say, and I faced him – three times."

"And lost three times, by my count."

Bartholomew took the cage door with both hands, shaking it so hard the hinges cried out. He slammed his face between two bars, baring his teeth like a wolf, a line of red glowing hot on his cheeks.

"Do not test me, girl. Do not test me, or I will show you what I am not afraid to do. Steele is dead. MacGuffy is dead. Lindsay Morgan is dead. Jim Morgan might as well be dead. I am the last man standing. There is no one left to rescue you from me!"

A rapid thump, like an urgent knock, beat against the inside of Lacey's chest. She pursed her lips to keep them from quivering and forced herself to inch forward, just a bit closer to the cage bars and Bartholomew's bared teeth.

"No one except your father, isn't that right?" She watched Bartholomew's snarl quiver at the edges. "Go on then. Show me what you're not afraid to do. Reach through the bars and kill me."

Bartholomew growled in his throat. He squeezed the bars so tight that Lacey could hear his leather gloves groaning against the steel. But he did not touch her. Lacey risked another inch closer. And another, until her nose was nearly touching Bartholomew's.

"See," said Lacey. "There is one person left to save us. Your daddy. And you *are* afraid of him."

"You know nothing of fear!" Spittle flew from Bartholomew's lips to land on Lacey's face. "Nothing!" He yanked again on the cage door, nearly pulling it off its hinges. But Lacey stood her ground. In that burst of rage she saw through the cold surface of Bartholomew's eyes. She caught a glimpse beneath the ice. Bartholomew did know fear. He knew it well.

"But I will teach you, little rat girl," Bartholomew railed on. "You will learn the very fiber from which fear is knit together. I came down here to tell you that we'll be going ashore soon. And after that you will know why we kept you street trash alive. When you stand as close to that thing in the cave as you stand to me, you will know fear."

Bartholomew shoved off from the cage and leveled a black-gloved finger at Lacey's face. "The same rules for the raven apply to you now, little girl. Loose your tongue again, and I loose my blade... on them." Bartholomew slowly panned his finger over Lacey's shoulder, to where Peter and Paul huddled behind her. He then spun on his heel to march back to the steps.

"You won't hurt us," Lacey called after him. "You need us to go through another door for you."

Bartholomew froze by the steps, his back still turned.

"Jim went into the Vault of Treasures. Jim went into the serpent cave on the Veiled Isle. I'll go into this cave. If you were any kind of man, wouldn't you be the one to go first through a door one of these days?"

Bartholomew's shoulders went still, the kind of still that requires all the strength in one's body and soul. His hand squeezed his sword. But the young Cromier said nothing. After a moment he simply took the stairs, all but flying back to the main deck.

"And you held my beak, shut," Cornelius said with a huff, flapping up to Lacey's shoulder.

"Cornelius is right, Lacey," said Peter. "What were you thinkin talkin to that crazy bloke like that? Did you see his eyes? He'll murder us all in our sleep!"

"Or murder us awake for that matter," agreed Paul. But Lacey was still staring after Bartholomew.

"Like you said, Cornelius," Lacey said quietly, "a battle is coming. And I told you all before, we're going to fight."

THIRTY

EGIDIO'S TALE
AND THE MAN IN THE DREAM

H ow much do you know of the Treasure of the Ocean, Jim?" asked Egidio. Jim and the old shopkeeper sat together in the cave, drenched from another flooding and exhausted from another bout of ogres' feeding.

"I know a little," Jim answered with a sigh, his eyes fixed on the stony floor. "I know that the Treasure is the key and the altar is the lock, and together they open a door to the world of magic. My mother told me that the door has to be held open for the magic to come through, that the magic needs a vessel. But I don't know what that means. I also know that all the carvings and paintings show that old, great city destroyed. That's all."

Egidio grunted, leaning back against Jim's cell wall, rearranging his rope to make himself more comfortable. Jim heard the old man wipe his greasy glasses on his filthy apron, as though it would do any good. Then Egidio sighed the sort of sigh that comes before a long story. His voice changed, dipping into that deeper sort of voice that opens the mind's eye.

"There once was a great city, the capital of the world, if you will – the greatest city that ever was. In this city there were two princes, the Elder and the Younger. The Elder loved the Younger very much, but the Younger brother secretly envied the Elder, for as the second son, he would never be king. Whoever sat upon the throne commanded great magic, for the crown and the scepter were powerful talismans. But the Younger, clever man that he was, always suspected there was more magic just beyond the king's reach. So he began to study. He delved deeper into the magical arts than any man before or since. In secret he crafted a scepter of his own, a weapon with which he would seize power for himself."

"The golden trident," Jim said, tracing that very symbol on the lid of his father's box with his finger. "The Treasure of the Ocean."

"Yes. But for all the Younger had learned of magic and power, there was one lesson he had yet to grasp. The Treasure opens the door between our world and the world of magic. But as your mother told you, in order for the door to remain open, something must hold it so. The Younger opened the doorway, and at once the magic began to fill him. It began to transform him."

"Transform him?" Jim finally turned his eyes from the stone floor to Egidio.

"You see, Jim, what the Younger failed to understand, what most men fail to understand, even good men like your father, is that to achieve ultimate power, you *become* the power. It is not only your enemies that are sacrificed. It is also your self. You have seen a small imitation of what the Younger nearly became, haunting your footsteps upon the seas."

"The Crimson Storm?"

"Yes. All that remains of Lord Winter – Count Cromier's first hired thug. But the Crimson storm is only a shadow of the power that can be unleashed if the doorway is opened. The Younger began to turn into such power. He could not control it. He destroyed the very city he meant to rule."

"Why didn't he end up destroying the whole world?"

"His brother, the Elder Prince, stopped him. He somehow managed to close the doorway between the worlds before it was too late – but not without cost. The Elder was thrown into the sea. The Treasure's transformative powers changed him as well. He became the first merman. The Younger, reduced by his folly, became a lesser version of the man he had once been. They are the fathers of our races, Jim. That is why you are able to use the Treasure. Your mother is of the Elder's lineage, and your father of the Younger. You are the Son of the Earth and the Son of Sea."

"So it doesn't really matter if Bartholomew or I use the Treasure," Jim said. "Neither of us could control the power. Both of us would turn into a storm."

"Yes, that is true."

"Then what's the point of it all, Egidio?" Jim cried. "Have all these people died for nothing?"

"The point is that ruling the world is a hopeless, impossible task, no matter the power you possess." Egidio reached out an old, trembling finger and tapped Jim twice on his chest with it, over his heart. "So focus on ruling this instead. The one who truly wins the battles waged there, the one who conquers the kingdom within, realizes he need rule nothing else in the world. He is the one that changes the world. That is what your father, Steele, and MacGuffy died for, Jim. It is a worthy cause."

Egidio leaned back again, folding his hands over his dirty apron. Jim went back to staring at the floor. His mind was turning Egidio's story over and over, trying to understand what he was supposed to do. But his father's box, resting on his lap, felt heavier than ever, like a large rock pinning him to the floor.

Jim's nightmare began where it usually ended, at the burning of Morgan Manor. The house fell to the flames. Count Cromier's and Bartholomew's faces appeared in the fire and smoke. The temple ruins climbed from the rubble that was once Jim's house. The Treasure of the Ocean was speared into the stone altar and the black hole ripped the sky open, releasing the powers from beyond into this world. It was the end of the dream…

…but Jim did not wake up. The dream changed again.

It was not the King of Thieves who appeared, as had happened on the Spectre. It was another shade from the past, one who had visited Jim's dreams before to warn him of the Crimson Storm. It was the shadow man, his face hidden in darkness, a red-hot sword in his hand. Now he pointed the glowing blade to the column of black smoke rising from Jim's burnt home – to Bartholomew's face still smiling in the billows. The winds from the black hole in the sky swirled the smoke into dark storm clouds. The thunderhead boiled and grew. Bartholomew's face stretched wider and wider in the folds, until he blotted out the moon and the stars, until his eyes burned with lightning and his mouth rumbled with thunder.

Lightning began to fall. The bolts clawed at the earth, churning up the soil and setting fire to the grass and the trees. The ground shook beneath Jim's feet, as if the world was going to tear itself in two.

Jim broke for the temple steps. He had to close the door. He had to pull out the golden trident. But before he could reach the stairs, a fist of rock and steel burst up from the ground, ensnaring him in a trap. It was his cell in the Dark Hole, but now the entrance to the cavity was sealed with iron bars. Jim threw himself against the cage. He pushed and pulled with all his might, but he could not escape.

Jim looked helplessly about as the earth fell into ruin. "Help!" he cried to the shadow man, for there was no one else to turn to. "Let me out of here. I have to stop this before everything is destroyed."

The shadow man said nothing, nor did he move.

"Please," Jim screamed. "If you won't release me, then pull the Treasure of the Ocean from the stone altar yourself. Stop this before we lose everything."

Finally, the shadow man stepped toward Jim's prison. His molten sword wilted the grass beneath its tip as he passed.

"I'm afraid I can't help you, Jim," said the man.

Jim knew that voice, but it had been a long time since he had heard it. The dark figure stopped just beyond the bars. He reached up and pulled at the shroud about his face. It came away like sticky spider webs. When it was gone, Jim knew the face underneath.

"Father," Jim whispered. He was here, as real as he had been in the Pirate Vault in London. "Father, you must help me. You must let me out. Or take the trident yourself."

"I can't, Jim," said his father. He stuck his burning sword into the ground and removed his hat, holding it in his hands. "I'm sorry. Much like in the Vault, I'm not much more than a ghost now – just a memory. Only the troubles I made for you remain."

Lightning sizzled everywhere, sparking fires and laying waste to everything that was green. The earth shook again, so violently Jim thought it would split open and swallow him whole.

"Then what can I do, father?"

In the middle of the world's ending, with Bartholomew's thunderous laughter rolling in the sky and fire raging across the land, Lindsay Morgan smiled – the most serene smile Jim had ever seen.

"Break free, Jim," he said. "Break free."

"I can't," Jim said, yanking once more on the bars. They seemed moored to the foundations of the earth. "I'm not strong enough."

"Yes, you are, son. Yes, you are."

"No, father, I'm not like you. I've been trying to be, but I'm not."

Jim hung his head, fighting his tears. "I'm not strong like you were."

"Who said you had to be like me to be strong?"

Jim lifted his eyes. He found his father still smiling.

It was his father's smile that gave him hope. Jim pulled at the bars with everything he had. He pulled until he screamed from the effort. The iron bars began to give. They bent and shook. Then they snapped in his hands. Jim pulled them down. He broke his cell to pieces, tearing it apart with his bare hands.

"I did it, father," Jim shouted, but only the thunder and the wind answered. His father was gone. Behind Jim, where he had broken out of his prison, lay not a pile of stones, but the remains of a shattered, wooden box, a familiar symbol carved into its lid. And before him, his father's burning sword was stabbed into the ground.

Jim took the sword. The broken box he left behind.

He climbed the stairs.

He neared the altar.

He waded forth into the dark storm…

Jim snapped awake. He felt feverish. Sweat poured down his cheeks. But the cold cave air soon chilled his body and stung his skin again. He sat up, stiff and slow, his back aching from the sharp teeth of the stone floor. The soggy rope cinched about his waist had chaffed his skin raw.

Sitting there in the dark, Jim's eyes fell on an even deeper black in the cavern, the chasm in the wall. It seemed strange to him then, how similar the chasm looked to the rip in the sky from his dream.

"Not a chasm," Jim said to himself after a while. "It's a doorway."

THIRTY-ONE

To the Cave in the Mountains

Beneath a dreary sky, a caravan of wagons rattled along a rut-strewn road. The road traced the edge of a lake, or loch, as the people of that hard country called it. But there were no birds or animals gathered about the waters. This was an empty stretch of land. In the back of one of the wagons Lacey, Peter, and Paul, huddled together, iron chains looped about their wrists and ankles.

The damp, northern air clung to Lacey's skin. It robbed the feeling from her fingers and toes and chilled her bones until they ached. She felt Peter and Paul shivering beside her. She tried to pull them close to share her warmth, but there was precious little to go around. The Corsairs had even kept the boys' jackets from them, and worse, Peter's pins within one of the pockets

"Well this is the most cheerless part of all England, innit?" Peter said. He stared morosely at the long stretch of field running away from the gray lake, his eyes chilly as the weather. "Even the grass looks hard as rock."

"I don't know about that, Pete," said Paul, pointing up ahead with a shaking finger. "I actually think *that* might be the most cheerless part of all England."

Lacey had no need to look. Several times already she had glanced ahead. She knew what lay before them. The rough road wound between two hills, lifeless and drab as old bones. After that, the path disappeared in a gray fog, thick as snow clouds in winter. Above the mist and beyond the hills, snow-capped peaks rose up like the tips of a monster's claws. The cold in Lacey's bones crept into her heart. But when she saw the forlorn looks in the Ratt Brothers' eyes, she clamped her teeth down tight and fought the cold away with what little hot anger she could muster.

"Whatever's up there, we'll face it together," she said. "I've been thinking. If Count Cromier has kept us alive, and dragged us this far into the north to get the treasure for him, he must truly believe we'll be able to bring it back. That should give us hope, don't you think?"

"Well, we are the greatest thieves in all of England, aren't we?" said Peter. "That's what George would say, right?" A brief smile flashed across his freckled face, there and gone again. Peter and Paul were longing for their brother, missing him every bit as much as she was missing—

Lacey gritted her teeth, harrumphing away the knot in her throat. There was more to think about than just their missing friends. The world itself was at stake. "Cornelius," she said, changing the subject. "Do those mountains up ahead have a name?"

"Indeed they do, milady," squawked Cornelius, lifting his head from beneath his wing, where he had been trying to keep warm as well. "They are called the An Cuilthionn, in the old tongue of this land. But modern folk call them the Black Cuillin. We are far to the north of England – in Scotland, my young friends."

"Know any stories 'bout this place, Darkfeather?" said Paul, rubbing his arms with blue-fingered hands. "Anythin to pass the time?"

"Maybe some legends that might tell us what we'll be facin up there?" added Peter. But Cornelius only ruffled his feathers and shook his head. He flapped his wings and made a short flight up to Lacey's shoulder.

"I'm afraid not, Master Ratt. Most of my stories are sea stories, you know. Did I ever tell you both about Freddy Nine Fingers? He—"

"Became Freddy Sevens and then Freddy the Stump," said Peter and Paul in a droning chorus.

"Only ten times already, Darkfeather."

"You really need some new material, mate."

"Well then, don't ask! And I assure you, the pages in my mind have been filling up with all manner of new stories over the last couple of days. I'm just hoping I'm around long enough to see how they turn out. So, if you're so keen on a story, perhaps you should learn to tell them yourself, Master Paul. You certainly have the mouth for it, my boy."

"I could tell about the time me and Pete fought with a giant owl on the Veiled Isle," Paul said. He and Peter immediately began to regale in the story, about how the giant owl had come to snatch them up near the Mountain's Tears, which was the river that split the Veiled Isle in two, and how they had overcome the owl, and ridden on its back to chase down Lacey, who had been captured. Of course, Lacey remembered that story a bit differently. Most notably, she recalled that both boys had been screaming like babies in the owl's clutches the entire way, but she let them tell it their way.

"You're not a very good liar, Cornelius," Lacey whispered to the raven on her shoulder while the Ratts carried on with their story.

"You do know legends of these mountains, don't you?" Cornelius coughed indignantly, puffing up his chest, about to launch into a long tirade defending his honor. But the bird's black eyes caught Lacey's honest blues, and he lowered his wings like shoulders slumping.

"Yes, milady, I do," he said quietly.

"Do I want to know what they are?"

"No, milady, you do not."

Some hours later, the wagons broke through the fog bank on the crest of a barren hill. The mountains spread out before them, armored in black rock and frosted in snow. In the heart of the range, one peak stood out from the rest, darkened in shadows. A cave opened up in that mountainside, like a crying mouth, an awful, moaning face in the rock. From the mouth flowed a river that ran down through the hills and emptied into the lake, miles behind them. It was to this place the wagons headed. Lacey could feel the cave's blackness reaching out to her, all the way to where she sat at the back of the wagon.

Not much later the caravan came to a stop. The Corsairs climbed down from their seats, stretching their backs and groaning with loud echoes into the mountains. Count Cromier and Bartholomew emerged from their carriage. Lacey, who could no longer feel her fingers or toes, thought the thick furs draped over their shoulders looked like the softest, warmest coats she had ever seen.

"Is this not a fitting end to my journey?" announced Cromier, stretching his arms to the mountains. "From the white caps of the sea to the white peaks of the earth we have ventured. Now my prize is at last within my grasp."

"Our grasp, don't you mean?" said Bartholomew. His voice was as icy as the snowcaps.

"Your glory is coming shortly, Bartholomew," said his father. "Let an old man have his moment. Bring us the girl and the whelps." Cromier snapped his gloved fingers. The Corsairs shoved Lacey and the Ratts before the count. No sooner had they come within reach than the count snatched Cornelius from Lacey's arms.

"Cornelius, no!" Lacey shrieked.

"Unhand me, you cur!" shouted the raven.

"Silence, the both of you." The count wrapped his fingers around Cornelius's throat. "Another peep and I'll end this chattering buffoon's life right before your eyes." Lacey shut her mouth. She suddenly felt her cheeks and her arms again, her old fury heating them up as her fingers curled into fists.

"Good," said the count, noting the simmering quiet. He nodded toward the Ratts. "Now, you two, once the payment has been accepted, you will bring me my prize. If you succeed, I will let you and the bird go free. After that, if you can make it back down the mountain, I'll have even spared your lives."

"Payment?" said Peter, narrowing his eyes on the count. "Whaddya mean, payment?"

"I thought we was gonna have to go through some traps and such, like Jim did before?" said Paul.

"Oh, no, no, no. This is nothing like before." A smile curled on the count's craggy face. He rested his dark eyes on Lacey. "Do you think I would force this beautiful, young girl to face such tasks? To brave dangers on my behalf? I would never – and she is so beautiful, and so sweet, with hair like autumn and eyes like summer, and a spirit like spring. She is nearly the mirror image of a young girl from so long ago – a princess from olden times." The count's wrinkled lips shivered on his face. "No, lads, I intend to offer her as a gift. I intend to trade her for my Treasure."

"You coward!" crowed Cornelius. "Where is your hono—" Cornelius's insult ended in a choked squawk. The count squeezed his throat between his fingers.

"No, Cornelius, stay quiet," Lacey cried, tears blossoming behind her eyes.

"If you value the bird's life, you'll do as I say. Now, tie her up," the count shouted to the Corsairs. Then to the Ratts, "And you two, once we've lowered her into the cave, you will follow and—"

"No!" Lacey shouted, her voice harsh and hot. The count's eyes, black bags dark as coals beneath them, flew open wide, as though he had been slapped. "No ropes. I'm not a goat that you lead to market, Count. I'm not a sheep that you drag to the shearers. I've sailed the seas with Dread Steele. I've learned the stars in the sky and I know their meanings. I've ridden the backs of water dragons with true friends. No one trades me for anything. I go where I choose. And I go for my own reasons. Now, Peter and Paul are cold. Give them their jackets at least and we'll all go in together."

The Corsair pirates stared at Lacey. The count stared at her as well, like seeing a work of art he could not quite decipher. But Lacey looked past them all, to Bartholomew, who seemed to want nothing more than to shrink into his warm furs beneath the flashing heat of her gaze.

"When I walk through that door, me, just a girl, at least I'll be able to do it with my head held high. And I'll know I had more courage than the great warrior, Bartholomew Cromier." As if in a trance, the pirates, who had only days before laughed at and mocked the boys, fetched their coats like butlers, and even set them on their shoulders. Another pirate handed Lacey a torch, keeping his distance, as though terrified she might turn him to ash with a blast of lightning from her eyes. Without a word more than that, Lacey turned on her heel and strode toward the cave, the Ratt Brothers running to catch up.

As she had whirled about to march away, Lacey was sure she had seen Bartholomew hang his head. And though Lacey had rarely held a sword in her life, she knew she had outdueled the raven-haired captain.

"That was somethin, Lacey," said Peter, nearly breathless. "That was something, alright."

"I think whatever is waitin for us in here should be more scared of you than you of it," said Paul.

Lacey smiled, but inside, her heart pattered. It was only a few paces before the blackness inside the cave swallowed her and her friends whole. Lacey wondered if it would be the last time she ever saw the sky, and she wished it had been on a summer night, when she could see the stars over the sea and perhaps hold Jim's hand. But a cold, gray sky over the mountains would have to do.

"Keep your distance once we get inside," she said to the Ratts. "We don't know much about whatever is waiting for us in here, but we know this – it wants me. It wants me more than even the Treasure of the Ocean. Whatever you do, don't let it take you when it comes for me."

The Ratts nodded, their faces pale. Lacey squeezed their hands in hers, perhaps for the final time. She swallowed down her fear, and then she and the Ratts descended into the dark.

THIRTY-TWO

Through the Chasm in the Wall

The floodwaters roared into the cave, tossing Jim about and snapping his body against the length of his rope, all but drowning him. As before, Jim held tight to his box, refusing to let it go.

But that is where the repetition ended. Since waking from his dream, Jim had not spoken one word, or hardly made even a sound. He had been waiting – waiting for this moment.

When the waters receded, Jim refused to choke and cough. He did not crawl on his hands and knees to his cell. He jumped to his feet and pushed the wet strands of hair from his eyes. The ogres, indulging themselves on the pitiful moans of the prisoners, ignored him at first, as he strode to where Egidio lay on the stone floor.

"Get up, Egidio," Jim said. "It's time to leave."

"Leave? Jim Morgan, where will we go?"

Jim threw his head back over his shoulder, toward the black chasm, smiling cruelly from the wall. Egidio's owlish eyes grew wider still. His old hands trembled as he adjusted his glasses. His chapped lips quivered.

"But Jim," he said. "The ropes. They're swollen from the water. We cannot untie the knots. It will take us days and days to unravel the cords that hold us here." Egidio gave a feeble tug at his rope. Jim doubted for a moment whether or not Egidio really wanted to untie his knot and face the tunnel. But he would not leave his friend here.

"Don't worry. I'm going to cut us free in just a moment. I have a plan."

"A plan, he saaaaays?" A slithering voice crept over Jim's shoulder. "There are no plans in the Dark Hooole, in this cave of soooorrows. There is morning and night, there is waters that drown, there is you and there is us!" Egidio shrank back as Grime rose behind Jim. Jim turned slowly to face the ogre guard.

"Yes," Jim said. "A plan."

Grime laughed. He threw his head back and roared. Bog and Slag came to the sound of their boss's chortling, leers painted on their freshly fed faces.

"Do you think, little maaaan, that this rope alone binds you to this place?" Grime leveled a warty, crooked finger at Jim's face. "The truth is, the only folks who wind up in this cave are the very folks that deserve to be here – the looosers, the defeated, the unworthy, and the faaaailures. Which of those are you, Jim Morgan? Oh yes, I have learned of you. When I taste the delicious sweetness of your despaaaair, I swish your memories in the back of my throat like a fiiiine wine. You have lost all that was left to you. You have abandoned your friends. You let your father and Dread Steele and MacGuffy die. And now, of all the riches and promise that were once yours, all that remains is that empty, wooden box. You have noooothing Jim Morgan!"

Grime jabbed his finger at the box. He thrust his scaly face into Jim's, his bulbous eyes bulging and his nostrils flaring. Jim looked down at his box, the small companion that had been with him ever since he'd run away, so long ago. For a moment, his fingers trembled. The plan wavered in his mind. He squeezed the box tight to steady his hand.

"That's not true," he said. Then Jim drew back his arm and slammed the box into the center of Grime's leathery head. The wooden frame exploded into shards and splinters. The ogre guard straightened up like a chopped tree, tipped over backwards, and fell flat on his back with a thud that reverberated through the cave.

"*Now* I have nothing. So I'll take my chances." Jim reached down and took the knife from Grime's belt. With the blade he cut himself and Egidio free from their binds. Bog and Slag, far from charging Jim to avenge their boss, fell back from him, gnarled hands covering their mouths and noses.

"Gads!" cried Bog. "What is that stench?"

"It's awful," screamed Slag. "It's the most awful reek I ever smelled. I think I'm gonna lose me lunch."

"It's courage," said Jim. He stalked over Bog, who was both fatter and slower than Slag. He grabbed the ogre by the ankle before he could scurry away and pinned the scaly creature down. He leaned in close over his face, so that the foul guard could do nothing but breath in Jim's new scent. "Haven't smelled courage in a while, have you? Well, get your fill, you poltroon. Learn this scent and learn it well."

"I'll hear your screams if you go down there," Bog wailed, twisting and turning to free himself from Jim's grasp. "I'll drink them up and laugh me head off when I know you're dead."

"You had better hope you hear me scream, you filth. Because if you don't, you're going to smell this scent again. When you smell it, you'll know I'm coming. And if I find that you have not released the rest of these poor souls from this place..." Jim let Grime's dagger gleam in the torchlight. "You'll learn what justice smells like next."

Jim finally released the ogre, who scampered away like a terrified lizard. Using the ropes that had once tied them to their cells, Jim and Egidio dragged down two torches from high on cave walls. Armed thus, with a dagger and firelight, they stood before the gaping black chasm in the cave wall. Jim climbed on the lip and stretched forth his torch. The black hole descended further than the light could reach.

"Jim, I…" Egidio began to say, his voice atremble. But Jim would not let the old shopkeeper finish. He grabbed the man by his shirt and pulled him onto the lip beside him.

"We'll hear you scream, you blackguards," raged Slag from the cave, though he dared not show his face. He was hiding in one of the cells, cowering behind some of the prisoners. "We'll hear you scream until you're dead from it!"

Jim ignored the ogre. He took a deep breath, grit his teeth, and held tight to his torch. He stilled the churning in his stomach and, pulling Egidio behind him, took the first step into the black.

Jim could not be sure how far into the depths he and Egidio had ventured after an hour or so of walking, but it was far enough to leave even the echoes of Slag's vengeful rant behind. For a long stretch there was only the rhythm of Jim and Egidio breathing, and the whisper of their torch flames burning.

"Jim, a question, if you please," whispered Egidio after a time, as though there might be many ears in the dark. "Your father's box – it certainly made a fine weapon with which to bludgeon that wretched creature in the cavern. But you seemed to relish its destruction. Why?"

"I think because, for the longest time, I used the box to keep safe everything I held dear. But that was the problem, Egidio. Everything I really hold dear can't possibly fit in a little box – and neither can I."

"Jim Morgan," said Egidio with a laugh, "I think you may become a wiser man than even myself, one day. And that is saying something. In fact I—"

A harsh rasp smothered Egidio's fact. Jim and the old shopkeeper froze, holding their breaths and straining their ears to hear over the whispering torches.

"Did you hear that?" Jim asked after a moment. The answer came before Egidio could speak.

Over here.

Jim flinched at the sound of the voice. There was no denying it now. Someone – or something – had spoken. Jim panned the torch back and forth before him. He saw nothing but rocks and shadows.

"Who's there?" he called. "Who speaks?"

Up ahead, just a little further. The exit is this way!

At the edge of the torchlight's reach, Jim thought he saw a flicker of movement in the tunnel. But he could not be sure. He drew Grime's dagger from his belt and held it before him beside the torch. Behind such defenses he and Egidio inched their way forward.

Trust me, my friends. I mean you no harm. I can help you escape... as I once did.

"It would be easier to trust you if you would show yourself," said Jim.

Must stay hidden, my friends. Must stay out of sight. But fear not. I will show you the way.

"Egidio," Jim whispered as he and the shopkeeper crept forward a half step at a time. "Do you remember anyone escaping during your time in the cave?"

"Not that I can recall, young Morgan." Egidio walked so close behind Jim that his own torch was stretched before Jim's face as well. "There were several prisoners that Grime and the others threw down here. Certainly, no one ever went willingly, until the two fools who did so today. But every time a prisoner went down, only screams came back."

I escaped long before the old man came to this place, young one. I have returned to help others find the way.

229

Jim and Egidio took a start at the voice's words. Whoever it was, Jim thought, he certainly had very good ears. Jim was just about to ask the voice how it stayed so thoroughly hidden in such a tight space, and why he and Egidio needed guidance in a straight tunnel, when they came to a split in the path. There were not only two ways in the fork, but three. One ran straight ahead, one turned sharply to the right, and the other slightly to the left.

See, my friends. A tricky maze this is. Take the wrong way, and only death awaits you. Take the right way, and freedom shall be yours. Follow me!

Another flicker of movement and a shuffle of feet came from the tunnel on the right. Jim and Egidio looked at each other, but with no better idea between the two of them, they turned to follow the unseen speaker.

Yes, yes, my friends. You've chosen wisely. This is the way. We must hurry, though, for the waters will soon rise again.

"Might you not slow down a bit?" asked Jim, for the flitting shadow was moving more quickly, always staying just out of the light's reach. Jim and Egidio found themselves shuffling faster and faster to keep up. "Might you not walk beside us, or with us?"

No time, my friends. No time. The waters are coming... and that which lurks at the end of the cave. Hungry it is... hungry for lost travelers like us.

Jim shivered at the thought of something lurking around in the tunnel behind he and Egidio – something with a taste for flesh. But there was a creeping doubt at the back of his mind. Why would the stranger not show himself? Why stay here after having escaped? But he and Egidio were now all but running to keep up, and they had come to at least three more forks in the way. Sometimes the whisper took them left, sometimes right. Jim was beginning to realize he had no way to retrace his steps back the way they had come.

"Please, slow down a bit!" Jim cried at last. He could hear Egidio beginning to wheeze, the old man's tired body weakened after so much time in the cave. "We need a breather." Jim stopped in the tunnel and let Egidio catch up. When the old shopkeeper finally came beside him, Jim motioned for him to lean against the tunnel wall and gather his breath.

No time for breathers. No time for rest. The water is coming... The creature is coming!

"But how do we know you're really a friend? How do we know this is the right way? If you would just come walk with us, perhaps we might get to know each other a little."

Do you know another way? Would you not only be guessing? I know a way. And trust your nose if you don't trust me. Breath of this air. Is it not less foul than it was before?

Jim did as the voice asked. Indeed, there was a sweeter scent in this part of the tunnel. The stink that had clung to him in the Dark Hole was replaced by a fresher odor, like the briefest hint of grass on a hillside. As Jim breathed in the cleaner air, his worries and his doubts began to slip away. His head grew light. Surely this was the way out, he thought to himself. The voice was a friend after all.

"Come on, Egidio," Jim said. "We must almost be out. Can't you smell the grass and fresh air?" Egidio, who had sunk down to his haunches, head bowed nearly between his knees, was about to stand, when he seemed to notice something on the ground.

"Jim, look at this," he said.

"There's no time, Egidio," Jim said, some impatience burning at the edge of his voice. "We're almost free."

"I'm not so sure, Jim. Look here."

"There's no time, Egidio!" Jim snapped. "Can't you smell the fresh air?"

"The fresh air?" Egidio asked. He stood up, but the moment he caught a whiff of the pleasant odor, he tore a shred from his apron and covered his mouth and nose with it. He ripped the strip in two and thrust the other scrap in Jim's face.

"Egidio, you old scatterbrain, what are you—" But Jim never finished. The scent of Egidio's apron, still full of the cavern's stench, was like a smelling salt in Jim's nose. He reeled back from the piece of cloth, but the sharp stink cleared his mind.

"Look!" Egidio demanded, pointing down at the floor, his voice muffled through his apron scrap. Jim held the other half of the torn cloth against his own face and kneeled down beside the shopkeeper. "From the water," Egidio said. He was pointing to rows upon rows of strange marks in the rock. Though the waving lines seemed to move all over at first, Jim finally noticed the pattern. The marks followed a path that led back the way they had come. Then Egidio pointed to their torch flames. The air in the tunnel pulled at the fires – again, in the other direction.

Jim looked into Egidio's round eyes. He cursed himself for being so foolish, but Egidio patted his shoulder with a comforting hand. The two nodded to each other before standing and beginning back the other way.

Wait! Where are you going? You're going the wrong way. You're going to get yourselves killed!

"No," said Jim. "We're going to get out. Come with us if you want."

No, no, no! Don't you trust your ears? I am a prisoner who escaped. Don't you trust your nose? The free air is this way. Please don't do this. Please don't throw your lives away!

But Jim and Egidio conversed no more with the unseen owner of the voice. They only pressed onward, moving as quickly as they could to make up for all the time they had lost. They followed the direction of the torch flames and the markings in the stone. But soon, the voice stopped pleading. Instead it began to curse and taunt.

You're both fools, do you hear me? Fools, fools, fools! You're never going to find your way out. You're both going to die down here. Do you understand? There's no escape from this place. There's no escape at all!

But after a time, Jim had heard enough of the voice's taunts. He stopped in the tunnel, raising his torch to the darkness and lifting his voice to the black.

"Silence, voice! Your promises of freedom were only lies and traps. Why would your taunts be anything else? So be quiet and go back to the crevice from which you crawled. We will hear no more of you."

And the voice spoke no more.

"I dare say, Jim Morgan," said Egidio. "You've always had the look of your father about you. But you have the sound of him now, too, don't you?"

"Thanks, Egidio, but I think if it weren't for you, we might have been stuck down here forever." With that, Jim and Egidio took up their trail again. But Jim wondered just how much time they had wasted following the false path. He wondered how long before the flooding waters, or whatever else dwelt in this horrible tunnel, came for them at last.

THIRTY-THREE

LACEY AND THE BEAST WITHIN THE MOUNTAIN

Lacey stood at the edge of a sharp cliff, beyond which the ground dropped off into nothing but blackness. She knelt down at the ledge and stretched her torch into the dark. The flames revealed a long outcropping in the rock below, like a stone tongue lapping at nothingness. At the end of the tongue stood a pylon, a cold torch set in the grommet at its top.

"That's where I'm supposed to go," said Lacey, staring at the edge of the rocky platform. "That's where I'm supposed to wait." But for what, Lacey did not know.

"Don't go down there, Lacey," said Paul, kneeling beside her. He gripped the cliff's sharp edge with white knuckles, his eyes searching the impenetrable depths of the cave. "Somethin ain't right down there."

"Do you hear that?" asked Peter. The three friends sat still for a long moment, straining their ears. Lacey heard nothing but the mountain wind swirling in the invisible cavern.

"It's just the wind."

"Do you feel any wind?"

No, Lacey thought to herself. No, she did not. She listened closer to what she thought was the wind through the cave opening, and discovered it had a long, particular rhythm.

"That's breathing," she said, trying to keep the torch from shaking in her hand.

"What do ya think could make breathin sounds like that?" asked Paul, inching back from the ledge. "It's gotta be gigantic. Like I was sayin, Lacey, don't go down there. I'd rather face old Cromier than whatever that is." Lacey's stomach was tying itself into a tricky knot, and a not so small part of her agreed with Paul. But the other part of her, the part that flashed bright behind her blue eyes, was too busy plotting to consider running away.

"No, it's Count Cromier who's made the mistake." She turned from the darkness and pulled the Ratts close. She put their heads together, whispering quietly as she could. "He sent thieves to fetch his treasure for him. And not just any thieves – the greatest thieves in the world. I'm going to go down there, and whatever it is that comes up will have its attention focused wholly on me, even if only for a moment or two. Remember what George always used to say about a perfect thieving?"

"It's all about distraction," Peter and Paul said together, a bit of the old Ratt mischief seeping into their faces.

"Whatever it is, whatever it does, keep your eyes sharp. Keep on the lookout for the Treasure, or for anything else we might be able to use to turn the tables on those villains outside. And if you see your spot – take it."

Lacey looked at the two Ratts, the torchlight glimmering in their wide eyes. Everything that had come before had been nothing but practice and games, she thought. Now would come the true test.

"You have been the best friends I could ever have," she said. "You took me in when I had no one, just like you took in Jim. You may be thieves, but you've given so much more than you ever took. Goodbye, just in case."

"Goodbye, Lacey." Paul squeezed his arms around her, giving a little sniffle in her ear.

"See you after, Lacey," said Peter, with as much confidence as he could muster, but he hugged her close as well.

"All right then, time to be off. Let's do our best, for George and for Jim."

"For George and Jim," the brothers agreed. With one more nod they went to work, attempting the greatest con and pocket pick in modern history, with nothing short of the world's end at stake. The Brothers Ratt stole into the shadows while Lacey dropped down onto the outcropping of stone. She walked to the very end, and there she leant her torch flame to the grommet on the pylon. When the light in the cavern doubled and spread, Lacey fought to keep back a scream.

"Who intrudes upon my dreams?" The question shook the cavern. "What fool has come looking for death?"

Lacey slapped a hand over her mouth as the creature unfolded beneath her. Great plates, like armor on a knight from olden days, scraped against each other with the grate of unspooling chains. Vast leathery folds unfurled like sails in the wind. A great horned head, set atop a serpentine neck, rose above stone outcropping, flanked on either side by outstretched wings.

"If you have come looking for that which I keep in my fortress of rock, despair. For you shall find only your doom."

Lacey had seen monsters before. She had faced the Kraken with Jim and George on the *Spectre*. She had been stolen away by giant owls on the Veiled Isle. She had even ridden upon the back of an ancient sea serpent. But standing on a thin platform of rock, with nothing between her and a hulking dragon but thin mountain air, fear nearly shook her to her knees. She took two steps back toward the entrance to the mountainside – but no more.

She held her ground.

The dragon opened his mouth. Teeth curved to meet each other. A crimson tongue lashed in their midst. But when the dragon looked down upon his prey, his threatening jaws slacked, even if only a little, and his eyes drew round on Lacey. The orbs in the beast's head were nearly black as pools of tar, with only blood red flecks within the colorless spheres.

"What is this?" the dragon asked. He lowered his head to study Lacey more closely. "Has a little fly flown into the web all on its own? Could I be so lucky? Or is this an offering meant to bribe me into giving up that which I hold? I have not given up a treasure that I guard for many, many years. Not since an old king offered me his own daughter. She was a princess, with hair like autumn, eyes like summer—"

"—and a spirit like spring," Lacey interjected. The Dragon seemed to take a start at being interrupted, but only for a moment. A long, sly smile stretched over his scaly mouth.

"Yes," he said, his forked tongue flickering. The dragon breathed deeply of the cave air, all over Lacey, and from the crack in the rock wall behind her. The smell of the monster's breath stank like burned meat. "I have not seen anyone to remind me of her in hundreds upon hundreds of years. And you do remind me of her. But you have not come alone, have you?" Lacey stiffened. Her stomach went cold. He had smelled the Ratts, she thought. The horrible image of the beast chomping them down in one gulp slipped into her mind. She closed her eyes tight to shut it out. "The reek of men is everywhere. One man in particular stands beyond my little hole, one with the scent of… something else upon his skin. How curious. But if you are a gift for me, where are your ropes?

Where are your binds? Where is the trembling coward, shaking in his armor, forcing you forth at the end of his spear?"

"They're all outside," Lacey said. Her words came out quiet and watery. She took a deep breath and forced herself to stand up straight, looking the dragon in his black eyes. "They're *all* waiting outside. They've come for the Treasure of the Ocean. I've come here so that you might give it to them."

"You came of your own free will?" The dragon swung its head about the stone outcropping, analyzing Lacey from the right and from the left. He began to sniff at her again, his nostrils so close that Lacey could feel the hot mist on his breath. "Auburn hair and sapphire eyes. You are a rare jewel indeed… just like she was. And yes, yes, you do have courage, don't you? Even more than your fear – but you are right to be afraid, little maiden. Surely you have never seen a beast like me. Surely you have never born witness to such power as that which I hold beneath my wings."

The dragon smiled. It was so very proud, Lacey thought, but it had somehow missed the Ratts – so far.

Peter and Paul wound their way down to the deepest bowels of the cave, working their way slowly, guided by only scant glimmers of light reflected from the dragon's golden scales. All of the young Ratts' past adventures had trained their feet and hands well, allowing them to creep over the rocks with hardly a sound. But it was nearly all for naught.

The moment the boys saw the wooden chest, resting on the cave floor at the dragon's feet, they despaired. The chest was far too heavy for the two of them to carry back. Its hinges were ancient and rusty, caked in burs. Paul shook his head vigorously *No!* when Peter went to lift the lid, motioning to his brother that the creaking noise would surely alert the dragon.

They were at a loss for what to do, when a gleam off the enormous beast's underbelly caught its ankle – its chained ankle. The dragon was imprisoned in the cave by a chain bigger than anything the boys had ever seen. Each iron link was taller than either Peter or Paul, and twice as thick around. This was not a chain that could have been made by any way other than magic. But forged by sorcery or not, the binds still gripped the dragon's claw by a manacle... a manacle with a large, dark keyhole.

Peter stared at the keyhole in the dim light, his fingers itching. He looked to his brother, who nodded back to him with wide eyes. Perhaps there was a chance after all... but it was a mad one indeed.

"I've ridden on a dragon once," Lacey said, taking her torch in both hands to hold it still. "In the ocean, in the rocks called the Devil's Horns."

"Ridden a dragon? In the water? You do not lie, but you speak false, my child. I know of this place, and I know of the doorway that is the Devil's Horns. You rode on a Water Dragon – what must be the last Water Dragon. But they are not *true* dragons, little maiden. Water Dragons are not of this world. They are creatures of magic, as are the so-called dragons of the east, which are creatures of wind. I was born of the earth, long ago, when it was but a ball of fire. Fire is my birthright!"

The dragon reared back, throwing open his jaws to the cavern roof, spitting flames so hot they were blue, then red, then yellow. The fire danced and crawled on the cave's ceiling, lighting the dragon's scales, gold like dirty coins. But in that brief moment of fire and light, Lacey saw three other things as well, down on the cave floor by the dragon's claws: a strong wooden chest, a chain, larger than could be made by men, and two silent, sneaking shadows.

"How is it then, that a true dragon, like yourself, has come to be chained in a cave?"

The dragon roared. His jaws opened so wide Lacey thought his horned head might split in two. She stared down the monster's throat and saw the furnace baking within his armored body. The dragon roared so long and so loud the stone outcropping beneath Lacey's feet threatened to crumble and break. But the dragon did not cast his flames, nor did he swallow Lacey whole.

"Cursed wizards! Cursed wizards of the north allied with knights on horses to capture me and put an end to my reign. They trapped me here and cursed me to watch over magical treasures and guard them from unworthy hands. The only pleasures left to me in the world are those lowered in by rope or chain. And I go so long without that I must, I *must* give up my prizes or I shall lose my mind. And so the cycle continues forever. Cursed wizards!"

"So, you only eat when someone brings you a girl for a meal?"

"Eat? Oh no, little maiden. Goats and deer and birds and bats often wander into my tiny hole... and foolish travelers from time to time. But a dragon needs no food to live. I eat only when it amuses me. Dragons live ten thousand years from the day we are hatched, no more and no less, and then we die. So many of my years have been wasted in this prison. But you, little maiden, you will not be eaten by me. I would not throw away such a rare jewel so quickly. You will *belong* to me as the princess once did, all those ages ago. You will sing when I am angry. You will laugh when I am bored. You will fetch things for me when I need them. You will pick the bones from my teeth after I have eaten and you will scratch beneath my scales. And many years from now, if you have not angered me, and I have not devoured you, or cooked you alive, or smashed you to dust beneath my feet, you will grow old and die. Then you shall be free."

Lacey's insides curled up like paper in a flame. She felt the urge to be sick, and every part of her body screamed silently to run. But she would not.

"You do not flee?" said the dragon. "You do not scream or cry out? You do not shed tears for this fate? Ah, now I see." The dragon breathed in Lacey's scent again, but more deeply than the first time. "I smell many scents upon your skin, my child, but three more strongly than the rest. You have courage. You have a strong will. But there is another, even stronger scent beneath those – is it love?"

Lacey said nothing, but the dragon knew what he smelled on Lacey's face, and on her skin, and in her hair.

"Yes, you are in love. A powerful feeling that is, child, and most powerful the first time. But not more powerful than fate. We dragons of the earth are not nearly as magical as those Water Dragons you have met before. But a single gift we do possess – the sight of fate. I see fate flowing through the air, like a river, curving and wrapping around the creatures of the world like water about stones. Your fate indeed is entwined with the one for whom you hold your hope."

Lacey risked a step closer to the giant creature. She looked into its deep, black eyes, splashed with crimson. She hardly trusted the arrogant beast, but she could not help but ask, "What do you see?"

"Stay a little longer... and I will tell you."

Lacey searched within herself for a solution, for a way out of this trap. She wondered for a moment, if she really would give herself to this creature, just for a chance that Peter and Paul might escape with the Treasure. She knew she would – but this was a trap indeed. Even if she stayed with the dragon, she could not be sure the Ratts would make it past the Cromiers. Lacey felt tears brimming behind her eyes. She was trying to keep them from falling when she caught a twinkle in the darkness below the dragon. It could have been nothing, she thought at first, but the twinkles kept coming. They kept coming in a particular order. A small pinprick of a hope crackled to life within Lacey's chest.

"Perhaps we could make a different arrangement," Lacey dared say. "Perhaps, if you were willing to make me a promise or three?"

"I make no promises, little maiden," the dragon roared, shaking the cavern over Lacey's head. "Here, in this cave, I am the only one that makes arrangements, and my visitors make promises to me."

"But what if you weren't in this cave?"

The dragon grew quiet as stone and listened.

THIRTY-FOUR

THE BATTLE ON THE MOUNTAINSIDE

Lacey saw triumphant greed fill the count's eyes the moment she emerged from the hole in the mountainside. It quivered into a twist of a smile on his lips. But it was not the count Lacey was worried about. Bartholomew kept looking from what Lacey carried in her hands to her face, and back to the dark cave behind her. He knew something was wrong, Lacey thought. He was going to catch her.

Lacey drew in a deep breath, reminding herself what Paul had told her about pulling off a good con. Don't say too much. Look them in the eye. And know when to run. Lacey exhaled to calm her nerves and reminded herself that she only needed to buy a few moments. She also adjusted her grip on that which she carried – the Treasure of the Ocean.

The gold was not nearly as shiny as Lacey had always imagined it would be. The hammer strokes were plainly visible along the shaft and on the spear points. The metal was dark and brassy, peppered with black imperfections. But ever since Lacey had pulled the Treasure from the wooden box beneath the dragon's claws, it had sung in her hands, trembling like a plucked string – a trembling that never faded away.

Lacey stopped ten paces from where Count Cromier and the Corsairs waited. Cornelius was still a prisoner in the count's grasp. But Cromier's grip loosened as he beheld the golden trident. His greedy mouth and eyes went wide. Lacey half expected the pirate thugs to rush forth and rip the Treasure from her arms. But as Paul had guessed, they all took two steps in the opposite direction, muttering to themselves and averting their eyes. Even Bartholo-mew, for all his bluster, slid his heels backwards on the gravelly road.

"At last," Cromier said. Lacey thought the old man might cry. "At long, long last. We have it, Bartholomew, we have it!" But Bartholomew did not smile or shout for joy. Perhaps it was his son's dour expression, but the count finally addressed the fact that it should not have been Lacey delivering his Treasure.

"Where are your friends?" Cromier demanded. "Where are the thieves? Why did the dragon not keep you?"

This was Lacey's moment, upon which the entire plan hinged. She pushed out two great tears, which rolled down her face, and she thickened her voice.

"The dragon ate them. But he let me go, because he said it was courageous for me to have come in with no ropes and no chains." The count pondered this for a moment. His hungry eyes kept falling back to the Treasure. After a long thought, he seemed to accept the story and let Cornelius go. The Raven flapped over to Lacey's shoulder and patted her on the back of her auburn hair in consolation.

"Set the Treasure down, girl. You have done well... So well. Perhaps it should have been you we sent in to the Serpent's Mouth on the Veiled Isle." Cromier laughed aloud, a cackling, merry chortle.

Lacey did as the count said. But she kept her hands close to her sides as she stepped away from the golden trident, hoping Cromier would not see the very thin tears in the sides of her dress. Her eyes she left on Bartholomew, who was staring back, very, very hard.

"So the dragon still gave you the Treasure?" Bartholomew asked. "Even though he did not keep you prisoner?"

"Yes," Lacey said. *Don't say too much*, she told herself.

"So what did the creature get out of all this?"

"He got to eat my friends," Lacey snapped. "Isn't that enough?" But she could tell, from the hardness in Bartholomew's icy eyes, that he had seen through her con.

"Father, wait—" Bartholomew began to warn the count, but before he could finish, he was interrupted by two, rather high-pitched wails, ringing out from the cave. From the black, two figures shot into the mountain air, kicking up dirt, high tailing it with arms and legs pumping. The count and the pirates, and even Bartholomew, were so surprised by the sudden reappearance of two, supposedly eaten thieves, that they all watched with furrowed brows as the two boys ran right past. The Ratts shouted for everyone to run for their lives, and also congratulated each other for being the greatest thieves alive at the same time.

The count glared at Lacey. He opened his mouth to tongue-lash her for her lies – when a roar from the cave silenced him. Fire and smoke poured from the hole in the mountain. The confident glee melted from the count's face. Seeing he was deceived, the count reached for the Treasure – only to watch it fly from his fingertips. The golden trident leapt back into Lacey's hands, by no trick of magic, but rather a trick of two, thin strings, almost invisible, unraveled from the hem of Lacey's dress.

The count gnashed his teeth like a rabid dog, cursing and spitting. He came for Lacey with outstretched hands. But Lacey did not run – not yet. She stood her ground and waited for the dragon to fulfill the first of three promises given for his freedom. The dragon sucked in a deep breath of mountain air. Lacey ducked as he released a spitting stream of liquid flame over her head. The count, Bartholomew, and most of the pirates dove aside, the flame forging a burning path through their center.

Then Lacey ran, as fast as she could, through the midst of the fallen men.

"I say, Lacey!" Cornelius squawked loudly in her ear. "How is it that every time one of you lot enters a cave, you come out with some monster at your backs. Every time!"

"Just lucky, I suppose, Cornelius."

The Ratts were waiting for them by the wagons, having already detached one of the carts and readied the horses. "You did it, Lacey," Paul shouted. "I can't believe that actually worked."

"What do you mean you can't believe it?" Lacey screamed back. "It was your plan!" But Peter was already shouting over them both.

"What I can't believe was that I picked a lock forged by wizards. I am the greatest lock pick of all time. I really — Lacey look out!" Peter's smile fell from his face and his eyes widened in horror. Lacey was only five paces and a leap from the horses, when a strong hand caught her by the back of the neck. She jerked to a violent stop, the collar of her dress catching against her throat. Her feet flipped out from beneath her and she landed hard on the rocky path. Cornelius tumbled from her shoulder, spilling onto the dusty road.

"You may have fooled my father, but you did not fool me, girl." Bartholomew's snarling face appeared over Lacey. With a gloved hand, he seized the trident. But Lacey refused to let go, hanging on tight as she could, though Bartholomew jerked with all his might.

"I won't let you have it," she screamed. The Ratts leapt in to help. Cornelius flew into the young Cromier's face, beating with his wings and scratching with his claws.

But it was the roar above them all that put a stop to the fight.

The dragon's great head swung into view, his wings spread wide, blocking out the sun. "I am sorry, little maiden," said the monster, a smile stretched on his crafty face. "I told you I would attack these men to help you escape. I told you that I would kill no men once I was free. But it seems that I can't do both at the same time. To help you escape, I would have to kill this man. So, if I can't keep one promise, I shan't keep any!"

The dragon drew in a great breath, the engine within his breast sparking the flames in his throat. A scream welled up within Lacey. Her arms and legs went numb. The treacherous dragon was going to kill them all. In Lacey's moment of fear, she slackened her grip on the Treasure. Bartholomew ripped it away.

Lacey cried in dismay for the Treasure, but the Ratts were already dragging her away from the Dragon. Bartholomew stood tall, removing his gloves. When his pale skin touched the gold metal, the trident gave off the glow Lacey had always imagined it would. Bartholomew held the Treasure before him, releasing a golden rush of magic to meet the dragon's fire. The magic plumed into a shimmering umbrella of power, strong enough to defeat the flame.

"Did you see that?" shouted Paul.

"No time, Paulie," cried Peter, lugging Lacey to her feet. "We gotta get a li'l wet and a li'l cold to escape, I think." With that, Peter pulled hard on Lacey, and the three friends, with Cornelius flying just above, splashed into the mountain river, flowing fast into the valley below.

Lacey gasped as she resurfaced, the icy water stabbing her body. She flung her wet hair from her eyes, looking back over her shoulder to the quickly shrinking mountain pass, where Bartholomew battled the dragon. The gold plated monster rose into the air on its bat-like wings, drawing up another shot of flames within his chest. But before the dragon could attack, a golden bolt of lightning burst from the trident. It struck the dragon in the chest like a flaming arrow, passing through the beast's armor like paper. Smoke and fire poured from the dragon's mortal wound. The beast plummeted through the sky with a dying growl, passing over Lacey and the Ratts like a shooting star, a trail of smoldering, black clouds marking its path through the air.

The cold river swept the Ratt Clan from the clutches of Bartholomew and the count, all the way down to the lake, miles away. But even as Lacey struggled to stay afloat, keeping Peter and Paul's heads above water at the same time, all she could think of was what she had just seen, and of what power had fallen into the Cromiers' hands. If Bartholomew could kill a dragon with the trident alone, what could he do once he had placed it into the altar, as Jim said must be done?

In the embrace of the cold waters, the three friends finally washed up on the shores of the lake. Lacey, Peter, and Paul dragged themselves onto land, shivering, coughing and spitting. There on the loch's edge, lay the dragon's body, wings broken on the hard ground, claws sticking up in the air. Fire still burned from the dragon's chest, and as morbid as it may have been, Lacey and the others came as close to the corpse as they dared, taking warmth from the flames.

"So, it would seem my freedom was short lived, little maiden," the dragon growled unexpectedly. The clan jumped together in a clutch, but Lacey did not run. The dragon's voice was weak. The creature neared death's door.

"It's no more than you deserve," she said, shrugging off Peter and Paul's attempts to hold her still. She approached the dragon's face. Both his horns had broken against the rocky earth. His red tongue lolled from his mouth. But even for the beast who had lied to her, Lacey felt a small stab of pity. She could not help herself from feeling it. So she stepped even closer and patted the monster on its nose.

"You could not see this coming?" she asked, but not cruelly.

"Not even a dragon may know his own fate. But I saw yours, little maiden, yours and the fate of the one you hold so dear. Cloudy and obscured by magic... even to my eyes... but I saw..." The dragon coughed. Lacey fell away from petting his nose, for a small ball of fire croaked from the dragon's mouth.

"I made three promises to you, did I not, little maiden? To help you escape... not to kill..."

"You broke those two," Lacey reminded.

The Dragon choked on a laugh. "So I did. But what was the last?"

"To tell me what you saw in my fate."

"That promise I shall keep," the dragon said, his voice going quiet.

"What did you see?" she asked him.

"Death." The dragon said. He wheezed once more, and then he died.

Lacey and the Ratts remained by the dragon's body as long as they dared, until they were dry from their escape in the river, but no longer than that. The Cromiers would be coming close behind. Lacey found she could not wholly warm herself, even in the flames. A chill sunk deep in her bones from the dragon's dark words.

THIRTY-FIVE

THE FINAL CAVERN

After many more hours of working through the stony maze, Jim and Egidio reached the end of the tunnels. They emerged into a large cavern, marked by rocky towers and squat boulders, worn into perfect spheres from centuries of flowing water. The cave's walls, eroded smooth as molded clay, twisted upward, all the way to an opening high above. A dreary light filtered into the cavern through the hole in the ceiling.

"Egidio, look," Jim said, pointing with his torch, which was very nearly burnt out. "There's light up there. It's the way out, I think. At last. Now we'll see if the guards spoke true or not about the boat waiting for prisoners."

"Indeed, young Morgan, we will," said Egidio, squinting through his round glasses. "But I don't much like that light up there."

"It's daylight, Egidio. How long has it been since we've seen any? I may like it more than anything else in the world just now."

"It is the gray of the light I don't much like. Gray light comes just before the dawn, and just before the morning flood."

To Jim, it suddenly looked like a very long climb to the cave's roof. "We'd better start up then, Egidio. These grooves in the cave walls look just wide enough to walk on. We could wind our way up, don't you think? It would be like the stairwell in the merfolk's crystal tower." Jim crossed the cave floor. His footsteps rang with clinking metal.

Jim looked to his feet and found a carpet of things covering the ground, glittering in the pale light – jewels, necklaces, rings, coins, and the like. There were some that did not shine as well – clothes, purses, and even children's playthings. Jim kicked at a small doll with his toe, its face long worn away by time and tide. He shuddered at the thought of living an entire life in the Dark Hole, knowing nothing but the horror of the dungeon behind him.

"I've never been to the great Crystal Tower," said Egidio, rummaging through the piles of rusted and ruined odds and ends. "I shall have to go, once we are free, and once we have stopped the Cromiers."

"It's been destroyed, Egidio. It's not there anymore." Jim's heart hollowed out at that thought, and of the Ratts, and Lacey. "We need to hurry," Jim said, looking back at Egidio, who took the news of the Crystal Tower with disbelief. "We need to set things right."

"And so we shall," Egidio whispered. He held Jim's eyes in his own for a moment, then went back to his search. "But first we must find my satchel. If we are to have any chance of escape, we must have it."

"What's in it?" Jim asked, kicking aside more piles of junk. He thought of searching for his mother's soul stone, but with an ache in his throat, he remembered it was emptied of everything it once held.

So he decided to leave it, as he had with the broken shards of his father's box.

"The satchel holds only all my best tricks and trinkets, my boy. I have a compass that points only in the direction a man should sail, Aeolus Feathers, to speed up the journey, a few skins filled with the most refreshing water, unbreakable rope, and – most important of all – that which once lay at the end of the path of riddles on the Veiled Isle, guarded by Percival the Water Dragon."

"What do you mean? I took the Hunter's Shell from there. Percival said my father left it for him to guard when he had answered the riddles."

"Yes, but Percival was already guarding something before your father left him the Shell, remember? It was something of great value indeed. I will show you, once I find this blasted bag."

Jim looked back to the hole above his head. The gray light grew brighter, a golden hue glimmering at the edges. Dawn was coming, and with it, another deluge to drown him. Jim searched with greater urgency through the piles of stolen possessions. He paused only when he came upon a suit of armor. It was ancient – a helmet, a shield, a spear, and a breastplate. The metal was rusted through and brittle, barely sturdier than wood. Jim picked the helmet up and found a hole in the crown. Whatever had pierced the metal had shorn it like thin cloth. The brittle edges of the gash were darkened brown, but not by rust – by ancient blood.

Click-Click-Click.

Jim dropped the helmet with a dull clang. He raised his torch high, turning in a circle, peering toward the edges of the cave, where shadows encircled the thin shaft of morning light. He saw nothing.

"Egidio? Did you hear that?"

Egidio's only answer was frustrated mumbling as he continued to rummage for his lost satchel.

Click-Clickety-Click-Click.

A thrum lit up in Jim's chest. He squeezed his torch tight with both hands. His heart pumped hard. He and Egidio were not alone in the cave.

"Egidio!" Jim's voice grew husky and hard. "Find your blasted bag and let's get out of here."

"Well, if I *had* the bag, I could have already *found* the bag," the old man snapped, hurling a moth eaten duffle over a rock with some disgust. "I'm sure I have a dozen seekers or such in there. Of course, they're *in* the bag, so what bloody good do they do us?"

Click-Click-Click-Click-Click-Click-Click-CLACK-CLACK!

"Egidio! Forget the bag! We'll take our chances without it." Jim ran toward the old man, ready to drag him out, kicking and screaming if need be, when the shopkeeper lifted his beaming face, a dirty, leather satchel raised above his head like a trophy.

"Found it, my boy. Now we may go."

It rose up behind the rock just past Egidio. The blood drained from Jim's face when he saw it. *Click-Click-Click* went its many legs, long, hard, and armored. *CLACK-CLACK* snapped its huge pinchers. It was like a great crab, shell white and dirty red, red like the old blood on the soldier's helmet. But from its plated body, a sickly gray torso sprouted, scaled hide like the ogres. It had arms like a man's, pale eyes, and a mouth twisted about two curved tusks, snapping in time with its powerful claws. Jim knew no name for this beast, only that it was the thing that had ended the lives of so many prisoners before him.

The creature shrieked with violent hunger.

"Egidio, run!"

Egidio realized just in time what now descended upon him. He dove forward. A giant pincher sliced the air where he had been sitting only a moment before. The old shopkeeper bolted toward Jim, who was already backpedaling from the beast.

"Up, up, up!" Egidio shrieked, pointing wildly at the winding grooves in the stone walls. Jim turned to run as well, but the creature was faster on its spindly legs than its prey. It circled around them, bounding over the boulders and balancing against the stone pillars like a spider in its web. It blocked their escape, unleashing another furious yowl.

"Egidio," Jim screamed. "Find something in that bag to help us!"

Egidio reached into the satchel, which somehow swallowed him up to his shoulder. He dug for something of use, but he was not fast enough. The creature rushed them again. Egidio ducked just quickly enough to avoid being cut in two by the snapping pinchers. But in his escape, he dropped the bag. The satchel tumbled just beyond his reach.

Jim rushed the monster before it could finish Egidio off, swinging his torch in one hand, and his small knife in the other. He wondered if fire might frighten the beast, as it would a wolf. The creature backed off a step or two and Jim thought he had found an answer. But the monster was merely surprised by Jim's foolish attack. It swept a fat claw across the chamber. The pincher glanced off Jim, hurtling him head over heels into a pile of stolen possessions. His torch and knife flew from his hands.

The crab-troll, if that was what it could be called, fell immediately upon Jim's sprawled form, raising a claw to strike. Jim reached for something, anything with which to fight. His hand smacked into the old helmet. He stretched past it and found the lip of the shield beyond.

Jim pulled the heavy armor over him as the claw came down. The pinchers snapped on the rim of iron-plated wood. The old shield trembled – but it held long enough. Jim pushed up with all his might until the shield snapped into matchsticks in the claw's grasp. The creature howled again, enraged. It snapped the tusks in its troll mouth and waved its mannish arms. With the shield destroyed, Jim searched for the spear, but he could not find it in time.

The crab-troll rushed again. Jim knew this was the end as the claw came down – until Egidio threw himself in the way.

"Back, you devil!" the old man cried. He had not recovered his bag, but he hurled a rock from the cave floor into the creature's face, breaking one of the tusks. But that did not stop the claw from dealing its due. The pincher's tip struck Egidio in the side, crumpling the shopkeeper and throwing him against a boulder. The old man fell and lay still.

"Egidio, no!" Jim screamed. His whole body went hot as fire. He found the spear, and with no thought for fear, charged the crab-troll. He came so fast that the beast missed him with both claws, swiping too late. Jim drove the old spear into the monster's gray chest. The ancient weapon snapped in two in Jim's hands, but it pierced deep enough to wound the troll. With a miserable groan, the crab creature staggered away, back into the shadows.

Jim gasped for breath and wiped the sweat of battle from his brow. He stumbled across the cave to where Egidio lay. As gently as he could, he turned the old shopkeeper over. The moment he saw the wound, Jim knew there was nothing he could do. Egidio's skin was ashen and cold. His breaths came shallow and weak. The old man's glasses were cracked and broken. So Jim took them off, fighting his own tears as he did.

"You do look like your father, Jim Morgan," said Egidio, smiling. His eyes were still large, even without his spectacles, large and kind. "It would seem I found my courage after all, didn't I?"

"Yes, you did," Jim managed, holding the old man's head in his lap. "You were brilliant, like a warrior."

A rumble shook the cave. Far away, the rushing sound of ten thousand running feet filled Jim's ears. The flooding waters were coming. Egidio would not have the strength to escape.

"Do not exaggerate, and do not weep, my boy. I sail on... as must you. And you must go quickly." Egidio pointed toward his satchel, which had fallen just beyond his reach in the fight with the crab-troll. "Take it with you. What is inside might save you. And here... I found something else while I was searching." Egidio held up Jim's mother's necklace, the silver dirty and dull. Jim took it, but as he did, Egidio squeezed his arm with what must have been the last of his strength. He pulled Jim close, close enough that Jim's tears fell on the old man's cheeks. "Jim, hear me now. There is only one way to lock a door forever. Only one. You must lock the key on the other side. You must lock the door behind you." Egidio gave another shuddering breath. Then his grip on Jim's arm went loose.

There was no time to mourn. Jim laid Egidio's head as softly as he could on the ground and ran for the satchel. The water exploded into the chamber the instant Jim took the leather strap in hand. The deafening roar was like a hundred canons firing at once, over and over. Jim tore for the winding groove in the stone wall, formed by decades and decades of this very water twisting its way up the tower. Round and round Jim ran, the water slapping at his legs. He threw the satchel's strap over his shoulder and slammed his hand over the flap to hold it shut. He would not be faster than the rushing tide.

The water caught Jim from behind and spun him into the whirlpool. It threatened to drag him back into the cavern, the prison's last, desperate attempt to trap him forever. But Jim had the blood of the merfolk in his veins. He kicked against the tide. He fought with all his strength, with more than his strength, with that of MacGuffy, Egidio, George, and Lacey's as well. He charged for the surface – and he reached the top.

Having failed to drown him, the Dark Hole spat Jim out. He tumbled down a rocky slope, rolling in the remains of the surge. After the flood abated, Jim picked himself up on a rocky beach. The wind off the ocean was on his skin. The salt of the sea was in his hair. The warmth of a morning sun touched his face, welcoming him back into the world.

THIRTY-SIX

MOVING SOUTH

Lacey, Peter, and Paul ran south from the loch for London, to find a ship that would bear them to Spire Island. They had to warn the pirates that Cromier had the Treasure, and Lacey also hoped against hope that someone there might know to where Jim had been banished. But London was a long way away. The land was hard, and the road was unforgiving.

The young clan had dared not bring a torch with them, for fear of being seen by the Cromiers and their cohort. So they shivered against the biting winds that whipped across the northlands. They had no vessel for water, nor did they have any food. So their mouths grew dry and sticky, and their bellies empty and aching. They had no map, and Lacey was so terrified that Bartholomew Cromier would spot a lone raven flying high in the air, and strike it down with lightning from his trident, that she entreated Cornelius to keep his scouting discreet and to a minimum. Their only saving grace was that Lacey knew the stars in the sky as well as any man of the sea. She could at least guide them south, toward London. But as far as any of them knew, London was hundreds of miles away.

At some point they all grew so weary that they stopped talking to each other, save only to warn when a spot on the horizon appeared that might have been a wagon or a rider. Even Cornelius ceased telling his stories, for the tales, all of which the three had heard before, began to fall on deaf ears.

But Lacey would not let them stop, even when pain pounded her feet. Blisters formed on her heels and cuts bled under her toes, but she kept moving forward. In her mind, she cursed herself for losing her grip on the Treasure, for allowing Bartholomew Cromier to take it. She could also see Jim, enchained and tortured somewhere, alone and imprisoned in some black hole, leagues and leagues away. But worse still, the Dragon's words haunted her steps. She wouldn't let the dragon's foretelling come true. She wouldn't.

At last, deep into the night, in the darkest hours before morning, Paul could go no further. He stumbled and fell onto the cold, hard dirt. When Peter and Lacey leant over to pick him up, they fell beside him in the rough grass.

"We'll just stop for a little bit," Lacey said, her tongue swollen in her mouth. "Just to catch our breaths." But her eyes closed. She slumped over on her side and knew no more for hours on end.

It was a splash of cool water in Lacey's mouth that roused her, along with the salty smell of meat, simmering in a stew. Her eyes stayed closed for a long stretch in that pleasant, warm place, where dreams are still a blanket under which the sleeper might crawl. It was the sound of wagon wheels on a bumpy rode that tore that blanket away.

Lacey flew awake. She breathed in a gulp of water, coughing and spitting. She jerked her hands up, as though fighting manacles she knew would bind them. But she found no ropes or chains, no sharp blade at her throat, and no bars caging her in.

"Peace, child, peace," said an old, kind voice. "You have been sleeping for a long vile. I have been keeping vatch over you and your friends. They voke just before you did." Lacey looked up to find Peter and Paul slurping on bowls of the delicious smelling stew. Paul waved at her, and when Peter tried to say good morning, it came out, "Bluud blorning!" with stew dribbling down his chin, he and his brother giggling as he wiped it from his mouth. They were in the back of a covered wagon, the bed lined end to end with strange odds and ends – dried animal bones, handmade musical instruments, wolf skins, and even a cage, with a monkey inside. The little creature was taking a nap on his perch.

"We worried for you, sweet Lacey," said Cornelius, hopping up beside her elbow. Lacey pulled him onto her lap and hugged him close. "You've been asleep for hours."

"Hours?" Lacey said, aghast. "We've lost so much time, then! I didn't mean to fall asleep. I'm sorry! We're still so far—"

"From London?" said the voice. Only then did Lacey look to the speaker. She must have been the oldest woman Lacey had ever seen. Her dry, craggy skin clung to her bones. Her lifeless gray hair stuck out from beneath a faded scarf about her head, like dry straw. Sharp black eyes peered at Lacey from overtop a large hooked nose. "Do not vorry, young von. Ve have been driving to London all through the night. Ve ver not headed that vay at first, but since you needed to go there, ve changed our minds. Ve vill arrive tonight."

With a brittle hand, the old woman offered Lacey a ladle of water from a bucket. For some reason, perhaps that the boys and Cornelius were alive and well, and eating stew, or simply because she felt a warmth in the woman before her, radiating through the ancient body, Lacey never questioned the water. She took the ladle and drank it down, quenching her thirst.

"Were any of us awake when you found us?" Lacey asked, wiping her mouth with the back of her hand. "Did you talk to Cornelius? It must have been strange for you to meet a talking bird."

"I have met many talking animals in my time, child," said the Gypsy woman, for that is what she was. "But your feathered friend vas very vise and said nothing at first. It vas you who told me that London vas ver you vanted to go. But that is not ver you vish to stay. Ver you really must go lies far beyond ver my vagons might take you."

Lacey stared at the old woman for a long moment, all but losing herself in the dark eyes that seemed to be smiling back at her. "I… told you all that?" she asked. "Was I talking in my sleep?"

"I heard," said the old woman. A smile on her old, fragile lips matched the one in her eyes. "And I saw. Do not vorry, young von. Old Baba vill take care of you. Eat your fill, then go back to sleep. Take your rest vile you may find it. Old Baba vill vatch over you vile you sleep." The old woman waved her hand over Lacey's face, and Lacey suddenly felt safer than she had in ages. She ate two bowlfuls of stew. She laughed with Peter and Paul. Then she fell back asleep and dreamt of freeing Jim.

THIRTY-SEVEN

WHAT HID BEYOND THE WINDOW

On the empty island, the rocky beach awash in sea froth, George Ratt sat in the shade of a brown palm beside the King of Thieves. He was leaning against the trunk, his belly full for the first time in days. The King had a hand on George's shoulder, like a father's hand on his son.

George had used the flute, as the King of Thieves had instructed him, to call for gulls to bring him some fish. He had recruited sea crabs to bring him driftwood. And with his greatest effort, stretching his abilities as far as they had ever been pushed, he called deep, deep down into the ocean, where a salamander lived in the fiery cracks of the seafloor. The salamander had come with great speed to the island and lit the driftwood, where George had cooked the fish and eaten his fill.

Some part of George, that piece of him that still felt awake and not dreaming, would have been in awe of these feats, were he told that he would one day accomplish them. But perhaps not if he would have known the cost. George hardly tasted the food. The cool breeze off the water pulled at his hair, but he never felt its touch. The glory of the whole ocean was stretched out before him, but he barely noticed. All of George's senses and thoughts were turned inside him, where they led to that window inside his head.

The window was opened very wide now, wider than it ever had been. That small, awake part of George feared he would fall through it and disappear into somewhere else. But once George had looked through the window, no matter how frighteningly wide, he had learned it was very hard to look away again. He saw things sometimes when he looked through – things he thought might be happening far away – perhaps things that had not happened yet.

"Today is the last lesson, George," said the King. "Are you ready?"

George nodded. When he spoke, his voice was quiet, subdued. "Yes, I'm ready."

George lifted the flute to his lips and began to play. As his fingers danced and his song blew, he stared into his little fire. But in George's mind, he once more went back to that window that was opened by magic.

George played and played. He stared harder and harder into the flames. It was almost as if he could see the flames burning in the window. An image appeared in the fire. It was an island, an island of rock. There was a building on the island, broken and old, older than any building George had ever seen. For some reason the building reminded him of a church. Jim was there, and Lacey, and his brothers. George was there, too. This could not be happening now, he thought. This was the future. The sea and the sky were crashing. There was a storm – and a battle. A fierce battle.

"Can you see, George?" said the King. "Can you see what you will face?"

Beads of sweat broke out on George's forehead. Calling animals took only a fraction of the energy he spent creating this image in the flames. But he managed to nod his head. Yes, he could see. It was a terrible battle indeed.

"Now you know how right I was, and how much Jim will need you. You will have to hold him back, George, and to do that, you will need to call up another great creature from the deep to aide you in the struggle. To do this, I think you will need more of my help. Will you let me help you?"

Again George nodded. He felt the cold of the King's long spidery fingers on the side of his head.

The image of the battle in the flames disappeared. A new figure appeared beyond the window in George's mind. It was a shadow. George leaned closer to the window, to try and discern the shape. By the time he realized what it was, it was too late.

It was the King of Thieves. The King reached through the window and grabbed George, pulling him through to the other side. George struggled and fought. He kicked and hit and shouted. But he was no match. The window was opened too wide, and he had wandered too close, as had been the King's intention the entire time. George was going to be pulled through. He had been tricked again by the King of Thieves.

"Come now, George, don't be afraid," the King cried, his voice booming from the far side of the window. "It's only a short drop to the other side, and once you're here my boy, oh the things you shall see and do." The King's face was hungry and cruel. His spidery fingers felt like iron bands on George's shoulders. George knew he would not have the strength to pull himself free.

But that small part of George that was still awake, and was still clever and still quick, was not prone to giving up. He grabbed onto the window ledge with one hand, hanging on for dear life, his fingers slipping one at a time.

Even though George was not as smart as Jim or Lacey, or maybe even as smart as his brothers, he still figured out that everything he saw inside his mind was just a picture – but a picture that meant something real. So, before he could be pulled all the way through the window, George took the hat from his head, the hat that Jim had given him for Christmas, and he threw it back to the safe side of the window. The hat, George hoped, was really a small piece of himself. Perhaps, when the time came, that small piece would be just enough.

Then George's last finger slipped, and into the blackness beyond the window he fell, into the waiting arms of the King of Thieves.

THIRTY-EIGHT

Shetew the Cursed

When Jim emerged from his wretched prison, he found himself on the strangest island he had ever seen. It was an unusual shade of green – unlike any land he'd ever set foot on before. Stranger still, the island seemed to be moving through the water – swimming even. Jim turned in a complete circle twice before realizing just where he was, and why no one ever could, or would, be able to find this hidden prison of misery, even if they searched for a thousand years.

The caves and tunnels from which Jim and Egidio had escaped were entombed in tall rocky towers behind him. It appeared to be a castle of stone built upon a hill. But the hill was not a hill at all: it was a shell – the shell of a turtle swimming through the sea.

Jim ran down to the place where the rock met the shell and

found himself standing on what appeared to be the turtle's shoulder. The morning sun was halfway up past the horizon, throwing golden light on the monstrous head and face as the turtle noisily chomped on an entire school of fish.

"Well, good morning, my young friend," said the turtle, looking at Jim with great, brown eyes, set into the sides of his warty head. "It has been a long, long time since I saw a person of any sort pop out of the stones upon my back. In fact…" The turtle took to chewing for a moment, many loud, sloppy bites, as though he was thinking quite hard, until he spoke again. "Actually, I don't know that any person has ever popped out of there before. You may be the first."

"Do you know what this place is that you carry on your back, sir, uh… Turtle?" Jim asked.

"My name is Shetew, little person," said the turtle. "And yes, unfortunately I am well aware of this awful place I carry upon my back. I am cursed, little person, cursed to carry this evil place for all time. Night and day, when the sun is in the sky or below the sea, I turn into stone. I become an island that is only shaped like a turtle. Only while the sun is upon the horizon, at its rising and setting, do I become real again. Then I must dive into the sea to find something to eat."

As much as he wanted to be angry at the turtle, for nearly drowning him and the other prisoners, Jim could not find it in himself to hate Shetew. In spite of the seawater on the turtle's face, Jim was sure he saw a great tear well up within his eye and fall down his face.

"Is there no way to break the curse?"

"There is a way, little person, but it is very long, and very hard, and there is no one to help me accomplish it."

"There is something I must do," Jim said to the turtle, keeping an eye on the sun, for it was ever closer to breaking the horizon. "The truth is, I don't know if I'll survive the task, but if you will help me find a way off your shell, or if you can drop me off somewhere, I promise I will come back to find you. In this bag are many kinds of seekers." Jim held up the satchel. "I know I could find you again with one of them. And if I can, I'll help you break the curse." It was not just for the sad turtle that Jim made this promise – it was for all the prisoners still trapped inside, and for the justice still owed to Grime, Slag, Bog, and the crab-troll at the end of the tunnels.

"I don't know why, little person," said Shetew, "but I believe you. I also do not know if you will live long enough to keep your word, but I at least believe that you mean to try. There is not time for me to swim you to any isle, but if you cross my shell to the other side, I believe a small boat has lodged itself on the far edge. It is a tiny thing, not meant for the deep ocean, but you may have it, little person."

"My name is Jim, Shetew. Jim Morgan, and I'll take it. And if I do survive, I will come back and set you free if I can."

"So be it, Jim Morgan. But beware – these are the Wastewaters through which I now swim. Dark creatures inhabit the islands out this way, and darker creatures still swim below the waves. It will take courage, strength, and luck for you to cross them in such a boat as the one I offer. But I wish you well, nevertheless."

Jim had not the time to thank Shetew for his advice. The sun rose into the sky, and the moment the burning disc crested the line of the ocean, the giant turtle turned to stone before Jim's eyes with a crackling like breaking ice.

Wasting no time, Jim ran across to the other side, and as Shetew promised, found a small skiff moored to the barnacles growing on his shell. The boat was nothing much to speak of, little more than a small hull, a rudder, and a single sail. But the sail had been wrapped up tight, and the mast sturdier than it looked, for in spite of being dragged around by the turtle for who knew how long, it was still seaworthy enough to sail.

And so Jim cut the little ship loose. He let down its canvas sheets to the wind. He reached inside the bag, and before drawing out anything else, found the compass of which Egidio had spoken, the one that could point the way to where a man needed to go.

Jim wanted to tell the compass to take him to Spire Island, or to England – anywhere he might be able to find Lacey again, or George and his brothers. But Jim knew where he had to go. He was on the Wastewaters, close to where his mother had directed him with the last words she ever spoke. He was close to perhaps the last person who could tell him how to reach the island of the ancient temple, where he would have to face the Cromiers.

"I must find the Island of the Silver Pool," Jim said to the compass. The needle turned East-by-Southeast. Jim turned the rudder. He reached into the bag once more and produced a handful of Aeolus Feathers. With the magic wind they called, he sped across the Wastewaters to the island, where lived Legeia – Bartholomew Cromier's mother.

Far behind Jim, on the edge of the horizon, a dark spot marred the morning sky. A lone storm cloud rolled through the blue. Crimson tendrils wound along the cloud's edges, and purple lightning flashed within the black folds.

BOOK IV

THROUGH THE DOOR AT THE EDGE OF THE WORLD

THIRTY-NINE

TO THE ISLAND OF THE SILVER POOL

Jim's voyage to the Island of the Silver Pool was fraught with danger. Great mountains rose up from the seabed and tore through the surface of the Wastewaters like talons. The corpses of shattered ships lay strewn upon the rocks. Sharks and eels flitted amongst the wreckage. As Jim sailed past, he imagined the creatures below still picking at the bones of pirate skeletons in their watery graves.

Jim was thankful for Egidio's satchel and the magic compass he had found within. Many times the rocks nearly shattered the small boat to matchsticks. It was as if the mountains were alive and reaching out to drag him down into the sea, but the compass led him safely through. There were also monsters beneath the waves — great beasts larger and fiercer than anything that walked the land. More than once such a giant creature threatened to swallow Jim and his skiff whole. But Jim found a few remaining Aeolus Feathers in Egidio's bag and used their magic to escape with his life.

When the feathers' effects faded and the skiff slowed, the Island of the Silver Pool came into view. At least Jim thought it was the island. It looked more like a floating cloud. Jim drew up his sail and slowed the skiff to a crawl. The first tendrils of the thick white fog slunk past his head like bony fingers, wrapping about him, pulling him further and further into the mist.

A black shape appeared in the white, and a chill sunk into Jim's bones. It was a Spanish galleon, a mighty ship of the sea, impaled upon a rock like a pike. Jim could still make out the faded title of the ship on the shattered hull as he sailed past – *El Halcón*. She was only the first. Jim passed broken hull after broken hull, as though he were sailing through a graveyard of murdered ships. What had drawn so many into such a deathtrap as this?

Soon Jim left the carnage of ruined ships behind, sneaking his small boat through a final set of rocky teeth, where the fog grew thin, and at least a little light fought through. A yellow beach opened up before him, and just past the shore, a jungle rose in a wall, tree trunks and bushes jammed together like an impassible fence.

Jim brought the skiff as close to the beach as he dared and dropped the small anchor, which was no more than a rock at the end of a rope. Before going ashore, he knelt down in the boat and reached once more into Egidio's bag. There was a powerful item still in the bag, Jim remembered. One Egidio had told him about. His father had taken some talisman from Percival the Water Dragon before leaving the Hunter's Shell. Jim envisioned his father upon the path of riddles, and no sooner had that image leapt into his mind than an object leapt into his hand.

Jim withdrew his arm from the satchel, and in his grip he found a cutlass, polished and shining as though it were new. Jim loosed a small whistle. The blade was pure, as though never used, with nary a nick or dent along the edge. The hilt was solid gold, with rubies inlaid upon the hand guard. Jim had never owned a sword of his own – especially not one so fine, or so magical. With the sword in his hand and the satchel over his shoulder, Jim splashed through the waves and onto the beach.

"The Silver Pool," he said to the enchanted compass. The needle wavered and swung in the direction of the trees. Jim took a deep breath for courage and plunged into the jungle.

Forging a path through the tangle proved hard travelling. Sweat streamed down Jim's face and rolled down his back. After a while he gave up wiping it away, for his clothes grew drenched with it, sticking to his arms and legs. Bugs whined in his ears and attacked his neck. Lizards and snakes fled from his footsteps, skirting around tree trunks as he came. When a thick vine barred Jim's way, he tried to hack through it with the sword.

The metal blade glanced off the branch as though it were merely a toy.

Jim slashed at the vine again. The blow left not so much as a scratch. Jim ran his thumb across the blade's edge. Not a drop of blood. Jim's shoulders fell and he dropped the tip of the blade into the dirt. What sort of magic sword was this? What good was a blade that would not cut?

But there was no turning back. Jim pressed onward, still holding the sword before him. He hoped at least that the sight of it might be enough to frighten off any potential foes.

For what felt like hours, Jim waded through the snarl. The jungle scratched his face, his arms, and his legs. Jim drank freely from the waterskins in the bag – but his supply was growing short. As he shoved the next-to-last skin back into the satchel, he reached out to brush a low-hanging vine from his way.

The vine drew back and hissed in Jim's face.

Jim froze. The viper he thought was a vine reared up before him.

The green body writhed in the air. Fangs gleamed with poison. Jim's mind raced. Could he swat the snake aside with the dull blade? Could he duck beneath its strike? If it did bite him… would he die?

The viper's attack came too fast for answers. The snake launched itself for Jim's face, fangs bared.

But the bite never landed.

Jim felt his arm swing. He felt the sword strike. The viper lay at his feet – dead. The magic sword hummed in Jim's hand. The metal rang high above the buzzing jungle. Now Jim understood the weapon's enchantment. It would not help him attack. But it would protect him from harm.

"Thank you, Egidio," Jim said. "Thank you father," he whispered to the sword. But even as Jim set off with renewed confidence, a new sound swam through the trees. It was higher and smoother than the ringing blade.

It was a song, sung by a woman's voice, and it was beautiful. Jim checked his compass. The song came from the direction of the silver pool.

Jim worked his way more quickly through the jungle. The song grew louder and louder as he went. As Jim drew closer to the silver pool and the source of the song, the less he heard from or saw any jungle creatures. The animals of the island did not go near this place.

Before he was ready, Jim burst free of the trees and stumbled into a clearing. A ring of rocks encircled a small pool. The water shone like metal in a thin shaft of light sneaking through the green canopy. Its surface was as still as stone, so smooth and flat that Jim thought he might strike himself dead should he dive in. Shadow lay over the rest of the clearing like a cloak.

The song filled the air. Jim looked up from the pool and at last found the source of the singing. A pair of eyes, blue as the summer sky, opened in the dark on the other side of the pool. The eyes seemed to shine, lighting the gentle curves of a face, and the full lips of a beautiful woman.

Legeia, Jim thought. The mother of Bartholomew Cromier. Her melodic tones soon turned to words as she continued to sing. And the words were death.

Come forward noble traveler,
Lean closer Son of Earth,
Walk but a few steps farther,
Follow the sounds of mirth.

Crash your boat upon the stones,
Throw your self into my pool,
By my song I bury your bones,
By stone and water I drown the fools.

Jim's toes neared the rocks about the silver pool. He stared into the blue eyes hovering in the jungle's darkness. The song filled his head. The words bade him destroy himself. Jim stepped onto the stone ring...

...and spoke.

"I will not be drowning myself today, Legeia." His voice silenced the song. Jim thought he heard a gasp from the bushes – or was it a growl? "I know what you are. You lure men to their deaths by your song. You're a siren."

"I give justice to wicked men, boy," said Legeia. Without her song, her voice came out hard and flat, like a club to the head. "I punish the vileness that is mankind. I have been given power over men to do so."

"You have no such power over me."

"No, it would seem I do not." Jim heard sniffing in the shadows. Legeia was testing his scent. "You are not wholly man, are you? I smell the blood of both Lindsay Morgan and Venia of the Sea Folk in your veins. But Son of Earth and Son of Sea or not, you are still mortal. And my song is not my only weapon."

Leaves and branches rustled and snapped as the beautiful face rose up from the darkness and Legeia surged into a shaft of light. Her skin was the silvery pale of a fish. Her black hair, matted and tangled, fell in twisted clumps about her face. She had the body of a woman, but limp, featherless wings hung useless from her back. Her fingers ended in curved talons and her legs became an eagle's gnarled claws below the knees. Jim retreated from the rocks. Legeia's face was as beautiful as an angel's – but she was a monster nevertheless.

The siren rushed about the pool, descending on Jim with claws outstretched. Her lips peeled back from her teeth. She meant to rend Jim limb from limb. But as with the viper, the magic sword came to life in Jim's hand, steel blade singing, leaping between Jim and the siren.

Legeia's claws clanged off the blade in a shower of sparks. She shrieked and howled, two of her talons shattered, blood the color of a dark bruise leaking from her hand. She shrank back from Jim, hissing and snarling, her wide blue eyes locked on the sword in Jim's hand.

"Cursed magic blade!" she spat. "Forged in the times of the ancients that was. Keep it away from me, Son of Earth, Son of Sea."

"Another taste of this steel would be no more than you deserve," said Jim. He advanced a step on Legeia, and as he hoped, she cowered before him. "How many innocent men lie at the bottom of the sea around this island? How many lie at the bottom of this very pool?"

"Innocent? There are no innocent men, young Morgan. Do you know any? Are you this innocent man? Have you always lived your life as this hero you show yourself to be? Have you never been the monster?"

Jim hesitated. He lowered his arm just a little, and the magic sword let him. Opening his left hand, Jim looked to the white rose scar in bloom on his palm.

"A man I met, not so long ago, said that it was not what other men had done that would make me lose faith in humankind – but what I was capable of doing that would. You're right, Legeia. I haven't always been a hero. I'm not proud of everything I've done."

"Then what gives you the right to demand anything of me, boy?"

"Because now I'm doing something different." Jim lowered his blade all the way, for it was no longer humming in his hand. He backed away from Legeia and sat down on one of the rocks that ringed the silver pool. "I know that you've met monsters that look like men before. I know of at least one."

"You know nothing," Legeia snarled. She slunk to the pool's edge and dipped her wounded hand into the metallic waters. The pool bubbled and steamed about her wrist. The siren hissed between her teeth. But when she withdrew her hand, her talons came out whole and her cut healed. She ran her sharp nails against one another, slashing in the air at Jim. But she did not come closer, and the magic sword remained quiet. "Why have you come to torment me, Son of Earth and Son of Sea?"

"I don't want to torment you, Legeia," said Jim. "But I need to know something. I need to know how to find the ancient temple. I need to know where the altar is, the one that can be used with the Treasure of the Ocean. No seeker can find this place, and you're the only one left who knows the way. My mother said you would tell me."

Legeia threw her head back and laughed. It was an ugly laugh, dull as a rusted knife. "You lie! Your mother is long dead. And why would I tell you such a thing? So that you might rule the world? You are as arrogant as your father, young Morgan. You are a fool to come here, for I will not help you."

"My mother is dead." Jim pulled the lifeless pearl from beneath his shirt, letting it glimmer in sun. Even in the shaft of sunlight falling through the trees, the emptied pearl looked dim. The jungle heat felt heavier on Jim's shoulders than it had the entire day as he tucked the silver charm away again. "But she told me you would help me nevertheless. It was the last thing she ever said."

"A soul stone?" Legeia asked, arching one eyebrow. "At the Well of Spirits? Then why did she not tell you herself? She knows the way."

"Yes, she could have," Jim whispered. "But the Well of Spirits was destroyed. My mother is gone forever."

"Then be grateful you were able to see your mother at all, to touch her, to speak with her even once in your life. Not all are so fortunate. Take your blessings and be gone with you. I will not help." Legeia turned from Jim and stalked back into the shadows. Jim was tempted to chase after her, to make her tell him what he needed to know. But he remembered what his mother had told him about the siren.

"I don't have the Treasure of the Ocean, Legeia. Bartholomew does. He and the count are probably heading for the temple even now." Legeia stopped, back still turned, her vestigial wings quivering on her shoulders. She was listening. "You know what will happen to him if he uses it. The same thing that happened to the Younger Brother in the ancient times."

"The same thing that will happen to you if you use it," snapped Legeia over her shoulder. "And the world will fall into darkness either way. So what's the difference?"

"There is another way, I think. There is a way to lock a door forever." At last Legeia turned to face Jim. She measured him in her glowing blue eyes.

"You have seen Bartholomew?" she asked after a moment. "You battled against him, I wager?" Legeia tried to keep her snarl fixed on her face, but her lips trembled too much, and her eyes were too fixed on Jim's face.

"Yes, I have. He looks like you... in a way."

"I have longed to look on him," Legeia whispered. "I tried through the power of the silver pool, but for some reason I could not. Is he... Is he misshapen?" Legeia looked away, to her reflection in the water. "Is he a monster? Like me?"

"No," Jim said, and for some reason, even though Legeia had drowned so many men, and had attacked Jim, he suddenly felt ashamed of the sword in his hand. "No, Legeia, he's not a monster. He is tall. He is strong. But his skin is pale like yours. His hair is black like yours. His eyes are blue like yours."

"Is he... Is he like his father?"

Jim thought about lying. But he could not.

"Yes, in many ways he is." Legeia's shoulders slumped. Her head fell.

"Then he is a monster. The count is a cruel man. He is a liar and a breaker of promises." The siren again turned to trudge back into the jungle.

"But in some ways he's not," Jim continued, as much to himself as to Legeia. He heard her stop by the pool. Jim reached up and touched a place on his cheek, where a small cut was still healing. "He let me go, Legeia. In the Kasbah of the Udayas, I was hanging by a ledge. Bartholomew stood above me. He pressed his sword against my face. But in return for a single kindness I had once shown him, Bartholomew pulled me up and showed me mercy. He let me go." Jim looked up, and found Legeia staring back at him – staring into him.

"You are not lying to me," she said. It was not a question. "About my son or about locking the doorway forever. You would do this thing?"

"Yes, I would."

Without another word, Legeia rose again to her full height and stepped up onto the ring of rocks. Looking down in the pool, she held her claws over the waters and sang her song again, but this time the words were beyond Jim's reckoning. The silver pool bubbled and frothed. Ripples flowed over the surface and the water glowed like the sun off a mirror. As Jim stared into the shimmering light, a map, showing the way to the ancient temple, was etched upon his mind. He saw the rocky island. He saw the temple ruins upon the stones. But in the shimmering vision Jim also saw a fleet of Corsair vessels on the seas, sailing toward the island. It was the Cromiers. They had the Treasure of the Ocean. Legeia ceased her song, and the waters stilled again in the silence.

"Now, go, young Morgan. Prove yourself and keep your word. But I must tell you this also – I too saw a vision in the silver pool… of the future. You told the truth, and so will I, and my truth is just as painful as yours was to me: The way before you is a dark path. Beware, for death and doom lie in wait, and I fear you cannot escape their clutches."

The siren retreated into the shadows. Jim opened his mouth to thank her, but her dark tidings stole the thanks from his lips. He turned to leave the clearing and begin the trek back to his skiff, but he heard Legeia call once more to him as he stepped into the trees.

"Your first test waits for you on the Wastewaters, Son of Earth and Son of Sea. The fruits of the count's evil deeds await you. The Crimson Storm comes for you."

FORTY

IN LONDON AGAIN

Lacey felt as though she had slept for days beneath the canvas shadow of the gypsy wagon. It was a magic sleep, for even her dreams were shielded from the dragon's prophecy, the foretelling of doom that had harried her along the hard road from the north. She regained her strength. The aches in her muscles subsided, the weariness in her feet melted away, and her cuts and bruises faded into scars.

But even more, her hope, which had all but withered and died, bloomed again. She was going find Jim. She was going to find George. Together they would defeat the Cromiers. Together they would find a home, and peace, at last. But a shaking on Lacey's shoulder told her the time for dreaming was over. It was time to wake up.

Lacey found Peter and Paul leaning over her as she blinked awake. The morning sun poured through the flap at the back of the wagon. It was plainly visible that the boys had taken the same rest as Lacey, for even the sun shone less brightly than the long lost smiles on their faces.

"We made it, Lacey," said Peter. "We're in London."

"It's time to go," said Paul, pulling at Lacey's arm. "Cornelius is already out, flappin around and what not, checkin things out for us." Indeed, Lacey found that all was quiet in the wagon. The rumbling of the wheels on the bumpy path had gone silent, and the steady sway of the rocking wagon bed had gone still. She yawned deeply, stretched her arms, and finally gave in to the Ratts' eager insistence.

"All right, all right. I'm up, I'm up."

"You seem vell rested, young one," said the dry voice from the back of the wagon. The old Gypsy, who was leaning up against some skeins of silk, her eyes half closed as though on the verge of sleep herself, smiled at Lacey. "Tis good to see the color returned to your cheeks, and the hope to your eyes. You vill need both for your journey, I think."

"Thank you for helping us. I'm not sure we would have made it if it weren't for you." As Lacey stared at the old crone, who had peered into her dreams and gifted her with an enchanted sleep, she was struck by a sudden, mad thought. "Excuse me for asking, but are you the Gypsy Witch? The one who cursed Jim's box all those years ago? You seem so much like the way he described you. But you can't be, can you? What would be the chances?"

"The chances, young one?" The gypsy laughed a tired cackle, wheezing at the edges. "Valk along the river and you vill see fish. Valk beneath the trees and you vill see birds. Valk the vays of magic and danger, and you vill meet heroes and villains. Such things should not surprise you, child."

"Jim did end up getting his box unlocked, after all. Of course, it was not without some trouble. But I suppose you already knew that, didn't you?"

"Yes, child. I knew this. But sometimes I vonder if it would have been better had he not. But then he would not be who he is now, would he? And I see that would be a loss for you, would it not child?" Lacey blushed. Her cheeks and her ears grew hot.

"Jim said you had a crystal ball. He said you looked into it and saw the future, that very same night you locked up his box. I was wondering if..." Lacey could see in the Gypsy's face that the old crone knew her question before she asked it, and that the answer was no. Already, after waking only a few moments ago, the dragon's words had wormed their way into the back of her mind, along with the visions of doom.

"Today has enough troubles, child. Do not carry tomorrow's as vell. Besides, I am old. My magic is not as strong as it once vas. But here – perhaps I have enough left for this." The Gypsy sat up with a groan and leaned over on her creaky arm. She reached out one hand, skin dry as sandpaper, and touched Lacey's cheek. Then she kissed Lacey on the forehead with lips like autumn leaves. Where the kiss touched, a warmth drifted down into Lacey's body. The worry in her thoughts and the flutter in her stomach eased enough for her to smile again. "Now go, young one. Go to the Inn of the Vet Rock, on the Isle of Dogs. You have been there before, yes? Go there and look for the dirty pearl... perhaps vith a rough polish, it might shine again, and help you on your way."

"So, it's back to the Inn of the Wet Rock, eh?"

Paul walked with his thumbs hooked into his lapels and the old Ratt swagger in his step. The three friends, along with Cornelius, who had found the clan soon after leaving the gypsies and now rode upon Lacey's shoulder, headed quickly for the docks. For the first time in years, Lacey and the Ratts were back on the cobblestone streets of London. Lacey found that she still knew her way, recalled the smells, and remembered the thrill of living life on the run in the alleys of one of the greatest cities in the world.

"That Inn was the scene of one of me greatest cons, I reckon," Paul continued. "Do you remember the pile of gold we had goin from all them scalawags?"

"I remember havin to give it all back," said Peter. "To be your greatest con, shouldn't you have gotten to keep the rich stuff, Paulie?"

"That wasn't my fault, Peter. That was Dread Steele we was up against. Not just any old bloke, now was he? He was a crafty old salt, he was."

"Indeed he was, lads," said Cornelius quietly, trying not give himself away as a magical creature in the heart of London. "And I will say, Paul, the captain once admitted to me that he nearly fell for your trick. Some of the fastest hands he had ever seen, and that is saying something."

"Ha!" Paul cried, raising his hands victoriously over his head.

"Well, your con was all right and all, Paul, but, in case you forgot, I did just unlock the magic chains that imprisoned a dragon for somethin like a thousand years." A sly smirk stretched across Peter's face as he polished his nails on his jacket. "I would say that qualifies me for greatest lock pick of all time. Not that I'm braggin or anythin."

"No, that doesn't sound like bragging at all, Peter." Lacey threw a look over her shoulder at him as they rounded a corner. "And don't feel too badly, Paul. As I recall, it was you who outwitted the three harpies on the Veiled Isle and allowed us to escape."

"That's right!" Paul shouted. "So there, *Peter*! If it hadn't been for me and me marble, you'd be just another set of bones in that big pile at the bottom of the harpy's nest. Although, I bet them harpies woulda spit you back out, cause you taste like—"

"Do not say anything disgusting, Paul," Lacey cut Paul off before he could start a smaller version of a famous Ratt Brothers' brawl. She had just led the clan across a street, and found herself at the front of a long-closed shoe factory, the windows boarded up, dust and cobwebs shrouding the shingle on the dirty brick wall.

"Oh," she said aloud, skidding to a stop on the walk. Peter and Paul, still trying to outdo each other with past exploits, ran into her back.

"Oy, Lacey!" shouted Peter. "What are you—" But both he and Paul saw what it was together, and let out their own *Ohs*.

It was their old home – the shoe factory. All by themselves, Lacey's legs walked her around to the alley behind the building, Peter and Paul following close behind.

The hole that led to the cellar was still there. It was smaller than Lacey remembered. How had they ever crawled so quickly in and out of there? Lacey knew they should be going. The Gypsy had told her to go quickly to the Inn of the Wet Rock, but Lacey could not help herself. She got down on her hands and knees and began to crawl inside. But the moment her eyes adjusted to the dim light, she wished she had not given into temptation…

…for a pair of gleaming eyes stared back from the hole in the wall.

Lacey scampered backwards into the alley. Just after her, slinking from the abandoned cellar, climbed three boys, all well on their way to becoming men. They were tall and thin, clothes not much more than stitched together rags on their lanky frames. Their wiry bodies were lean and strong, muscles taut as cords, with calloused eyes and cruel smiles.

"Well, well, well. Wouldya look at this boys? Never thought I'da seen the day," said the first of the street toughs who now lived in the cellar beneath the shoe factory, "when such a pre'y, pre'y girl would come a knockin on our door, so to speak."

"Pretty li'l thing indeed," said the second.

"Knock, knock, knock," said the third.

Peter and Paul squeezed close to Lacey. She checked quickly to the end of the alleyway, thinking of escape, but the pale lads from the hole had already begun to close in around her and the Ratts. Cornelius spread his wings on Lacey's shoulder, giving his identity away in a brave attempt to frighten off the street haunts.

"Be gone with the three of you! We have come from caves deep in the earth, and faced fire breathers of ancient days. We have come too far and fought too long to be bothered with the likes of you."

The three toughs paused for a moment, just long enough for Lacey to hope that Cornelius's bravado had worked. But it was not fear that broke over their greasy faces – only widening smiles.

"That really is a neat, neat trick, my li'l feathered friend, but it won't work on us quite as well this time."

"Won't work at all, feathered friend."

"A neat trick, it is, it is!"

"Again?" said Lacey. But she suddenly realized where she had seen these three lads before – when they were but children themselves. "You were with Red's Clan, weren't you? You were there that day in the snow." Lacey remembered the day as though it were yesterday. She and George had just been in a fight and Jim was trying to make her feel better, when they were set upon by Big Red and these very same street toughs. It was the day she had first met Cornelius.

"Indeed we was, pre'y li'l girl. Indeed we was. Your li'l bird friend there, he frightened us good, but we was just kids back then. I also remember you knockin ol Big Red flat on his pants in the street, yes we do. But neither of them's gonna work again. We's become proper criminals these days, while it seems your mates have become proper gents… and you's become a proper lady."

Lacey let not a drop of fear cross her face. She had, after all, just faced a dragon with the power of whole armies in his wings. But inside, she felt her heart begin to hammer. For during her time with the Cromiers, Lacey had learned that sometimes men could be worse than dragons.

Lacey balled up her fists. Cornelius readied himself for battle on her shoulder. Peter and Paul raised their own guards at her side. But before the tussle could begin, a long shadow stretched over the scene, a giant silhouette all but filling the entrance to the alley with a cloaked frame. The dark shape held a great staff in his hands, tapping its end into his open palm with a thump, thump, thump.

"I think that'll be just about enough out of the three of you," said the shape. "The next time I catch you causin trouble to the people on my streets, it'll be the cell for you… or worse." The man slapped the staff against the palm of his big hand with finality.

The cruel sneers on the toughs' faces fled, and they suddenly looked more like the dirty little urchins Lacey remembered. They scampered out the other end of the alley, all but falling over one another to escape. But the danger was not yet passed. Lacey turned to face whatever the shadow revealed itself to be – something frightening enough to scare away three street-hardened lads. But when the shape spoke again, his voice was kinder, and more familiar than it had been a moment ago.

"As I live and breathe," said the shadow. "If it ain't the Brothers Ratt and little Lacey, returned from who knows where to the streets of London Towne." He stepped further into the alley, and with the morning light off his shoulders, his face came into view. He was a mountain of a man, dressed in a blue cloak and tricorn hat, the badge of the King's Men upon his breast. A bright smile broke beneath a droopy mustache and above a thick curly beard.

A sigh of relief escaped Lacey's lips. She let her fists fall back to her sides and a smile cross her cheeks. "I never thought I would say this, sir," she said, "but it's good to see you again, Constable Butterstreet."

Not a few minutes later, Lacey and the Ratts sat in the constable's office, sipping on mugs of hot tea. Though summer had ended only a few weeks before, cool autumn winds were blowing through the streets of London, and the clan warmed themselves by the stove in the corner, coals glowing orange and rippling the air within.

"Thank you for the tea," said Lacey. "I wish we could stay longer, but we'll need to be going soon."

"I won't try and stop you, my young friends," said the constable. He was sitting in a chair by the cell, leaning back with his huge feet propped up on the deputy's desk, which was empty. "There were rumors, of course, of where you all disappeared to after that night in the streets. Goodness, it's still the talk of the pubs and the inns from time to time – pirates battlin soldiers, Dread Steel hisself in London, magic on full display. I certainly never saw anythin like it before or since. But I was always wonderin where you all had gotten off to. No need to explain it all, if you don't like, but I've been a King's Man for a long, long time, and I can tell when folks have somethin important to tend to. I could always tell by the look of your friend, Jim Morgan, that he was up to important things. Maybe even terribly important things. Where is he, by the way? And Georgie?"

Lacey gripped her teacup in both hands. Her lips pursed tight around the words she wanted to say, but they seemed stuck in her throat. "That's why we have to be going, sir," she finally managed.

"I see," said the constable, taking his feet off the desk. "I don't suppose this is anythin with which I could lend you aid, is it?" Lacey shook her head. The constable stood and approached the stove, staring into the glowing coals, nodding his head grimly. "Can't say I fully understand why, but there have been evenins, especially the stormy sort, when the wind was blowin and the thunder crashin, that I looked through this window, or the one in me little house, and thought of you young ones. Somethin important they had to do, I would think. Somethin more important than anyone would figger for a bunch of kids off the street. But you never know who'll play a part in the fate of things, do you? Which might make this next introduction a bit less surprising."

Constable Butterstreet nodded his head toward the door just as his deputy came in off the street. He was as tall and lanky as the three lads who had just nearly caused a great deal of trouble for Lacey and the Ratts, but the smile he wore on his freckled face was so much kinder, and his face so much brighter than theirs had been. When he pulled his own tricorn hat from his head, a tangle of red hair, very nearly bright as a carrot, came tumbling out.

"It can't be!" said Peter.

"Big Red, is that you?" asked Paul.

"Most people call me Bill, these days," said the deputy, and the sweet smile on his face grew wider by twice. "But you can still call me Red if you like, Paul Ratt. I always knew I'd see you all again. Don't know why, but always knew I would."

"Red, you're a deputy?" Lacey was unable to hide the surprise in her voice. "Whoever would have guessed?" Red blushed nearly as brightly as his hair, folding his hat in his hands.

"Not me, that's for sure."

"You see?" said the constable, smiling again. "You never know how a body will turn out till you see for certain. Red even sings in me church choir. Best tenor in the lot if you ask me. And he really did believe he would see you all again. Bill, our guests will be leavin soon, so if you wish to give 'em what you found, now's the time."

Bill, who had once been Big Red, the meanest lunk Lacey and the Ratts had ever known, nodded his head and rushed over to his little desk. He opened a drawer and pulled out a few folded pieces of parchment, held together with a brown string.

"I went back to St. Anne's not long ago, more to apologize to the nuns for what a terror I was back then, you know." Bill stared more at his feet than looked at Lacey and the Ratts. "And to say sorry for runnin away. But they let me have my paper when I was there, the one that tells me who me mum and me dad were. And I don't know why, but I thought of you all, and I thought for sure I would see you again one day, so I took yours too." Bill gave the papers over to Lacey, who took them with trembling hands.

"Thank you, Red... I mean, Bill."

"Milady," was all he said in return. He threw his hat on his head, tipped it once to Lacey and the boys, and dashed back out in the street without another word.

"Sweet boy is Bill, sweeter than you ever thought he could be," said Butterstreet. "Feels something awful for the way he was, and works hard every day to make up for it. He's the best deputy I ever had. Well, I must be back to work meself." Butterstreet took up his cloak and his staff, and put his own hat back on his head. "I wish the three of ye the best luck you might have, and I'm sorry I have naught more to give ye than that. Let yerselves out when ye go, and Godspeed." The constable tipped his own hat, and then he was off.

"A kind gift indeed," said Cornelius, who had been keeping quiet this entire time. He flapped down from Lacey's shoulder onto her lap, peering curiously at the parchment in her hand. "I've never heard you make mention of your surname, Lacey. I imagine it is as sweet and noble as you deserve."

"I forgot what it was," said Lacey. She turned the paper over in her hands. "My mother never told it to me after my father went away." Without a word more, she threw the parchment into the stove. It blackened and crisped in but an instant, turning to smoky ash and swirling away up the chimney. Lacey was glad Red, or Bill the Deputy as he was now known, had left, so he would not see her destroy his gift.

"What did you do that for, Lacey?" asked Peter, staring into the stove, his mouth hanging open. "Now you'll never know your last name."

"Let's go," was all Lacey said to this. What she did not say was that names were important to her, for they partly said who a person was. It was why Big Red went by Bill now, for he wasn't the same person he had once been. It was why Jim never again went by James, which is how he had been called before he came to London. And if

Lacey was going to have a last name ever again, she wanted it to be one that meant more than just running away. "We need to get to the Inn of the Wet Rock."

Out the door Lacey marched, with Cornelius on her shoulder and the Ratts behind. They needed to go in search of the filthy pearl, whatever that was, and a way back out on the high seas – a way back to George, and Jim, and possibly to whatever doom the dragon said lay in store for them all.

FORTY-ONE

THE WAR ON THE WAVES

Jim saw it on the horizon an hour after he left the Island of the Silver Pool, when night was closing its fist about the world. It was a deeper darkness lurking on the edge of the sea, snuffing out the first stars like candles. A flicker of demon red flashed across the surface of the spreading black.

Jim glanced down at Egidio's enchanted compass. He felt the cool wind at his back. He listened to the canvas sails ruffle and pull him across the waves. All three of them, the compass, the wind, and the sail, pointed the way to Spire Island. And all three of them pointed a way through the Crimson Storm.

Jim reached into Egidio's bag to check his stores, finding one Aeolus Feather, a single waterskin, and not another scrap of food.

There was less than enough of anything remaining, especially time, to sail around the storm, and Jim knew he could not escape.

Night came quickly, the storm on her heels.

Jim sheeted in his little sail as the winds began to whirl. He tied the canvas tight to the cross mast. From the satchel, he took all the rope he could find. He lashed Egidio's magic bag down to the back of the little boat and tied another length around the till, winding its end about his wrist. The last coil he wrapped about his waist, cinching it tight, looping the other end about the mainmast of his small boat. It would be his lifeline. He checked the compass one last time and took one last drink of water – then away with those things in the satchel.

In Jim's left hand he held the line on the till. In his right, he took the magic sword. He went to the bow of the boat – only he, the ship, the sea, and the storm.

The storm stretched out in the sky. The crimson fire burned at the edges of the clouds, setting its blackness apart from the night. Purple tongues of lightning lapped at the ocean water in flashing silence. The peals of thunder rolled after. They rumbled across the waves to where Jim stood, alone at the prow. This was the storm from which even MacGuffy ran, one of the bravest men Jim had ever known. This was the storm that had killed Dread Steele, the Lord of all Pirates. This storm was a taste of the Treasure of the Ocean's power.

Jim's rising and falling breaths matched the rush of the waves, running faster and stronger beneath the boat. His heart beat the war drum within his chest. A brief surge of panic welled up in his throat, but he swallowed it back down.

"A boy doesn't know what sort of man he'll be until he's sailed through the storms," Jim said to himself.

The lightning cracked sharper. The thunder crashed harder. The waves smashed into the ship like the first charge of cavalry.

But Jim did not move from the prow. He had been taught to sail by the greatest men of the sea ever born: by MacGuffy and by

Dread Steele. He had the strength of his father and the magic of his mother in his blood.

"Come on then," Jim whispered to the sky. "Come do your worst, and let's see if I'm still here when you're done."

The magic sword began to whine at Jim's side, singing its high note, trembling in his hand.

"Come on then," Jim said to the wind and the waves.

The thunder clapped in return, and the lightning tongues lolled from the black clouds.

"Come on then!" Jim cried to the storm. And it answered with fury.

A canyon opened up in the water. The boat tilted over the edge and careened into the gulf. Jim learned what it was to be swallowed whole. The water was all about him like the jaws of some unfathomable beast, a maw great enough to swallow a fleet of ships in one gulp. Jim and his boat were but a speck upon its frothing tongue.

Jim strained against the rope lashed to the till. He pulled with all his might to hold it straight – to sail himself into the wave. He would ride it and climb to the top of the rolling mountainside. He finally reached the bottom of the valley of water, and when he struck the trough, the wave bore him up.

Jim all but stood on the nose of the boat. It rose straight into the air like an eagle climbing into the sky. The rain lashed him hard on the face, falling like arrows. The lip of the wave loomed over his head. And above the foaming ledge, curling to tumble over and bear down on Jim, the crimson clouds waited. Lightning burned like cannon fire within its roiling folds.

Jim crested the wave. The face in the storm greeted him with a deafening war cry. Its maw was open, as if to gnash Jim within its teeth and rend him to pieces. A fire burned within the mouth and behind the eyes. The storm threw its first bolt of lightning – a spear of fire white hot enough to melt stone.

The enchanted sword leapt up in Jim's hand. It sang louder than the roar of the waves and the boom of the thunder. It met the lightning head on. The flash dazzled Jim's vision. The heat singed his hair and burned the skin at his nose and cheeks. He felt the strike crash against the sword and sail off to the starboard, parried by the enchanted blade. For an instant, not even a full moment, Jim thought he saw a flash of concern in the storm's eyes. Then fury washed all else away. The storm threw itself upon Jim Morgan. The face in the clouds descended in a whirling funnel. The waves towered over the boat and more than once they washed over Jim. But his lifeline was made of Egidio's unbreakable rope, and it held true.

The storm hurled bolt after bolt down on Jim's head. It swept the lightning from side to side, slashing at Jim to slice his little boat in two. But the enchanted sword would not surrender a blow. The magic blade, humming in Jim's hand, began to jerk him by the arm less and less. He and the blade began to fight together.

Still, Jim knew he could not battle forever. His arm was bleeding from the rope. His shoulder burned from dueling the storm. His legs ached from holding fast at the prow. The storm smelled blood in the water, and it took the moment to strike hardest yet, to finish this fight forever.

Power gathered in the storm's gut, coiling from all edges of the churning clouds. When all its might was readied, the storm unleashed a lightning strike strong enough to burn a hole in the world.

Jim raised his sword. The bolt slammed into him like avalanche. Jim's knees buckled. His arm quivered. A cry escaped his lips. But he did not let go of his sword.

The lightning grabbed at the edge of the blade. The heat of all the storm's hatred and vengeance burned down through the metal and into Jim's hand. Jim summoned all his will and all his hope from somewhere deep inside, from that place where little boys, battling imaginary enemies with wooden swords on white sand beaches all across the world, call up the courage to stand against all darkness for the sake of the light.

Jim pushed back against the storm. He threw the great bolt back at its maker.

The lightning exploded in the storm's crimson face. It blew a hole open in the clouds, straight through for Jim to see the stars on the other side. The black clouds fell back in on themselves, flinching about the wound.

The eyes flashed once more in the clouds – flashing with fear.

The black clouds shrank from Jim. They curled up into a ball and rolled away across the sky like a cowed bully, running for home. The rain ceased in the sky. The waves calmed themselves. The stars and the moon once more filled the night with light.

Jim held the magic sword up before his face. It burned hot orange, like a blade just pulled from the blacksmith's forge. Jim jabbed its point into the prow of his ship. The heat burned its way into the wood, and the sword stood tall on its point.

"Still here," Jim said to the shrinking black cloud. Then he let out his sail once more and made for Spire Island.

FORTY-TWO

BACK TO THE INN OF THE WET ROCK

ray clouds and an autumn wind had crawled over London by the time the clan reached the Isle of Dogs. The Gypsy Witch said they might find help there at the Inn of the Wet Rock. But as Lacey led the way, weaving between packs of sailors and huddles of old salts, she sensed a deeper chill behind their wary eyes. There was little of the hearty growls and coarse laughter she remembered from the first time she'd come, when Jim and George were so intent on finding the Amulet of Portunes all those years ago. Now the men whispered low amongst themselves, and more than once, Lacey caught them casting up furtive, fearful glances to the sky.

"It's quiet down on the docks," said Cornelius into Lacey's ear.

"And there ain't many ships in port," added Peter, nodding

toward the piers lined up down the Thames River. "Not like last time anyhow."

"What's gotten into them all, Cornelius?"

"They know, young ones. Gossip travels fast upon the water, leaping from ship to ship like fleas. They know the Crimson Storm is on the prowl. They've heard that the Red Count has closed in on his prize. Some of them may have already guessed that he has it in his possession."

"So where have they all run off to then?" asked Paul. "From what Jim was sayin, there ain't gonna be no safe place nowhere if Bartholomew gets that Treasure to the temple. No safe place on land or sea at all."

"Men of the sea are odd sorts, if you hadn't already figured that out for yourself. They trust a deck beneath their boots more than the tallest mountain on the earth. Some of them will sail as far away as they can, but the braver souls will be headed in the same direction as we hope to go – to Spire Island. Not that we shall be safe there, mind you. All the world is at risk, and will be, for as long as both the Treasure of the Ocean and a Son of Earth and Son of Sea exist at the same time."

"Well, not if Jim got a hold of the Treasure, right Cornelius?" asked Peter. "I mean, then the world would prolly be better off, right?"

Lacey glanced out of the corner of her eye at the raven, riding upon her shoulder. The raven was looking back. They were both afraid. Neither she nor the black bird answered Peter's question, but she quickened her pace toward the Inn of the Wet Rock.

Time had grown short.

If there was one place on the Isle of Dogs that seemed to hold at least a measure of cheer, it was the Inn of the Wet Rock. Within the stone walls and beneath the thatched roof, the ale still flowed, the fireplaces still crackled, the scent of roasted meat still wafted, and the laughter of men still rang true.

"Don't this lot know that the world's about to end?" asked Peter, standing close behind Lacey at the door.

"Enough ale and a fool will laugh in the face of Death himself," answered Cornelius. "Then he'll simply be a dead fool."

"You don't reckon the old barkeep still remembers everythin from the last time, do you?" asked Paul. "I believe his exact words, after throwin us out on our ears, was 'Don't come back... ever.'"

"I don't know, Paul," said Lacey. "And I don't want to find out. Besides that, we don't have time to waste, so let's be to our business."

"And what exactly are we lookin for?"

Lacey was about to answer, when a chorus of howling laughter and bawdy cheers rose over the inn. One of the bar backs was screaming like a monkey, hobbling around a barrel of ale — a knife protruding from his substantial left buttock.

"Sorry about that, Johnny," bellowed a slurred voice from across the inn. "I don't suppose One-Buttock Johnny is a very good name at all, is it?"

"A filthy pearl indeed," Lacey said, glaring at the man who had just thrown the blade into poor Johnny's rear. "We're looking for him." Lacey stormed into the heart of the inn. If the Gypsy Witch had not told her she would need this arrogant pirate's help, she would have been plotting revenge on him for abandoning her and the others on the waters above the merfolk's city.

"Nouble or Duthin!" F.W. Pennington Sharpe was just saying to the pirate audience gathered about his table, another sizeable pile of doubloons, jewels, and silver pieces stacked before him. He still wore a tricorn hat with a large white plume, and his powder blue coat, unspecked by even a hint of dirt. From his pocket, once again, he withdrew the magnificent pearl, and laid it on the jumble of treasure.

"Good evening, Captain Sharpe," shouted Lacey, loud enough to be heard by everyone in the inn. "I was wrong about you, you know.

I thought you were a smart enough man to at least pull a different scam in each port to which you sail. What do you think, Paul?"

"You even used the same jokes, mate." Paul shook his head, a disappointed frown creasing his face, his arms folded over his skinny chest. "That's for amateurs."

"And just how many bar backs have you knifed in the hiney?" asked Peter, aghast, checking on poor Johnny and clucking his teeth. "It's not right."

The pirates about the table, and even those gathered about the various fireplaces around the inn, craned their necks and scratched their scruffy jaws. Their eyes darted back and forth between Sharpe and Lacey, who stood with a midnight black raven upon her shoulder, and whose blue eyes flashed with fury. But true to his words before, Sharpe never missed a beat and never showed a single crack in his mask. He doubled over, spewing out a wheezing laugh, and slammed his fist on the table so hard that the gold jumped and the drinks spilled.

"Look!" cried Sharp in his drunken slur, laughing so hard he was crying. "I do b'lieve thass an angel who's losss her wings... and if she's wounnup here, she's more loss than any angel I ever seen!"

A few of the pirates began to laugh at Sharpe's joke, but Lacey was in no mood for humor and had no time for lies. She flashed out her hand like a snake strike and seized a heavy tin right out of the hand of the pirate about to drink from it. She hurled the cup, still full of ale, straight at Sharpe's face.

The captain was a clever liar indeed, and a practiced con, but he was also a skilled warrior. Even he could not outwit his own reflexes. Sharpe snapped to attention and his sword flashed from its scabbard, slashing so fast and so true that it sliced through the tin, spraying all the pirates about him with ale, and leaving the two halves spinning on the floor.

The crowd stared in open-mouthed silence at the captain's impressive display of swordsmanship for a long moment... until they realized what it meant. Then their open mouths curled into sneers, and their wide eyes narrowed into hateful slits. All the while, a slow smile spread over Lacey's face.

"I can't even begin to tell you how good it is to see you all again," said Sharpe, darkly, stalking down the cobblestone street, checking over his shoulder every few paces or so, just to make sure he'd lost the angry mob of pirates he had just cheated.

"Where is your honor, Sharpe?" cawed Cornelius, as he and the others followed close on the captain's heels. Sharpe stopped so quickly that Lacey and the Ratts nearly ploughed into him. He turned on the raven, leveling a gloved finger at his beak.

"You all knew where my honor had gone the day you hired me, Darkfeather – to the bottom of the ocean. So don't ask questions to which you already know the answers. It is unbecoming of we men of the sea. And as for MacGuffy..." A shadow passed over the captain's face. "If I had lifted even just a finger, I and all the men who once sailed with Steele would be lying cold beside him. We were outnumbered and outmatched. We stood no chance."

"The F.W. Pennington Sharpe I once knew laughed in the face of such odds," said Cornelius.

"Well then," said Sharpe, finding his sly smile once again and staring back down the street. "I wish you the best of luck in finding him. But this one just lost out on a year's worth of gold, and I'm not going to find any more in this town, thanks to you lot. So if you'll excuse me."

"You still owe us a voyage, Captain Sharpe," raged Lacey, storming in front of him and blocking his way, stomping her foot on the cobblestone. "You only took us one way the first time, you owed us a trip back. So I'm here to collect."

"And you still owe me one thousand gold pieces for the first trip, young lady. Do you have it on you? Let's not even mention the one thousand you would have owed for the second leg of the journey. I used a great length of magic rope the first time, if you don't recall, and that stuff doesn't come cheap."

"The world is about to end, Captain," said Lacey. "All of it. The Cromiers have the Treasure of the Ocean. Doesn't that mean anything to you?"

"Yes. It means if you're headed in that direction, I should probably point myself in the other. So, again, if you'll excuse me."

Sharpe skirted around Lacey, stretching his legs and picking up his gait to speed away. Lacey's shoulders fell. The thickness in her throat that she'd been suppressing finally burst loose. Her nose stung and her eyes burned. Captain Sharpe's rushing figure blurred in her vision.

"What would you do if someone stole your pearl, Captain Sharpe?" she yelled after him. "That one in your pocket – the one that came from the merfolk? It's the only thing you care about besides yourself, isn't it?"

"That's why I don't lose the things I care about, young lady," Sharpe called over his shoulder as he patted his coat pocket. "I keep it close to—" Sharpe froze. He patted his coat harder and frantically reached inside.

"Not close enough, mate," said Paul Ratt. On the tips of his clever fingers he held the immaculate pearl, a sly grin spreading over his cheeks. "She is a beauty though, innit she?"

The trademark smile on Captain Sharpe's face fell away. His eyes blazed with a sudden fury. He covered the distance between himself and the Ratts in the blink of an eye. His sword rang from its sheath like lightning. The point hovered an inch from Paul's nose.

"Little Ratt," the captain rasped. "Unless you want to see your hand on the street beside you, you will give back what is mine at once."

"What's so important about it, anyway?" asked Peter. "You don't even sell it for money."

"That pearl is all I have left of—" Sharpe's voice caught. His usually smiling lips quivered. "It matters not. What should matter to you is that I would fight an entire army to get it back. And if you ran from me, I would chase you ten times 'round the world to hunt you down."

Lacey ran the back of her arm across her face, spilling a few tears down her cheeks. She stepped between the captain and the Ratts. With one hand she took the pearl from Paul and with the other she gently pushed Sharpe's blade aside.

"Now do you understand, Captain Sharpe? Our pearl was taken from us. It's not the Treasure of the Ocean, or revenge against the Red Count, or all the gold in the world. We would do anything to get it back. I would do anything. I would sail across the sea. I would promise myself to a dragon. I would beg a captain who already abandoned us once to help us again, just to get back what I'd lost."

Lacey held the pearl out to Sharpe. He took it from her and held it before him. He stared into its perfect surface for what seemed like a long time, until finally he looked up to meet Lacey's eyes.

"I'm not asking you to sail ten times around the world, Captain," she said. "I'm only asking for once. Please."

FORTY-THREE

To Spire Island

L acey stood on the *Spectre's* prow with Peter and Paul, petting Cornelius. The ocean wind swept her auburn curls from her face, giving her a clear view of the stone tower, rising above Spire Island.

F.W. Pennington Sharpe, scoundrel that he was, had been convinced at last to sail Lacey and the Ratts to the pirate isle. He had used his one remaining coil of magic rope to pull the ship the entire length of their journey in but a single night. Although morning gray lay cool over the waves rushing toward the small island, Lacey's skin felt warm and itchy, her insides afire with ticking time. The Cromiers had taken possession of the Treasure of the Ocean days ago. And though Cornelius assured her that they would surely have known if Bartholomew had already inserted the Treasure into the altar, the count and his son were drawing near to their goal – to the ultimate power and the darkening of the earth.

It was bad enough to be so far behind in such a race as this, Lacey thought, but it was worse without Jim and George beside them. Lacey had no idea where to even start looking for her lost friends.

A hopeless lump swelled in Lacey's throat, but she swallowed hard and forced it down. Her whole life had been rather hopeless, really. She probably should have died on the streets of London as a little girl, alone and abandoned. She probably should have perished at the hands of the King of Thieves, or Count Cromier, or the dragon. But somehow she had survived them all. And what chance had a girl with no family, no past, and no name, in the eyes of a boy born with royal, magic blood? Yet here she was.

"Look at all them ships," said Peter, one foot on the railing, pointing to the island. "I never seen so many here at one time." Lacey saw at once that Peter was right. Spire Island bristled with pirate ships from the world over. The mighty vessels were packed in a tight ring, like a thorn bush fence about the piers, masts and bowsprits like a leafless forest on the waters.

"It would seem I was correct," said Cornelius. "Those of us who know what danger looms have either fled, or gathered here, looking for news… or hope, if any of it remains."

"Cornelius, is there anywhere we could go?" asked Paul, checking the sky with round eyes. "Could we go where the others sailed? Could we go where they ran away if Bartholomew uses that spear thing at the temple? Is there somewhere to hide?" Cornelius flapped over to Paul, resting on his shoulder and patting the back of his head with a feathery wing. Lacey also leaned over to the youngest Ratt, taking his hand in hers.

"How I would like to say there is, Master Ratt. But even I don't know for sure. This magic is older than any being that still walks the earth or swims the sea. This power is greater than any army or navy in the world. I don't know what hope there is if the Cromiers win the day... but I do know there is still hope to stop them – even if it is only a sliver. That is where we should focus our thoughts."

"Well, I will say this: The young lady gave one speech that softened a heart of stone," said Captain Sharpe, approaching the prow with his hands behind his back, while Mister Gilly steered the Spectre into the last empty berth in the island's docks. "If any of you here really do hold heart that the side of good might win the day – which I do not, for the record – let's hope she has another one ready behind those earnest blue eyes of hers."

"Me?" said Lacey, releasing Paul's hand and fighting that lump in her throat all over. "Why would any of these pirates listen to me? I'm nobody to them."

"Well, this is an island of cutthroats, scoundrels, thieves, raiders, and poltroons who don't think about much of anything beyond themselves. You might be the one person in a thousand leagues that honestly believes in anything else. And, whether you know it or not, sometimes a bit of honesty to a bunch of liars sounds like the best idea any of them has ever heard."

"Be that as it may, Sharpe," cawed Cornelius, "we hardly have time to chase down every captain on the island, don't we?"

"Darkfeather, that is the one problem you won't have." Sharpe nodded his head to the docks, where the wooden piers met Shelltown's cobblestone streets. The entire edge of town was swallowed in a tumultuous crowd of pirates, as jammed together as their ships were packed about the isle. From where Lacey stood, she could see fists waving and fingers pointing, and she could hear voices shouting and curses rising over the mob.

The hot, itchy prickle on her skin began to burn.

F.W. Pennington Sharpe led the way down the pier, Lacey and the Ratts in tow, with Mister Gilly, Murdoch, Wang Chi, and mighty Mufwalme bringing up the rear. Lacey peeked around the captain's elbow and found that the pirates were holding some sort of town meeting, having erected a small podium on the street. On the wooden stand, Lacey recognized the two pirates currently managing the crowd's attention. They were the other pirates MacGuffy had nearly recruited at the start of this adventure – Lo Fang and Golden Ginny. As Sharpe and the Spectre's crew approached, it seemed the entire throng turned their way, waiting for them to join the deliberations.

"Each time I lays eyes upon the *Spectre*," said Lo Fang, shaking his bald head, "my heart still hopes to find Dread Steele at her helm, and to hear his voice cry out over the waters. We are surely in need of his counsel now."

"Well, if matters continue upon their present course," said Sharpe cheerfully, stopping the small party at the edge of the wooden platform, "it may not be much longer before you can find him in the afterlife and speak freely again." Several of the pirates in the crowd laughed bitterly, but most began to murmur amongst themselves, deep frowns upon their faces and worried furrows on their brows.

"This is hardly a time for jokes, Sharpe," said Golden Ginny, not a trace of a smile upon her perfect face. "Scuttlebutt is that Count Cromier has found what he long sought. That he's killed young Morgan. That nothing now stands in the way of his mad quest. All that being said, I thought for certain you would have high-tailed it for the New World by now with the rest of the cowards."

"Oh, you know me, Ginny," said Sharpe. "I go where the wind blows, and the wind just happened to blow me here with you cheerful lot. Perhaps after, we can all cozy up for another bout of knives?"

"This is a pirate council, Sharpe," said Lo Fang, glowering. "We are trying to decide what to do. Some say this is all just madness and fairy tales, others that we should track down Count Cromier this very moment, and others still that we should set sail for distant waters and never look back. Do you know something that might help us? You command the *Spectre* now, and that ship, for good or ill, has always been at the heart of these grave matters. What say you, Captain?"

"All I say is this: If you're all going to decide to do something foolish, or cowardly, or brave – which is really a lot like foolish, isn't it – then you best know what you're up against. And perhaps you should hear it from an eye witness."

Sharpe stepped aside. Lacey felt the weight of nearly a thousand eyes fall upon her slender shoulders. Her insides turned to water and that itchy feeling upon her skin became hot as a fever. But Cornelius flapped up to her shoulder to give her courage, and Golden Ginny reached out her hand to help Lacey up to the podium.

From atop the platform, Lacey looked to the crowd. They were quiet as ghosts, their faces – darkened by the sun, wizened by the years, and scarred by the hard life of the sea – were set upon her. Lacey grabbed the sides of her dress and squeezed them in her hands. She shoved that hopeless, fearful lump aside and spoke, the morning breeze off the ocean carrying her words over the mob.

"The Treasure of the Ocean is real. I saw it with my own eyes. I touched it with my own hands. Count Cromier has it. He took it from the last fire-breathing dragon in England, and he's had it for almost four days."

The pirates erupted into a wave of voices, which washed over Lacey and nearly drove her off the platform. Some shouted that they'd known it all along, others quailed in unintelligible fear, but most scoffed and laughed. Lacey could hear the derision in their voices, and could see it in their eyes. Why should they listen to a pretty little piece of street trash from London? That question, ringing in the back of Lacey's mind, while the pirates fought amongst themselves, loosed the lightning she kept bottled up behind her blue eyes.

"I'm not a liar!" she shouted, stepping so far forward on the platform that her toes stuck over the edge. Whether it was the glare in her eyes, or the absence of fear, which Lacey's anger had just driven from her body, the pirates quieted themselves to a murmur and listened. "And for those of you who think I am, you should see this." Lacey nodded to Peter, who reached into his pocket and threw the object he'd kept hidden there for the last few days up to Lo Fang. The pirate turned it over in his hands. The color drained from his face as he realized what he held.

"It is a dragon scale," the pirate said. "And it has been pierced by some weapon."

A dismayed murmur floated over the crowd. Pirates threw up their hands or shook their heads. Some began to walk away.

"Please! Please, we must try!" Lacey cried. She searched the faces in the crowd for even one that offered some courage, or at least some hope. But all she found was despair. The pirates now believed the only option left was to run for their lives. "Surely there is something we can do. We can't let the count and Bartholomew take the Treasure to the temple. It will be the end of everything." Lacey looked to Lo Fang and Golden Ginny, but they too held their heads low.

"Wait!" said a tired, nasally voice from beside the platform. It was Mister Gilly, but he was not facing the shouting crowd or Lacey. The plump old sailor was staring out over the waters, peering into the rising sun, which had just slipped its first golden crescent over the horizon. "There's another ship comin in, sirs and ladies," said the sharp-eyed salt.

"I hardly think one other chap is going to make much a difference at this point, old boy," said Sharpe. "I believe we've heard all we need to hear today."

"Beggin your pardon, Cap'n," said Gilly, still staring hard. "But I think thissun just might."

A small skiff, only a silhouette before the rising sun, took shape as it neared the pier, its lone sail pulling it across the waters. Lacey knew it the moment she saw the figure at the front, one foot on the prow, one hand on the rudder rope, standing carefree in the ocean wind. She knew that shape like she knew her own, and a smile at last broke free on her face.

The morning sun warmed Jim's back as he sailed into the port at Spire Island. The ocean breeze rushed into his skiff's sail, running through the wild curls on his head. Jim stood tall at the prow, Egidio's satchel over his shoulder and the magic sword in his hand. He held the rudder true to course with his rope, steering himself toward the end of the closest mooring.

It seemed to Jim that an entire army of pirates awaited him on the pier. Almost every seaman he had ever met or known was there, including the crew of the *Spectre*. Cornelius was flapping his wings like mad on Mister Gilly's shoulder, and Mufwalme's great arms were raised in the air, shaking his fists in celebration. But when Jim looked past the sailors, he saw Peter and Paul, and between the two of them, he saw the face he had been thinking of since Count Cromier had sent him away with the black powder.

Jim kicked off the skiff and onto the pier, not even bothering to tie it down. He meant to run straight for Lacey, but the pirate horde set upon him at once, patting him on the shoulders and back, shouting his name over and over. Peter and Paul threw themselves on Jim at once, wrapping their arms around him tight.

"Thought we might never see you again," said Peter, his eyes wet.

"Glad you're back, Jim," added Paul.

Jim pulled them both close, telling them each how glad he was to see them as well. But when he finally released the Ratts, he met Lacey's eyes, and he suddenly found he was every bit as terrified as when he had faced the Crimson Storm on the open ocean. He had no idea what to say or what to do. But as she so often did, Lacey did the thinking for him. She put her hands on the sides of his face and pressed her lips on his. A warmth deeper than the morning sun poured through Jim into his bones, and he felt as though he might fly. The pirates laughed and whistled and cheered. Peter covered Paul's eyes. And Cornelius squawked in dismay. But Jim cared not one whit.

"Welcome back, Jim Morgan," said Lacey, once she had pulled away. She wrapped her arms around his neck, and Jim was sure he felt some wetness on her cheek as it rested against his own. Still holding Lacey close, Jim caught Captain Sharpe's knowing grin out of the corner of his eye.

"Well... now I am impressed," said the pirate. "Well done, Lord Morgan."

"Lord Morgan indeed," said Cornelius, and he too bowed his feathered head to Jim.

"There's no more time for congratulations, I'm afraid," said Jim. He finally let Lacey go and faced the pirates before him. "We have to leave, this very moment. I know where the island is. The merfolk are probably already there, and they're sure to give the Cromiers some trouble. But not even Nemus and his army will be able to stop Bartholomew when he's armed with the Treasure."

"I will sail with you, Lord Morgan," said Lo Fang. "To the end, if need be."

"And me," said Golden Ginny. "To the death."

"The crew of the Spectre is with you, Jim, as we always have been," said Cornelius, flapping down to Jim's shoulder.

"You're not goin anywhere without me and Paulie," said Peter.

"Or me," said Lacey, grabbing Jim by his hand. Jim squeezed it back.

"Well, I suppose I don't want to be the only chap left out of this party," said F.W. Pennington Sharpe. "That is, if you will have me, Lord Morgan."

"There's no gold in it, Sharpe," said Jim. But the captain only smiled.

"Oh, I don't know about that. I'm sure the odds against our

success are about a hundred to one. A well placed bet might net me a large sum indeed – should I lay it on the right party, wouldn't you say?" He smiled at Jim, stretching out his hand. Jim took it in his and gave it a firm shake.

"I would," said Jim, but he failed to return the smile. Legeia's words still rang in his ears as he thought about the battle to come, and about what he must do to end all this madness once and for all. Death and doom, she had said to him. Death and doom.

FORTY-FOUR

AT THE TEMPLE RUINS

From behind a twisting black ribbon, George Ratt appeared on a small rock, the last of five rising up through the ocean waves like knuckles on a fist. The late afternoon sun was growing fat and red, casting wavering shadows from the barren isles in the water, as if the knuckles were bleeding. On the second rock, by far the largest, the crumbling remnants of a derelict temple stood as gray and lifeless as the stone beneath it.

The ocean mist hung in the air over the islands, but George could not feel the droplets on his skin. The waves were crashing against the rocks, but all George could hear was the voice of the man beside him.

"Long, long ago, this place was called the Fist of the Gods," said the King of Thieves, still gathering the black tendrils of his power back into his shadowy form. "That was in the time of the ancients. An entire city laid to waste in but a day, such is the might the Treasure of the Ocean holds." The King's sallow face was stretched tight around his mouth, staring over the waves like a hungry animal. The only thought George seemed able to muster was that he agreed with every word the King said.

"The fighting will be fierce tonight for such a power, more deadly and dangerous than anything you have ever faced. Jim Morgan will be fighting hardest of all. He will use all his cunning, all his skill, and every trick available to him to win the Treasure of the Ocean from the Cromiers. He will claw tooth and nail, George, to be the one to drive the trident into the altar. Whatever you do, you must not let him do this. For he would surely be destroyed."

"I'll be ready," George said in a sleepy voice.

"Then ready yourself, for it begins." The King stretched a long, bony finger toward the waters around the temple isle. A swirling current was beginning to turn and turn around the rock, like a whirlpool above a drain.

"What is that?"

The King showed George through the circle of his entwined arms. Hundreds of merfolk surrounded the stone isle. Around and around the rock they swam, coral weapons in hand, mouths open, shouting unheard war cries and silent battle chants. Out before the army, King Nemus himself floated, his great spear grasped in his fist. Queen Melodia stood in her chariot, drawn by hammerhead sharks, hovering beside the ruler of the sea people. Even through the magic looking glass of the King's arms, George could see the crestfallen look on Queen Melodia's face. Heartbreak showed through her eyes. The Queen's sadness seemed to give strength to another voice in George's head. A voice that didn't agree with everything the King said.

The King dissolved the circle again, pointing toward the horizon. A fleet of Corsair ships sailed in fast, at least twenty strong, the dark hulled *Sea Spider* at their head. The King's eyes then snuck to their corners, toward the opposite horizon. George followed the King's gaze and found a black stain marring the evening sky.

"The Crimson Storm," George whispered. He had a sudden memory then, of himself and Jim, fighting together, fighting the Cromiers under that very storm. That memory at last gave the whisper at the back of George's mind enough strength to be heard. The whisper gave George a different plan than that of the King of Thieves... A mad plan.

"All the pieces on the board are here, and all will play in this final game." The King set his thin, spidery fingers upon George's shoulder. George could not feel their weight, but an icy cold settled into his chest, trickling down his arm. The cold touch silenced the whisper in George's head, but not before it had its say. "You and I, George Ratt, we shall be history's unsung heroes. It will be you and I, my boy, just like I always promised. You and I will shape the course of the world."

"Yes," said George. "We will."

FORTY-FIVE

LAST VOYAGE OF THE *SPECTRE*

Jim stood on the *Spectre's* quarterdeck, sailing at the head of twenty pirate ships, cutting across the ocean toward the ancient temple. The setting sun fell quickly behind the edge of the world, leaving the wind cold on Jim's back. But he felt warm enough in the dark coat Captain Sharpe had leant him, and the tall boots as well, which all fit better than Jim imagined they might. His magic sword was sheathed in a scabbard at his belt, and the emptied soul stone hung around his neck.

The distance from Spire Island to the ancient temple was thousands and thousands of leagues, and at first, Jim had feared they could not possibly make it in time. But Lo Fang had called for aid from an old friend. The dragon who had given him a crown jewel was an air dragon, a master of the four winds. Lo Fang cried out on the morning breeze for the dragon to help him one last time.

Through the air Jim had watched them come, nearly invisible, twisting ripples in the sky in the shapes of wingless dragons. The mystical winds had rushed into the pirate sails, and faster than even Sharpe's rope or Egidio's Aeolus Feathers, the pirate fleet had soared on the waves toward the ancient temple, and into the battle that awaited them there.

"Well, Lord Morgan, we near the place you charted on the map," said Captain Sharpe. Jim hardly recognized the man when he looked his way. Captain Sharpe had shed his powder blue coat in exchange for one as black as Dread Steele's had once been. He had removed his brown curl wig and plumed hat. His hair, blonde and shaggy, was pulled back from his face in a small tail behind his head.

"You know," said Jim. "A very brazen pirate once told me that when a man showed his true face, that was the hour of his doom." Sharpe laughed.

"It is quite possible that we may be in trouble then, milord."

"May I ask you something, Captain? What made you come back?"

"Your young lady can be quite persuasive when she doesn't get her way," said Sharpe, still smiling, but the roguish grin had faded away. His eyes drifted toward the setting sun. From his pocket, Sharpe withdrew the fantastic pearl again, turning it over in his gloved fingers.

"I really was a friend of your father's and Dread Steele's, once. Like Lindsay, I too, fell in love with a mermaid. Not hard to do, once you've met one, you know. They are beautiful, and every single one has a perfect singing voice." It seemed to Jim Sharpe was making a joke, but he wasn't laughing. "But there was one... the purest soul I had ever met. She... well, I was a poor man, Jim. Debt hung around my neck like a heavy stone, dragging me into the depths. Fulkern, the captain of Queen Melodia's guard, caught wind of my romance. He hated humans. But I suppose he had me pegged right, didn't he? He offered me this pearl to walk away from my love forever." F.W. closed his fist around the jewel. "Halfway home I turned the ship around. I tried to give it back. I tried to tell her what a fool I'd been."

Sharpe opened his fist and stared at the pearl, before placing it back in his pocket and finding a halfway believable smile again. "Anyway, once you've given away your honor, Jim Morgan, it's almost impossible to get it back again."

"That same pirate who told me about the masks, also told me that it wasn't what other men did that would make one lose faith in mankind, but what he would do." Jim held his scarred palm out to Sharpe. "I know what he meant. But I think the same may be true in reverse. If you want to get back your faith, you're the one who must do something worth believing in. And here you are."

Sharpe's half-hearted grin grew into a full smile. "If we survive this, Lord Morgan, you may just make a fine nobleman. And that is a very rare thing indeed."

"I've always said that, you know," cawed a raven's voice. Cornelius swooped down to land on Jim's shoulder. "You will make a fine Lord Morgan. However, I'm sorry to say, that is a rather large if attached to our survival."

"Don't say that, Mister Cornelius." Lacey had arrived as well, followed by Peter and Paul. She took Jim's hand in her own, lacing her warm fingers through his. "I thought that same thing myself when Jim and I stood in front of the Pirate Vault, and when we were lost on the Veiled Isle, and when the Crimson Storm was about to kill us again. But each time, we've come through. I think we're *supposed* to make it through. Like it's written in the stars."

Jim was glad for Lacey's cheerful words, but he saw some doubt lurking behind her blue eyes, some question she seemed to be silently asking, about whether or not it really would all be right in the end. For Jim's part, he hoped he was better at hiding his doubts than Lacey. He had not told anyone what Legeia said awaited him at the end of this journey. For all they knew, as long as he was the one to use the Treasure of the Ocean, all would be well with the world. And Jim swore to himself that it would be him, no matter what, so that he might execute Egidio's plan. As long as Lacey, Peter, and Paul, and perhaps, somehow George as well, would finally be safe, it would all be worth it in the end.

"Look at that." Paul pointed over the railing toward a spark burning against the blackening sky. A second flash followed the first, and then another, and another. The rapid bursts lit the scene, approaching fast upon the horizon, faster than Jim was ready.

Only a few leagues away, a fleet of Corsair Ships sailed toward a row of black rocks, five in the sea like the tip of a fist. From the lead vessel, what must have been the Sea Spider, golden lightning lashed. White-hot fingers of power lanced back from the waters before the largest rock, trading magic blows back and forth. Bartholomew was wielding the Treasure of the Ocean. And Nemus was battling back.

Above the battle, shrouded purple blossoms unfurled in the sky. A churning blackness lay over the waters, scarred with bloody red tendrils along the edges. The Crimson Storm had come. But it did not join the fray, Jim noticed. It only hovered over the great rock – waiting. The magic bursts lit the night, throwing into brilliant silhouette a ruined building upon the stony outcropping.

It was the temple – and the altar within.

Jim's fingers wrapped themselves around the hilt of his magic sword. He could feel it trembling within its scabbard, begging to fly out.

"It would seem the festivities have begun without us," said Sharpe, without his signature smile. The flashing lights glowed in his eyes. He pulled his gloves snug and tightened his belt. "How I do love a good party."

"Cornelius," said Peter, squeezing in closer to Jim and Lacey.

"Have you ever..." The question faltered on Peter's lips, but Cornelius was already answering.

"No, Master Ratt, I've never seen anything like this... never in my life. But stick together, young sir, and you and I shall see this through to the end."

"Well, written in the stars or not, time for you three to get below," Jim said to Lacey and the Ratts. "This will be more dangerous than any of that other stuff we've been through before, so—" He tried to pull his hand from Lacey's grip, but she squeezed it so violently, Jim thought she might break his fingers.

"No, Jim Morgan, we will *not* be getting below anything. Boys are the most ridiculous creatures on earth. They kick and scream and throw fits like children the moment someone tells them they can't do this or that, or to run and hide, or to save themselves, but then they just can't wait to tell a girl to go do the same. I've faced down a dragon for you, Jim Morgan, so don't you dare think you can tell me to leave you on your own for anything ever again."

Jim opened his mouth to argue, but he could not think of a single intelligent thing to say in return. It was Lacey, after all, and he half feared she might slap him silly before the real fighting even began.

"Well then, stay behind me for heaven's sake, will you?" Jim tried to glare at the three of them, especially Lacey, as hard as he could, for what it was worth. "The magic sword protected me from even the Crimson Storm, it can protect us from this."

"Nevertheless," said Sharpe, "better safe than sorry, or so some fool somewhere once said." He withdrew a short rapier from behind his back, flipped it in his hand, and offered it handle first to Lacey. "Nothing to it really, milady. If an unsavory fellow gives you any trouble, prod him a bit with this. He'll think twice about doing it again." Without even a moment's hesitation, Lacey let go of Jim's hand and took the rapier, testing its weight with a few practice jabs.

"And I thought she was dangerous before," Peter whispered to

Paul. The brothers snickered together, but all the same they drew even a bit closer to Lacey's sides, and seemed a little more confident in her armed company than they had the moment before.

From behind Jim's three friends, enormous Mufwalme, sly Murdoch, steady Wang Chi, and even portly Mister Gilly stepped into the light of the magic battle. They held naked blades in their hands, and their belts and bandoliers were loaded with pistols, knifes, and every other weapon imaginable. The faithful pirates, who had sailed with Jim across the oceans of the world and back again on this quest, stood beside him once again.

With the lights of magic powers glowing all around him, with the sounds of battle growing louder in his ears, and with the weight of all his friends' and comrades' eyes upon him, Jim discovered a surprising irony. Here he stood, those he cared for at risk, the Treasure of the Ocean within reach, pirates and thieves surrounding him, obstacles of magic and mayhem between him and his goal, and a talking raven upon his shoulder. The end of the journey was so much like the beginning it nearly made Jim laugh. It was only he that had changed.

Jim drew his magic sword. The blade hummed in his hand, quivering its high note.

"Shall I stay on your shoulder again, Lord Morgan? Should I remind you that fear is thinking on all in the world that might happen to you, and courage is thinking on what you shall happen upon the world?"

"Yes, Cornelius, just like before," said Jim. "Through every door but the last. That one I must enter alone."

And with those words, the *Spectre* sailed into her last battle.

FORTY-SIX

THE BATTLE BEFORE THE TEMPLE

Jim saw at once that the Corsair fleet had planned for the arrival of the *Spectre*. About half the ships turned from the fight with the merfolk as the ragtag armada from Spire Island came into view, springing what was meant to be a well-laid trap. But the Corsairs had failed to take into account the ferocity of Nemus and his army.

The merfolk had pulled no less than five of the count's ships into the waves by the time Jim and the others sailed into the fight. The waters before the temple's rocky island were littered with the drifting, broken, and burning shells of defeated Corsair ships.

And the *Spectre* and her ships had a plan of their own. Lo Fang and Golden Ginny broke off, leading several ships each in two lines before the *Spectre,* like a protective wall on either side. Cannon fire erupted. White smoke ran over the waves like fog. Just as Jim and Sharpe had planned, the small fleet engaged the Corsairs at the *Spectre's* flanks, forming a tunnel into the heart of the battle – straight for the Cromiers and the *Sea Spider*.

As Jim's ship closed the distance, he tightened his grip on his sword and gritted his teeth, witnessing for the first time the Treasure of the Ocean's power. Bartholomew stood on the *Sea Spider's* prow, his father all but on top of him, gripping his son's arms in his hands, screaming into his ear. The golden trident was aflame, and from the three spear tips, firebolts burned through the air, falling one after the other on a lone figure, floating in the water before the Temple Rock.

King Nemus stood his ground in the waves. With his magic spear, he batted aside the Cromiers' assault. But Jim could see that Nemus was beginning to tire. He blocked three magical strikes for every one he threw back. His own magic was swallowed up in the Treasure's golden power. Nemus's huge shoulders heaved, and the tip of his spear dipped lower and lower toward the water.

Jim's stomach clenched. He willed the *Spectre* faster into the fight. Nemus would not last much longer.

Above the fighting, the Crimson Storm rumbled and growled. It opened its fiery eyes into thin slits, following the *Spectre* as she sailed into the fray. But it did not attack. No bolts of purple lightning rained down from above, nor did any gale winds or blinding rains lash the decks. It held its place above the temple – brewing and threatening.

"What do you think it's waitin for, Jim?" asked Paul, eyeing the red clouds warily. "Why's it just sittin there? Normally that thing just can't wait to destroy somethin."

"It's waiting for me," said Jim. "It's waiting for me or Bartholomew."

"One of you two shall be there soon enough," whispered Cornelius.

"Prepare to ram them!" Captain Sharpe cried over the din. The crew rushed up behind Jim and his friends, to the *Spectre's* prow, weapons drawn and teeth bared. "Prepare for boarding!"

"Whatever happens—" Jim hissed to Lacey, Peter, and Paul. But before he could finish, his magic blade sang loudly, the sword jerking to Jim's right. Three high-pitched pings pierced the roar of battle, and three coral arrows, fired by mermen off the starboard bow, clattered harmlessly to the deck. "Stay behind me!"

"Brace yourselves," Sharpe called.

Jim and the others ducked low. Pistol shots from the deck of the *Sea Spider* whistled over their heads. The *Spectre* slammed into the count's ship. The bowsprit slipped over the *Spider's* railing, sending Corsairs sprawling. The fore crunched into the opposing hull with a sound like breaking bones. Jim, Captain Sharpe, and all the others used the force of the ramming to catapult themselves over the railings and pour onto the *Sea Spider*.

Jim's magic blade quivered in his hand, but the Corsairs never got close enough for Jim to need it. The crew of the *Spectre* cleared the way for him and his friends, forming a protective bubble around them. He felt Lacey and the Ratts right on his heels, crouching low, as pistol shots, coral arrows, and cannon smoke drifted over their heads.

Sharpe, Mufwalme, Murdoch, Wang Chi, and all the rest attacked with such abandon that the Corsairs fell back before them, crying out in fear. Some even threw themselves overboard, where the merfolk dragged them down into the depths. The boarding party fought their way up to the fore of the ship more quickly than Jim was prepared to face the Cromiers. But the Red Count, screaming like a madman at his own son, had his back turned. He and Bartholomew were so caught up in their battle with Nemus that they took no notice of the fight on their own ship.

For just a moment, a wild hope leapt in Jim's heart. He could take the Cromiers by surprise, he thought. He could strip the

Treasure from them. He could explain to Nemus what he was going to do, how we was going to lock the trident away for all time. All this could be over in but a moment...

...but Jim had forgotten how clever was the count.

Cromier had only been waiting.

He pulled at Bartholomew's arm, spinning his son about, bringing the crew of the *Spectre* into his aim. The tip of the trident glowed the brightest gold.

Jim broke free of Lacey's grip on his arm, shrugged Cornelius from his shoulder, and threw himself before the pirate crew.

"Jim, no!" Lacey cried behind him. But the magic sword was their only hope.

The blast came. Jim's sword leapt up to protect him. The bolt struck the blade with ten times the force of the Crimson Storm's lightning. Jim's feet skidded back on the *Sea Spider's* deck. The magic's heat burned his knuckles and singed his face. He felt pitiless hate burn in the bolt as it locked onto his sword, the power overwhelming even his enchanted weapon.

At the last moment, just before Jim thought the power would consume him, he turned his blade downward, throwing the attack into the deck. Wooden planks exploded at Jim's feet. The blast threw him backward, where he landed in a heap beside Lacey and the Ratts. Jim's ears rang. The world tilted and spun around him. Captain Sharpe and all the others had been knocked to their backs as well, dazed and helpless.

Bartholomew stalked forward, his father, Count Cromier, clinging to him like a withered leech, his hands clawing into his son's arms.

"Now, Bartholomew. At last, finish that which you have waited so long to do." The count narrowed his eyes on Jim. "Send these fools to the next world – for this world belongs to us!"

Bartholomew raised the trident again, summoning the gold fire. But he and his father had turned their backs on Nemus for a moment too long. Another explosion shook the *Sea Spider*. The bowsprit, along with the entire fore, shattered into kindling. A wave of light and heat washed over Jim where he lay.

Somehow, the second blast shook Jim's head clear. He climbed to his hands and knees, coughing in the smoke. The *Sea Spider's* prow was a flaming wreck. Silence fell over the deck. All the pirates and Corsairs were slowly picking themselves up – including the count and Bartholomew. The two Cromiers lay face down…

…and the Treasure of the Ocean had slipped from Bartholomew's grasp.

Jim took his sword in his hand. With a running start he leapt over the smoldering hole from the bolt he had parried into the deck. The Treasure was only a few feet from him, just out of reach. He lunged for it, when a swirl of black, like twisting ribbons, spun into being, blocking Jim's path.

Jim slid to a halt. His heart sank. He had been so close, and he knew who now stood in his way. The King of Thieves had appeared at his opportune moment, looming like a wraith over the deck — George Ratt at his side.

FORTY-SEVEN

THE TRIDENT AND THE FLUTE

eorge!" Peter and Paul screamed. Never minding any fear or confusion as they beheld the resurrected King of Thieves, the two Ratts and Lacey started toward George. They ran around the hole in the deck with open arms, ready to pull him into their embrace and take him back as one of their own.

But Jim stopped them. He raised his magic blade at his side to hold them back. From what Lacey had told him of George's disappearance, Jim had guessed who it was that had taken him. Jim had only just found the strength to turn the King away, but it was clear that George had not.

George's face was as pale as Bartholomew Cromier's. A shimmering mist clouded his eyes. Worst of all, wrapped about George's shoulders like a fatherly arm, one of the King's coattails rippled like a black serpent. Jim felt his chest go hollow at the sight of it.

"George Ratt, you come over here right this moment!" Lacey shouted. Peter and Paul waved their arms over their heads, tears in their big eyes as they called for their brother as well.

"Come on, George!"

"Run, George, run!"

"He can't hear you," Jim said to them. "He can't hear or see any of us. The King of Thieves has him. He tried to take me, but he got George instead."

"Hello, my friends," said the King. "It has been too, too long." That honey smile spread over the King's lips.

"Let him go, King," Jim shouted. "Let him go, or I'll make you." The King laughed and shook his head, pointing a long, spidery finger at Jim and his friends.

"I am not of this world any more, Jim Morgan. You have no weapon against me. You have nothing with which to threaten me now."

Jim held up his magic sword, brandishing it toward the King. The blade quivered and hummed. It nearly shook loose of Jim's hand with every inch closer he drew to the King. The honey smile on the King's face faltered.

"Sure about that? You're not the only one who's been on the hunt for magical treasures." Jim dared a step toward the King. To his right, he saw Captain Sharpe and the *Spectre's* crew picking themselves off the deck. But before him, Bartholomew Cromier and his father stirred as well, shaking their heads clear of Nemus's attack. The Treasure of the Ocean, the golden trident, lay in the middle of them all.

Jim knew the time was now. He lunged for the Treasure. But he never reached it.

The King of Thieves snapped his bony fingers. At his command, George lifted the enchanted flute to his lips. The tune poured over the deck – punctuated by fountains of water erupting from all around the ship.

A slithering coil wrapped around Jim's waist, pulling him off his feet and hoisting him into the air. Five more arms writhed into view. They snatched up all the most dangerous threats to the King and his plan – Sharpe, Mufwalme, Murdoch, and Wang-Chi. Lacy, Peter, and Paul were all swept up in a single tentacle. It was the Kraken, Jim realized, the very one that had attacked the *Spectre* on her way to the Veiled Isle. George had used Philus Philonius's flute to summon it back.

"Yes!" The King of Thieves was laughing again. "You have gone and found some magical trinkets, haven't you, my boy? But I have been collecting magical friends. Who would have thought that young George here, once just a dirty little pocket pick in London, had it in him to become a great sorcerer? Certainly not me. But now he is my servant."

"George, stop," Peter cried to his brother from the coils of the Kraken's arm. "We need you, mate. You're the leader. We just ain't the Brothers Ratt without you."

"The cheer starts with you, George," said Paul, tears running down his face. "George, Peter, and Paul... We are the Brothers Ratt!"

But the boys' cries fell upon deaf ears. George stood still as stone, the flute to his lips, playing his tune.

Jim scanned the deck for any sign of hope. He thought he found it in the most unlikely place. Bartholomew Cromier was on his feet – staggering toward the Treasure of the Ocean. Even without the altar, the golden trident was the most powerful magic on earth. Surely it could destroy the King.

"Bartholomew," Jim gasped, the Kraken's arm squeezing his chest like a vice. "Use the Treasure on that shadow. He wants its power for himself."

Bartholomew Cromier, still dazed from Nemus's blast, looked

up at Jim, confusion in his eyes. But it was the King of Thieves who answered.

"Oh, Jim, you fool. Why do you think I knocked on the door of your mind? I am a wraith – a formless shadow in this world. How could I possibly seize anything for myself? Especially that which can only be possessed by a Son of Earth and Son of Sea? Don't you know how I work? No, foolish boy, I don't seize such power for myself... I have others do it for me. And you were not the only Son of Earth and Son of Sea I visited in his dreams."

The King of Thieves stretched out his spindly arms. They lost their shape, wriggling from his body like the rippling coattail that held George beside him. The black ribbons took Bartholomew Cromier by his arms, jerking him up straight. That same misty cloud that shrouded George's eyes, fell over Bartholomew's as well. He dangled at the end of the King's grasp like a pale marionette.

An icy cold stabbed at Jim's heart. He truly had been a fool to think the King of Thieves would have targeted him alone. He had gone after Bartholomew as well – and he had wormed his way into the young Cromier's mind. Jim watched, helpless in the Kraken's grasp, as the King moved Bartholomew under his command, forcing the young man to take up the Treasure of the Ocean once more. At Bartholomew's touch, the trident erupted into golden flames.

Green sparks crackled in the King of Thieves' eyes and rippled along his body. He howled into the air. His legs twisted into one, shadowy pillar, lifting him into the air. "At long last!" He cried into the night. "At long last – I can feel the power! So much power!"

"But it shall not be yours, vile creature," thundered an unseen voice. From beside the ship, another figure rose into view. Nemus raised himself up on his own pillar, this one formed of foaming seawater. "It shall not be yours or any man's."

Nemus fired a stream of white-hot magic from his spear. The fiery tongue struck the King. The shadowy wraith screamed in pain. His murky shape twisted and writhed under the attack. Jim dared to hope that Nemus had done it – even if Jim and Bartholomew were to be next – that he had struck down the King of Thieves. But Nemus had been weakened by his battle with Bartholomew. His last, mighty blow had not been enough.

The King of Thieves pulled his form back together. He snapped his arms like whips, and at their lash, Bartholomew turned on Nemus. Surges of green magic poured down the King's arms into Bartholomew and into the trident. Jim felt a sick churning in his stomach at what was about to come.

Bartholomew fired on Nemus, and this time, the mightiest of all the mermen's strength failed him. He caught the magical bolt with his coral spear, but the golden power broke Nemus's weapon in half. The magic struck Nemus in the chest. His shoulders went slack. His eyes closed. The Ruler of the Sea Folk, Jim's grandfather, fell beneath the waves.

The King of Thieves gloated in triumph. He snarled and clapped his teeth, snapping his arms, turning Bartholomew back on Count Cromier. The Red Count had only just come to his senses, staring at this unexpected turn of events with vile contempt dripping from his scarred face. But contempt turned to fear as Bartholomew unleashed the magic upon him. The golden light enchained the count, tying him down to the Sea Spider's deck.

"Release me, shadow," raged the count, gnashing his teeth. "Release my son. He is mine! The Treasure of the Ocean is mine. The power is mine!"

"I shall deal with you in time, my dear Count," said the King. "But I can't kill you yet. You see, you are your son's motivation. It was his hatred of you that let me into his mind. But, first things first, eh, Jim?"

The shadowy King rose up over the deck on his black pillar, floating to where Jim hung in the Kraken's arm. He twisted his black arms, strung to Bartholomew, and at his command Bartholomew released another stream of magic. The bolt cut into the Spectre, slicing the hull in two. The great ship, which had been Jim's home for so many days and nights upon the sea, broke in half, flames engulfing the mast and the sails. It sunk quickly beneath the waves, leaving only a trail of smoke in its wake.

"You should have joined me when you had the chance, Jim Morgan," said the King. "Twice you spurned me. I offered to be your mentor, your father. I offered to lead you down the paths of power. But you spat in my face. You have no amulet to shatter at my feet now, do you? You cannot reach me with your magic sword. You will only watch, as Bartholomew Cromier unlocks the ultimate magic, and together, we rule this world for our own."

"Don't you know what will happen to Bartholomew when he places the Treasure in the altar?" Jim pleaded, the tentacle about his chest squeezing tighter and tighter. "He will *become* the power. It will destroy him and the entire the world."

"No, no, my boy," said the King, shaking his head. "Bartholomew will lose his body, but I will control his mind. At last, through the power of Bartholomew Cromier, I will be able to touch this world again. I will shape the nations with my fingertips. I will wield the power of the ocean in my hands. I will force the whole earth to bend its knee at my feet. And the wind and the rain and waves of my storm will wash even your name from memory. Goodbye, Jim Morgan."

The King floated aside. Below him, from the deck, Bartholomew raised the trident. He pointed it at Jim. The spear tips lit with golden flame.

FORTY-EIGHT

THE BATTLE'S END

Jim's magic sword was screaming in his hand. He tried to raise it and defend himself. But the tentacle wrapped about his body held him fast, his arm pinned to his side. Lacey, Peter, and Paul were shouting at the tops of their lungs, trying to get Bartholomew or George's attention, but the two were slaves to the King of Thieves.

Jim forced himself to keep his eyes open. If this was to be his end, he would not die in the dark. But before the blast came, a screeching caw cried over the *Sea Spider's* deck.

"Preoleum!"

Cornelius, forgotten by the King of Thieves and the Kraken, dove down from the night sky, claws bared. Behind him sailed scores of coral arrows and spears, and the sound of pistol shots rang in his wake. The raven had rallied Queen Melodia, riding her chariot, and Lo Fang and Golden Ginny. The merfolk and the pirates had now stopped fighting each other and were closing in on the *Sea Spider* and the King of Thieves. But none of them, not Cornelius, nor the arrows, nor pistol shots, were aimed for the shadow wraith – they fell upon Bartholomew.

The King of Thieves snarled and whipped his black arms again. At the last moment, before Bartholomew could be skewered by raining arrows or well-aimed shots, the King turned him from Jim and toward the attack. Golden fire leapt from the Treasure of the Ocean, turning the coral arrows and iron missiles to ash in the air. Cornelius circled around the blast, diving down, clawing for Bartholomew's face. Bartholomew swatted and swung for the raven, keeping the King busy as the merfolk and pirates advanced.

But the King still had another servant under his command.

The rippling coattail wrapped about George's shoulders tugged at him, and George played another trill on his flute. With a roar that shook the *Sea Spider*, the Kraken hoisted its mammoth body up from the waves. The snapping beak, that had once nearly been the end of Jim and all the pirates on the *Spectre*, rose into view. Under the spell of George's flute, the creature moved itself between the ship and the attackers, blocking their arrows and shots.

But as the fight now fell upon the Kraken, Jim caught an unintended consequence. For every blow the giant monster absorbed, George flinched as well. The two were tied together through the flute. The Kraken's pain was also George's, and it seemed to shake him from the King of Thieves' control.

"Cornelius!" Jim called as best he could, his body aching beneath the tentacle's grip. "The Kraken! Tell Melodia and the pirates to attack the Kraken." Cornelius took off at once, only just evading a fire bolt from the trident. In but a moment, the Kraken began to roar and bellow. Jim could hear Melodia's battle cry and Fulkern's war chant as they battled the sea monster. George flinched and staggered on the deck again. The Kraken's grip on Jim loosened ever so slightly.

"Enough of this!" said the King of Thieves. He brought Bartholomew's aim to bear on Jim again. Jim tugged his arm with all his might, and against the tentacle's weakened hold, pulled it free.

The blast came and Jim met it with his sword. But this time he did not attempt to catch it. He only deflected it, glancing it off his blade and sending it careening into the Kraken's flank.

The giant squid screamed in pain. Jim winced, hoping that he had not killed the beast, for it was as innocent in this as was George. But the creature's injury served its purpose. The tentacles wrapped about Jim and his friends unraveled, dropping them all to the deck.

The moment Jim landed, he looked for George. His friend had dropped to his knees, and the flute had fallen from his hands, clattering on the deck. George's eyes were squeezed shut, closed tight against the Kraken's pain that was now his own.

"George," Jim cried. "You don't work for the King of Thieves any more. You're not a member of his army. You don't believe in his lies. You are the greatest pickpocket in the world, and you're my friend. Together we can do anything, remember? Wake up and help us, please!" George shook his head in pain. He collapsed and rolled onto his side. Peter and Paul ran to their brother, but there was no time for Jim to do the same.

The King of Thieves dropped down onto the deck beside Bartholomew, his spindly legs materializing again beneath him. Green power crackled down the King's arms and into Bartholomew. The trident lit up and a wave of energy poured forth, threatening to roll Jim under its fire. The magic sword leapt to Jim's defense, but there was nowhere to parry the blow. The Sea Spider's deck was nearly destroyed, and Jim's friends were all about him. So he held onto the attack, locking blades with the stream pouring from the Treasure.

Jim pushed with all his might. The magic sword sang louder than even the battle din ringing over the waters. Jim wrapped both hands around the grip. The heat pouring down the metal blade burned his hands. Just when Jim thought he could bear no more, an explosion snapped his head back. He felt himself tumble backward. The crash of a thousand breaking windows filled his ears.

Jim sat up at once, choking on a cloud of smoke. But as the ocean breeze cleared the haze, Bartholomew and the King of Thieves appeared – advancing upon him with the trident still aglow.

Jim forced himself to his feet. But as he prepared for another bout, his shoulders fell. He still held the magic sword's grip in his hand, but the steel blade came to a ragged end only a hand-length up from the guard.

The enchanted sword had been shattered.

The smile found its way back onto the King's face. His dark eyes glowed green at Jim and his broken weapon.

"And this is but a taste of the Treasure of the Ocean's power, boy. But a taste. It has destroyed your only protection from me." The King flicked his arms and Bartholomew raised the trident. "Better to have been a slave and lived, Jim Morgan, than a hero and have died."

"That'll be just another one of your stinkin lies, King!" a familiar voice called from Jim's right. "And I think me and me friends have had enough of 'em!" George was back on his feet, face still pale, but eyes bright again, narrowed on the King of Thieves. Peter and Paul stood beside him, fists clenched and raised, the Brothers Ratt reunited once more.

"I no longer have a use for you, George Ratt, so what you think of me or my lies are of little consequence," said the King with a sneer. "Your beast has retreated under the sea, and your greatest act will go down in history as summoning the fish that destroyed the crystal tower. You are a failed sorcerer, a failed thief, and a failed friend."

Those words struck George hard. His eyes misted over again, this time with tears. But he did not back down. He did not hang his head. He only brought the flute back to his lips.

"Maybe so, King," George said. "But I have friends – real friends – and even though I was your slave, there was still enough of me awake inside to call on one more – a magic friend. And I think he'll be arriving just on time."

George played on his flute. The answer came in a rush of water behind the *Sea Spider*, with a mighty roar that silenced all else in the battle upon the waves. A great head rose up from the waters, looming on a purple-scaled body, round as the broadest tree, golden eyes glowing in the night.

Percival, last of the water dragons, had returned.

George ceased his song, pulling the flute from his lips. He had not been commanding Percival, Jim realized, only asking him to come, asking for help.

"Percival," George cried. "That's the one. The shadow man. Only you can stop him!"

"And I shall, friend of Jim Morgan," rumbled Percival. "With pleasure!" Percival surged back beneath the waves, spiraling his armored body down and under the *Sea Spider*. His head reappeared on the port side, mouth open, rowed with teeth long as swords, eager to tear into the King of Thieves.

"Creature of magic spawn!" The King howled. His smile disappeared. Fear ran over his pale face. "This cannot be." The King of Thieves whipped his shapeless arms at Bartholomew, spurring him to fight this new foe with the Treasure of the Ocean. But when the King had been taken by fear, terrified at the arrival of Percival, he had lost some of his control over the young Cromier. Jim saw the ice blue in Bartholomew's eyes glimmer, free of the magic mist that had covered them.

Jim felt his chest go empty. That old, murderous hate blossomed again on Bartholomew's pale face. But Bartholomew was no longer obeying the King of Thieves. He kept his sights on Jim. The flame at the end of the trident flared gold.

"Jim!" Lacey screamed from somewhere beside him.

Magic fire lanced forth. It streaked for Jim's heart. At the last moment, before what should have been his death, Jim felt a shove at his side. He tumbled to the deck. The heat from the blast singed his shoulder and the side of his face.

Jim landed hard on his side, his eyes still locked on Bartholomew. Percival's head slammed into the deck at the same moment, pouring through it easily as water. Wooden shards and splinters splashed and fell like rain. Bartholomew went flying, his body and fate hidden from Jim's sight. For the King of Thieves, however, there was no escape.

Percival pulled his head from the hole in the *Sea Spider's* deck, the King of Thieves in his teeth. The King scratched and clawed. He tried to melt into the night to escape. But Percival was a creature of magic blood, and the King's shadowy form was like flesh to the water dragon. Jim heard the King howling, cursing his name as the sea serpent finally swallowed him whole. Percival reared back and roared at the night sky in triumph.

Jim could have laughed, but his body hurt too much. Only a relieved smile split his face. All went still. The ocean breeze swept across the deck, ushering away the battle smoke, and also blowing an auburn curl into Jim's face. Jim's smile widened.

"Good timing, Lacey," he said. "A moment later and I would have—"

Jim's words caught. He felt Lacey's weight atop him, where she had fallen after pushing him out of the way. But she was heavy, too heavy, and too still. Jim rolled her over. A smoldering mark blackened her dress.

Jim looked at her face, but her eyes were closed. He touched her lips, but her breath was gone. He put his ear to her chest, but her heartbeat was quiet.

FORTY-NINE

TO THE STONE ALTAR

Jim knelt beside Lacey on the deck. George came over slowly, followed by Peter and Paul. When they realized what had happened, Peter and Paul began to sob. George wept silently. He twisted his hands around the flute, as though to snap the cursed thing in two.

Cornelius landed on Jim's shoulder, and the Pirate crew of the once mighty *Spectre*, now sunk to the bottom of the sea, gathered in a ring around the boys. Even Percival, only a moment ago roaring in triumph, leaned his great, spiny head over the deck in silence.

"Oh no," said the raven. "Of all of us, would it have not been her."

Jim opened his mouth, but his voice was broken. Nor did tears fall, nor did he cry out. It was as though all the life within his body was drained, floating away with the columns of smoke. He reached out and took Lacey's hand in his. It was already cold.

"Is it over, at least?" asked Mufwalme, tears glistening on his giant face. "Is it done?"

"No sign of the count or his son," said Murdoch, scanning the deck. "And the Corsairs are making a run for it." He nodded his head out toward the ocean, where what remained of the Corsair fleet sailed at full speed for the horizon.

"No, there is no sign of the Cromiers," said Captain Sharpe, "but nor is there a sign of the Treasure of the Ocean. The trident is gone!"

Jim lifted his eyes from Lacey's face. It was not the mention of his enemies, or even the thought that the battle might be over that sent a spark through his deadened body. It was the Treasure... the Treasure of the Ocean, and all its power.

Jim searched the deck. Above the scorched wood and shattered holes ringed with fire, he caught a swirl of black dust settling down on an empty patch – settling down in the shape of a ring.

"That bloody count and that coward Bartholomew have gone off again," raged George, who had followed Jim's stare. "They've run off with the Treasure."

"No," said Jim. "They haven't run." Thunder rumbled in the stormy clouds above the temple. Lightning burst within the black folds. "They've gone for the altar."

Jim scooped up Lacey's still form in his arms and took off for the *Sea Spider's* fore, shorn away by Nemus's blast.

"Percival!" Jim screamed. He leapt from the broken end of the ship without a moment's pause, and faithful Percival, still a friend to Jim after all this time, caught him on the top of his scaly head. But Jim did not land alone. The Ratts and Sharpe had followed.

"Percival, to the temple, hurry!" Jim gripped Lacey's body tight against his chest as the water dragon tore through the waves, reaching the rocky shore in the blink of an eye.

"We'll help you stop him, mate," swore George, fists and teeth clenched. "We'll give them villains what they deserve."

"Young Morgan," cawed Cornelius, swooping in low and gliding beside Jim's shoulder. "What are you planning on doing?"

"We can't let the Cromiers use the Treasure, Cornelius," Jim barked, but he would not look Cornelius in the eye.

"No, Jim, what are *you* planning on doing?" the raven cawed again. But Jim gave no answer.

Percival did not stop at the shore. He stretched his body over the island, smashing through two ancient columns that had once lined the inner temple, breaking through the old rock and turning it to dust. The altar, nothing more than a square block of carved stone, sat atop stone steps in the center of the courtyard.

Bartholomew Cromier and his father were already on the altar's steps. Jim half expected them to have speared the trident into the stone, but something had slowed them – each other. The count and Bartholomew both had their hands upon the Treasure, battling for its possession. Not even the destructive arrival of Percival put an end to their struggle.

Jim leapt from the water dragon's head, landing in a run, even with Lacey in his arms. The Ratts hit the ground beside him, with F.W. Pennington Sharpe just behind and Cornelius flying overhead. Together they charged the battling Cromiers.

"Release me, you old bag of bones," screamed Bartholomew. "I shall do this alone. This is mine to do. It is my destiny to take!"

"You shall do as I command. You are mine," the count rasped in return. Cromier's blood-red wig had fallen from his head. Nothing but gray wisps on a bald, spotted scalp remained in its place. The long, purple scar, given to him by Jim's father so many years ago, writhed on his face. He was a ghoul, now, Jim thought, his wretched spirit clinging to his body and refusing to die. The count had latched onto Bartholomew's wrists, digging into his son's pale flesh.

Only at the last moment, when Jim and the others were all but on top of them, did the count take action. He raked the back of Bartholomew's hands and then kicked his own son in the stomach, knocking him from the steps of the altar. In one spinning turn, Cromier drew his sword, bringing it over his head to strike Jim down.

But another blade came between Jim and death at the count's hand. Captain Sharpe rammed his shoulder into Cromier, knocking the old man down. Sharpe threw off his coat, crossing his blade before himself and coming to stand between the count and the altar.

"Sharpe, you fool," raved Cromier, spittle flying from his lips. "Do you know how many heroes have died trying to stop me? To keep me from this destiny?"

"Well then," replied Sharpe, "it's a good thing I'm not a hero." Sharpe and Cromier fell on one another, blades echoing off the ruined stone of the temple.

So too did the Ratts dive on Bartholomew, who was still picking himself up from his father's kick. The three brothers, who for so long had practiced such heedless brawling on each other, now unleashed it on Bartholomew. They landed on him, fists flailing, shouting and screaming at the tops of their lungs.

Jim paused just long enough to gently lay Lacey on the ground, taking only a moment to brush her curls from her colorless face. Cornelius circled over Jim's head, desperate for Jim to hear him.

"Young Morgan, I know your heart, and I know what you now plan to do. It would seem like nobility. It would seem like love. But think, boy, think! I beg of you! Is this what she would have you do?"

"Maybe I can save her," Jim finally said. "I can save her."

"At the cost of the whole world, Jim?"

"I can save her, Cornelius!"

Jim took the rapier, which Lacey had cinched with the ribbon from her dress, and thus armed, strode forward to wrench the Treasure of the Ocean from Bartholomew's hands. Cornelius could only caw shrilly, circling above the fight.

But the young Cromier had proved to be a more capable foe than the Ratts had expected. He rose up in the midst of the three, crying out, kicking and punching. An elbow smashed Peter in the side of the head. A knee caught Paul in the stomach. George was the last Ratt standing, but Bartholomew butted his head against George's, staggering the oldest brother. He followed up by swinging the trident in a wide arc, catching George in the arm, leaving three, bloody gashes behind. George stumbled and began to fall. Jim caught him just before he hit the ground, but he did not stop. Jim kept moving forward, charging Bartholomew, who was already lunging for the altar.

Jim met him on the stone steps. He seized the Treasure in one hand and swung his rapier with the other. Bartholomew twisted the trident, blocking Jim's slash with the end of the spear. Face to face, the Treasure of the Ocean between them, Jim and Bartholomew wrestled their way up the steps of the altar.

The Treasure burned at Jim's touch. He felt the heat coursing through his arm. As he and Bartholomew grappled for control, golden bolts of power ripped from the spear tips. Stone columns toppled when struck. The fiery blasts burnt into the ancient rocks. Percival roared and spiraled away, just ducking beneath a stray bolt. Jim could only hope that the Ratts and Captain Sharpe were fast enough to get out of the way, for he could not afford to let go of the golden trident.

Bartholomew was stronger than Jim. Years of hatred burned in his eyes. More than once he threatened to throw Jim aside and stand alone before the altar. But Jim had lost too many friends. He would lose no more. He refused to let go or give in.

Whether on purpose or by effect of their fight, one of the two, Jim or Bartholomew, drove the trident into the stone square. As if drawn to the altar by the pull of the earth itself, the golden spear points slipped into the three holes.

The trident turned.

A column of white light erupted from the stone, shooting into the sky, piercing the Crimson Storm, burning a hole through the dark clouds, and revealing the stars above. A ripple of power rushed over Jim's body. It struck him with such force that he was thrown from the altar, and from the Treasure of the Ocean.

Just before Jim flew through the air, tumbling head over heels, he felt his fingers slip from the golden trident.

FIFTY

IN THE PLACE BETWEEN PLACES

Jim lifted his head and opened his eyes. For a moment, he thought he had somehow fallen through a hole in the temple floor and crashed into a hidden cave below. He could no longer see or hear the ocean. All around him was black and gray, misted over like rain clouds. It was as though he were standing inside the cathedral heart of a storm.

But in the center of what Jim thought was a cave, the stone altar remained. In this place, wherever it was, the rock from which the altar was cut now gleamed like the marble floor of a royal palace. From the altar's heart, the tower of light rose into the night, higher than Jim could see, perhaps all the way to the roof of the world. Somehow, Jim was still in the temple.

The ruined columns rose about him, but now they looked like cloudy obelisks. And beyond the courtyard, the billowing thunderhead upon which Jim stood dropped off, like a cliff, and spread out farther than Jim could see in all directions, just like the ocean. A sudden terror gripped Jim then, and he scrambled to his feet, hoping he was wrong. But just near him, cloudy statues stood on what had once been the temple floor – statues like those in Jim's dreams.

The shapes of three young men, two kneeling, cradling a third between them, with the lump of a bird upon one of their shoulders, were the closest. Farther away were two larger sculptures, of men locked in combat. In between, on the ground, lay the outline of a girl. Her eyes were still closed, and she looked to Jim as though she could be asleep.

Jim tore his eyes from the shapes of his friends and back to the altar, where the column of light reached to the heavens. The Treasure of the Ocean was gone. In its place, lying atop the altar, lay a golden key, shining as though on fire. Across from the altar, not twenty paces, there stood a door, one without hinges, without a frame, without even a handle. In the middle of the door was a steel plate. And in the center of the plate was a black keyhole.

It was the final door.

Jim went to investigate, but as he came closer to the altar, another face appeared beyond the tower of light. A pair of surprised blue eyes stared back at Jim from the other side.

Bartholomew Cromier.

"Morgan," Bartholomew hissed.

As one they bolted for the key. Jim brought forth Lacey's rapier, still in his hand and every bit as real as it had been in the ancient temple – as real as Bartholomew's own blade. Also as in the real world, Jim was still faster than Bartholomew. He leapt onto the altar, took one step to the far side, and hurled himself down upon the young Cromier.

Their blades met, and only their snarls echoed louder than the ringing steel. Bartholomew was strong and fast. All his life he had trained for combat, and for war. But Jim was quick and deft. For years he had lived among pirates and scalawags and thieves, learning to sail, to fend for himself, and to fight. But something more miraculous had happened to Jim over the past few days – the magic sword had taught his arm how to move, how to parry, how to defend himself from harm.

Round and round they turned, swinging at each other with all their hope and hate, leaving no reserve of strength untapped. This fight was for the world itself, Jim knew. The fight was to the death.

Bartholomew brought his blade down hard upon Jim's slim rapier. The young Cromier took Jim by the wrist with his free hand and pulled him close. He rasped at Jim between bared teeth, lips peeled back like a wild dog's.

"This is mine, Morgan! It is the only thing that has ever been mine. My destiny. I will not be robbed of it. Not by you! Not again!"

"You killed her!" Jim screamed. "You took her from me, and I'm going to get her back!"

Jim threw Bartholomew off him and charged after. He no longer cared for parrying or blocking. He swung and stabbed and sliced. Bartholomew's eyes opened wide, caught off guard. He reeled from Jim's blows. The young Cromier retreated farther than he first intended. Jim pushed him back between the cloudy shapes of the temple columns. He pushed him to the edge of the thundercloud that had once been the rocky isle beneath the ruins. He drove him to the cliffs.

Bartholomew's heel hit the ledge. His balance tilted. His free hand wheeled in the air. Jim did not miss the chance. He swung with all his might. Bartholomew only just blocked the slash, but the force of the blow sent him over. Backwards he fell into nothing, crying out with despair.

Jim paused, his whole body humming. His breaths came in ragged swallows. His teeth were clenched so hard his jaw began to ache. Had he done it? It had happened so fast, and Jim was horrified to think that he actually had – that he had pushed Bartholomew Cromier to his doom – until a desperate grunt sounded from below the ledge.

Jim inched closer to the drop, his rapier held high. He leaned over, and there he found Bartholomew. The pale man had somehow managed to grasp the cloudy rocks, firmer than they appeared. He struggled to hold his purchase, adjusting his grip and hanging on with what little remained of his strength. Far down below, Jim heard the metallic clatter of Bartholomew's sword, only just striking the ground.

"I told you, Morgan," said Bartholomew. "Do you remember? I told you this could only end with one of us on his knees, and the other with sword in hand. Now here we are. Go on then and finish it."

"It's what you deserve," Jim shouted. "You and your father both. It's what you deserve after what you did to her... what you did to me!"

The tears that would not come earlier, when Jim knelt beside Lacey, now blurred his vision. He wiped them away with the back of his hand. When he had cleared his sight, he found Bartholomew looking back, not with murderous hate, but with a glaze of tears turning his eyes blue as the sky.

"It's all fate, isn't it? Destiny?" He said. "It was all along. You are the son of a hero and a princess. I am the son of a monster and a madman. How could I have ever been anything but a villain? Is this not how all fairy tales end? This is the way it was meant to be from the beginning. It is what I deserve. So, finish it Morgan. Take the key – it's yours. Save her if you can. She was a brave soul."

Jim pulled back the rapier.

But something held him. It was not the rose scar on his palm, though it was burning. Nor was it guilt, or pity exactly. It was a

356

weight at his side. He felt it again – the phantom weight of his father's box in his pocket. Bartholomew bore that weight as well. Jim could see it in his eyes.

"Do not toy with me, Morgan," Bartholomew cried. A single tear crawled down his cheek. "If you lack the stomach, I will prove my courage at last."

Bartholomew let go.

But he did not fall far.

Jim caught him.

Bartholomew's weight nearly pulled Jim over the side. He jabbed the rapier into the cloudy rocks and somehow it held. The two of them strained and groaned. The rapier blade bent, but it did not break. Their arms, already burning from battle, nearly gave out. But all the ferocity with which Jim had tried to kill Bartholomew a moment before, he now called upon to save him.

Nearly falling to their deaths more than once, Jim and Bartholomew dragged themselves over the ledge. They collapsed there together, chests heaving and gasping for air. When they finally found the strength to sit up, Bartholomew's eyes flicked to the rapier, still in Jim's hand. Jim tossed the blade over the cliff. He was about to ask Bartholomew what they should do now, when a voice that was not his and was not Bartholomew's spoke instead.

"Well, that's not how I imagined this going at all."

Jim and Bartholomew leapt to their feet, exhaustion forgotten, standing to face a shape looming over them, silhouetted before the tower of light.

"Perhaps you should not have tossed aside the rapier, Morgan," said Bartholomew, raising his hands to fight. Jim meant to agree, when the figure came into view.

He was old, old as time, it seemed to Jim. White hair flowed from both his head and his face, reaching his back, and the beard to his belt. But the old man still stood tall, with broad shoulders that must have once cut an imposing figure.

"Yes, we will miss the rapier indeed," whispered Bartholomew. His mouth dropped open and his eyes went wide.

"You know this man?" Jim asked.

"As a child, I did. He was the Warrior, the fourth Pirate of the Black Skull. He is Lord Winter."

FIFTY-ONE

THROUGH THE DOOR
AT THE EDGE OF THE WORLD

Was, Bartholomew," said the old man, taking another step forward. He walked with his hands clasped behind his back, appraising Jim and Bartholomew more like a curious schoolteacher than the bloodthirsty swordsman Jim had always imagined him to be. "I *was* Lord Winter. In truth, that may not be most accurate either. It may be most right to say that I was part of Lord Winter."

"Was part?" demanded Bartholomew. "You look the man to me. Older, yes, but yours is the face I remember. My father told me stories about you. Told me the things you did. Told me of the men you killed... hundreds of men. You were the monster in my dreams,

Lord Winter, and glad to be such, as I recall. So do not play friend to me." Bartholomew drew closer to Jim, whispering from the side of his mouth. "We must take him together, Morgan."

Before Jim could even gather his wits for another plunge into action, he caught a sudden surrender in the old man's eyes. It was the startled gaze of a man cut so deep that surely the very life was bleeding from him.

"Was it so many?" Winter said. His colorless lips trembled and his old eyes wetted and glistened. "It was, wasn't it?" Lord Winter hung his head. His broad shoulders fell. Jim lowered his fists.

"I thought Lord Winter became the Crimson Storm," Jim said. "In the story, you were stabbed by the golden trident. Your blood flew into the sky and became the storm clouds. I fought you... or so I thought. I fought you on the Wastewaters with my father's magic sword."

"Indeed I was, young Morgan. And indeed you did." Lord Winter took a deep breath, blinking away his tears. "The magic in the Treasure of the Ocean is a curious thing. I cannot say I fully understand it. But somehow, all that was angry in me, all that was violent, cruel, bloodthirsty, and wicked, all of that became the storm. What remained of me, what little good lived in my black soul, became the frail figure you see before you now, trapped here, in this place, for all this time."

"Looks like you weren't left with much," said Bartholomew, glancing from the old man's figure to the sky, where even in this gray world, the darker clouds of the Crimson Storm still swirled.

"There are two men in all of us, young Cromier," said Winter. "But only one throne."

"You've been here since that night?" asked Jim. "For over fifteen years? Which I guess begs the question, where is here?"

"The answer to your first question is yes. I have been a prisoner in this place ever since the day I fell to the temple floor. I think, were I still the man I was, my solitude would have driven me mad...

if I wasn't mad already. But those more vile parts of myself were left free to roam the world." Lord Winter squinted to the sky, to the churning storm above. It was not hate exactly that Jim thought he saw in the old man's face, but some sentiment both colder and hotter at the same time.

"As for your second question, this more quiet fraction of my soul has pondered this place for some time, and come only to this conclusion: this is the place between two places. It may exist in some small bubble of the ether, or perhaps inside the Treasure of the Ocean, or inside the altar, but it is not truly a place of its own. It is neither here nor there."

"What do you mean by *there*?" asked Bartholomew.

"Why, beyond the doorway, of course."

Lord Winter turned and walked back to the altar. Jim and Bartholomew shared a glance, a glance Jim thought surely the two of them would never share – one of being glad they were not alone. Together, they followed the old man.

"Early on, when I first came here – or rather, when I was first brought here. I tried many times to take the key and go through the door. I may as well have tried lifting the entire island. It would not budge for me. But I think it will move for the two of you."

"And then what?" asked Bartholomew. He seemed to Jim nearly heartbroken. "Where is the power? Is it beyond the door? Must I travel farther still to take it?"

"You can't take it," said Jim, staring at the key, remembering all his mother and Egidio had told him, finally and fully understanding. "The power is behind the door. If you open it, the power can come into this world, but something must hold the door open. The power passes through you... until you become the power."

"Yes," said Winter. "This I believe as well. As my hate became the storm, so you would become also, only more, more than could be contained by even all the skies above the world. It is strange, I think, that the barrier between life and death, for all who walk upon the earth, could be as thin as one oak door. I have wondered sometimes if it was simply by good fortune that this door fell here, between our world and the next, closed instead of open, or if someone long ago shut it for all our sakes."

Jim let his eyes drift upward, to the boiling clouds, and then over his shoulder, to the still form upon the ground behind him, shrouded in the gray mist, her eyes still closed, sleeping forever.

"I can't save her, can I?" he asked, his throat aching. "Not even with all the magic that lies beyond the door. I wouldn't be able to control it, would I?"

"I think that, should you open the door, the world would cease to be a place of flesh and blood to you, just as much as you would cease to be so to it," said Lord Winter. "It would become like this cave, cold and lifeless. And you would become a force, like a wave, and the world just a rock, upon which you would crash, over and over again, until you pounded it into nothing. I have finally learned, after so much time alone, that to change the world, you must remain a living, breathing part of it. No power, no talisman, no magic, save that which each man holds over himself, will ever renew it for us."

"What now, then?" asked Bartholomew. "We are prisoners here, like you? Or we open the door and destroy the world? Are those the only choices left to us?"

"I reason," said Lord Winter, "as I have found no way out of this place, that only use of the key will return us to our world... and also doom it to a fate of darkness."

"What fools our fathers were," lamented Bartholomew. He slammed his fist onto the corner of the altar and hung his head. But Jim's heart was beginning to quicken inside of him. He finally had come to the moment he had been building towards his entire life – to the moment of his destiny.

"No," he said. "There is another way. We can unlock the door, take the key through, shut the door behind, and then lock it again from the other side. No one, not even a Son of Earth and Son of Sea could ever open this door again. The world would be safe from its power – forever." Lord Winter and Bartholomew regarded Jim for a long moment, wondering if his plan would work, and if he was serious about going through with it.

"It just might work," said Winter. "And, it just might return the one of you who remains back to our world."

"But not you?" asked Bartholomew.

"No, lad, not me," said Lord Winter. He seemed to Jim remarkably unshaken by this dire prospect, and perhaps even eager. "My soul is split in two. Half of a man cannot return to life, I don't think. I imagine that this part of me will evaporate, escape out into nothing, and I don't think my other half will survive on its own either. The Crimson Storm may have one last stab of hate left to it," Lord Winter's eyes drifted past Jim and Bartholomew, settling with a cold gaze upon the misty, fallen form of Count Cromier. "But then it too shall be no more."

Lord Winter returned to their conversation, but not before catching sight of Jim's necklace, still hanging about his neck.

"Your father's?" he asked Jim, nodding toward the charm.

"My mother's," Jim corrected. "But now it is empty. She's gone." Somehow, saying those words made up Jim's mind for good. Perhaps, in some misguided, unfortunate way, his father's designs for him had finally come full circle. Lindsay Morgan had sired a Son of Earth and a Son of Sea, one of only two that could unlock this door of magic, and one that could finally rid the world of its threat forever.

Jim turned his back on the two men and walked back toward the cloudy statues. He paused by the Ratts and Cornelius. He thought back to that day in the court of the King of Thieves, when he was still a spoiled, unlovable toad, and how these three had taken him in and made him their fourth brother. They would never get credit for such a deed as that, Jim thought, but how could they be labeled thieves, when they were willing to give for free what so many would never sell for all the gold in the world?

Jim patted Cornelius, his constant companion, on the head, and then he wandered over to where Lacey's form lay on the ground. No matter what became of him beyond the door, or what doom or adventures he would face there, he would remember her smile, her hand in his, and her kiss upon his lips for as long as he would live.

Those were the best goodbyes Jim would manage. As he had done so many times before, he picked up the pace, turning on his heel and walking with a quick purpose, which was the easiest way to do something hard or frightening without losing the nerve to see it through. It was how he had raided the Pirate Vault of Treasures. It was how he had walked the Path of Riddles beyond the Serpent's Mouth. So it was how Jim Morgan would walk through the door at the edge of the world. But when Jim reached the altar he paused, just long enough to ask a favor from one person he never dreamed he would.

"Bartholomew," Jim said, his voice shaking. "I know I have no right to ask, but would you please do one thing for me?" Bartholomew stared back at Jim, his ice blue eyes unblinking. "Please... if you have a little money to spare, will you bury Lacey on a hill for me? Not in London, but somewhere out in the open, somewhere under the stars."

Bartholomew nodded, it was nearly imperceptible, but enough of a yes for Jim to hope it would happen.

"Lord Winter," Jim said with a nod. "Good luck." Then he reached for the key.

A gloved hand caught him by the wrist.

Jim flinched in the grasp. For so long he had fled from the Cromiers, endured their treachery, and fought their schemes. Even at the end of his journey, he prepared himself to battle once more. But Bartholomew, Jim's wrist in his hand, was not even looking at him, or at Lord Winter for that matter. His eyes were fixed upon the door.

"Lord Winter," Bartholomew said. His voice was a harsh whisper, full of fear, Jim thought, but tasting the fear like catching the first snowflake of winter upon his tongue. "What lies beyond the door? What besides the power?"

"No one knows for certain, young Cromier. Perhaps magic, like an ocean, which would drown a man should he try to swim it. Or perhaps only emptiness or eternal darkness. But maybe, and this is what I believe most of all, somewhere beyond the door lie the shores of another world."

Jim felt Bartholomew tremble, from the hand that seized him down to his black boots. "At last," he said, so quietly Jim barely heard him. "At last." Bartholomew released Jim's wrist, and took the key in his hand. "I'm afraid, Morgan, that I will not be able to do your favor for you. In fact, I will need you to do a favor for me."

Jim stared hard at Bartholomew. He wanted to say no – to say that he did not trust Bartholomew to do it. But in Bartholomew's eyes, Jim realized that walking through a door that led to an unknown fate, even to death, of his own free will and courage, was Bartholomew's treasure. It was this prize he had fought so hard to claim. It would be tantamount to murder, Jim thought, to take that prize away from him.

Bartholomew reached into his pocket and withdrew two tiny figurines, one of a woman and one of a child.

"You must mind these very carefully, Morgan, and let them come to no harm, until you have gone to Shade Manor and released the two prisoners held there. They are the wife and child of Abdullah, the shopkeeper, and they should be returned to him at once. And one more thing." Bartholomew turned and took one last look at his father, his face hard as stone. "After you have let them go, burn that place to the ground."

With that, Bartholomew gave Lord Winter a curt nod, turned on his heel, and strode toward the door. Jim gaped after him, feeling the delicate, wooden shapes in his palm. Bartholomew had kept them safe, through all these misadventures. He had kept them safe from his own father.

"I met your mother," Jim shouted suddenly, stopping Bartholomew just before the door. Bartholomew did not turn back, but he tilted his ear over his shoulder. "She loves you, Bartholomew. She asked after you. She asked if you had grown up into your father. At first, I told her you had... but then I changed my mind. I told her you had not. I was right after all."

At those words, Jim was sure Bartholomew stood taller, shoulders straighter, and head higher. He stepped to the door. He took a long, deep breath and placed the key in the lock.

"Goodbye, Lord Morgan," Bartholomew called over his shoulder.

"Goodbye, Count Cromier," Jim said.

Then he turned the key.

The door flew open. An avalanche of sound poured into the cloud cave. Light streamed in white, and gold, and blue from the other side. A great wind blew Bartholomew's coat about him, throwing him back from the door, whipping also at Jim's clothes and his face.

Jim feared that he, Bartholomew, and Lord Winter would all be swept aside, that the magic would force its way into the world in spite of their efforts and plans. But Jim watched as Bartholomew fought the final battle of his life. Step by step, against the waves of power, the young Cromier willed his body forward. The magic seemed to fight harder the closer Bartholomew drew to the door. His body became nothing but dark lines in the midst of the blinding light. But Jim saw the silhouette take the door in his hand and pull it behind him.

"Hold on, Lord Morgan!" shouted Winter. The old man took Jim around the shoulder, holding him fast against the wind. As he supported Jim with one arm, the old man took the pearl charm about Jim's neck in a fist. Lord Winter leaned in close, shouting a few words into Jim's ear.

Somehow, with strength Jim wondered if he would have possessed, the dark-haired son of Villius Cromier and Legeia, Siren of the Sea, shut the door. The thunder snuffed out in an instant. Jim heard the lock latch in the silence that followed.

FIFTY-TWO

SAILING ON

Jim blinked. When he opened his eyes again, he found himself returned to the temple ruin upon the rock. He stood with one foot braced against the stone altar, exactly as he had stood when he had been fighting Bartholomew for the Treasure. Bartholomew, though, was nowhere to be seen. He had vanished without a trace, as though he had never been there at all. Only the evidence of his struggle with Jim remained, strewn across the courtyard.

Stone columns smoldered in toppled piles. Scorch marks scarred the hard ground. Only a few paces from the altar, George lay in a heap amongst his brothers, his arm slashed and bleeding. Across from the huddle of Ratts, F.W. Pennington Sharpe stood over Count Cromier, holding the villain at bay by the point of his sword.

The Treasure of the Ocean turned cold in Jim's hand. The gold faded before his eyes, turning gray. The thrumming power, once running through the trident, grew still. The great Treasure of the Ocean became nothing more than a piece of metal, a lifeless artifact from an ancient people, long fallen beneath the waves.

When the last drop of magic within the Treasure died, a thunderclap exploded in the sky above Jim's head. The thunder rolled, building into a deafening crescendo. This was no taunting laughter or booming threat from the Crimson Storm. This was the agonizing cry of a creature clawing at the precipice of death.

Lightning burned in the black clouds. But each flash was like a blow to the Storm, eating away at it, piece by piece. The face in the storm opened its flaming eyes wide and roared with its molten mouth. It screamed in pain.

With its last gasps, the Crimson Storm poured out of the night, falling from the sky like a blood-red ribbon, purple tendrils of power crackling along its length. Jim braced himself. He pulled the trident from the altar, preparing to make his last stand. But the hateful stream of magic streaked over Jim's head. It wound through the air, coiling above the fallen form of Count Cromier.

"Away, foul spirit!" Count Cromier shrieked, scampering back on all fours until he rammed himself into the stump of a stone column. "Be gone with you, Winter. Was I not your oldest friend? Was I not your ally? Be gone and leave me be!"

Cromier begged for his life, but the blackest parts of Lord Winter's soul, bound up in the Crimson Storm, showed no mercy. The last curl of red struck Cromier like a serpent. It latched onto his body, twisting about his arms and legs, until it finally swallowed the Red Count and all his screams whole. With a final snap of purple fire, the Crimson Storm evaporated into nothing, leaving only wisps of smoke in its wake.

Quiet fell over the temple. Jim's heartbeat thumped in his ears. The moon and the stars shone down through a suddenly cloudless sky. Compared to the suffocating blanket of darkness that had covered the rocky island only a moment before, the soft blue light seemed bright as day.

Jim ran from the altar to where Peter and Paul held George between them. As pale as the eldest Ratt appeared from his wound, still bleeding through his shirt, more color warmed his face than had in many months. Jim looked to the ground at George's side. The magic flute lay broken to pieces upon the stone.

"He will be all right," said Cornelius, nodding his beak toward George. "As long as Mister Gilly still draws breath, I think he shall be just fine. Old Gilly could stitch a hay bale back into grass on the earth, given enough time, I'd wager."

"You did it, Jim," said Peter. His eyes were still red from tears. A great black bruise was rising upon his cheek where Bartholomew had struck him, but he managed a weary grin nevertheless. "You saved us."

"You saved the whole world, I reckon," added Paul, thumbing at his bloody lip. The Ratts, it seemed to Jim, were trying to supply the proper measure of cheer such a moment deserved, but they seemed so tired, and Peter kept looking over his shoulder, toward Lacey.

"Actually," said Jim. "I didn't save the world. It was Bartholomew."

"Did he now?" said Captain Sharpe, sheathing his sword and coming to stand beside Jim and the others. "I would never have thought even a shred of hero lived beneath that pale skin."

"A person might surprise you, every great once in a while," Jim said, nodding at the captain, "if given a proper chance."

"Every once in a while, Lord Morgan. Every once in a while," Sharpe agreed. "Of course, as for the older Cromier..." The captain gave a dismissive sniff over his shoulder, where the last curls of smoke were drifting away on the ocean breeze. "I think the whole world smells a bit fresher now than it did a moment ago."

"I'll say," said George with a grimace. He sat up in his brother's arms, holding one of the shattered flute shards in his bloody fingers. He flicked his eyes from the broken instrument to the lifeless trident in Jim's hand. "I suppose there's also a bit less magic lurkin about than was a few moments ago, too. Wonder if there's any left at all in the world after tonight."

"There's still a little," said Jim. "Enough for one last trick." He set the trident down and unclasped his mother's chain from around his neck. Holding the silver shell on the tips of his fingers, Jim flipped it open. A white glow, dimmer than it had been when Jim's mother's soul had dwelt within, but a glimmer still, splashed over Jim's face.

Without another word, Jim ran to where Lacey lay on the stone floor. The Brothers Ratt – George lifted between Peter and Paul – and F.W. Pennington Sharp, came quickly after him. Cornelius flapped through the air and came to land beside Lacey's head.

"I thought the soul stone to have gone empty, young Morgan," said Cornelius. "I thought, begging your pardon, that your mother's spirit was lost."

"It was empty. But Lord Winter filled it again – with everything left that was good about him. He told me I could have it. He told me to do something good with it."

Jim reached back and smashed the pearl upon the stone ground – once, twice, three times. On the third strike the pearl cracked. A swirl of white light, sparkling beads like bright stars floating amongst it, danced in the air from the broken pearl. It lit up the entire temple, throwing long shadows back from the small circle of friends. After pluming in the air, the sparkles fell like snowflakes upon Lacey's body. They rested upon her skin for only a moment, before melting into her, disappearing like winter dust does upon a warm face.

The light faded. The quiet took deeper hold. Jim's whole body trembled, all within him clinging to a fingerhold of hope... until

Lacey drew in a breath and opened her eyes. Peter and Paul began to laugh. George slapped his hand against his face, swiping away at tears. Even Cornelius, wise old raven, ran his feathered wings across his beaked face, great drops, as large as a full-grown man's, pattering onto the ground beside his clawed feet.

But between Jim and Lacey there was only a smile – tears, laughter, and words wrapped up within it.

"Hello there, Lacey," said Jim.

"Hello there, Jim," she replied.

Jim pulled her into his arms. George, Peter, and Paul followed. The five friends once more became a single tangle of arms, legs, laughter, and tears.

Jim, Lacey, and the Ratts made their way down the steps, carved from the age-old rock, toward the stony shore. Cornelius rode on Lacey's shoulder, chattering into her ear about all that had happened while she had been "asleep." F.W. Pennington Sharpe came last, walking easily and whistling, as though all this had simply been just another day in his tremendous life. In Jim's left hand he carried the dead Treasure of the Ocean, in his right, he held Lacey's.

All the fighting had stopped, the Corsair ships having long since fled and Queen Melodia having taken charge of the Sea Folk. Yet, beside the Queen's chariot, supported by Fulkern and another of his warriors, King Nemus floated in the waves, still alive. He bore a great wound on his chest, and any fire of war had dulled in his eyes. Lo Fang and Golden Ginny, pirate crews at their backs, stood in rowboats just off the rocks, white flags of truce rippling above their heads. All of them, pirates and merfolk alike, lifted their eyes at the Clan's approach, a measure of wonder in their gazes, Jim noted, and not without satisfaction.

"Grandfather," Jim said to King Nemus. He let go of Lacey's hand and stepped to the edge of the rocky shore, his feet in the water. Bowing his head, Jim extended the Treasure of the Ocean to the king. "What was once taken from you is now returned." Nemus said nothing, but weakly reached out and took the trident.

"It has gone cold," he managed, his voice quiet.

"The door it was meant to unlock can never be opened again. There's no danger in it any more. I know this doesn't bring back my mother, or rebuild the crystal tower. But you can have me, if you will. You can call upon me if ever you need me, and I'll come." King Nemus said nothing. His old eyes left the trident, and drifted to the shattered pearl, now hanging about Lacey's neck. Queen Melodia spoke for him.

"We are glad you are safe," she said. "And I hope we might call on you for more, or less, than heroic deeds in the future. But for now, let both sides heal on their own." The Queen swam forward and kissed Jim on the cheek, then she, Nemus, and all the Sea Folk swam back into the ocean, disappearing beneath the waves.

"Lord Morgan!" cried Lo Fang from his little boat. He waved at Jim and the others, bowing his head with grace. "It would seem that you have written the first of many great deeds upon the scroll of your life, and I am honored to know you."

"Well he didn't do it on his own, did he?" said Peter, coughing into his hand. Lo Fang laughed, bowing his head again.

"I have not forgotten you, master thieves. Truly you are the greatest thieves in all the world. You have managed to steal the respect from my very heart."

"Did you hear that, Georgie?" whispered Paul. George let a smile cross his face. He looked like the old George then, fresh off the streets of London, lighting in a bottle.

"Finally," he said to his brothers. "Finally somebody knows what we knew all along. About bloody time, if you ask me."

"However, my new friends," continued Fang, "it would seem things are now back to normal, and it also appears that you have lost your ship. The mighty *Spectre*, great lady of the sea that she was, now lies beneath the waves, with the *Sea Spider* soon to follow. However, I, the most generous Lo Fang, will gladly offer you passage back to Spire Island – for only the price of the pearl in Captain Sharpe's pocket."

"We would rather swim, Fang," said Sharpe, fingering the handle of his sword. "And the next time we toss knives, you should mind your own buttock, you scoundrel."

"We would?" asked Lacey, throwing Sharpe a glance. But the mischievous pirate only winked in her direction.

"How much for a trip back with Golden Ginny?" asked Paul, hope spilling from his face.

"Ten times the worth of Sharpe's Pearl," said the lady pirate, but she offered the Ratts a glowing smile nevertheless.

"That sounds like a deal, don't it?" Paul whispered to his brothers, absolutely serious. "We could pay it off over time, couldn't we?"

"I thank you all," said Jim, laughing. He bowed low to both pirates, then gave a sharp whistle as he stood back up. "But I think we have a ride."

The pirates were very nearly drowned by two large waves, all but turning their little boats over, as Percival the water dragon splashed between them, laying his head low for his friends to climb aboard.

Some hours later, the moon dipping beneath the waves to the west, and the morning sun rising in the east, Jim Morgan stood atop the head of a great sea serpent, looking toward the horizon, salty breeze tugging at his hair. Lacey sat behind him, patting Cornelius on her knee as the water dragon sped them along to Spire Island. The Ratts were gathered beside Mister Gilly, who was still checking his stitchwork on George's arm.

The rest of the *Spectre's* crew had said their goodbyes and joined up with either Lo Fang or Golden Ginny, sailing off for parts unknown. Even F.W. Pennington Sharpe, the rascally pirate, had somehow won a coin toss with Golden Ginny to earn himself a free voyage home.

"So long, Lord Morgan," Sharpe had said to Jim, as the two parted ways. "Send old Darkfeather out to find me in some years, will you? I've been looking for another sailor with which to share some adventure or another on the far side of the world. You're not a half bad pirate, really, and I'm not just saying that because you battled a magic storm or saved the world, either. You've got grit, my boy, real grit."

"Thank you, Sharpe," Jim had said, laughing, even as Lacey rolled her eyes, waving at Sharpe from Percival's head. "I do have a few things I need to do that might require a fellow of your skills. But you know, it will all be that hero sort of thing."

"How unbelievably dull, Morgan. But, you never know, do you?" With that, and a smile, the pirate sailed away.

"You know, boys," George said, catching Jim's attention from over his shoulder. "Now that we're officially the Greatest Thieves on Earth, I'm thinkin it's time we retire. Go out on top and all that, just like our father used to say."

"You didn't know our father, George," said Peter and Paul together.

"But do go on, Georgie," said Peter. "If we aren't thievin, what are we gonna do with ourselves all day?"

"Well, I figure old Egidio, rest his soul, would have wanted someone to carry on his work, you know? And seeing as how the three of us know a thing or two about magical artifacts, we're just the lads to do it."

"I like where your head is at, Georgie," said Paul, tapping his fingers in front of his face and smiling dangerously. But just when Jim thought George might reach all the way back in time, and invent an all new, ridiculous cheer, the oldest Ratt's eyes got lost somewhere far away, and his roguish smile softened on his face.

"We just need to make some changes to the Turtle Shell," he

whispered. "We'll need to build a bit beside it. That old pier needs a lighthouse I think. A white one, right there on the beach."

"I think that sounds beautiful, George," said Lacey. "I imagine the top of that lighthouse will make a good place for stargazing, don't you?"

"It's only too bad you lost your book, Lacey," said Peter, "so you could know all their names and everythin."

"I think I'll write my own," said Lacey. "A book about the stars, and about the people who sail beneath them."

It was then that Cornelius flapped up from Lacey's lap and settled upon Jim's shoulder, gazing out with him at the golden dawn. "Well, my boy," said the raven, "I'm afraid, even after all our adventuring, battling, and derring-do, we never really found the treasures we were looking for at the first."

"I suppose we didn't, did we Cornelius?" said Jim. Though he threw a look over his shoulder, to Lacey and the Ratts, laughing and teasing each other about stars in the sky and lighthouses at the edge of the sea. "But maybe we found better ones in the end."

"Indeed, young man, indeed. So what now, Lord Morgan?"

"A long time ago, on the beach outside my home, my father told me that the world was full of heroes and villains, monsters and beauties, and marvelous treasures."

"Did he now?" asked Cornelius, a knowing smile at the corners of his beak.

"Let's go find some," said Jim. Cornelius spread his wings and cawed, and Jim laughed. It was a boy's laugh, a boy with the smell of the ocean on his skin, and the salt of the sea in every curl upon his head.

THE END

Acknowledgements

It is far more difficult than I imagined it would be to write the last words in this book. Not that it's hard to say thank you to those who deserve it. That's too easy, in fact, and less than the wonderful people I'll soon mention deserve. But it's hard to say goodbye to the world of Jim Morgan.

The Jim Morgan books are not perfect novels. And, for better or for worse, it's not up to me to decide how many readers will eventually stumble upon their stories. But as I sit here, the first two books stacked beside my keyboard, I can at least let them go with a smile. Writing these books has brought me some of the greatest joy I've ever known to my life. And if in turn these little novels bring their readers, however many, whatever age, a bit of that joy, then what does it matter if they weren't perfect? They did what they were supposed to do, and that makes me happier than I deserve to be.

My first thanks are to Lora Lee, for creating artwork that so perfectly captured the spirit of the series.

To Julie Gray, Meg Mardian, and Tamson Weston, thank you for pushing me, always forward.

To Steve Martinez, Sam Winokur, Richard Smith, Jenny Minniti, and Nikki Katz, for your friendship and wisdom, but also for the strength and courage to tell me I could be better.

To the Cottinghams, the Smiths, the Phams, the Johnsons, Chad Perkins, David Berger, and Ditter Kellen, thank you for believing in me.

To my mom, Heather, Mickey, Oma, Opa, and all my family, thank you for your pride and your faith.

And to the readers, thank you for taking this journey with me. I hope it helps you, even in some small way, along your own amazing adventure.

Made in the USA
San Bernardino, CA
13 May 2018